TREY: EUROPEAN REDEMPTION

SHANDI BOYES

Edited by
NICKY @ SWISH EDITING & DESIGN

Illustrated by
SSB COVERS AND DESIGN

COPYRIGHT

Copyright © 2020 by Shandi Boyes

Photography: Furious Fotog

Model: Dylan Horsch

Cover Design: SSB Covers and Design

✿ Created with Vellum

WANT TO STAY IN TOUCH?

Facebook: facebook.com/authorshandi

Instagram: instagram.com/authorshandi

Email: authorshandi@gmail.com

Reader's Group: bit.ly/ShandiBookBabes

Website: authorshandi.com

Newsletter: https://www.subscribepage.com/AuthorShandi

ALSO BY SHANDI BOYES

*** Denotes Standalone Books**

Perception Series

Saving Noah *

Fighting Jacob *

Taming Nick *

Redeeming Slater *

Saving Emily

Wrapped Up with Rise Up

Protecting Nicole *

Enigma

Enigma

Unraveling an Enigma

Enigma The Mystery Unmasked

Enigma: The Final Chapter

Beneath The Secrets

Beneath The Sheets

Spy Thy Neighbor *

The Opposite Effect *

I Married a Mob Boss *

Second Shot *

The Way We Are

The Way We Were

Sugar and Spice *

Lady In Waiting

Man in Queue

Couple on Hold

Enigma: The Wedding

Silent Vigilante

Hushed Guardian

Quiet Protector

Enigma: An Isaac Retelling

Enigma Bonus Scenes (Two free chapters)

Twisted Lies *

Bound Series

Chains

Links

Bound

Restrain

The Misfits *

Nanny Dispute *

Russian Mob Chronicles

Nikolai: Representing the Bratva

<u>Nikolai: Resurrecting the Bratva</u>

Nikolai: Ruling the Bratva

Asher: My Russian Revenge *

Trey *

Nikolai: Bonus Scenes (10+ chapters from alternative POVs).

The Italian Cartel

Dimitri

Roxanne

Reign

Mafia Ties (Novella)

Maddox

Demi

Ox

Rocco *

Clover *

Smith *

RomCom Standalones

Just Playin' *

<u>Ain't Happenin'</u> *

The Drop Zone *

Very Unlikely *

False Start *

Short Stories - Newsletter Downloads

Christmas Trio *

Falling For A Stranger *

Enigma Bonus Scenes (Two free chapters)

Nikolai: Bonus Scenes (10+ chapters from alternative POVs).

One Night Only Series

Hotshot Boss *

Hotshot Neighbor *

The Bobrov Bratva Series

Wicked Intentions *

Sinful Intentions *

Devious Intentions *

Deadly Intentions *

Martial Privilege Series

Doctored Vows *

Deceitful Vows *

Book Three

Omnibus Books (Collections)

Enigma: The Complete Collection (Isaac & Isabelle)

The Beneath Duet (Hugo & Ava)

The Bad Boy Trilogy (Hunter, Rico, and Brax)

Pinkie Promise (Ryan & Savannah)

The Infinite Time Trilogy (Regan & Alex)

Silent Guardian (Brandon & Melody)

Nikolai: The Complete Collection (Nikolai & Justine)

Mafioso (Dimitri & Roxanne)

Bound: The Complete Collection (Cleo & Marcus)

DEDICATION

To the women in Shandi's Book Babes,

Behind every strong woman is a group of even stronger women propping her up.

You guys make me thrive harder.
Thank you for that!

Shandi xx

PROLOGUE

TREY

Six years earlier...

The dark room we're fucking in amplifies the scent of her musky perfume. While flaring my nostrils to suck in the addictive smell of her heated skin against mine, I grip her ass firmer, increasing her moans from breathless whimpers to ear-piercing screams. I pump in and out of her on repeat acting as if my desire to claim her won't start another war.

For years, the Dvořáks have had footholds in this half of Europe. My father's sanction in the United Kingdom is strong, but he doesn't just want to rule his side of the pond. He wants to govern the entire world. After the Berlin and Paris chapters crumbled with death tolls almost as high as ones recorded during the Cold War, Prague was the next natural choice.

I'm here to infiltrate their camp, seek out their weaknesses, then helm the raid that will see the streets of Mikulov littered with the bodies of Sahib Dvořák's men.

Instead, I'm fucking Sahib's daughter in the butler's pantry like she's one of the many whores he's offered me the past three months.

I was born evil. Hate is buried deep inside me, but the temptation to make India mine was too strong to consider the carry-on effect our fuck will cause my birthright. Her oceanic eyes and untouched skin deserved further exploration. Her response to my gall tonight brought brightness into my bleak and miserable existence and has me wondering if there's more to life than victory, murder, and mayhem.

I can kill a man without blinking, feel his pulse fade to nothing without an ounce of remorse, but right now, all I'm hearing is my heart in my ears. It's thudding nonstop, drowning out everything and everyone, including the warnings about how disastrously my campaign will end.

India doesn't know I'm here to take down her father. She has no clue about the number of men I've killed and how many widows I've made.

She also isn't mine.

She was betrothed to a man three months before I arrived on the scene. They're set to wed next week. That's why I moved as quickly as I have. I only caught the back end of her as she entered the industrial-size kitchen in the underbelly of her family's compound.

Although a dingy, dark room isn't an ideal location to authenticate the hidden glances, whispered words, and slight touches India has bombarded me with the past three months, it's rare for her to be alone, so I took advantage of the situation.

Her nails clawed at me when I pinned her against the first solid surface I could find before I sealed my mouth over hers. It wasn't solely in fear, though. She was also turned on, incapable of denying the sexual chemistry teaming between us.

I've fucked many women in my almost twenty-two years. My crew's victories are regularly celebrated with gallons of whiskey and an endless number of whores. However, not even someone as perverted as me anticipated for my kiss to turn into a lust-filled fuck against shelves of food brought in specially for India's wedding to Achim Novak, son of a prominent European aristocratic family.

Their nuptials will merge old money with new blood-tainted money *if* I allow the wedding to proceed as planned.

As my teeth gnaw on India's bottom lip, mine shift into a smug smirk. I'm acting as if I have control of the situation when that's far from the truth. India's virginal blood is smeared on my cock, and her salty tears are flavoring our kiss, yet all I did was seal my mouth over hers. India crept her hand into the waistband of my jeans. She undid my belt and removed my cock from its trunks to line it up with her fragrant-smelling cunt. Just like it was her who slammed down on my rock-hard erection to impale herself with one quick thrust.

Don't misread what I am saying. I'm not a saint by any means. I've met the rock of her hips grind for grind, toyed with her clit when the clenches of her greedy cunt almost suffocated my cock, and gripped her tighter and tighter when the fiery way our bodies are connected slicked our skin with sweat. I just didn't instigate the fuck that'll switch her from being a real-life princess to a mafia monarch. That was all on India... as will my seed if her cunt doesn't stop sucking at me like it is.

After adjusting the tilt of her hips, widening her more for me, I give her the last inch of my cock. She calls out, her moans equally erotic and earth-shuddering. Needing her to be quiet before our romp is caught by one of the many guards who walk these corridors at night, I remove my hand from her sweaty hip to her mouth. I can't see shit in the poor conditions, but my hand is so large, it swamps a majority of India's face, so it'll soon take care of her moans.

"If you don't want your husband-to-be to know the reason you'll have to dye your wedding dress before festivities next week, take it down a notch." My words are grunts jutted by the brutal slams of my cock.

The tightness of India's cunt guarantees her father's claims about her once saintliness were true, however, I can't hold back. I love to fuck, and although I've dreamed about this day for weeks, it's above and beyond anything I could have imagined.

Not all virginity fucks have to be uncomfortable. You've just got to find a man who knows what he's doing. I doubt soft-cock Achim would have been up to the task. That's why he fools around with the help, so he doesn't have to worry about anyone's needs bar his own.

"Or perhaps we should let Achim hear your screams, then, once I'm done claiming every inch of you, we can dye your dress in his blood," I growl when India's pussy tightens around my shaft. She tugs at me, gripping my cock as well as her dislike of her husband-to-be tightens the noose around his neck. "Do you want a war, Duchess?" I ask while rubbing my thumb over her clit. "'Cause I'm ready for battle. I was built for carnage, so perhaps we should play the fucker at his own game."

My gravelly reassurance I'll fight to the death for her sends India freefalling into ecstasy. She comes apart in my arms, her entire body used to climax. I continue pumping into her, unafraid of the fiery wreck I'm steering us toward. My cock is not sheathed, and the sucks of her cunt are greedy, but the only way I'm pulling out without coating the walls of her cunt with my seed is if someone puts a gun to my head.

Even then, there are no guarantees.

This feels too fucking good to let a threat of death end it.

"Let them hear you," I say as I drop my hand from her mouth to her hip before doubling the rock of my hips. "Let *him* hear what I do to you, and how well the Corbyn men fuck. Let the war begin without a single bullet being fired. I'll give you the crown you're craving, Duchess. It just won't be pronged with jewels."

India begins to shake like she's about to have another orgasm. "You like that, don't you, Duchess? You want to rule a kingdom, not sit in a crystal tower." I pin her closer to the shelving with my hips before returning my hand to her face. I grip her cheeks firm enough she'll feel the sting of my fingers as long as her pussy will feel the burn of taking my cock unprepared. "I'll give you what you want. I will give you the entire world... *after* I've taken it all away from you first."

As cum erupts from my cock in roaring spurts, I seal my lips over India's. My kiss is as cruel as the way I claimed her—as will be the war our fuck instigated.

ONE

TREY

Present Day

The moans in my dreams sound real, as does the wetness coating my cock. There's just one difference. I'm not fucking India in a pitch-black butler's pantry as my deranged mind has once a week for the past six years. I'm being fucked, from above, by a whore who should know better than to serve herself a helping of the monster dick memories of my past instigate.

I didn't get my cock pierced solely for the women I fuck without knowing their names or their life history. They're to remind me of the tightness of India's cunt, and the way it rippled around me when she moaned into the cool night air. They are for the coolness of my veins when I watched her blood drain from her body and heard the chilliness of her screams.

They're so I'll always feel pain even when I'm being pleasured.

They are *not* for dirty whores who don't understand a drug-fueled gangbang isn't an open invitation to ride my cock anytime she feels like it.

"You good?" I ask, gripping her hip firm enough to mark.

She's got a nice rack, a super flat stomach, and an ass with plenty of bounce, but she's like every other whore in this compound. There's nothing unique about her. Not even her scent is one-of-a-kind.

The woman's name I'll forget within a second of release scrapes her teeth over her lower lip before she nods. We've got an audience. She doesn't care. Hell, she looks hopeful one of my brothers will come over and join us like they did last night.

They won't.

Not if they know what's good for them.

I'm all for fucking. I have been since I was sixteen. However, this shit doesn't fly with me.

If I want to fuck you, you'll be the first to know. If I don't, you sure as fuck don't get to take yourself for a ride and expect me to be okay with it.

The whore releases her lip with a moan before she drops her eyes to mine. They're icy and blue and have my veins cooling even more than her clit grinding against the steel bar in my pubis. She's super greedy today, acting as if the six studs pierced in my shaft aren't enough to get her off. And don't get me started on my length and girth, or my mood will grow even more pissy.

If she hadn't been run through the mill last night, my cock would be wearing as much blood now as the smears I washed off in the shower after stealing India's virginity. Guaranteed.

"It feels so good, baby."

"Is that right?" When she nods for the second time, her moans doubling in appreciation of the British accent I've yet to get rid of even after being surrounded by Russians twenty-four-seven for the past three years, I twist my lips. "I think this would feel better."

Since she's as thin as a rake, I lift her off my cock without so much of a strain on my pinkie. When I stand to my feet to bend her over the couch in the middle of the compound teeming with ruthless men and half-dressed whores, she perches her ass high in the air, praying I'm about to stretch her puckered hole as well as my cock did her pussy.

I'm tempted, but I am also frustrated, so her begging ass will have to wait.

"Open wide. If you graze me with your teeth, my hand will get friendly with your cheek." It dawns on me that my threat would be better suited for another whore when she shudders at the prospect of being hit. There are a handful of girls at Clarks who like being slapped around. I usually steer clear of them.

Wife-beating isn't my kink.

Her moan when I ram my cock to the back of her throat pulls my balls in close to my body. Even in my pissy mood, I can admit her tongue dragging over the curved barbell piercings in my shaft feels good.

Her dedicated attention to my cock deviates my plans for a few minutes. Not long enough for me to forget my purpose, but long enough I forget there are the eyes of over two dozen men on me and my cock.

Fortunately for all involved, I don't get stage fright.

After another handful of minutes, I remove my cock from the her mouth, give it two good pumps, then watch cum squirt out of my crown.

It lands on her lips and cheek and covers a good portion of her right eye.

"Nuh-uh," I growl out with a moan when her tongue attempts to lick up the droplets coating her lips. Her tongue will never reach the murky white substance on her cheek and eye, but when I teach a whore a lesson, I do it the right way. "You want to be a whore, so I'm gonna treat you like one."

Careful not to trip on my jeans huddled around my ankles, I take a step back before yanking the rigid material up my tattooed thighs. Once I have my still-throbbing cock tucked away, I nudge my head to the parking lot at the back of Clarks. "It's late, so you better get home before your daddy gets worried about you."

Although shocked at my dismissal, especially since it's barely noon, the blonde dips her chin before her hands dart up to clear away the mess on her face. "Nuh-uh," I repeat, louder this time. "You're a whore, remember? It's about time your daddy learns of your career aspirations."

Smiling, I smear in the blobs of cum that'll most likely fall when she stands before shifting on my feet to face August, or Eight as he prefers us to call him. He's a newbie to Nikolai's crew, so he's the best one to free from the bunkers while we wait for an update from Nikolai on where we're going next.

He's preparing to send his girl back to Hopeton, aware a war is about to begin. If I were smart, I would have done the same thing with India. Alas, back then, I was only twenty-two. I had no clue how fucked-up this world is, much less the people who *think* they run it.

"Follow her home. If she touches her face during the commute, revoke her privileges to Clarks." The whore gasps in a sharp breath. It's barely heard over the chuckle of Nikolai's men.

Nikolai is my brother-in-arms. He took me in when my wish to make India mine almost caused my demise. He's Russian, fucking filthy, and hates the man who raised him with every fiber of his being.

I want to say I had the same issues with my father. Regretfully, it was the respect I had for him that got him killed. Have you ever thought about who you'd choose if forced to pick between the woman who made you realize you had a heart in your chest and the man who gave you life?

It wouldn't be an easy decision for the strongest man to make, much less one who had a gun held to his head and a threat to kill them both if you didn't pick one.

Did I pick right? You tell me. I'm in a foreign country, second-in-charge of an entity turning over three billion dollars in assets a year, and fucking whores who can stir my cock even without drugs lacing my veins.

Some will say I'm living the life.

Others would fight for better.

I say quit complaining and take what you're given. Things aren't the best, but they could be much worse. I could be in the ground like my father, his entire existence ruined because his son couldn't keep his dick in his pants.

As Eight marches the whore with my cum on her face to his car, I slump back into the two-seater couch I woke up on. This place fucking reeks of sex and blow. It's a smell I usually crave. However, the havoc brewing in my gut is snuffing my body's usually positive response to the lifestyle I was raised in.

This is life for me—drugs, whores, and guns. I was raised around them, craved them, and have been destroyed by them, yet they're the only things that make me feel alive, although not once have they caused my heart to patter in my ears.

TWO

SALES DOCKET NUMBER 12574

Bile burns the back of my throat when I ram my fingers down as far as they can go. I can't believe I was so stupid not to check the food they slid through the slot this evening. I'm starving, and my body is showing signs of malnourishment, but still, I can't believe I trusted these men.

They sell women as sex slaves. As if that isn't bad enough, this sanction doesn't do one-and-done sales. They auction the same women over and over again, only stopping when they're either killed by one of the brutes paying to spend an hour with them, or they die from starvation.

I'm teetering close to having both causes of death placed on my death certificate.

The men in this sanction pay top dollar for a woman to occupy their time for an hour. The thousands they hand over ensures their stipulations are the highest I've seen. They don't just want beautiful, charismatic women with flawless bodies and tight vaginas, they also want them to be full of tenacity and to have the gall to get through the four or so men a night they're expected to 'entertain.'

When I was given to Vladimir Popov, founder of this sex-trafficking ring, I had the curves needed to entice top dollar, the wavy blonde locks men like to grip, and bright blue eyes that were full of life. But since I also have the shyness of a mouse, I've been overlooked more than the women I arrived here with.

Don't get me wrong, I am not complaining I'm not fetching top dollar. I'd rather starve to death than be brutalized by men who see women as nothing but commodities more than necessary, but I don't know how much longer I can live like this.

The small portions of food they've been giving me the past ten weeks are now laced with hallucinatory drugs with the hope of sparking a personality out of me, and the once meaty parts of my body no longer exist.

I'm nothing but skin and bones.

That won't stop these men, though. Some will beat me to rouse a response from me. Others will stroke themselves from a distance, happy for my nudity to get them off. Then there are the ones who won't care if I never speak to them. They paid for me, so they'll do whatever they want to me.

They're the men who scare me the most.

Once I'm certain the food in my stomach has been expelled, I fraily climb the cracked bathroom sink to wash my vomit-smeared hands. As I stare at myself in the scum-coated mirror, I try to recall a time when I felt pretty and cherished. It was so long ago, the memories are fading from my head as quickly as the light is from my eyes. I barely recognize myself, so I doubt anyone who saw me previously would. I'm not out to impress anyone, so I guess it doesn't really matter how I look, does it?

Ignoring my grumbling stomach, I step over the sloppy meat concoction I think was supposed to be shepherd's pie before making my way to the main part of my 'room.' It's more a prison cell than a bedroom, and the fact I have a mattress and attached bathroom doesn't glam it up in the slightest.

If anything, it makes it worse.

Only the women Vladimir wants to 'entertain' his guests for the night get mattresses. The thought alone has me wanting to vomit again. I would if it would bring up anything but my stomach's lining.

When I slump onto the bed, too tired to remain standing, my eyes stray to the goop I knocked over when I realized it tasted funkier than it should have. It looks like someone had an accident on the floor, and it pops a brilliant idea into my sluggish head.

———

"You think you're smart, don't you?"

My teeth crunch together when Vladimir backhands my cheek for the second time. He must be super mad because he usually makes his goons do his punishments on his behalf.

"You wasted both my time and my money this evening."

The urge to bend in two overwhelms me when he gets right up in my face. For a guy pushing seventy, he's fit and healthy, but his insides are so hideously ugly, no number of good genes can save my stomach from heaving about his closeness.

"And to think I was going to invite you to the feast after this round of guests." He taunts me with food as he knows it hurts me more than his earlier threat about selling me twice this week. "Now, you won't even get the scraps left on their plates."

I deserve to be punished. I wasted food, but at least I put the sloppy meat of my 'dinner' to good use. I coated it from the apex of my thighs to the back of my knees. The man who paid three thousand dollars to spend an hour with me was less than impressed he didn't get a woman close to the image Vladimir uses to sell me each week, and it had nothing to do with the fact I looked like I had pooped my pants.

He wanted the woman I was before I was shunted into this life, the one who exuded freedom even though she's never truly been free. He wanted Kristina, a woman I no longer am, and will most likely never be again.

After delivering the rest of his scorn solely with his eyes, Vladimir releases my face from his clutch before stepping back. The chains holding me hostage from a U-bolt in the ceiling jangle on the protruding bones of my wrist in rhythm to his boots tapping across the concrete.

When I unearth the reason his punishment was reduced to two slaps tonight, they clank even more. A large brute of a man is standing in the doorway of my room. He has a fire hydrant hose in his hand and an abhorrent smirk on his face. Even if my ruse was real, it won't be effective the instant he switches on the nozzle that's dribble has more pressure than the shower in my bathroom.

Confident I've caught the gist of what's happening, Vladimir smirks a smug grin. "Get her washed up now. I'm feeling generous enough tonight to share her with the men unable to bid... *once* she's finished serving the ones stupid enough to pay for her."

As my throat works hard to swallow, my eyes rocket to Vladimir in silent pleading. He's dressed to the nines, which reveals his guests tonight are more aristocrats than the bottom-dwelling mobsters he usually caters for, but still, I'm worried. Vladimir only ever gives away his whores when he has no intention to sell them next week.

This isn't an industry you leave alive. If I'm done being sold, I am *done*. The lights once in my eyes will be permanently extinguished, never to be relit.

"Do you have something you want to say, little girl?" Vladimir asks when he spots my pleading stare, his tone mocking.

Pleas sit on the tip of my tongue, but no matter how hard I try to relinquish them, I can't. I'd rather die silently than speak a ton of words I can't take back.

"Ah, such fight," Vladimir croons like he's four decades younger than he is. "If only the men could see that via a video lens."

After clicking his fingers two times, he exits the room. Not even two seconds later, I'm blasted with icy-cold water. The pain is horrific. It feels like my skin is being scraped off with a cheese grater. The sting ripping through my body has screams roaring up my throat and whizzing out of my nostrils with breathy gasps, but not a peep escapes my lips.

I won't give these brutes the satisfaction of seeing me cry. I could. The only good thing about being hit with enough water to fill a lake is the ability to deny the salty blobs wanting to slide down my cheeks, but I won't because I told myself I'd never cry in this room. I made a promise to remain strong no matter what, and although this shouldn't count because it hurts more than I could ever explain, it does.

I will not cry for these men.

I will not break.

I will win, even if it kills me.

By the time the unnamed man turns off the hose, my clothes are shredded off my body, my bedding is drenched through, and the silver tray my dinner was delivered on is wrapped around the pipe I was cuffed to my first five days here.

When the hose's nozzle drops to the concrete ground with a clang, I collapse against the chains holding me hostage, incapable of balancing on my tippy toes for a second longer. Although I'm sparkling with the cleanliness I haven't experienced in weeks, every inch of my body is aching. I feel like I've run a marathon, but there will be no reprieve for my tired muscles. That isn't the way these men work.

Another silent scream pops into my head when the brute fists my hair to yank my head back. His evil eyes glide over my face, down my neck, and across my collarbone before he stops on my breasts. Compliments to good genes I got from my mother, that's the only part of my body with any meat left on it, and even then, it isn't much. It would be barely enough to fill a hand.

"You scrub up good," the goon grunts, half laughing, half moaning. "Let's hope your line of visitors isn't too long this evening. I'm not into necrophilia."

I'm so dead on my feet, I fall into his arms when he releases my wrists from the contraption bolted to the ceiling. I am anticipating for him to carry me back to my bed, so the parade of men he mentioned can commence getting their money's worth, so you can imagine my shock when he heads for the door Vladimir exited minutes ago.

The air outside of my room isn't any less stuffy, but I suck it in like it's full of the nutrients I've been lacking the past ten weeks. Once I have my lungs as revitalized as my determination to live, I ram my palm into the brute's nose, kick out of his arms with a grunt, then hightail it down a corridor lined with padlocked doors.

I should bolt straight for the closest exit, but since that would make the torment of the last ten weeks utterly worthless, I shout one name on repeat before bobbing down to peer through the keyholes on a handful of doors.

With none of the words shouted back at me done in Czech, I make it almost six doors down before Vladimir's goon catches up to me. He punches me in the stomach, winding me even more than my sprint before he tosses me over his shoulder like I'm a rag doll and stomps down the corridor.

Most women would kick, thrash, and wail when they're being

carried so brutally. I'm way past normal. I don't fight him at all. I merely still my movements and prick my ears so I can listen for an accent similar to mine.

There are so many women, more than I could have possibly imagined. Their accents are from wide and far. It takes him marching us down a third corridor before I hear one close to mine, but when I do, it launches my heart into my throat.

"Ana?"

The fight I failed to give earlier roars out of me in uncontained violence when the faintest voice whispers back, "Kristina?"

"Ana!" I fight and fight and fight to be freed. I dig my nails into his huge shoulders, bite at him, and kick him with all my might.

The harder I fight, the tighter the goon holds me.

"I'll come back," I promise in Czech, on the verge of tears, scared I'm so close to my dreams, yet still so far away. "I will find you. I promise."

A grunt rattles my ribcage when the man tosses me into a room at the end of the corridor Ana is in. Even with my lungs void of air and my backside sporting an aching sting, I spring onto my feet and race to the door, praying I can stop it from shutting before I'm once-again locked away in the nightmare of my thoughts.

My effort comes too late. I'm not just naked in a room too elaborate to belong to a slave, I've caught the eye of Satan, and he isn't a man who's happy to look from a distance.

"Mika is right, you do scrub up nicely, little girl," Vladimir mutters, stepping closer. "Now I just need to find a way to discover if your moans are as sweet as you taste."

A war is coming. I can sense it in my veins and feel it trickling through the fine hairs on my arms. It's the same sensation I got in the butler's pantry six years ago. Not only are Nikolai's men thirsty for bloodshed, so are men who don't belong in this fight. The Popovs own Las Vegas. Nothing happens here without their consent, so why the fuck does Alexei have his crew barricading the hospital Roman was taken to?

Roman is Nikolai's advisor. He's at least mid-fifties, if not sixties, yet he has no issues keeping up with the rest of Nikolai's crew. Nikolai chose well when he demanded for Roman to take Justine back to Hopeton to save her from a wayward bullet. He learned lessons from my failed takeover bid years ago and put steps in place to ensure his outcome was better than mine.

Regretfully, Vladimir had the jump on us. Roman was shot earlier today. If reports are anything to go by, Vladimir's goons needed more than a bullet to take him down. They also chloroformed him.

It's all part of Vladimir's game. He can't fuck with Nikolai if

Nikolai has no clue he has his girl. He kept Roman alive for a reason, which is why I need to get him out of the hospital he's holed up in and back to the compound so we can unearth his reasoning.

I drag in a long drawl of my recently lit doobie before devoting my focus to Eight. "How many men do we have in total?"

He checks the figures scribbled in his notepad. "Four each on the front, back, and side entrances, three at the crossover, and two spotters on the overpass heading west."

"Nero?"

"Tying up loose ends." He fans his hand in front of his face to ward off the smoke plume escaping mine. "We'll be down to the final four soon." The direction of his eyes reveals who he's referencing.

While following the direction of his gaze, I push down on the old crank mechanism on my window, understanding not everyone is a fan of secondhand smoke—even when it's the best weed in town. "How far out is recon?"

Eight twists his lips before he shrugs. "Twenty, thirty minutes. Give or take."

"We can't wait that long. Justine has been gone for hours. Time isn't on our side."

He jerks up his chin in agreement. "Then what do you want to do? Nikolai wants Roman no matter the cost, so perhaps we should think outside the box."

I take a few seconds to deliberate on his suggestion. It awards me nothing but a surly attitude. "Have you ever considered just walking up and knocking on the front door?"

Over the game of men believing they're in charge when they aren't, I slide out of my 1966 Shelby GT350 and hotfoot it across the street. Eight, although quiet, quickly catches up with me. I'm not surprised with how long his strides are. We don't just call him

Eight because his name is August, and he was born in the eighth month of the year. It's because his super long legs would have you believing he's eight feet tall, and during drug-fueled benders, he usually has eight whores going at once.

I won't mention the fact he also only has eight fingers, or that his cock may only be in the eight-inch category. He's a little sensitive about those parts of the equation, so it's best we keep those facts between us.

Approachability isn't something gangbangers often use, but I give it a whirl. "What's up, boys? Alexei got you chasing ambulances now. Did you miss the memo? You don't need a prescription for marijuana anymore. You can get that shit at a shop."

T, a low-ranked gangster from Alexei's crew, spins around to face me. "What's the bet that nasty shit is still better than the low-grade crack your men were pushing last week. My grannie couldn't even get off on it."

My teeth gleam in the early morning sunlight. "Lucky your girl didn't face the same issues, eh? She was so up in my blow, she left my bed with it all over her face this morning." I still can't recall the whore's name who woke me up by riding my cock for free, but I've seen her around T enough to know she was once one of his favorite girls before she upgraded the men she likes to get off on. "She's so desperate to get out of the shit your crew is snowballing, she'd rather get around with my cum on her face than lose her 'whore' title with the Popovs."

My smile doubles when T fists my shirt. He's such a hothead, I would have only needed to insult his shoes to have him fisting up for a fight. This way was more fun. What can I say? I'm an asshole who's always ready for a war.

"What do you want, Trey?" he sneers in my face, his words as hot as the ash on the end of the joint dangling out of my mouth.

While pushing him off me, I give him a stern look, wordlessly warning him the next time he puts his hands on me, he'll lose fingers.

Confident he's got the message, I say, "Roman."

When I sidestep him to enter the hospital, he gets up in my business. "Can't let you do that. We have orders Roman is to stay here."

"I wasn't asking your permission, twat-face."

I stab out my half-smoked joint into his chest then sidestep him for the second time. My jaw quivers when his getting up in my business occurs this time around with the muzzle of a gun being shoved into my ribs. "As I said, can't let you do that. We have orders."

"Orders for a war you don't belong in. This is Popov turf. You have no sanction here," I growl without the slightest quiver to my words. He may have his gun on me, but I'm not close to being dead.

T has bigger balls than I realized. "Says who? A British immigrant too weak to rule his own kingdom." My jaw ticks when the men surrounding him laugh. I'm all for jokes. I love them as much as I do fucking, but I won't tolerate being laughed at, and T and his fuck-face friends are two seconds from learning that the hard way —even more so when he snickers, "Go home, foreigner, your time here is done."

I tighten my jaw but keep a cool and collective head—for the most part. "I'm asking you politely, T. Step back before I remove the walnuts from your sack and use them as anal beads the next time I fuck another one of your sisters in the ass." That was my calm response. This is my menacing one. "Or perhaps you'd rather me give your mother a good once-over, so, for once, she can climb a pole that doesn't have the word bastard associated with it."

Like a fool not in fear for his life, T steps up to me until we stand chest to chest. "Do all the Popov men go on parent-hating rants when they're scared? Or just the parentless motherfuckers like you, Trey?" He spits out my name as if it's vomit. "You're so pathetic, when you buried your father, I bet you bought up all the plots around him for his many whores, unsure which one was your mother—"

His words are replaced by garbles when I shut him up with my knife.

As T tilts my way, his footing as unsteady as Eight's grab for his gun, I raise my knife another four inches up his gut to ensure the tip pierces one of the valves around his heart.

Bullets halo my head, but I can't see anyone but T. Although, if I am being honest, I'm not really seeing him either. I'm standing across from Achim, knifing him as I wish I'd done years ago.

"I asked you politely. I told you to step back. You didn't listen. You never fucking listen." My last four words are roars from my past coming back to haunt me. "You wanted the castle, I gave you the entire fucking kingdom, but it still wasn't enough for you, was it?" I remove my knife before jabbing it back in more forcefully, untrusting of his still chest.

I made a mistake once believing someone was dead when they weren't.

I won't make the same mistake twice.

I only return from the darkness of my past when Eight steps in front of me. "Grab his shoulders. We'll dump them later. Your ploy worked. While we occupied the front, Nero got Roman out the back entrance."

With sirens wailing and my mind still a little lost on what the hell just happened, I help Eight place T into the back of my Shelby along with one of his gang-popping pals. I don't know how Eight took down the second member of Alexei's crew, but if the blood splatter of his face is anything to go by, it was violent.

"How many casualties?"

"Just these two. Nero's group cleaned up the rest." Eight curls T's legs so they can fit into my trunk before jerking his head to the rotating hospital doors. "Two sought shelter in the hospital." He lifts and locks his grassy-green eyes with mine. "They won't talk, but if they do—"

"Nero will take care of it."

Eight smirks, winks, then slams down the trunk. "Come on, Nikolai is en route to the compound. Things are about to get heated."

After gathering up the nine or so shell casings coating the ground, I slip into the driver's seat of my car. With Eight's legs longer than mine, it takes him longer to join me. I've only just cranked over the engine when I see the clean-up crew arriving in my rearview mirror. Most of T's blood was soaked-up by my shirt, but they'll ensure not a droplet will be found by the CSI team I hear racing to the scene.

When we glide past lit-up police cruisers racing in the direction opposite to the way we're fleeing, Eight slumps low in his seat. He's so tall, his attempt to hide makes laughter rumble in my chest.

If he sinks any lower, he'll be eating his cock.

Hearing my laugh, Eight socks me in the arm. "Laugh while you can, Trey. You may lose the ability by the end of the week."

I push off his worry with a laugh. "*Pfft.* Whatever. You said Nikolai wanted Roman no matter the cost. I got him for him. Might've lost two soldiers in the process, but those are the casualties of war."

My voice waivers when Eight interrupts, "Holy fucking shit. You don't know who T was, do you?"

"A low-ranked wannabe gangster—"

"Whose father doesn't care he was birthed by a whore. He loves his sons all the same."

As my throat works hard to swallow, my eyes stray from the

road to Eight. "What the fuck are you on about, August?" The fact I used his real name reveals the urgency of the situation. I'm at a complete loss as to who he's referencing.

Eight sits up straighter before twisting his torso to face me. "T is Tristan *Vasiliev*. Alexei's son. Fuck, man. I thought you knew. Why do you think I'm missing *numero uno* number one?" Although he's asking a question, he doesn't wait for me to respond. "I beat up his son in a *paid* fight, yet I still lost a finger for it."

"T is Alexei's son?" The thump of my heart is heard in my question. When Eight nods, I ask, "His *blood* son?"

When he nods again, I get nervous for the first time in six years.

Fingers crossed it ends better than my last farce.

After checking on Roman in the makeshift hospital room in the dungeon of the Popov compound, I make my way outside to call Nikolai. I'm barely halfway across the foyer when he enters via the main door.

"Where is he?" He doesn't need to mention Roman's name for me to know who he's referencing.

I point to a door at the end of a long corridor. "Dok's with him. Not sure what happened yet. We just ran logistics as you requested." Not exactly as requested, but I keep that snippet of information to myself. Nikolai is a killer in every sense of the term, so I've never seen him this worked up. Usually, he acts first, asks questions later—*who do you think I learned my hang-up from?*—but I get that he has to mix things up this time around. It isn't just his livelihood at stake, his entire crew is in jeopardy. It's not a good set of shoes to be in. I've done it once. Don't plan to do it again anytime soon.

Needing to get something off my chest, I step closer to Nikolai. The change in position has me stumbling onto a dark-haired man with a face as hard as stone standing left of us. Although I'm reasonably sure I've seen him before, I can't pinpoint where.

After following the direction of my gaze, Nikolai demands the dark-haired man to move on. Once he disappears into the shadows, Nikolai drifts his massively dilated eyes to mine. "What is it?"

Never one to sugarcoat things, I get straight to the point. "Alexei's men had the hospital barricaded. I had no choice. I couldn't get to Roman without taking down two of his men first."

What? I'd rather tell him a little white lie than admit I acted like a pansy who can't get over his past. When the time is right, I'll tell Nikolai what really happened.

Now is *not* the right time.

Air whizzes from Nikolai's nose, but he isn't surprised by my revelation. "Loss of life is a casualty of war, Trey. Alexei knows that better than anyone."

"Yeah, I get that," I agree, nodding. "But I don't see Alexei willing to accept that excuse when he discovers I murdered his son."

Nikolai looks a little uneased while asking, "Which son?"

I swish my tongue around my mouth to loosen up my words. "Tristan."

Nikolai's relieved breath fans my cheek for barely a second before he sucks it back in. "Is Alexei aware of the incident?"

I shake my head. As much as Eight's disclosure rocked my core, I wasn't so stupid not to realize we need to keep Tristan's death on the down-low for as long as possible. "No, we cleaned the scene as thoroughly, if not better, than you would have. Their bodies are still in my trunk."

"Good. Keep them in there until I say so." Before I can get in a word, he continues talking, "Once Justine is home, I'll deal with

Alexei. Until then, his son's body will remain in my possession." Nothing but honesty is seen in his eyes when he says, "Negotiating Tristan's return is the only bartering chip I'll have for you to see out the week with your pulse not flatlining."

I'm about to say it's too late to worry about a flatlining pulse, but I realize the day he discovered his girl is being held captive by his murderous father may not be the best time to have a conversation about my empty chest.

"All right, I'll gather the men and head to Jim's. Hopefully, some ice will keep away the vultures." Jim's is a storage ground where we keep deceased bodies until the heat dies down. Jim is almost deaf, half-blind, and has freezers big enough to house fifty men. It's one of the joys of owning a pig farm. The pigs come in handy, too, but I'll keep that story for another day.

"Once you've got them on ice, gather the rest of the men from Clarks, then come back here." Nikolai's jaw gains a spasm. "Until we know what Vladimir's plans are for Justine, none of us are getting any sleep."

With my crisis diverted by a seemingly level-headed Nikolai, my inquisitiveness gets the better of me. "Is that who I think it is?"

The man hiding in the shadows has no similar features to Nikolai, not even their eye coloring is a match, but they give off the vibe of brothers. If my intuition is right, and the stranger is still breathing, that can only mean one thing. He's the infamous Rico Nikolai's men talk about all the time. The *dead* Rico Popov.

I realize I'm on the money when Nikolai asks, "Have you ever seen a ghost, Trey?"

Although incapacitating memories have me wanting to nod, I shake my head instead.

When Nikolai's spots its waggle, he murmurs, "You have now."

I watch him cross the room with my mouth hanging open and

my mind shut down. I knew he was tiptoeing toward a minefield when he gave up his favorite whore just for the chance to slip between his lawyer's sheets, and don't get me started on the possessiveness that beamed out of him when his crew spent the weekend shacked up at his girl's crash pad, but this, this goes beyond anything I could have predicted. He isn't just tiptoeing toward danger anymore, he's gone full tilt, blind to the warning signs flashing before him.

I can only hope this mafia prince's sprint through a battlefield doesn't end as disastrously as mine did, or hell will be empty from all the devils uniting to execute his revenge.

FOUR

SALES DOCKET NUMBER 12574

As I rock in the corner, I cover my ears, fighting to ignore their screams. I'm so angry at myself—so very, *very* mad. I let *him* break me. And for what? To have him smile at me before he threw me into a room even barer than the one I was in before he stole the last bit of dignity I had left. The food he promised me isn't even served on a tray. My toilet no longer has a lid. I'm not even allowed to shower anymore.

That's for the good girls.

The ones who say please and thank you.

He might have me forgetting who I once was, but he didn't force me to speak. I whimpered, and my eyes filled with tears, but I didn't utter a syllable.

I think that's what saved me from him. He hit me, kicked me, and screamed words at me I didn't understand, and he did it while I was naked, but he was as sickened by my soundless sobs as me, the only part of his body that came close to mine was his shriveled-up penis when he requested for me to spit on it.

I wanted to tell him to go to hell.

I wanted to spit in his face.

But instead of doing either of those things, I broke.

I wouldn't have if Ana's cries weren't still ringing in my ears. I gave in for her as much as I did for me. I'm too hungry to keep fighting and way too tired. I can't keep doing this day in and day out. You don't realize how exhaustive fighting is until it finally dawns on you that it'll never end.

Whether here or in Prague, my life has always been one struggle after another.

Once Vladimir finished, which I'm pleased to say wasn't long enough for me to remember, he tucked away his penis while warning me I better surpass his expectations tonight, and that every man who enters my room better leave with a smile, or I'll be punished again. Except this time, no amount of tears will save me.

I should be pleased I'm not dead, but in some ways, that just adds to the torment. Death is the coward's way out, and even though I'm a sex slave, I'll *never* be a coward.

I awaken startled when the screams return. These are different than the ones that lulled me to sleep several hours ago. They're not begging for the pain to stop or for food. They're begging to be freed.

That can only mean one thing.

It isn't a new bidder being shown the ropes.

It's a new victim.

Concrete dust kicks up around my knees when I crawl across the filthy floor. I don't know who had this room before me, but it's clear they lost the will to live long before they died. The vomit at the side of the door looks like it's been there for weeks.

It takes me blinking three times in a row before the visual

through the keyhole clears enough that I see a redheaded woman being marched down the corridor. She appears as heartbroken as I feel about the numerous pleas for her help.

Although she's naturally slender, the meat on her bones reveals she's either brand new or her owner took good care of her. She has a bump on her forehead, but other than that, she's well put together. Her face isn't gaunt like the rest of us, and although her skin is pale, it shows the gleam regular time in the sunlight awards it with.

"Be careful," I warn her in Czech when the goon stops outside the room I was just freed from. Vladimir scraped the bottom of the barrel when he forced me to give him head, so he most likely won't go gentle on her.

My heart thuds in my ears when the pretty redhead replies, "It's all right. Help is coming." She didn't speak her words in English. She spoke them in my native tongue

"Děkuju," I reply, hopeful she's being honest.

The determination in her eyes is so startling, I'm scared within an inch of my life when the man clutching her arm bangs his fist on the lock I have my face pressed up against. "Get back in bed. You've got another three visits before your night is over."

Even with fear being my strongest emotion, I still issue the stranger a warning, "Devil. Watch out for the devil."

While the door opposite mine slowly creeps open, I scamper back into the corner I've been hiding in the past few hours, praying the shadow filling the gap under my door isn't one of the men Vladimir's goon mentioned earlier. I'm too woozy to give Vladimir's guests the special attention he believes they deserve, and being silent takes more effort than fighting. It takes everything I have to emerge into the dark that saves me from the nightmares of the light, and I have barely an ounce of strength available tonight.

I realize just how unlucky I am when the shadow from the door jumps to the lock. As steel keys jangling against a solid door trickle into my ears, I swallow down the bile racing up my throat. Even with poor lighting hiding the man's face, I know he's been here before. He's paid for me three times the past ten weeks. The first time he was happy to watch me from afar. The second time he wanted a lot more for his money. I can only hope he's feeling friendly tonight because there are no nail marks on the walls for me to concentrate on, and no boarded-up window to look out of. I'll either be stuck here in the torment, feeling every disgusting thing he does to me or trapped with the demons in my head.

Neither are pretty.

⸺

Whips hurt more than fists. The crack they make with my back adds to the blistering heat racing across my back. I guess that's why they whipped people back in the olden days. It both humiliates and hurts, and if Vladimir has his way, it'll have me toeing the line.

I didn't spit as requested the second time tonight.

I bit.

Despite my weakness, I had the strength to gnaw my 'guest's' cock right off, but, unfortunately, his screams alerted Vladimir's goons to his mauling before I could get halfway through. That resulted in me being punished, again. It could be worse. I could have been beaten *after* being raped. This way, I'm just beaten.

The lash marks on my back will heal, but I doubt my mental stability will ever return after this. I feel humiliated, broken, and for the first time in my life, utterly worthless.

When a knock sounds at the door, the man whipping me doesn't put as much power behind his next hit. He's too busy snooping on the conversation Vladimir is having with the man who interrupted their sickening nighttime entertainment.

I can't understand a word they're speaking, I don't understand Russian, but one name is mentioned frequently. 'Dimitri.'

I don't personally know Dimitri, but I have a newfound appreciation for him when his arrival ends my punishment after only five strikes. My back is stinging, and if the dribble running down the middle of it is anything to go by, I have open wounds, but it could have been so much worse. I've seen women enter this room walking and exit in a body bag.

You're not supposed to survive this space.

"Take her to her room."

I think I'm free from additional torment.

It's silly of me to believe that would *ever* be the case.

After lifting my hanging head, Vladimir locks his wide-with-lust eyes with mine. "I'll be in to visit you later, little girl. We have much to discuss."

I had hoped my silence would disgust him since he wants me to scream so badly. Only now am I realizing my determination may be the very thing causing me additional torment. He now knows I'm not shy, and that I've been fighting him with silence, so he'll work even harder to make me crack. It's how he gets off. He doesn't want the purity he stole from me my first week here. He wants to suffocate my soul one painful minute at a time, and I'm on the verge of letting him do it.

The concrete my feet are dangling mere inches above digs into my knees when Vladimir's goon releases the chains holding me hostage. This time, when he tosses me over his shoulder, I don't put up any fight. There's an unusual sensation bristling in the air. It feels like I am dreaming even though I'm trapped in the sickening throes of a recurring nightmare.

I'm probably on the cusp of dying.

It could be worse. I anticipated the knowledge to bombard me with horror, whereas all I'm feeling is peace.

Once I am returned to the room across from Vladimir's private abode, a thin nightie is shoved into my chest. "Put this on. Vladimir will happily tear it off you later. He likes unwrapping his favorite whores."

The idea of giving Vladimir any pleasure repulses me, but I slip the thin material over my head, nonetheless. It barely covers my nipples and the faint hairs between my legs Vladimir refuses for his captives to remove, but it's better than remaining naked. A thin barrier of protection will forever exceed nothing.

The goon has only just stepped out of my room when the lady I saw earlier sprints past him. Although her clothes are torn open, her body isn't harnessing any of the marks I anticipated her to have after her visit with the devil.

Is that because she's already marked? If so, I wish even more now that I didn't attempt to take out one of Vladimir's guests with the blade of a razor my first week here.

If scars will save me from Vladimir, I'll wear them with honor.

"I'll come back. I promise I will be back," the redhead shouts in multiple languages as she darts down the corridor.

When my door slams shut at the same time she comes to a grinding halt, I race for the keylock. I can't see the person responsible for her frozen stance partway down the corridor, but I don't need to see him to know who he is. The redhead's face is holding the same sickened expression mine did when Vladimir forced his cock between my teeth my first week here.

I press my ear against the door when accented voices boom through it. Although I can't speak a word of English, I do understand it. My father loved English-speaking television shows. My mother and I regularly watched them with him, so we caught onto the lingo.

"Is she as you remember?" asks a familiar, arrogant tone. Vladimir sounds like he's still hard from watching me being punished. I'm not surprised. He's a sick fuck who would have enjoyed watching the welts in my back bleed more than my pathetic attempt to give him head.

"Yes," answers a male voice I don't recognize. "You can starve off your hunger for years, but it doesn't make your desire to eat any less rampant."

If I were half the woman I once was, I would have agreed with him.

Now I doubt I'll ever be desired again, much less *feel* desire.

It dawns on me that my earlier assumptions about the redhead's scars saving her from Vladimir were true when he spits out, "Even knowing she's marked?" He sounds as disgusted as his abhorrent face makes me feel.

After a few seconds of painstaking silence, the second man replies, "Scars don't bother me. It's the marks you can't see that are the hardest to heal."

His words hit me harder than I care to admit. I'm damaged both inside and out, so if what he's saying is true, it'll take more than a hearty meal and a long shower to fix me, and unfortunately, not all the damage occurred here.

My focus returns to the confrontation occurring outside of my room when Vladimir grunts out, "To each his own. Just don't mark her any more than you already have. There are a long list of men waiting their turn."

I want to scream for the redhead to run again, but she has more gall than all the women in this compound combined. "He will kill you if you touch me." Her threat is stern and to the point, fortified by a strong backbone. "When Nikolai discovers what you have done, he will kill you both."

I peer back out of the keyhole when the shuffling of feet

sounds through my ears. It has me missing what a dark-haired, blue-eyed man replies, but no amount of thickness can detract from the roar of war that thunders down the corridor a few seconds later.

"He's here! Nikolai is here!" bellows up the stairwell a mere second before gunfire gobbles up the man's shouted warning.

The corridor fills with men as the redhead strays her eyes to Vladimir. "I told you he'd come. It's time to pay your penance, Vladimir. The prince has arrived to collect his throne."

The back of Vladimir's hand collides with her cheek so forcefully, even my teeth feel the brunt of his hit. "The sale has been canceled. I'll refund your money by the end of the week."

I bang on the door, wordlessly pleading for Vladimir to leave the redhead alone when he drags her down the corridor by her hair.

He doesn't pay me any attention. He's too busy repeating to the man not happy his sale has been canceled that it's his way or death.

There are no in-betweens when it comes to this man.

When Vladimir and the redhead disappear into the room I was just punished in, I press my back against my door so I can cradle my head in my hands. The sound of a chain being run through the pulley is too much for me to bear. It reminds me that the pain skating across my back isn't the pleasurable version some women love. It's because I was humiliated in the very room Vladimir plans to kill the redhead in.

I saw the gleam in his eyes. He only ever gets that look when death is on the agenda.

With my head occupied by horrible thoughts, the time between Vladimir dragging the redhead to her death and a funky wet substance seeping under my door darts by remarkably quick. When I dab up droplets of the liquid onto my fingers, I'm torn between being excited and uneased. The sickly smelling liquid is gasoline, and there are more than a few droplets.

When I return to staring out of the peephole, my heart launches into my throat. Four men are splashing gasoline on the doors lining the corridor while another two soak Vladimir's room from top to bottom, dosing it with way more gasoline than needed.

Vladimir is a madman, but not even someone as evil as him would burn down an entity bringing him in thousands upon thousands of dollars every night. That's why my emotions don't know which way to swing. If they're planning to burn this place down, that can only mean one thing.

Vladimir is dead.

That should be a good thing, but the fact gasoline is being tossed around while padlocks remain on doors reveals it isn't.

Vladimir's captives are being sent to hell right along with him.

We'll be tortured even more than we already have been.

That isn't acceptable.

That's not right.

We're not animals, so why are we being treated as if we are?

"No!" I shout in Czech, annoyed that Vladimir's victims will be forced to hell with the men who brutalized them. "You promised you'd come back! You said help was coming." As tears threaten to slide down my cheeks, I bang my fists on the thick wooden door. "You lied. You lied to all of us."

I don't know why the redhead's deceit is hurting me as much as it is. She was a stranger, so I should have treated her promise as if it were a grain of salt, but for some stupid reason, I trusted her.

How foolish was I?

I continue shouting until the potent smell of gasoline becomes too much for me to bear.

It's time for me to give in.

To give up.

I'm not strong enough to keep fighting.

"I tried," I whisper after raising my eyes to the ceiling. "I gave it my all. I'm sorry I failed you again. Please don't be mad at them. I did the best I could. It just wasn't enough." *It's never enough.*

As madness steamrolls into me, the deafening thud of people running booms into my ears. Although I'm broken and confused, I peer out of the keyhole again, gasping when I spot the female I saw earlier outside my door.

Is she keeping her promise?

Did she remember us?

Did she remember me?

"Move away from the door," she requests in Czech, peering at me through the hole. She looks different than she did mere minutes ago—stronger and somewhat relieved.

When she gestures for me to move back, I scoot to the far corner of the room I generally hide out in. I block my ears when the bang of a gun being fired is closely followed by a boot being kicked against my door. When the fortified material shoots open with a whack, I bury my head into my knees. The redhead isn't alone. She's with a man who has dark hair, bright blue eyes, and the sneer of a murderer.

Although I don't immediately recognize him, the dingy conditions Vladimir made me entertain his 'guests' in means I must remain cautious. He's attractive, but that doesn't mean anything. Only my 'guests' lack of morals made them hideously ugly, so I can't be certain he wasn't one of them.

I peer at the duo through lowered lashes when the unnamed

man instructs for the redhead to stay behind him. He's so protective of her, his possessiveness is almost suffocating. I haven't seen that from a man before, especially not in this country.

"It's okay," the redhead mutters in Czech, stepping closer to me. "We're not going to hurt you."

My eyes bounce between her and her partner when he warns, "Not too close, *Ahren*."

I shouldn't like the fact he thinks I'm a fret, but I do. It means I'm not wholly broken. There's still some life left in my eyes.

Nodding so he's aware she heard him, the woman the man refers to as *Ahren* slowly bridges the gap between us. Although my intuition is warning me to remain cautious, there's something in her eyes I can't disregard. She's been hurt before, the scars peeking out of her shredded shirt exposes this, much less her soul-exposing eyes, but she also looks at peace. Like she has the world at her feet.

I discover that *is* the case when she whispers in Czech, "The devil is dead. He can't hurt you anymore."

I want to burst into tears. I want to shout my relief into the humid night air, but instead of doing either of those things, I accept the hand she's holding out in offering.

The wetness in my eyes jumps into hers when she drags her thumb against the week-old welts on my wrists. I was handcuffed to my room last week when I attempted to escape while dinner was being served. Vladimir's goons put them on extra tight, hopeful the pain would discourage me from moving too much when they punished me with more than their fists. All it did was leave slash marks embedded in my skin and grew my determination to escape to an unprecedented level.

"Thank you." My praise doesn't feel adequate to truly express the emotions pumping through me, but they are all I have, so they're all I can offer. "Thank you very much."

The weeping wounds on my back sting when I trudge toward

the door of my cell. It's amazing how euphoric it feels seeing it hang from its hinges. It's so badly damaged, it won't hold a woman captive again any time soon.

The entanglement of emotions already holding me hostage take on an entirely new meaning when my slow trek to the stairwell that'll lead to my freedom has my eyes locking in on a face I swore I'd never see again. "Ana!"

Forgetting about the pain rocketing through my back, I galloped down the stairs to greet the woman I went to hell and back for, praying the hard times are now behind me.

Ana's eyes are as wide as mine, her cheeks just as pale. "Kristina, you're here. How are you here?"

I don't answer her questions. I can't. I just wrap her up in a firm hug before sending my thanks to God. I fought the devil and won. That's a victory worth praising even if I had to go to the depths of hell for it to occur.

FIVE

I stop assisting a badly beaten woman into the back of an SUV when Nikolai and Justine arrive at my side. I'm pleased to report Justine is uninjured from her time with Vladimir... *if* you exclude her massively dilated eyes and the nasty red welt on her neck.

"Is this everyone?"

While jerking up my chin to Nikolai's question, I assist another two women into one of the SUVs that drove Nikolai's men straight onto Vladimir's battlefield. We lost over a dozen men to free Justine from the sex-trafficking ring Vladimir was planning to shunt her in.

It could have been worst. I was a second from flicking a lit match onto a gasoline puddle when Nikolai ordered us to search the compound for the women Justine promised to free.

I won't lie. I'm a cruel fuck who could be accused of mistreating women more than once, but even I struggled to keep a level head when door after door exposed Vladimir didn't just store his favorite whores here. He had victims—many of them.

Some were on the verge of death. Others had succumbed to their injuries. Then there was her, the petite blonde standing at the back of the pack, unsure whether she should flee or stay.

If any of the inane thoughts in my head have a chance of transpiring, she should run. She can barely walk, she looks like she hasn't eaten in days, and her hair is matted and tinged with blood, yet my cock still stirred when my eyes landed on hers.

I want to say it's because she has similar features to India, a girl I wanted but couldn't have, but that would be a lie. It was only when our eyes locked and held did my cock begin to twitch, and I started my assessment of her enticing body from her feet.

If all I wanted her for was her cock-thickening body, the thickness in my pants would have stood to attention the instant my eyes landed on the tiny apex at the top of her grubby thighs. Her nightgown is so thin, she's practically naked, yet it took me returning her prolonged stare before my cock commenced paying attention.

Her eyes are her most exposed feature. They reveal she's a fighter, she just has no clue how strong she is. If I were a real man, I'd show her how no amount of torture can bend the toughest spines. Regretfully, I lost who I was long before she became Vladimir's captive, so I have no right to act heroic.

When Nikolai kicks my ankle with his boot, I'm reminded that I failed to answer his question. "Yes, but we need to move quickly."

Like a perfectly-timed skit, sirens break through the joyous sobs of the women seeing daylight for the first time in weeks. Even the unnamed blonde is sheltering her eyes with her hand as she peers up at the rapidly blackening sky. She doesn't mutter a peep like the dozen or so women surrounding her, though. It's as if she finds sanctuary in silence as I once did many moons ago. It makes her even more intriguing.

Needing to keep my head in game mode before the ugliness of

my past rears it horrid head, I shift my focus back to Nikolai. "Where do you want them taken?"

"Take them to Clarks, but no one is to move until I say so." His reply pleases me greatly. If this were a standard whore-for-exchange program the Popovs generally run, Nikolai wouldn't care what happens to these women. The fact he's issuing a hands-off order means he's hoping to move his sanction away from the sex-trafficking industry Vladimir has been pedaling the past decade.

Vladimir was only removed from his throne mere minutes ago, but the benefits are already rolling in.

That's extremely rare.

I nudge my head to the left when Nikolai asks, "Where's Rico?"

"He's getting our guest ready for transport."

When a smug grin tugs my lips high, the blonde watches me as I did her earlier. The almost extinguished blaze in her eyes burns brighter the longer she stares at me. I can tell her hands are itching to cover the rosy pink buds sitting high on her chest, but she keeps them balled at her side, aware her secrets won't be exposed by her thin nightgown.

She really should close her eyes.

Our stare-down is interrupted by a commotion at my side. Malvina, Nikolai's ex-fiancé, is being marched down a set of stairs by Nikolai's once-dead big brother.

Even ghosts resurrect when news circulates about Satan being sent back to hell.

From what I've overheard the past few hours, Rico and his wife were country hopping the first two years of their son's life. They only settled down in a coastal town many miles from here when Blaire's father fell ill. Although he's now recovered, I don't see Rico packing his suitcase again any time soon.

He's not here for Vladimir's throne.

He came to help Nikolai seize it, knowing Nikolai's reign is the only chance he'll have to live the remainder of his life in peace. If I had the same comradery with my sibling six years ago, I'm reasonably sure my father's bid to seize control of Prague would have been successful.

Alas, not every man who carries your blood is your ally.

With sirens growing stronger, Nikolai guides Justine to the first fleet of SUVs while I finish loading up the ones that will follow him. We're looking at piling over a dozen women into three SUVs.

With figures not stacking up, I take advantage of the situation. "You can travel with me."

The petite blonde's eyes rocket to mine when I stop her from entering the vehicle on the heel of the woman she hasn't let out of her sight for a minute. Dirty blonde hair falls in front of her face when she vigorously shakes her head.

I can see the denial in her eyes, smell it pumping out of her, but what can I say, I'm an arrogant prick who doesn't like taking no for an answer. "I wasn't asking."

After shoving a woman with more meat on her frame than the one standing in front of me, I slam the door shut, tap on the roof to signal for Nikolai's fleet to commence moving, then shift on my feet to face the unnamed blonde.

I've barely cranked my neck halfway around when the crack of her fist on my jaw thrusts my head back further than what's natural. She swung at me so hard, my jaw will ache for a week.

What did I tell you? She's got spunk.

Even though I usually retaliate to violence with violence, I don't do that this time around. Not only are my fists not close to being clenched, the blonde is hightailing it away from me. For how fragile her legs look, they shouldn't be able to pump as well as they do.

She races up the stairs at the speed of lightning, only stopping when I growl out, "If you want to see your sister again, get your ass in my car."

Confident about my assessment of her desperateness, I jog around to the driver's side of my car, crank open the door, then slide in behind the steering wheel. A voice inside of me screams for me not to be a prick, but it isn't the only noise I'm hearing.

My heart is also thudding in my ears.

It hasn't done that in a very long time.

I stop assessing the rarity of my pulse beeping in my ears when the crank of a handle breaks through the oddity. The blonde slips into the passenger seat so soundlessly if her unique scent didn't stir my cock, I wouldn't have realized my ruse had worked. She doesn't have a pure smell, but it's most certainly enticing. It is roughish and dark and has me recalling a damp, obscure place where two people could cause a heap of trouble.

While wringing my steering wheel, I push out, "Put on your seat belt. Don't want you getting hurt."

I don't look at her, but I feel her eyes on me for eight long heartbeats before she does as told. Once the familiar click of a latch being locked into place sounds through my ears, I crank the engine, pull my car next to the stairs she raced up mere seconds ago, then grab a box of matches out of the glove compartment. Although I have no clue what the fuck my game plan is tonight, this feels as right as it did when I followed India into the butler's pantry at her family compound.

I can only hope it doesn't end as disastrously.

"Do you want the pleasure, or shall I?"

When I shove the matches the blonde's way, she peers at me with wide and apprehensive eyes. I'm dying for her to talk, to say one of the many thoughts I see in her head, but I also like her quiet. I get an immense amount of satisfaction from silence, and I won't mention how it doubles the tension teeming between us, or you'll think I'm as insane as Vladimir once was.

"Go on," I say with a nudge of my head. "Send the bastard to hell where he belongs."

With a faint dip of her chin, she pulls one of the matches out of the box before dragging it down the flint. I realize just how weak she is when she can't run the matchhead down the side of the box with enough force to get a spark. Believing I was the only thing standing between her and freedom, she put all her strength into hitting me, so she doesn't have an ounce left to give.

"Here, let me."

When she grunts while snatching the matchbox back, a smile tugs at my lips. She wants Vladimir to burn in hell as much as she wants to take credit for helping with his demise. That isn't the reason I'm smirking, though. Her grunt—*Fuck. Me.* I've only heard one noise more seductive than it. It was years ago, and it cost me everything, so a second-best noise shouldn't make me as hard as it does, but it does. I'm so hard, my cock's head is knocking at the zipper in my jeans, begging to be freed.

After warning my cock to calm down, I say, "We'll do it together."

With sirens growing louder, I grab her hands a little more roughly than intended. She stops shaking when our joint drag of the matchhead down the flint sparks it to life. She stares at the flickering flame for what feels like hours before she tosses it out the window.

With Nikolai's men being super friendly with their gasoline cans, it only takes seconds for flames to lick the walls of Vladimir's private compound. They race up the wooden shutters before engulfing the thick rafters holding the roof up.

Within minutes, the entire building is lit up with hues of orange and red.

Confident no amount of water will douse the raging inferno, I plant my foot onto the gas pedal of my Shelby. With recent rain making conditions muddy, the tires slip and slide in the wet conditions before they eventually grip the tiny shards of gravel Vladimir laid to ensure none of his guests at his house of horrors would get bogged down.

The knowledge of the courtesies he offered his 'guests' has my jaw working side to side. The woman seated next to me has clearly been used and abused, yet, I'm still putting my needs above hers. And for what? Because she reminds me of a girl I hardly knew and a past I'd give anything to forget.

Clearly, I need to cut back on the drugs. My head is getting too fucked-up.

SIX

For most of our trip through the sloshy fields, the blonde in my passenger seat keeps her eyes fixated on the side mirror. She watches the black plumes of smoke rising from Vladimir's compound until it becomes one with the pitch-black night.

Although hues of orange are seen for some time, within minutes, her focus shifts from the past to the present. She stares at her reflection for several long seconds, moving closer the more the sticky night air combs the knots out of her hair.

The wind whipping past her face from my fast speed makes quick work of her tears, but I don't need to see wetness on her cheeks to know she's crying. I can smell the saltiness of her tears lingering in my nostrils. It's an addictive scent that shouldn't be as arousing as it is.

When I take a right at a T-intersection, I spot what the muted blonde wrote in the condensation her heavy breaths made to the side mirror. It's the letter K.

"Is that what your name begins with? K?"

The tightness in my jaw grows when she scrubs her fingertips over the gleaming glass. I'm not frustrated she's putting massive barriers between us. I wouldn't have expected any less from a woman who's been through what she went through. It's the thinness of her wrist that has my molars grinding together. I could circle her wrist with my thumb and index finger, and I guarantee there'd still be a gaping hole between us.

"When was the last time you ate, K?"

She's shocked about me calling her K, however, it's barely seen through the truth on her face that it's been a very long time since her belly has been full.

Her bright blue eyes snap to mine when I slam on my brakes before completing an illegal U-turn. Although Clarks has enough food in its industrial confines to feed an army, it'll take the once-whores a good twenty to thirty minutes to rustle something up. I can't wait that long to put food in K's stomach. If I do, guilt will eat me alive, and we're not going to mention the ghosts of my past, or I'll force her to eat until her stomach pops.

With the night still early for Vegas locals, I pull straight up to the Sonic drive-in speaker without needing to wait. "What do you want to eat, K? You can have any fucking thing you want. Beef, chicken, wings. You can have it all if you want."

K's stomach growls in hunger, but she remains as quiet as a church mouse, only gasping when my desperateness to show her not all men are pieces of shit sees me placing an order for one of everything on the menu. I might be an asshole, but not even the hardest gangster could look at someone as frail as K and not offer them a bite of their sandwich—not even Nikolai. You'd have to be completely heartless not to feel some kind of remorse, and mine is ten times worse since I knew the game Vladimir was running, and I didn't do anything about it.

Yeah, I could be accused of treating the whores at Clarks like shit, but they're there because they want to be there. K and the women being transported to Clarks never had a say in the matter. Even pimps treat their hookers better than Vladimir treated his captives.

The bills I toss to the cashier at the window haven't been laundered, but since I don't see much of it landing in the cash register, I'm not worried.

With my order obsessive, I anticipate for my car to be full to the brim with bags of greasy food. It would be if I didn't tell the cashier to hold all the drinks bar two. I can't guarantee K won't hurl the instant one of the burgers reaches her stomach, so I'll keep her drink selection to plain ole' bottled water.

"Are you going to eat something?" I ask K after tossing the final bag of food into the back of my car and recommencing our trip.

I don't get words, but she does shake her head. Her response frustrates me more than the whore who took herself for a ride on my cock yesterday morning. I'm finally capable of doing a good deed, but the person I'm testing the rarity out on doesn't want my help.

What the fuck?

"Why not? You're hungry, aren't you?" A tick impinges my jaw when a reason behind her hunger strike pops into my head. "You won't be expected to repay me for the meal. You don't owe me shit. I can get my dick sucked without handing over a dime, so you've got nothing to worry about."

I don't know whether to be pleased or pissed when she continues clutching several grease-laden bags in close to her chest. I'm glad she isn't holding back because the idea of sucking my cock repulses her enough she'd rather starve, but still, I wish she'd eat something. Just looking at me is making me hungry, and no, I'm not solely referring to the feast only women can serve me.

K's breaths come out ragged when I pull my car down the long driveway of the Popov compound. People usually drool over the thirty-plus room mansion. K looks far from impressed. She's more panicked now than she was when she spotted my gawk from afar forty minutes ago.

Her worry is warranted. P's is elaborate, but no amount of glamor can mask the scent of desecration.

The same can be said for my aftershave.

I angle my head to hide my smirk while saying, "I need to drop something off real quick. You can come with me or stay here..." My words trail off when K tugs bags of food in closer to her chest, denying my request without words. "All right. I'll be back in a tick. Don't go anywhere." My last comment was more in jest than a demand. Manned guards are on every corner of P's. Even if she wants to run, she won't get far.

After slipping out the driver's seat, I hotfoot it up the side entrance most of the once-whores-now-maids use. Just as I reach the foyer, Nikolai and Justine enter from the other side. Considering she was sold tonight to a bunch of worthless pricks with more money than sense, she looks well put together... *if* you exclude her out-of-control body shakes.

The same can't be said for Nikolai. He looks a little lost—*kind of like me.* A weird sensation is bristling in the air. It could be because a new monarch just seized his throne as my brother tried to do years ago, but in all honesty, it feels more than that. It's a strange sensation but highly addictive.

I stop at Rico's side just as he offers for Nikolai to leave business to us. "Go take care of Justine. Trey and I will get everything under control down here."

My lips quirk into a smile, smug-as-fuck Rico sees me as an

equal. I doubt he will if any of the rumblings out of Nikolai's crew the past eight hours reaches his ears. Supposedly, we're each other's biggest competitors. I thought our placement in Nikolai's life would make us more allies than enemies. It appears as if Rico agrees with me.

With that in mind, I lock my eyes with Nikolai and say, "We know where to find you if we need you."

He lifts his chin at our suggestion. "Take care of everything *but* her." He strays his eyes from me to Malvina sitting wonky on a single-seater couch since her arms and legs are still bound. "We've got a few matters to discuss before she returns to Russia. *If* she returns to Russia."

With three sets of murderous eyes on her, Malvina's throat works hard to swallow. It appeases Nikolai's worries in an instant.

Confident we're more than capable of holding down the fort, Nikolai commences leading Justine to the stairwell. I wait for him to disappear down the corridor on the top level of the compound before shifting on my feet to face Malvina. The quicker I get her into lockdown, the faster I can return to K, who I'm hoping like fuck is still waiting for me in my car.

My steps to Malvina halt mid-stride when Rico says, "You appear to have your hands full, so why don't you leave Malvina for me."

When I peer at him, lost as to what he means, he nudges his head to the door I walked through only thirty seconds ago. K is peering through the spotlessly clean glass. It's clear from the expression on her face she's scared, but her fear isn't high enough for her to place it above the person she's seeking.

It's that side of her that intrigues me—her strong side.

Even from a distance, I can't deny my body's response to her fragile, broken appearance. I don't want to fix her. I'm fascinated as fuck to discover if she can fix herself. If an abused sex slave can claw her way back from the brink, who's to say I can't do the same.

Upon spotting Rico and my gawking stares, K's eyes pop so far out of her head, I'm certain they'll feel the burn of her dehydration for days to come before she pivots on her bare feet and dashes down the stairs.

"Shouldn't you go after her?" Rico asks, concerned she's running.

I shake my head. "She isn't going anywhere. I have something she wants." And for the first time tonight, I'm not referencing the woman she wouldn't let out of her sight.

Broken people attract broken people because they know better than anyone that only when you're at your best, do you attract your worst. K doesn't trust me any more than the man standing next to me, but she isn't scared of me. That's why she hit me.

You can't fear someone who lives in the same shadow as you.

Needing to end one injustice before taking up another, I dig a sheet of paper out of my pocket. It's covered with dirt, but its importance is highly notable, even more so since a sex slave wrote a single letter into the fog of her heated breaths.

"While you're tucking Malvina in for the night, perhaps you could ask her about this."

Rico's dark brows stitch when I hand a sale docket I found in the room Malvina was hiding out in during our raid. If I were to believe what it says, Nikolai purchased a whore by the name of Kristina Svoboda for one point two million dollars earlier this week —days after falling dick first for Justine.

"Is this legitimate?" Rico asks, his tone pitched with annoyance.

It's obvious I'm not the only man in the room with a dislike for the sex-trafficking industry. I get it makes a lot of money, and to some men, that surpasses anything, but you've got more issues than a fucked-up head if you need to force someone to sleep with you. You must have a dog's ass for a face, or worse, a limp dick. There's no other explanation. Clarks is swamped with whores willing to do anything to become one of my brothers' old ladies, and they don't get handed a dime, so if you're paying for it, it's time to check yourself.

When Rico arches his brow, prompting me to answer him, I shrug. "I had Mikhail take a quick look at it after the raid. A matching set of funds left Nikolai's bank account hours after Kristina's sale."

Rico works his jaw side to side before telling me to leave it to him. "Even dead Vladimir is still fucking with Nikolai's head."

I jerk up my chin, agreeing with him. "There's something murky going on here. Nikolai is—"

"As pussy whipped as the rest of us, so he'd never pay for a side-whore? Yeah, I get that."

Although I agree with most of his comment, I scoff about my inclusion in his equation. I'm as free as a bird *and itching like fuck to get back to my car to check if K is back inside.*

Pretending his rile has no basis whatsoever, I play it cool while Rico guides Malvina toward the 'dungeon' half of the mansion. The instant he's out of earshot, I hotfoot it to my car.

I'm not surprised to spot K sitting in the passenger seat. However, I am as smug as fuck.

With my cocky smile hidden by an angled chin, I slide into the driver's seat of my Shelby and fire up the ignition. K keeps her eyes front and center when I tell her to put her seat belt back on, but I hear the nervous bob of her throat. She isn't fearful she was busted being disobedient, she's uneased about me calling her Kristina. That can only mean one thing. Either she isn't Kristina, or she hates the name.

Whatever the reason, I won't use it again.

Knowing her name won't have me understanding her story any better.

Only she can do that.

We travel the four miles to Clarks in silence. It's quicker to go over the rugged landscape than around it, but the lapse in time gives me a chance to get my head screwed on straight. Only one time have I acted this reckless. It ended disastrously, so I'll do anything to skip another shit-fest.

When K's body temperature notches up a couple of degrees from me pulling my car into Clarks, her unusual scent doubles. I suck in the fear bubbling in her veins like it's a line of coke while searching for a spot to park. I don't want to walk far while carrying dozens of bags of greasy food.

Although Clarks is newer, cleaner, and more up-to-date than the compound K was rescued from, I can understand her panic when she drinks in the modern fortress. The men here are as rowdy as they are horny. She has no reason to fret, though. Nikolai put a no-touch order on the women rescued, so unless they have a death wish, the men will follow Nikolai's command.

"I'm just helping you take the food inside," I assure K when a growl rumbles in her chest about me snagging the bags from the backseat. "We'll camp out here until the heat dies down, then work out where we go from here. The rest of the girls are inside, so how about we get them the food before it's stone-cold?"

In silence, she watches me gather up the rest of the bags before she joins me outside my car. She looks more scared than strong as we make our way inside, but I still see the tiny flicker of hope in her eyes. Her strides are as lengthy as mine, just ten times shakier.

"No one will touch you. I promise you that." Since my assurance was straight-up honest, it sounded that way. It was also possessive, but we'll keep that snippet of information between us. With the adrenaline high of a raid having my head teetering between the past and the present, I've got a set of fucked-up circumstances fueling my emotions, so a little leeway wouldn't go astray.

Eight's eyes lift to mine when I enter the main living area of Clarks with K shadowing just behind me. With a handful of the men sporting bullet wounds, the smell of blood is stronger than the chemicals pumping out of the jacuzzi housing half a dozen topless whores. Well, I assume they're topless. I can't see their lower halves, so there are no guarantees. Most of the women get around here naked. It's how the men like it. They battled hard today, so they'll celebrate just as intensely.

I'm usually just as eager, but my mind is elsewhere right now. Once I get K settled, I'll work on getting my head screwed on right.

"Where are the rest of the girls?" I ask Eight, talking loud so he can hear me over the music pumping out of the stereo at his side.

Eight nudges his head toward the sleeping quarters at the back of the space. "Nero said to put them in the bunkers. Is Nikolai staying at P's tonight?"

P is what my brothers call the Popov compound. Nikolai usually resides at Clarks, but I can see how that would be awkward for his girl with the number of naked women wandering around, and don't get me started on the horndogs in his crew. They'll bat one off right outside your door if your hookup's moans are enticing enough.

I lift my chin, answering Eight's question before gesturing for K to head in the direction Eight nudged his head at. Nikolai's order for the girls to remain untouched pops back into my head when I notice a handful of eyes following K's slow retreat. Bags of greasy food hide her chest from view, but they don't do shit for the lower half of her body.

Even with her being tiny enough for my cock to snap her in half, the shadows under her nightgown are mighty enticing, and my brothers in arms are more than happy to drink them in.

Generally, I'm happy for them to look as long as they don't touch, but that isn't cutting the mustard today. "If anyone needs a reminder about Nikolai's directive, I'll be back in ten."

You'd swear K suddenly turned ugly when numerous sets of eyes drop to the floor. I'm not surprised. The punishment for disobeying Nikolai's direct order is death. Mine is almost as bad. You'll be wishing you were dead by the time I'm done with you.

Proof K can understand me is awarded when I tell her to take a left at the end of the hall. Although I'm pleased she has no issues following instructions, unease melds through my veins when her quick pivot causes the hair hanging to her waist to swish away from her back. Blood is seeping into her nightgown. It isn't coming from the lower extremities of her body—*thank fuck*. It's a diagonal pattern across her back, similar to how a sash would be draped if she won a beauty contest.

Rage unlike anything I've ever felt pummels into me when reality dawns. Those fuckers didn't just rape and starve her, they beat her as well. Vladimir was a sick fuck, but this is worse than I realized. I've seen a lot of sanctions in my twenty-eight years. None have been this fucked-up. Nikolai has his work cut out for him, even more so when he discovers the full extent of Vladimir's quirks.

Several grubby faces snap to the door when we enter the dormitory the women are being held in. When they spot the bags of food in our hands, the once-dormant mob activates. They race our way like scavengers discovering a giant X on a sandy island to snatch the greasy food out of our hands.

I let them have it without so much as a fight, suddenly not hungry. K isn't as willing to give up her stash. She's more than happy for them to take two of her bags, but she fights to keep the third one.

Grunting, K pushes the women back with the aggression she used to sock me in the face. Although she's half the size of most of the women, she gives as good as she's getting.

I discover the fuel behind her gallantry when her victory sees her joining a woman at the back of the pack. It's the blonde I'm assuming is her sister. She has a similar shaped face and eyes, but hers aren't holding the fighting gleam K's have.

When Eight bumps me with his shoulder, I work my jaw through the annoyance of K handing her entire bag of food to the woman she was glued to earlier. "I asked the cooks to rummage up some grub. They should bring more supplies in around twenty." After following the direction of my gaze, he asks, "Who is she to you?"

"She's no one." That was harder to articulate than it should have been, and Eight is happy to call me out on it with a mocking grin.

After backhanding him in the chest, wordlessly warning him to stand down before I rearrange his face with my fists, I instruct, "Come find me when the food arrives."

I'm not hungry, I just need to make sure K eats. At the moment, everyone in the room is taking advantage of her selflessness, including her sister.

That shit needs to stop.

People become fucked-up when they place themselves at the top of the agenda, but that doesn't mean the people stuck on the bottom rung have to take their shit. You can rule without being an asshole. Both K and her sister need to learn that, and perhaps the men I once called my brothers, but that's a story for another day.

SEVEN

SALES DOCKET NUMBER 12574

When a chunk of the patty from Ana's burger she's practically swallowing whole falls out of its packaging, I try to catch it before it lands on the filthy floor. Although this holding cell is newer and cleaner than the ones I've seen the past ten weeks, there's no denying it is dirty. Just the soot off the women's feet when they scampered to steal the food the bearded man purchased for us has me cringing when I miscalculate the fall of the fat-laden meat.

It lands on the floor a mere inch in front of me. It's flip-flop-flap routine almost breaks my heart. Not because I hate wasting food, but because I snatch it up and shove it in my mouth like my desperateness won't have the bearded man peering at me with even more sympathy.

I don't want his sympathy.

I want my freedom.

A string of whimpers breaks throughout the crowd when my swallow of the greasy meat causes the thud of boots to race across the room. The brooding stranger who made me feel safe for the first time in years when he saved me from the yearning gawk of his friends charges across the room. His jaw ticks like it did when I couldn't get the stupid match to spark, and his fists are clenched into tight balls.

When he stops a foot from my dirty feet tucked under my bottom, I slant my head to the side with a flinch, prepared for the sting of his strike. He didn't retaliate to my violence earlier when I struck him, but men are less forgiving when they feel humiliated.

Me eating food off the floor mere seconds after standing up for me like I'm worth something would most likely humiliate him.

Although my cheek doesn't feel the scorn of his annoyance, my wrist sure does when he uses it to pluck me from the floor. I don't know if he's hurting me on purpose, or he doesn't realize how strong he is. Whatever it is, whimpers rattle my ribcage, although not a snivel escapes my lips. I don't want him to see me cry, even with my willpower having nothing to do with my time in captivity.

When he walks me toward the door we walked through only seconds ago, I shoot my eyes to Ana, hopeful she'll fight for me as hard as I fought for her in the past. Her eyes, along with a dozen or so more, watch me being dragged out of the room, but her lips don't twitch in the slightest.

Mercifully, help arrives from someone I never anticipated. The giant standing at the door scrapes his hand across the stubble on his chin as his eyes lock with the man separating me from the pack. "Trey... you know Nikolai's orders. He won't be happy if you disobey him."

My eyes snap to Trey's so quickly, I make myself dizzy, but before I can work through an ounce of my confusion, he growls out, "I'm not fucking her. I'm going to feed her. If Nikolai has an issue with that, he'll have to tell me himself." With my pulse roaring in my ears, I could be forgiven for mistaking his last growled sentence. "Because I won't have her eating off the fucking floor like a savage."

After instructing the giant to keep an eye on the other captives, Trey commences walking me down the hall. He takes a left at the end before he marches us past a jacuzzi full of scantily-clad women.

I cover my chest with the hand Trey isn't clutching, not just shy about the number of eyes I have on my almost-exposed breasts from the men we race by, but embarrassed my body looks nothing like the women eyeing Trey with interest. Even before I was imprisoned, I didn't look like them. They have perky breasts, flawless faces, and perfectly made-up hair that looks professionally done each morning. They're beautiful, even with them being seen more as a commodity than a person.

How is that possible?

Aren't they ashamed of who they are?

Before I can find answers to my questions, Trey bursts us through a large stainless-steel swinging door. The smells streaming into my nose has my stomach flipping. I can't tell if it's a good flip or a bad one. I'm as hungry as hell, but I've never been given anything without a consequence attached to the action, so I must remain cautious.

I also don't trust anyone. I'm a good enough person to forgive someone who does me wrong and admits it, but trust isn't something that comes easy for me. I've been burned too much in the past to hand it around lightheartedly.

"Out!" When the half-dozen middle-aged women working in the super-size kitchen fail to jump to Trey's snapped command, he hits them with another. "If I'm forced to repeat myself, it won't just be your pay I'll slice."

When they scamper out of the room, I want to follow them. I would if I could. Trey is clutching my wrist too firmly for me to escape. Even being held captive as a sex slave hasn't improved my knowledge of the opposite sex, but I'm confident his hold is as possessive as it is aggressive. It prickles the fine hairs on my arms as well as his underhanded glances do.

He doesn't look at me how most men do. Very rarely do his eyes drop to any of the areas below my face. It is like he can see my secrets in my eyes, so he doesn't need to assess the damage firsthand.

I'd be scared by that fact if I couldn't see his just as easily. He's dark and dangerous, but he wasn't always this way.

Someone broke him too.

Is he damaged beyond repair like me? I honestly don't know, but I can't stick around to find out. I didn't endure years of hell to forget my objectives now.

"Don't even think about it," Trey mutters under his breath when he veers us past a butcher block brimming with super sharp knives. I barely glanced at them for a second, however, his worry is very much warranted. It only took a nanosecond for me to conjure up numerous ways I could escape with one knife, much less half a dozen of them.

My stomach gurgles for an entirely new reason when Trey says, "I don't want to hurt you, K..." He strays his eyes to mine. The gleam in them certifies my earlier assumption that his hold is as possessive as it is aggressive. "But I will if forced."

Either trusting me in a way he shouldn't or hoping I'll force him to hurt me, he lifts me to sit on a part of a bench not covered with apple peels and cores. Although the knives used to peel the apples aren't as large as the ones we walked past, they could still cause a lot of damage to the vein in Trey's neck that hasn't stopped thumping out its own tune for the past twenty minutes.

After dropping his eyes to the high rise of my nightgown for barely a second, Trey floats his eyes up to mine. They're familiar, yet foreign. Both dangerous and welcoming. Beautiful and tormented.

Dead, yet still alive.

When his lips furl into a smirk, my heart matches the mariachi beat of the vein in his neck. He isn't laughing at me. He is smirking about my brutal clutch of an apple corer. I would have preferred to protect myself with a sharp blade, but the apple corer was closer, so I worked with what I had.

Like a man not in fear for his life, Trey hits me with a frisky wink before he turns his back on me. As shock bolts through me, my mouth falls open. I could strike now and hightail it for the screen door on my right, but for the life of me, I can't. It isn't just my wish to take Ana with me that has me ignoring the many inane thoughts in my head. It's him, the man who felt the crack of my fist, yet doesn't display an ounce of fear about me brandishing a weapon.

I'd be impressed by his gall if it didn't make me feel so pathetic.

"I'm assuming by the chunk of meat you popped into your mouth, you're not a vegetarian." Although he isn't technically asking a question, when he spins around to face me with a bowl full of meat, potatoes, and vegetables, I nod. "Good, then you can eat this. Although I suggest you go easy, so your stomach doesn't get upset."

I accept the bowl he's holding out for me, but I don't touch the contents inside making my stomach grumble so fiercely, I'm afraid our gathering will soon be interrupted by spectators wondering where the rumbles are coming from. If I leave the hot dish in his hands, I risk being scolded by more than his eyes when I refuse his generosity. As far as Vladimir was concerned, being discourteous was as punishable as being disobedient.

With his hip balanced on the counter next to my practically

bare thigh, Trey's eyes bounce between the bowl of stew and me for the next several minutes. They're darker than they were earlier, somewhat fortified.

"Eat," he commands a few seconds later, his tone gravelly. I shouldn't find his accent comforting, but for some reason, I do. It reminds me of home even with it belonging to a country thousands of miles in the wrong direction.

Trey's jaw is covered by a wiry beard, but I still spot its tick when I timidly shake my head. I'm starving, but how can I be sure he didn't turn his back on me for no reason? The burgers were safe. I saw them prepared in front of me, and they barely left my sight during our trip.

This meal wasn't scrutinized in the same manner.

Furthermore, I don't know this man, so I have no reason to trust him.

As his pupils dilate, Trey gives credit to my distrust. "Don't force me to hurt you, K." He brings his six-foot-three height down a couple of inches so he can meet me eye to eye. "You need to eat. If you won't do that without me ramming food down your throat, so be it, I'll do that. I will shovel it into your stomach until it bursts if that's the only way I can get you to eat." His words are barely whispers when he adds, "Then the hungry growls of your stomach might stop fucking killing me."

I peer at him through scrunched brows, shocked. I thought his threat to hurt me centered around a sexual preference. I had no clue he was referencing my refusal to eat.

Although the knowledge has me wishing I could sample the food warming my hands as well as his prolonged gawk heats up my dead-cold heart, I can't. He isn't the first man to bribe me with food. Vladimir starved me for three days straight before he entered my room with a sandwich. It was bland and boring, a combination many residents of the United States are a fan of, but it cost me a fortune.

That was the first time I broke.

I've not yet forgiven myself for it.

I will never eat a peanut butter and jelly sandwich without tasting Vladimir's cum.

With my stomach flipping in contempt, I thrust the bowl of stew back toward Trey. My refusal to eat means not a speckle of blue can be seen in his eyes. His nostrils flare as he rakes his hand across his jaw, pondering. He looks torn between wanting to back-hand me or forcefully spooning the food into my mouth as threatened.

I realize it's the latter when he jabs a spoon into the meaty goodness with so much force, broth spills over the edge of the bowl and splashes onto my thighs. It sizzles on my skin, but I'm too stunned by Trey shoving the spoon into his mouth to worry about a little burn.

"Do you trust it's not laced with drugs now?" he asks through a mouthful of meaty goop. "Or would you like me to feed you like you're a baby bird? I'm up for both, K, so spell out what you'd prefer."

I freeze, both shocked and excited by his comment. How is it that he already knows me well enough to know I'm panicked my food is tainted? We've only just met, haven't we?

I freeze again when panic slams into me. He couldn't have been one of Vladimir's guests. He hated him. I could feel the dislike pumping out of him when he helped me light the match that sent Vladimir to hell, but that doesn't mean he wasn't one of Vladimir's goons. This isn't an industry where you must like the man throwing around orders. As long as it pays well, some men have no limits on how far they'll go for a man they hate.

I learned that the hard way many times the past twenty-two years.

The knocks keep coming when another disturbing notion smacks into me. What if we weren't saved? What if we've been captured by another sanction as demoralizing as Vladimir's—or worse, one shoddier?

I barely survived my last trade.

I won't survive a second one.

Preferring to die fighting than be seen as weak, I kick out with a grunt. Trey's jeans wear as much of the stew as mine when my shove knocks the bowl out of his hand.

When his back slams into the six-burner stovetop opposite the counter I'm sitting on, I leap off it with a soundless grunt, confident I'll have the speed needed to reach the open screen door before him.

I'll come back for Ana the instant I find help.

I'll save her once I've saved myself.

My plan goes to shit when my bare feet slip on the mess I made on the floor. I fumble like a newborn giraffe, my campaign for freedom undone in a matter of seconds.

Trey's earlier clutch on my wrist has nothing on the one he wraps around my waist. He pulls me into his fit body before he drops our weird, tangled mess to the floor with a thud.

"Stop it!" he demands when my nails digging into his tattooed arms agitate him more than my wish to escape. "I'm not going to hurt you. I am trying to fucking help you."

When his roared words reach the ears of his crew, we're joined in the kitchen by three of his men. I thought their humored faces would end Trey's charade in an instant. It couldn't be further from the truth. With one of his legs wrapped around my waist, and his arm pinning my back to his thrusting chest, Trey demands a dark-haired man to bring over the pot of stew simmering on the stovetop.

Once he has a generous helping sloppily served into the bowl I kicked out of his hand, he fishes out a large chunk of meat before steering it toward my face. I clamp my lips together as firmly as I can, but they're no match for the strength and girth of Trey's fingers. He strains the chunk of beef through my lips, and then my teeth in a matter of seconds before adding a warning to the deadly gleam in his eyes.

"If so much as a drop of stew spills from your lips, I'll feed you like this every fucking day for the rest of your life. Do you hear me, K? I'm not fucking playing. I've got all the time in the world to force you to eat, so there won't be any skin off my back if moments like this are added to my daily routine."

With my shock higher than my belief my food is tainted with drugs, my lips part to accept the next chunk of the food Trey fishes out of the bowl. Its texture and starchiness tells me it's a piece of potato. It is tastier than the chunk of steak, although my body will never admit that. It is shut down in shock, muted and confused as to why this rough, rugged, and pierced man is so pedantic about me eating. It's not like he'd be upset if I starved to death. No one cares about me, not even people I classed as family, so why does a stranger feel the need to take up the campaign?

I peer at Trey through a different set of eyes when he mutters, "Good girl. Keep eating." He feeds me like a father would their sick child. His hold is anything but gentle, but his eyes are brimming with unusual tenderness.

By the time I realize Trey's Adam's apple matches the bobs of my throat when I swallow his offerings into my stomach, I've consumed half a bowl of stew. It feels good to have food in my tummy, but no amount of heaviness stops its flips. I feel out of my element here, even more than I did when I 'entertained' my first lot of guests.

After wiping away the meaty dribbles running down my chin with his hand, Trey lifts his eyes to something above us. When I follow the direction of his gaze, I'm anticipating to see three humored faces peering back at me, so you can imagine my surprise when I discover the kitchen is empty. It's just Trey and me, alone, and in a lighted room.

With no concerns about waste, Trey uncurls the leg wrapped around my midsection to knock down a bowl of bread from the counter. I don't know whether to laugh or cry about his worry I'll attempt to escape the instant he releases me, so I smile instead. It's not a big smile. I don't think I'm showing any of the teeth that were hard to keep clean with a lack of accessories, but Trey notices it in an instant.

As his lips lift in a similar fashion, he asks, "Are you smiling 'cause I look like I shit my pants? Or are you excited about devouring some fresh bread?" Although he's asking a question, he continues talking as if he didn't. "I can still recall the first time I sampled bread straight out of the oven. It was warm and spongy... almost as delicious as a woman's cunt." A flare darts through his eyes when he drops and locks them with mine. "This isn't warm, K, but I swear to you, it's fresh."

My heart beats out a funky tune when he rips off a chunk of the bread and pops it into his mouth. After angling his head so I can see the bob of his Adam's apple from him swallowing it down, he tears off another generous chunk for me. He doesn't force it into my mouth this time around, though. He holds it out in front of me, offering it up as if there won't be any stipulations attached to his generosity.

It takes me longer to accept than I care to admit. My mind is still spiraling with debilitating confusion, so a lack of respect can be excused. Furthermore, men I once called friends hurt me for less than a chunk of bread, so it'll take a lot longer than an hour for me to trust one I hardly know.

"More?" Trey asks when our turn-for-turn on the bread roll sees it consumed in under a minute.

Although I still feel hollow on the inside, I shake my head, confident the empty feeling has nothing to do with a hungry stomach.

"All right." Trey stands to his feet without the slightest bit of discomfort fettering his features from my monkey hold. "Then, how about we get cleaned up."

Don't misconstrue his wording. He isn't suggesting we should do this. He's telling me what we're doing. It's a known trait of all men in this industry.

Usually, I hate it. It isn't irking my nerves as much tonight, though.

After placing me back on my feet, Trey curls his tattooed hand around mine. His hold is less aggressive than it was previously, but there's no denying its possessiveness.

When we enter the common area in the middle of the compound, my eyes float up from the floor to Trey when he says, "Give the women access to the shower stalls. They'll need clothes and toiletries. If the whores don't have enough to share, send someone out to get supplies." He's speaking with the man he was talking to earlier, the giant who's missing a finger from each of his hands. "And have some of Nero's men guard that side of the compound tonight, but ensure they're aware of Nikolai's order. If they are touched—"

"There will be hell to pay," the unnamed man interrupts. As his tongue fiddles with the circular ring in the corner of his bottom lip, he drags his eyes down my body. His prolonged gawk of my stew-stained nightgown doesn't make my stomach flip, but his questions sure do. "What about her? Want me to take her back to the dorm?"

I doubt he'd touch me, fear was the first emotion that flared through his eyes when he finalized Trey's threat. It is Trey's reply that has my stomach twisted up in knots. "No. She's staying with me."

I don't know why his answer shocks me. I paid horrendously for a peanut butter and jelly sandwich, so why would I anticipate a lessor response for a much more heartier meal? Nothing in life is free, and I'm about to learn that the hard way for the third time in my life.

EIGHT

TREY

"Eight is going to get you some clothes, but for now, you can wear one of my shirts."

After double-checking the temperature of the water pelting out of the shower, I spin around to face the main section of my room. Clarks is like a fortress. It's made out of concrete, glass, and steel, and has an impressive amount of floor space, however, its sleeping quarters aren't hideously ugly like the rooms Vladimir held his captives in. They're like hotel rooms with king-size beds, double-headed showers, and state-of-the-art equipment.

I swear the person who built this compound was either gay or a chick because even the roughest and meanest members of Nikolai's crew have hairdryers in their bathrooms. I've had my room the longest. It was the first space I was given that didn't represent a prison cell after my failed bid to take down the Dvořáks, and the only place I go when I'm feeling lost.

K is making me feel lost. The dark bleakness in her eyes, the frailness of her skin, and the pained expression on her face that never quits has me wanting to go on a killing spree. Considering our heist today notched my tally up to thirty-three deaths this year alone, the craving shouldn't be as strong as it is, but fuck me, the urge is fierce, even more so when my entrance to my room has me stumbling onto a butt-naked and frozen-stiff woman.

K is lying in the middle of my bed. Her nightgown is dumped on the floor. Because she doesn't have enough meat on her bones to cover up the shadows I could see long before she removed her grubby sleepwear, she's fully exposed.

Her tits, although smaller than I guess they'd be if she weren't starved, are perky and sit high on her chest, her lips are naturally plump, and her seductive-smelling cunt is barely concealed by a thin layer of blonde hair.

For how bruised, nicked, and malnourished she is, she shouldn't look enticing, but she does. She looks ravishing enough to eat, and my cock isn't ashamed to admit it. He sits heavy against the zipper in my jeans, throbbing with both need and desire.

As I close the distance between the bathroom and my bed, I tell my cock to calm the fuck down. It's twitching like K is a whore waiting to be consumed. Even if I wanted to pretend that's the case, I can't. The whores are too scared to come into my room without permission, so no amount of pleading from my cock could have me pretending I don't know what this is really about.

Although her eyes are open and her chest is rising and falling as she sucks in shallow breaths, K isn't here. She's completely fucking gone, swallowed by the blackness of her miserably bleak existence.

I know better than anyone that sometimes the only way you can escape the torment is by fully emerging yourself in it. More times than not, the darkness in your head is worse than anything you'll face in the real world, but when you're beyond broken, you've got no choice but to let it overwhelm you occasionally.

While tugging the bedding out from beneath K's immobile frame, the reason I was so desperate for her to shower smacks back into me. It isn't her smell. For someone who lived in the equivalent of a dungeon, her scent is intoxicating. It's the dry blood on her back and the marks that look like she was whipped.

"What the fuck did he do to you, K?" I murmur to myself while carefully rolling her over.

An itch to kill steamrolls into me when I see the full extent of her injuries. She wasn't whipped once. She was struck multiple times. The slashes across her back are so red and blistering, I'm confident they're brand new, like they were done mere minutes before she was freed from hell.

The torment tearing me up inside grows so perverse, within seconds, I'm trapped in the darkness in my head right along with K...

The breaths I suck in to cool the fire roaring through me does little to reduce the shakes wreaking havoc with my body. My hand holding a gun is shuddering so much, even with my target selected, I may end up killing the wrong person. I spun the wheel, her fate has been chosen, but no matter how hard I fight, I can't inch back the trigger.

It was one fuck, *I remind myself again.* It meant nothing. A hessian bag is pulled over her head. She won't even know it was you.

But I will know it was me. I'll remember how our night in the butler's pantry was the only time my pulse has fluttered in my ears. How her heat wrapped around my cock was the best it had felt. And her scent, my fucking God, her scent when she came undone will never leave me. It wasn't pure, it wasn't even sweet, but it was the most addictive scent I've ever sucked in.

If I kill her and live off the memories, my father won't pay for my crimes. If I don't, they'll both die. Those are the terms Achim spelled out when he caught me off-guard. I was still relishing her scent, still caught up on how her skin heated under my touch, I didn't realize I was walking into a trap until my leg was already snared by the prongs of an invisible bear trap.

My father shouldn't be here. I had not yet sent for him or his men, so not only was I surprised when I saw him bound and gagged at the round table Sahib makes all his decisions at, I was angry— really fucking angry. My father is stronger than Sahib and Achim combined. He has killed men by the thousands and is feared by millions, yet he sits in a chair, defenseless and weak.

And now I stand before him just as spinelessly.

I should take a risk. I have a gun in my hand, and the killer instincts to take down Achim long before the man with his pistol butted to my temple will yank back his trigger. It will most likely see us all go down in a fiery gun battle, but it has to be better than dying like a coward, right?

Ugh, it shouldn't be this fucking hard. Hate was born inside of me. It was nurtured by every man I took down and grew to a point I shouldn't give a shit about anyone, not the man who raised me or the woman who made my heart thud in my ears. I just need to get her smell out of my head, her taste from my mouth. If I can free myself from the memories debilitating me, I'll be able to inch back the trigger without a single worry. Killing is who I am. It's all I know.

So pull back the trigger! *Roars the evilness inside of me. Kill her as you had planned to do only weeks ago. Begin the war you crave more than the heat of her cunt wrapped around your cock.*

With a roar, I inch back the trigger as I was trained to do. The gun clicks, but the barrel fails to bang. The chamber is as empty as the now-gaping hole in my chest. I chose my family over her, yet the torment still won't end. Not just because India heard the empty coil of the chamber when I chose her fate, but because of the man entering the room from my left, clapping like he just watched the performance of his life.

"Bravo, Trey, Bravo. Blood is clearly thicker than water..." He angles his head to the side to fully free his smile before he adds, "... for you. I wasn't so lucky, was I? He didn't pick me over her. He left me to die."

"She was our mother," I argue even though I'm not truly sure if the ghost of my brother is standing across from me or if I'm over-dosing on the adrenaline surging through my veins. "She should have always been his first choice."

"I was his son!" Cole's roar shudders the dishware lining the far wall. They're china plates for each year the Dvořák's have been in power. I should have paid attention to how many there were before I agreed with my father that this takeover bid would be easy. "I was his blood, but that still wasn't enough to save me. I was still taken by his enemies, maimed, tortured, and beaten without him feeling a single ounce of remorse."

"That's not true, Cole. We searched for you for months. We killed men across the globe in the hopes of finding you. We've never stopped looking."

My older brother steps closer to me. His chest is flaring as hard as his nostrils. Although we're only a year apart, his face is wearier than mine, aged by the hardness of the war we were born in. "Yet, this is the first time I've seen you in the flesh in years." After straying his eyes to our father over my shoulder, he snarls. "We were never important to him. We were not his sons. We were soldiers used for war. Pawns in a game we never signed up for. He used us as much as Achim used his whore to get to you." He returns his eyes to mine. They're not wet with the tears they had when the enemies of our family made my father pick between his wife and his almost-grown son. They're dark and evil, an equal match to mine. "Was she worth it, Trey? Will the memories from your fuck in the pitch-black room keep you alive long after your soul leaves you?"

The tactical side of my head tells me not to fall for his tricks, the man standing across from me isn't my brother, so he shouldn't be treated as if he is, but I've always been more emotionally responsive than impersonal.

Cole's lips curl at one end when I dip my chin. "Yet, you still chose our father over her. I wonder how she'll handle the news?"

Confusion twists through me when he clicks his fingers together two times. I assume one of the many men surrounding me will yank the bag off India's head so I can see her disappointment as readily as I feel it, so you can imagine my surprise when they draw back the curtain separating the royal-size dining room from the crystal ball-room on our right. India is standing on the other side, uninjured and wide-eyed.

How can that be? She can't be in the ballroom and seated in front of me. She must be a doppelgänger. I can smell her heated skin lingering in the air. The bulletproof glass separating us wouldn't allow that. Cole must be playing tricks on me. He's fucking with my head as well as the years he was missing screwed our father's mind. He couldn't forgive himself for giving in, even when he would have lost everything if he didn't, so he drove himself mad to fix the injustice.

He destroyed anyone who played a part in Cole's demise, yet it still wasn't enough. He wants every man responsible to be held accountable for their crimes—himself included.

Now I understand why we're here, and how my father was taken down minus the bloodshed I'm accustomed to.

This isn't a takeover bid.

It's a mercy kill, a beg for forgiveness. Even if he ends up dead, he'll be freed from the torment that's been eating him alive the past four years. He will finally be free.

Refusing to let my family's legacy die without so much as a fight, I disarm the man holding a gun to my temple before turning his weapon onto Achim. It was foolish of me to do. I forgot blood is no longer thicker than water to Cole. He fires at our father a mere second after I gun down the man stupid enough to put himself between Achim and me. Cole doesn't just discharge one bullet, though. He pops three into our father's chest, ensuring there's no way I can mistake how he's hoping today's battle will end.

It's a pity he underestimated his little brother. After knocking over the blonde my hazy mind still believes is India to drop her lower than the line of fire, I take cover behind one of the massive concrete pillars holding up the top story of this compound.

From my vantage point, I take down another three men without injury. India isn't as lucky. A howl roars from her throat when her shoulder catches a wayward bullet. It isn't a kill shot, but the sob of pain tearing from her throat does have me leaving my hidey-hole.

Like a real-life motherfucking mafia kingpin, I walk straight toward my death, firing my gun as if bullets aren't being shredded through my stomach, my chest, and my shoulder. Even when my knees buckle beneath me, and blood pools in my mouth, I don't give up. I continue firing until my gun runs out of bullets, and the blood streaming from my body joins India's on the floor.

I can't see anything through the wooziness of my head. Her screams, though, they will never leave me, they'll haunt me through the botched surgery to remove six bullets from my body, through the shudders of an infection when forced to recover in the equivalent of a dungeon, and for the endless amount of torture Cole puts me through, having no clue the years he was missing were just as torturous for me as they were for him...

They are even with me now. They're just too quiet to break through the thud of my pulse in my ears. It's thumping nonstop, only ripped away when the pulse fading under my fingertips is torn from my grasp just as brutally.

Nero tackles me so fiercely, I splinter the drywall behind my bed when I crash into it with a bang. The ripple of pain my collision with the wall causes my body has nothing on the convulsions K's body makes when it fights to fill her lungs with air. She shudders all over, fighting to live with a will I thought she would have lost months ago.

"What the fuck, man!" Nero glares at me with icy, ready-to-kill eyes, looking prepared to wallop me as I want to pound into myself. "You were choking that girl. What the fuck were you thinking? Nikolai will kill you if he finds out."

After a final shove to my chest and a glare that reveals I royally fucked up, he stands to his feet and paces back toward the bed.

"Don't touch her," I growl out when he moves his hand near K's neck.

His words are spat out of his mouth as quickly as vomit races up my throat from his reply. "I'm checking she has a pulse, dipshit."

I'm pissed at myself, but I don't back down when I'm worked up. "I said don't fucking touch her! For all we know, she'd rather be dead than be touched again without permission."

Hearing the threat in my tone that I'm five seconds from killing him, Nero steps back from my bed with his hands held in the air like he's being arrested. Since his eyes aren't anywhere near K's frozen and naked form, the torment tearing me in two fails to augment my worded threat to an all-out violent one.

Sensing my lowering temperament, Nero mutters, "Mercy killing isn't what we do here, Trey." He slants his head to lock his brown eyes with my blue ones. "If that girl wants to end her life, that shit is on her shoulders, not yours. I thought you knew that better than anyone. Silly me."

After a final shake of his head, revealing his disappointment in me, Nero exits the room as quickly as he entered it, leaving me defenseless to a woman I thought I could save from the darkness by taking her place, having no clue I'm already there.

I should have known better.

I don't live in the darkness.

Darkness lives inside me.

SALES DOCKET NUMBER 12574

I wake up gasping like I can't breathe. It feels like I'm suffocating, like more than fear is stopping my lungs from filling with air.

As my hands shoot up to loosen the tightness squeezing my windpipe, my blurry eyes dart around the masculine, yet homey space. It is empty, which isn't surprising. It's rare to wake up to an audience. Once the men get what they want, they leave. It's the fact I fell asleep that has me gasping.

I emerge into the blackness in my head because it's the lesser of two evils. I feel their beatings for days after they leave, and my muscles ache for almost a week, but not knowing exactly what they do to me offers some weird sense of comfort. I feel safe even when I should feel anything but.

However, I'm not supposed to fall asleep.

That's dangerous.

It should have gotten me killed.

Mercifully, my heart is still pumping.

Most days, I'd relish the victory. Today, I'm not sure I won. I'm alive, but I can no longer see the light at the end of the tunnel I've been crawling toward for years. It has vanished, up and left. I've just got to work out if it's a good departure or a bad one. I'm leaning toward the negative. If I don't have goals to aspire to, I may as well be dead.

Incapable of ignoring the uneased churns of my stomach for a second longer, I race into the bathroom attached to the lavish room I awoke in. The heaves of my stomach are so violent, they bring up the meal I ate last night with only two big churns.

Once I'm confident my stomach is empty, I rest my backside on my feet before removing a square of toilet paper to clear away the mess on my lips. It's funny how the simplest things can make a deranged woman even more unhinged. The softness of the toilet paper as it scrapes my lips is one of those things. The paper—if you were lucky to get any—in my cell was as rough as sandpaper. It added to the pain I experienced every weekend—*a pain I'm not noticing this time around.*

Confused as to why the lower half of my body isn't aching, I stand and pace backward until the mirror perched above a double vanity exposes me in all my hideous form. The lifelessness of my eyes is still apparent, and the red welts on my neck are standard, however, there are no grab marks on my breasts, and my vagina isn't bruised and bleeding. Just from looking at me, you wouldn't think I had been assaulted tonight. I look untouched.

Well, as untouched as a sex slave can look.

Certain my head is playing tricks on me, I use the facilities, slip a shirt four sizes too big I found on the bed over my head, then exit the room. Upon discovering there's no lock on the door, much less a guard, I increase the length of my strides. Even with this being a dream, I plan to make the most of it. Usually, my dreams are as horrific as the nightmare I'm living, so a change-up isn't just nice, it's highly craved.

My steps slow when accented voices boom into my ears. For the most part, they're male, but the occasional female ones are added to the mix. Although they're more moans than words, they most certainly don't belong to any woman doing something against her will. They're brimming with too much pleasure to be mistaken as sobs.

I halt partway down the corridor when a sparkling of silver illuminates my pale skin. There's a skylight above my head. Although the darkness of the sky reveals it's nighttime, not a cloud hides the moon. It beams through the clear glass so brightly, my usually pasty skin lights up like the window in my room the past ten weeks wasn't boarded up.

Something so simple shouldn't be so joyful, but it is. It burns my eyes with tears while reminding me no matter how dark things get, there will always be light. It's hidden inside of me waiting to be released. I've just got to be brave enough to set it free.

After absorbing the moon's rays long enough to recall I have a beating orifice in my chest, I continue down the hall. When my trek has me stumbling onto a group of people in various stages of undress, I pivot on my heels, prepared to find another way back to the room Ana is in.

I've barely tiptoed two steps when I spot a man coming from the other end. He's large, thick, and stroking himself through his pants. Although his face doesn't register as familiar, he is the type of man I was expected to entertain when Vladimir kept the members of his crew happy during the quiet weeks.

"Are you lost, little one?"

Shaking my head, I step back.

"Are you sure? I think you're lost. I can show you the way home." His lips curl into a cruel grin. "*After* you've proven yourself worthy of my help." When I shake my head for the second time, his smile grows. Just like every man in this country, his evil thrives off fear. "Ah, the silent type. I'm not usually a fan, but I'm willing to give it a whirl for you."

When he takes a step forward, I take another one back. A squeak almost pops from my lips when my attempt to flee is thwarted by a body just as rigid as the one approaching me. I used to believed there was safety in numbers. I don't anymore. Men are crueler when they're showing off in front of their friends.

My silent pleas get answered when a thick, gravelly tone growls out, "Go find a whore to play with Rory. This one isn't on the cards." His voice doesn't have a British accent like Trey's, however, it's just as violent. It sends Rory scampering in the direction opposite to the one he was traveling and has my heart rate returning to a safe level, albeit hesitant.

"Stupid piece of shit," my rescuer mumbles as he spins me around to face him. He's the man Trey was speaking with earlier tonight. I can't recall if I've heard his name. "What are you doing awake, K? I thought you'd sleep for ages."

Although he's asking a question, he doesn't wait for me to reply. He just continues spinning me until his arm wraps around my shoulders, and he guides me toward a group of people drinking, laughing, and smiling like they didn't lose any members of their crew tonight. I saw the number of bodies sprawled on the floor during my escape. Not all of them were Vladimir's men. Even without knowing their names, I knew most of the men in Vladimir's crew—*regretfully*.

Halfway to a coffee table lined with bottles of alcohol, packets of smokes, and a variety of drugs, the reason for the prickling of the hairs on my arms comes to light. Trey is in the jacuzzi. He isn't alone, and none of his late-night bathing companions appear to be fans of personal space. They're draped all over him, front and back, and everyone one of them is blonde.

My eyes stray from Trey when the man shunting me out of my

comfort zone for the second time in my life offers up an introduction to the people seated in the massive living area. "This is Nero, Lexa, Haley, Nathan, Max, and Nerissa." He shifts on his feet to face me before shoving a frothy pink concoction into my hand. "Everyone, this is K."

"Hi, K," the group hums in sync, oddly friendly.

Only Nerissa adds to her greeting, "You're pretty, K. Perhaps you should come sit with me?" She taps on the minute snip of material next to her meaty thigh.

"Yeah, nah. She is off-limits." When the unnamed man pushes me into the plush leather chair my knee was balancing against, some of my drink spills onto Trey's shirt.

I stop panicking about how much trouble I'll get in for making a mess when a second man's backside fills part of the chair my skinny frame doesn't take up. "Taken by who? Nikolai said the women were off-limits, so who could she be taken by, Eight?"

When Eight's narrowed gaze swings to the other side of the room, I follow the direction of his gaze. I'm not the only one experiencing discomfort by the stranger's closeness. Trey seems put-off by it as well, but instead of being angry at my chair-hogging companion, he glares at me as if I requested for him to sit with me.

I don't know what has him so worked up. I'm not the one entertaining five people in a hot tub. They may only be kissing, but that's the most intimate act there is. Rape, torture, and deprivation of liberty rarely include kissing. None of the men I was forced to 'entertain' were interested in kissing me. They wanted my mouth for one thing and one thing only. Although glad none of the women in the jacuzzi are doing that to Trey, for some stupid reason, watching them kiss him hurts just as much.

Needing to settle the flips of my stomach before I hurl on the expensive-looking rug under my feet, I take a sip of the drink Eight shoved into my hand. The burn the liquid hits my throat with is worse than the dryness Trey's glare instigated. It has me coughing like I'm on the verge of an asthma attack and sends laughter breaking across the room.

The only person not laughing is Trey.

He's glaring—still.

"Slow slips, baby girl," encourages the man warming my thighs with his heated gaze. He's cute, but I'm not interested. *I'll never be interested.* "Nothing around here is done in halves. Not even cocktails."

My drink is a cocktail? I thought they were supposed to be yummy. This is far from tasty.

I grow worried I said my comment out loud when the dark-haired man laughs like he heard my private thoughts. "Eight is a shit mixer. How about I fetch you something more appetizing?"

After inching back far enough, his hand falls from my face, I shake my head then place my barely-touched drink onto the coffee table. Seemingly incapable of understanding the word no, the man snatches up my glass before he moseys to a bar in the corner of the room to mix me a new drink.

Although panicked about how my rudeness will be handled, I've had enough of the festivities to risk being punished. When the group breaks into rapacious laughter about Nero saying balls should be excluded in measurements, I slip off my seat and tiptoe away from them. I'm not here to make friends. I need to find Ana and then the closest exit before the unexpected attention has me forgetting I'm no more important than the women imprisoned in a room at the back of this compound.

I'm no one.

I almost make it to the corridor that leads to the dormitory the women are in when a dripping-wet body blocks my exit. Since my eyes are planted on the ground, it doesn't take me long to realize the person confronting me is naked. Although his cock is flaccid, it's still large enough for me to know it won't matter how gentle he is, you'll hurt for days after sleeping with him.

"Where are you going, K?" His possessive tone gives away who he is, much less his British accent. "Don't you want to party with your new friends anymore? Eight seems willing to lose another finger for you, and Logan only mixes drinks for the girls he wants to fuck, so why aren't you taking advantage of their generosity?" The bad slur of his words reveals his level of intoxication, and don't get me started on his massively dilated eyes, or we will be here all night. He isn't just drunk, he's drugged as well. "You trust them enough not to check if your drink was spiked, so why are you running as if you're scared of them?"

When awareness on what his anger centers around smacks into me, I roll my eyes before attempting to sidestep him. His annoyed sneer makes it obvious he believes he didn't get adequate payment for the meal he provided me, and his jealousy is doubling the obviousness. He's acting as immature as Vladimir did anytime his guests went over their allotted timeslots. Instead of taking his annoyance out on those responsible, Vladimir punished the women like they purposely deceived him. We barely knew if it was day or night, so how were we to know his guest's time was up?

Instead of letting me leave without making a scene, Trey crowds me against the outer wall of the west wing. "I asked you a question, K, and I'm not letting you leave until you answer me."

He steps closer and closer and closer until the visual of his rapidly thickening cock is pinched from my sight. Instead, it pokes me in the stomach, stealing the last snippet of my sanity. The silver ends of the barbells partway down his shaft feel cool against my roasting body temperature, and the tattoos accentuating his cock makes it more attractive than ugly.

I've never seen a penis and thought it was sexy. They usually make my stomach flip in repulsion, especially the ones I've seen the past ten weeks, but Trey's isn't close to ugly. It actually makes me feel desired, which is ridiculous considering how hard he's snarling at me.

"You trust Eight enough to drink from a glass not prepared in front of you, but you don't trust me to shower and take care of you. What the fuck is that about, K? What did I ever do to deserve your distrust?"

I stare at him as if he's absurd. I don't trust anyone, much less men I don't know.

Incapable of standing the heat of his wrath for a second longer, I stray my eyes to the other side of the room. Our charade has gained us an audience. Not a peep projects across the room because everyone, even the women Trey was entertaining before he chased me down, are staring at us with amusement slashed across their faces.

That hurts more than the clutch Trey places on my face to coerce my eyes back to his. "Don't worry about them. They're nobodies. Your focus should be on me, K. It should *always* be on me."

When I give in to his silent demand, his cock digs into me deeper, making me hot all over. It's like he gets off on having my undivided attention. I have no clue why. The women pining over his return are far more attractive than me. They also don't seem like the type to blank out during intimacy. I'm a sex slave with no identity whatsoever. There's nothing in my file but a sales docket number. That's how worthless I am.

I am a nothing.

A whore.

A woman not worthy of *any* man, let alone one who looks at me like I haven't been chewed up and spat out more times than she can count.

With his head slanted and his pupils massive, Trey says, "Tell me why you trust them more than me, K, then maybe I'll go easy on them when I show them what happens to insolent men who disregard my direct order." I want to tell him his jealousy is unwarranted, but before I can, he continues talking, stopping me, "Is it because I choked you? Are you mad I thought you wanted to be freed from the madness? I was trying to save you from additional harm, K. I wouldn't have if you had given me any indication you wanted to live."

As my lungs struggle to fill with air, my hand darts up to caress my neck. Is he the reason for its extra thump of agony? Did he try to kill me? If so, why is he acting irrational now? If he wants me dead, he shouldn't care whose cup I drink from. He should be grateful they took up the slack his failed attempt to murder me bogged him down with, then he'd be free to get back to his bevy of beauties without burden.

Some of the anger making me want to slap him hard across the face weakens when he mutters, "I didn't do it to hurt you, K. I thought I was helping you." There's a truth in his eyes I can't ignore. He either truly thought he was saving me or he's a narcissist. I don't know which I prefer. They're both confronting in their own right. "Are you mad at me, K? Do you want to hurt me?"

When he fills the minute gap of air between us with his impressively large frame, I'm torn between wanting to gouge out his eyes, blacking out, or kissing him. My latter thought is the most ludicrous of them all. Not even his wiry beard can hide the lipstick smears on his mouth. However, I'm more disappointed the stains weren't put there by me than recalling there's more than one set of colors.

God, this country has made me mental.

A sensation I haven't felt in years pumps through me when I attempt to wiggle free from Trey's clutch for the second time this evening. It's hot and knee-knocking and has me hoping I may not be as broken as believed. Although it's been a while, I'm reasonably sure the warmth heating my veins is desire.

It grows more rampant when Trey angles his head to better align our lips. "You're not angry at me, are you, Duchess? You want me to kiss you? To make you mine?"

The strong scent of liquor bounding out of his mouth could excuse the wooziness of my head, but that would be the cheats way out. It isn't the alcohol leeching from his pores making me dizzy nor the arrowing of his lips toward mine, it's his nickname.

I've been called Duchess before.

It was by a dead man.

"Your every wish is my desire, Duchess. I'll give you the crown you're seeking. It just won't be pronged with jewels."

With the world crumbling in on me, I twist my head in just enough time to stop Trey's lips landing on my mouth. I need air, badly, and not even the furious growl rolling up Trey's throat can take from that. He's mad I'm rejecting him, when in reality, I am doing everything I can not to pass out. My past is clutching my throat even worse than the past ten weeks of torture did. It's asphyxiating me, killing me with the same painstaking slowness of the past six years.

Trey doesn't realize that, though. "My kisses not good enough for you, Duchess? Do you have someone else you'd rather kiss? Perhaps a rich aristocrat who likes fiddling with his staff?" Vomit races up my food pipe when he growls in my ear, "From what I heard, you still married him. How long did it take you to forget me? A week, possibly two?"

I almost bend in two when reality smacks into me. This is just another game. A sick and twisted mindfuck that'll maim me more than any of Vladimir's guests.

Haven't I been through enough?

Will this nightmare ever end?

It won't end until I make it end.

Grunting, I push Trey away from me before attempting to slap him across the face. My hand barely skims his cheek when he grips my wrist so hard I'm certain it's seconds from snapping.

After roaring like the torment inside of him is as dark as mine, he tugs me away from the wall, wraps an arm around my thighs, then throws me over his shoulder as if I'm the weight of a feather. "If you want to play with the big boys, Duchess, I'll show you how we truly play."

Through the thumps of my fists colliding with Trey's back as he stomps us across the room, I hear someone mumble, "Trey... it's my fault she's out here. I invited her to sit with us. If you want to be angry at anyone, be angry at me."

Trey either doesn't believe Eight or he's disinterested in what he has to say because he wants any excuse to punish me, which he does not even two seconds later when he slips into the warm water of the jacuzzi with me attached to his front.

To anyone without open wounds, the soothing water would be heavenly for their exhaustive bodies. To me, it's like being dipped into boiling lava.

The screams ripping through me are soundless. Trey can't say the same thing. He howls like a wolf under a moon when I claw my nails into his pecs so I can climb up his body. I want to run as far away from him as possible, but the pain is too intense. It's taking everything I have for me not to cry, so I can't waste an ounce of energy fleeing.

After burrowing my head into Trey's neck, I use his stiff-as-a-board body to weaken the severity of the shakes hampering mine. Although my screams are soundless, I'm certain Trey hears every one of them. My breaths batter his neck as forcefully as my nails dig into his shoulders. I can also feel his raging heart. It's as sky-high as mine.

I'm so deep in my pain cycle, I don't realize Trey is moving us until his shouted words overtake the frantic thumps of his feet. "Get Dok!"

After bolting down the corridor I walked only minutes ago, holding me tighter with every step he trudges, he kicks open his door, heads to the bathroom, then yanks on the faucet in the free-standing shower. Even with it being super muggy this evening, my teeth chatter in protest to the cold water pumping out of the showerhead when he steps us into the stall. Although the rest of my body is freezing, my burning back soaks up the water like a desert being hit with its first sprinkling of rain. It's heavenly to my oozing welts.

"I'm sorry, Duchess, I'm so fucking sorry," Trey mutters through the heavy thuds of his heart booming into my ear. "I forgot about your marks. My fucked-up head forgot about them." He bangs himself on the forehead two times, hopeful a couple of hard thumps will draw him out of the drug-fueled binge he's on. "I didn't mean to hurt you. I was just mad. Not at you. At myself... *and at fucking her.*" His last four words are barely whispers, and they rip my heart to shreds.

After pulling back the strands of dirty hair hanging in front of my eyes, he lifts my head via my chin, locking our eyes. "You're fucking with my head. Having you here is fucking with my head. I thought the past was dead. You're reminding me it isn't."

I want to say something, but even if I could get my mouth to follow the prompts of my brain, he wouldn't understand me. I don't speak English, and he doesn't understand Czech. We have no way of communicating, not to mention the fact I truly don't know what to say. My head is reeling as much as his, so I doubt anything I could say would offer much help.

After running the back of his hand down my cheek, Trey tracks his rough thumb over my lips before he pulls me in close to his chest. We stay huddled in the shower until the burn on my back cools right along with the heat trekking through Trey's veins.

Once he has me wrapped in a thick, fluffy towel that should be more comfortable than his rigid body but isn't, he sits me on his bed. He grabs a tube of ointment off a big set of overflowing drawers in his room, shouts out the door for them to hurry the fuck up and find Dok before returning to my side.

"It's just ointment," he assures me after joining me on the mattress and tugging down the back of my towel. "It'll take away the remaining burn. Dok gave it to me earlier when you were sleeping. Before I..." He doesn't finalize his sentence, but the sorrow pumping out of him does. He's sobering up remarkably fast, which isn't surprising considering the circumstances.

My teeth grit when he rubs the ointment into my skin. It doesn't burn as much as chlorine, but it still isn't pleasant. Trey is being as gentle as possible. He's touching me with a kindness I haven't experienced in years, however, worry still flows through me. He's only being gentle *after* hurting me. That's not okay, and something I thought I'd stop experiencing once I left the dungeon Vladimir kept his captives in.

Mistaking the second grit of my teeth as upset instead of determination for a better life, Trey says, "You can cry, K. It's okay to cry." His switchback in nickname reveals his drug binge is coming to an end. I don't know whether to be relieved or worried. I'm more stunned than anything. If any of this is true, I've just been thrust from one nightmare to another.

After rubbing his ointment-sticky fingers onto the towel wrapped around his waist, Trey gently tugs on my shoulder, wordlessly requesting for me to twist around and face him.

When I do as requested, he looks like he has an arsenal of questions he wants to ask me. I have just as many, but before either of us can work through our confusion, much less categorize the importance of our questions, the shuffling of multiple feet sound from outside his door.

I'm covered by a towel, but you wouldn't know it when Trey darts up to place himself between me and the doorway. Although his treatment of my wounds soothed the burn, and I tell myself time and time again that Trey's visitors won't hurt me, nothing can keep my head out of the dark place it convenes in when the shadows of my past catch up with me.

Darkness doesn't scare me. I've been hurt, beaten, and raped in the light, so I'll never fear the dark. Furthermore, evil doesn't live in the dark, it thrives off people too scared to realize it's worthless without fear.

> *Evil is powerless*
> *if the good are unafraid.*

> *--Ronald Reagan.*

TEN

SALES DOCKET NUMBER 12574

Six years earlier…

After checking the coast is clear for the third time, I dash for the corridor where the 'help's' rooms are located. I broke protocol for a late-night snack, still hungry since the meal I shared with one of Achim's newest staff members saw her gobbling down the entire dish without coming up for air. I barely got in a spoonful, and my hunger was too apparent to ignore.

I snuck into the butler's pantry for a chunk of bread. I left with my virginity no longer intact.

That isn't something I ever anticipated to occur from breaking the rules.

Well, not in a joyous way.

In all honesty, I should be sickened with myself. I couldn't see the man's face I gave my virginity to, and he thought I was someone else, but it still felt magical. I don't know if it was the dark *surrounding us, or the way his attention made my pulse thud in my ears, but whatever it was, tonight was the first time I acted on impulses instead of orders.*

My family has been servants for the Novaks for several generations—cleaners, cooks, chauffeurs, and gardeners. If a position needed to be filled, a member of my family usually filled it. I've been a chambermaid since the age of twelve. For the first four years, I completed my schoolwork between four and six in the morning, and my household chores kept me occupied until nine at night. The hours were exhausting, but the conditions made it bearable. I had my own room, was served three good meals a day, and was given all my school supplies and clothing free of charge.

Things changed when Mr. and Mrs. Novak's eldest son requested India Dvořák's hand in marriage. India didn't want to leave her family's estate in Mikulov until after the wedding, so Achim went to her.

He couldn't do that without bringing members of his team with him—myself included.

My schedule has been starkly contradicting here. I'm expected to work from sunup to sundown, my school hours no longer exist, and I have to share a dorm-like room with another five women.

The only good that came from the change was anonymity in numbers. Achim doesn't choose his 'help' merely on acceptability. Their looks always enter into the equation. I haven't seen a dark-haired woman near him in years. It's always the same petrified, blue-eyed, blonde-haired women.

His preferred choice.

As I round the corner partway down the hall, I bump into someone coming from the other end. Instinctively, I drop my eyes to my shoeless feet before muttering out an apology about not looking where I was going. Even if our collision wasn't my fault, I'm expected to take blame for it.

A scratch impinges my throat when I absorb the expensive silk material draped over the person in front of me. They're not the satin sleeping pants I strive to ignore when a visitor pops into my room every night for the past three months. It's the material of a night-gown—a regal nightgown.

"Ms. Dvořák, is there anything I can help you with?" India's demands are the sole reason my days are so long now. Her needs are even more exhausting than her husband-to-be's. "Perhaps I can bring a nightcap to your room?"

I can't have her going to the pantry. If that happens, I'm dead. It's clear the man I just slept with thought I was India. He didn't directly mention her name, but he referenced parts of her life I can't brush-off as being coincidental.

His disclosure occurred to late into our exchange for me to respond to it. It was at the end, right before I imploded with an array of emotions I've never experienced before. Talking was above me. I couldn't even refuse his request for us to meet again tomorrow night when all was said and done. That's how scuttled my brain was and still is.

Furthermore, who's to say he won't kill me the instant he real- izes he fucked the help. Achim has a fondness for sexually cavorting with the female members of his staff, but not many other men are like him—thank God. They'd never lower their pigheadedness enough to ask a member of their staff to suck them off since their fiancées refuse to.

When India remains quiet, I gingerly lift my head. Although she's standing directly in front of me, her focus isn't on me. It's on someone behind me. I don't need to peer over my shoulder to know who she's staring at. I can smell his aftershave from here. It's also embedded in both my dowdy nightclothes, recently washed hair, and the air, and I'm not going to mention the deep grumble of his British accent when he wishes his 'Duchess' good-

night. His tone is super flat and low as if worried I'll expose their secret.

They have nothing to be worried about. I'll keep their secret as long as I plan to hold mine. It may be the only way I'll stay alive.

Seconds after the clomping of boots sounds through my ears, India lowers her eyes to mine. They're not kind. That's not unusual. They are never kind. "Come with me." When my lips twitch, preparing to respond with any excuse I can find, she snaps out, "I wasn't asking."

My knees knock the further we walk down the isolated corridors. I've been down these hallways before. It never ended well. This is the men's side of the residence, and more often than not, the rooms are brimming with monsters whose morals are lower than Achim's.

"Back so soon? I shouldn't be surprised." A man with golden blonde hair, a gaunt face, and a sneer oddly familiar stops talking when he spots two shadows entering his room. "Who is this?" he asks, peering at me, somewhat amused.

The humor on his face doubles when India replies, "She's the key to your kingdom." Her smile is so evil, I don't see the dark creeping up on me until I'm struck across the temple and knocked out.

———

When I come to, I'm bound to a chair, a hessian bag is shoved over my head, and I'm gagged. Although my temples are thumping, and the conditions are poor, I can determine I'm in a room with approximately three or four people. One is more familiar than the rest. I'll never forget his scent, let alone the comfort he gave me in the dark. The memories will keep me warm even while recalling how he has his gun pointed at my chest.

I can feel his torment, smell it slicking on his skin, but at the end of the day, we both know he'll pull back the trigger.

I'm the help.

The slave.

The woman who deceived him.

I deserve to die.

The belief doesn't lessen the amount of moisture burning my eyes, though. I thought we had a connection. A unique closeness that was tripled because of the dark.

I, for once, thought I was worthy.

Silly me. There's no price tag associated with my name. No wealth. I'm nobody. And it's proven without a doubt when the man who saved me from the darkness yanks back the trigger...

Gasping, I jackknife into a half-seated position as my hands shoot up to check my chest for a bullet wound. There won't be one. There never is. My hazy head often confuses the emptiness in my chest as the gaping hole of an invisible bullet. Not even the real bullet that shredded through my shoulder only minutes later that morning hurt as much as the fake one that rocketed out of the man from the pantry's gun.

As I struggle to regulate my breathing, I scan the room I'm waking up in. It's starkly contradicting to any of the rooms I've awoken in previously. It is masculine but with a touch of the sophistication I admired anytime I was a chambermaid for a female member of the Novaks' family.

The skyrocketing blood pressure I'm only just getting under control spikes again when my eyes land on the chest of the tattooed man sleeping across from me. It's the same tattooed chest I was confronted by only hours ago, but now his identity is slowly being unveiled, I'm looking at it through an entirely new set of eyes.

Tattoos can conceal scars, but they can't fully hide them, and Trey has more than his fair share.

When I scoot across the mattress, being extra cautious not to pull on the bandages plastered to my back, the sound of gunfire booms into my ears. The noises aren't real, they're from jaded memories. However, the smell most definitely is. It is the scent of death and desecration. A smell I've become well accustomed to the past six years.

Hopeful the drugs hazing his mind earlier are still in effect, I stop an inch away from Trey's slumped frame before raising my hand to his chest. My breathing grows shallow when my fingertips trace a bullet wound hidden by the large fan of eagle feathers stretched across his chest. There's another one just to the right of his ribs, two in his stomach, and one partially concealed by the waistband of his Calvin Klein boxer shorts.

The final piece of the puzzle slots into place when my finger outlines a circular scar high on Trey's left shoulder. Six bullet wounds may seem like a lot, but when you learn how many shots were fired that morning, you realize it could have been so much worse.

Part of me wants to believe the man from the pantry lowered his gun to my stomach before taking his shot was because he was aware the likelihood of surviving a bullet wound to the stomach was far more probable than one to the head. He also pushed me out of the line of fire *after* taking his shot.

It all seems very heroic... until I recall the hell his gallantry put me through.

There have been many times I've wished to be dead since that day. Death was far kinder than anything I've faced after India told Achim what I had done. He said I was a whore, and as such, he would treat me like one.

That was the first time I was raped.

It continued a minimum of once a month for the next six years, growing more violent with each one. I've been abused both physically and mentally, defiled, and had my family name shamed all because, for the first time in my life, I acted on impulses instead of orders. And now, just as I'm on the cusp of being freed from the torment, the same man is about to steal it away from me again.

I can't let that happen. I'm barely surviving as it is. The thread is extremely thin. If I don't fight for my freedom now, I may never get the chance again. That's how dire things are, and it's the sole reason I slip Trey's cell phone off the table next to him and punch in three words into a messenger box I never thought I'd use.

> I have Ana.

TREY

The guilt eating me alive gets a moment of reprieve when a faint tap hits the edge of my boot. Peering down, I spot an untouched orange teetering back and forth next to my covered foot. It's from the bowl of fruit the women devoured within a second of it being placed in front of them earlier today. It's untouched because the person lucky enough to scavenge it up doesn't trust anyone.

How fucked is it that the only person K trusts is me? A drug-fucked idiot who got so possessive about a woman he hardly knows, he hurt her to prove a point. I'm not talking about the chlorine in the jacuzzi. I truly did forget about the welts on K's back when I slid into the warm water with her in my arms. I'm talking about how I made out with whores *after* spotting K's unexpected entrance into the main living area of Clarks.

Seeing Eight's arm wrapped around her shoulders snapped something inside of me. It fucked with my head even worse than the drugs I took to try and pretend I hadn't attempted to end K's life as I wish someone had my miserable existence years ago.

I don't recall much of the night Nikolai's crew found me in a dungeon starving, naked, and shackled to a stonewall like winter wasn't below freezing. However, I do remember pinning Nero to the wall of my holding cell with a shank I'd made in case anyone was game to walk in with my moldy, undercooked food once a week, instead of sliding it under the door as they had the previous three years. I wanted them to kill me, to free me from the torment I hadn't built the courage to end myself. My father raised me with so much self-worth, no matter how many times I pierced the shank through my frail skin the prior twelve months, I couldn't end my life as Cole had tried years earlier.

Nikolai saw straight through my ruse. He knew I was taking the coward's way out, so instead of killing me as I was hoping, he walked out of my torture chamber, grunting that Nero would have been dead if I had truly planned to kill him.

I dug the tip of my shank in deeper, determined to prove Nikolai wrong.

All it did was display the courage I assumed I'd lost.

Upon seeing this, Nikolai gave me two choices. Kill Nero and remain captive in a compound now controlled by Russians, or put down my shank and join him in returning rightful order.

"I'm British," I said to him that night, speaking for the first time in years.

Nikolai smiled a grin that revealed he had once been as broken as me. "Bloodlines mean nothing when kingdoms are merely conquered provinces."

When confusion bombarded me, I received help from the last person I expected.

"He means princes don't necessarily wear crowns," Nero said, unconcerned about the sharp, rusty blade piercing a vein in his neck. "And darkness is a realm that needs more than one leader."

With uncertainty higher than my wish to die in that instance, I lowered my shank before collapsing to the ground, my exhaustion too apparent to ignore for a second longer. I had hit rock bottom that day as I did last night, yet K still rolls the orange she's been holding the past hour my way, hopeful I'll prove it isn't tainted with drugs so she can eat it.

Even after ensuring Dok dressed her wounds without touching her in a way that could be deemed unacceptable, and sitting by her bedside for hours on end to ensure her slip into a deep, dark void for the second time wasn't interrupted, I don't deserve her trust. I hurt her even knowing she's been hurt in unimaginable ways.

That makes me a fucking monster.

That makes me unworthy of her faith.

But more than anything, it makes me want to protect her even more. Not just from additional harm but me as well.

Knowing K will never eat until the food she's consuming is proven safe, I bend down to gather up the orange. When I bite into the tangy, bitter fruit without bothering to peel it, K's eyes drop to watch the bob of my Adam's apple. Once the clump of citrus is sitting in my stomach, she returns her eyes to my face, soundlessly begging for me to return her orange.

I should roll it across the floor like it isn't dirty, pretend I don't care she's eating food too acidic for her shrunken stomach to handle, but for some fucked-up reason, I can't. Just like I couldn't walk away last night, I can't this morning, either. I'm drawn to her. I just have no clue why. For years, I've cared about no one but myself.

Panic floods K's impressive eyes when I spin on my heels and walk out of the room. I'm clutching her orange in my hand, hopeful the gall I saw in her eyes in less than a nanosecond is as strong as I'm anticipating. If she wants to eat, she'll have to bring out her strengths again because only someone strong enough to leave the darkness unaccompanied deserves a second chance.

I learned that the hard way three years ago when I followed Nikolai out of the dungeon I'd been held captive in for three years. He wasn't giving me a free pass. I worked for everything I've achieved. It wasn't fucking easy, but glory doesn't come to those too scared to fight for victory.

"Let them wander freely. They're not prisoners here," I say to Rory who's manning the corridor with an AK-47 in one hand and a packet of cigarettes in the other. "Just remember, no one is to make a move until Nikolai says so."

I wait for him to lift his chin in confirmation before heading for the kitchen at the back of Clarks. When I enter the industrial-size space, my jaw gains an involuntary tick. Instead of flour coating the wooden chopping blocks the cooks prepare food on, cocaine is.

"Get that shit out of here." Rick's wide eyes lift to mine for the quickest second before he scoops the coke into his hands like its worthless and hightails it out of the kitchen. The three girls he's hoping to get doped up enough they'll forget he's a bottom-dweller quickly chase him down.

I've only just cleared away the mess that will have K being more distrusting of her food than she already is when a second body joins me in the fragrant-smelling space. Regretfully, it isn't who I'm hoping. It's Logan instead of K. He's looking smug like the drugs he encouraged me to binge on last night didn't fuck with his head as well as they did mine.

I'm still as high as a fucking kite.

I shouldn't be surprised. The Popovs only sell the good shit.

"How you feeling this morning, T-Man? You were pretty shit-faced last night."

Logan musses my hair like he's not in my shit-book for the stunt he pulled last night. I'm not talking about the blow. If I weren't down with getting high, I wouldn't have dabbled in my drug of choice. I'm talking about his overfriendliness with K. I warned him earlier she was off-limits, yet he still acted like a man who's never had his dick sucked last night when she was placed on his radar. He was so up in K's business, I could smell his aftershave on her face before I threw her over my shoulder. Why do you think I was so desperate to get her clean? I hate that she smelled like him. It fucked with my head more than the drugs I use to forget.

A note for future reference, just because you're taller than someone doesn't mean you're tougher than them. They'll put you on your ass as I do Logan five seconds after his fingers leave my hair. "What the fuck, man? I was just saying hello."

After working his ribs over good enough he'll feel me for a week, I pin him to the industrial-size fridge by his throat, then get up in his face like he did K's last night.

"You messed with my head, Logan. I don't fucking like it. Do it again, and I'll have Leroy pummel your ass... and I don't mean with his fists. He's been dying to stretch your puckered hole for years, and I'm about in the right frame of mind to let him."

My taunt is delivered with the menace I was aiming for. Regretfully, it isn't just Logan quivering in his boots. So is the woman who built the courage to walk through a compound full of murderers just for the hope of eating a half-chewed orange for breakfast.

"K..."

She rockets out of the kitchen as fast as her quivering legs will take her, aware my threat was more honest than a scare tactic.

After imprinting the fridge with Logan's body, I take off after K. I reach her just as she enters the corridor leading to the dormitory the other women are in. I hate that she woke up there this morning, but considering she snuck out of my room in the middle of the night, there wasn't much I could do about it.

She didn't tell me she was too scared to remain sleeping in my room. I could see the fear in her eyes when I found her in the dormitory after my frantic search this morning. It maimed me as much as the whimpers she releases when she's sleeping.

Confusion draws my brows together when K takes a right halfway down the corridor instead of left. My shock is pushed aside for worry when the sound of glass shattering booms out of the bathroom she entered two seconds later.

When she returns to the corridor, clutching a shard of glass so tightly blood drips from her hand, I hold mine out in front of my body. Her eyes are murderous, and she doesn't just have me in her sights. She waves her shiv around as if it's a knife, threatening anyone stupid enough not to feel the fight to live beaming out of her.

"K... put down the glass."

The commotion of her shattering the mirror has gained her an audience. The once-captive women eye her without a peep escaping their lips. My brothers are much more vocal. They tell her to drop the glass or they'll shoot her. One even goes as far as saying he looks forward to fucking her corpse when he sends her to hell for her stupidity.

He's the dumb fuck I take down first.

K was smart to snatch-up the apple corer last night. It makes a quick and clean entry point to Bailey's neck. If multiple strikes to his juggler don't kill him, he'll bleed out long before Dok can save him.

While wiping Bailey's blood from my face with my equally

bloody hand, I warn the rest of my brothers that I'll remove their stomachs via their nostrils if they don't immediately back the fuck down. "I swear to God, if anyone touches her, I'll gut you like Bailey," I add to my threat, lessening the number of guns in the corridor from a dozen to four.

Once I'm confident I have the situation under control, I step closer to K. She isn't eyeing me like the violent killer I am. If I'm not mistaken, she looks pleased I stood up for her.

Her admiration has me tempted to kill again. I would if it weren't Nikolai's men surrounding me. Nikolai has only just seized his throne. He needs all the help he can get. Furthermore, half of these men aided in my recovery, so even with my desire for a rampage the strongest I've felt, it'll have to stay on the back-burner—for now.

With my eyes locked on K's, and my hands held out to ensure her I mean her no harm, I say, "I need you to put down the glass, K. I can't protect you if they think you're a threat." When she remains quiet, I step even closer. "Do you want me to protect you? Do you want me to keep you safe?" The tightness around my chest slackens when she dips her chin a few seconds later. I honestly hadn't expected her to say yes. "Then, I need you to put down the glass."

I don't understand a word she replies while shaking her head. Her voice isn't just faint since it's barely used, she's speaking a different language. "*Vzal ji. Zlý muž ji vzal.*"

"If this is about the orange, there's a heap in the fridge. I was getting you a fresh one. That's why I walked away." I'm lying, and she knows it. I wanted her to show the strength she's showcasing now. I just wish it were being done in a non-violent manner. One life should never be worth many, but as I stand here right now, I'll kill them all if it guarantees K walks away uninjured.

She's been hurt enough.

I can't let her suffer more.

My voice is rougher when I ask, "Tell me what you want, K. Let me help you."

"Jako jste tehdy tehdy? Nikdo mi nemůže pomoci." Her already gaunt expression grows worse when she garbles out, *"Chci být volný. Bez Ana to nedokážu. Tentokrát mě zabije. Zemřu."*

I can feel the fear beaming out of her, taste it on the tip of my tongue, but I'm still fucking lost as to what has caused the swift change in her composure. If it has anything to do with the nail-wide scratches scoured down her arm, I'm about to become as violent as her, if not worse.

Desperate for answers, I say, "I can't understand you, K. You need to speak English."

"Byla tady. Právě tady. Přišel a vzal ji," she replies, stepping closer to the room where the women are huddled. Her change in position allows Dok to drag Bailey out of the hallway to check him for a pulse, but it does little to ease my hesitation. She still has four red dots on her chest. That's four too many.

"I want to help you, K, but I don't know how. You're not making any sense—" My words stop, shunted by the shock of K redirecting the glass to her throat.

"Měl jsi pravdu. Měl jsi mě zabít. Zasloužím si zemřít." As tears fill her eyes, she locks them with me. *"Ale pokud umřu, tyto ženy také zemřou. To jim nemůžu udělat,* Trey. *Nenuťte mě, abych jim to udělal. Prosím. Jsem unavený. Tak velmi unavený."*

"Step back!" I scream at Nero when he lines up the perfect kill shot. "Don't shoot. She won't hurt anyone." I stray my eyes back to K, aware she is seconds from death but determined to get her out of this alive. "You won't hurt anyone, will you, K? You just want to help them, right?" When she nods, agreeing with me, I suck in my first breath in what feels like hours. "Then you need to tell us what you want." *And for how fucking long you want it.* With my last comment being more a personal reflection, I only say it inside my head.

My neck cranks to the side when a voice at the end of the hall murmurs out the last name I expected to hear in this confrontation. "Justine." Eight walks gingerly down the hall, still feeling my anger from last night when he arrived at my room with Dok. I worked his ribs as good as I did Logan's minutes ago, ensuring he knows K isn't a gimmick to toy with me. "She understood K last night. Perhaps she will today as well."

As much as it kills me to admit, he's right. Justine communicated with many of the women last night, so perhaps she can help me get K out of this alive.

I jerk my head to the quad bikes stationed outside. They make the trip to the Popov compound ten times quicker than a normal mode of transport. "Good idea. Go get her."

"Fuck no," Eight instantly replies. "I don't have a death wish." He peers at K with the tip of the glass pierced through her skin before doubling the shake of his head. "You might survive Nikolai's wrath from bringing his girl into this situation, but I most certainly won't. I like my nuts, so I'd rather keep them a little longer." He returns his eyes to mine. They're brimming with an equal amount of truthfulness and cheekiness. "If Nikolai punishes me instead of killing me, I doubt he's a finger-removing type of guy. I'd rather be dead than lose my nuts."

"Fine." Over his humor in an extremely volatile and dangerous situation, I shift on my feet to face Nero. "If *anyone* touches her, even you, disobeying Nikolai's direct order will be the least of your worries. Do I make myself clear?"

Nero has no problems holding his own. He is as feared by Nikolai's men as he is respected, but he also knows I'm not one to be messed with.

If you want to fuck a whore straight after me, go ahead.

If you want to cut up my drugs with shit that could kill me and I'm stupid enough to give them a go, that's fair as well.

But if you mess with something that's mine, which for some fucked-up reason is exactly what I consider K as—mine—you sure as fuck better be prepared to die for it.

"They won't touch her." Smirking, Nero strays his eyes over the two dozen or more men huddled around us. "I warned them this morning she was your girl, so they'd do best to listen." He returns his eyes to mine. They're tougher than stones. "But you've got to know I ain't lowering my gun until Nikolai gives me the order. One life is never worth more than another. You know that better than anyone."

Not in the mood for another one of his lectures, he's worse than Roman when his gums get flapping, I jerk up my chin. After giving K a final reassurance that she is safe, and that no one will touch her, I hightail it to one of the many quads surrounding Clarks. The motors were built to give maximum performance, but I still thrash the living shit out of it over the rugged, sandy plains.

When I arrive at the Popov compound only minutes later, my brows stitch. It's different than it was only twenty-four hours ago—as am I. It's more settled, somewhat heartening.

Although my first thought is to head to the sleeping quarters on the top level of the mansion, something redirects the direction of my course. I want to say it's intuition, but since none of my actions the past six years have been driven by that, I'm not willing to use it as an excuse. It is the thump of my pulse in my ears, an experience I haven't felt in years, and it's there because of K. I'm certain of it.

The craziness I've been working like a stripper does a pole the past twenty-four hours gets a pat on the back when I find Nikolai in his office at the back of the Popov compound. He's deep in thought. I don't see that as a bad thing. Sometimes mix-ups are as cleansing as a bloodbath. That's one of the reasons I stayed on with Nikolai's crew after my recovery. I could have sought vengeance like Cole did, but honestly, where would that have gotten me? Back into the dark, hidden void I barely creep out of for more than a day a week.

Fuck that.

I'd rather be dead than become anything like my brother. He killed our father because he valued the love of his life more than his sons, failing to realize the only people you can pick to be a part of your life are the ones who don't share your blood.

Blood isn't always thicker than water.

My placement in Nikolai's crew is proof of this.

When I rack my knuckles against Nikolai's office door, his eyes pop up from a heap of paperwork on his desk. His office is fancier than it was when I arrived stateside. It was nothing but shards of glass and twisted metal.

I was too merged in my own nightmare to realize Nikolai was facing just as many demons. Only weeks earlier, he had lost the only man he classed as his brother. Little did he know, his life would go full circle only three short years later.

I'm beginning to wonder if I am about to face the same set of circumstances. A particular sensation is bristling in the air. It is similar to the crackling of energy that zapped through me when I followed India into the butler's pantry. Greatness was set to happen that night. I just had no clue it would be quickly chased by hatred so black, evilness would thrive off it.

I can only hope today's sensation ends differently.

When Nikolai arches a brow, prompting me I'm the one interrupting him, not the other way around, I recall the reason for my visit. "We've got a problem at Clarks."

"Handle it," he replies, more than aware his crew is capable of tackling any dilemma thrown at us.

Although I agree with him, this isn't something I can do alone. "Can't."

Nikolai dumps his pen onto a stack of paperwork before slouching low in his chair. He looks tired. It isn't just his girl keeping him awake at all hours of the night, though. Vladimir's fuck-ups will take months to clear away, if not years. He ran a tight ship that amassed a substantial amount of wealth the past fifty-plus years, but his operation was a fucking mess.

With enemies willing to do anything to see his kingdom fall, he was the most hated man in the country. That hate has now been passed to Nikolai. If that doesn't keep him on his toes, his wish to keep his girl away from additional harm sure will.

"Why can't you handle it?"

When his question is asked with a ton of jeering, my Adam's apple bobs up and down. "Because we need you... and your girl." When he straight-up shakes his head, denying my request, I speak faster, "Justine is the only one who can understand these women. They have demands we can't meet. Unless you want to break your promise to Justine that they'll remain untouched, we need her help." I'm low-balling using his girl against him, but when you're clutching at straws, you better hold on tight. "It'll take barely a minute. I cross my fucking heart and hope to die."

My analogy is lost on him, but it does get his ass moving out of his seat. "She is supposed to be resting."

I smirk at the unease in his tone. Nikolai doesn't get ruffled about anything, so I'm aware his panic has nothing to do with his girl catching up on sleep and everything to do with him knowing he'll want her the instant he locks eyes with her. If I'm stopping that from happening, he's fighting not to kill me as I'd hoped he would have three years ago.

Do I still want to die? If you exclude last night when I hurt K, no, I don't. Although having her around is doubling my wish to reclaim who I was. I'm living a life most men would cream their pants to experience, yet I don't believe I'm truly living until my heart thumps in my ears.

K makes that happen.

Why? I have no fucking clue, but I'm eager to find out.

Impatient to make sure Nero kept his word, I nudge my head in the direction Clarks sits. "I'll meet you at Clarks."

Although unhappy about my request, Nikolai dips his chin in agreement. I don't see him being keen to agree to future requests when he discovers the environment I'm about to step his girl into. I'll risk it, though. It isn't the first time he's stuck his neck out for me. Don't see it being the last.

TWELVE

SALES DOCKET NUMBER 12574

"Calm down. We're not going to hurt you," a man I was introduced to last night assures when I grasp the shard of glass so firmly, blood dribbles off my arm to puddle around my bare feet. "But you need to know, this won't help anyone."

That's easy for him to say. He wasn't dragged down the corridor by a man double his weight and height. If I didn't use all the strength I gathered last night from tussling with Trey and winning, I'd be holed up with him like Ana is, most likely fighting for my life.

I don't speak a word of English, but I have no trouble understanding it. The things he said he was going to do to me was the reason I fought so hard.

I won.

Ana didn't.

Her screams were still echoing in my ears when I raced toward the kitchen to seek help. I thought Trey would protect us, he pledged exactly that only mere hours before, so you can imagine my surprise when my quest for help had me stumbling onto him assaulting a man while issuing the threat of rape as if it's a game.

That's when I realized I had to take matters in my own hands. I want to be free, but only now am I realizing the only person who can free me is me—*and perhaps Trey.*

He killed a member of his crew for me without a single snip of hesitation crossing his features. I was shocked, and it had me replaying how he tossed me out of the line of fire on repeat in my head, but since it wasn't the time to sit down and work through my confusion, I got my head back into game mode.

As I do again now.

"He took her," I repeat in Czech. "She was right there. He snatched her away." Sick of the horrifying life I've been forced to live the past six years, I dig the tip of the glass in deeper to the vein in my neck that won't quit pumping out its own tune. It's been that way since I unearthed Trey's true identity last night. "If he kills her, I will die. Do you understand? I'll be dead." Tears prick my eyes when a wish to live overwhelms me. They've been so far and few between the past six years, even I'm shocked by my mumbled confirmation. "I don't want to die. I've barely lived. It's not time for me yet. Please help me. That's all I'm asking. I just need some help."

Nero ensures his gun is pointed at my heart before he steps closer to me. "Don't," he pleads when his closeness has me piercing the glass in further to my vein. "I'm trying to help you. You want my help, don't you?" When I nod, he inches closer. "Then put the glass down." I stop shaking my head when he asks, "Is it your sister? Is she who you're after?"

It takes me a few seconds to click on to who he's referencing, but when I do, my heart launches into my throat. It isn't a good launch. It reminds me how Achim never strays from his preferred choice—blonde hair, blue eyes, and a slender frame. Even his wife has the same features, so it's understandable Nero is mistaking Ana as my sister. We often used our likeness to our advantage when the pain of Achim's demands became too much to bear.

Even knowing Nero won't understand a word I'm speaking, I can't help but reply. "I need her back. If I return her to Achim, I'll be free. He's sending men to collect her. He knows she's here."

Before Nero can reply, Trey returns to the room. He isn't alone. The man and woman who freed me from captivity only twenty-four hours ago follows him into the room. "What the fuck, Trey?" the dark-haired man grinds out when he spots the glass piercing my neck.

When Trey notices the droplets of blood coating my feet, his response is barely legible since it's chopped up by the anger clutching his throat. "She doesn't speak English, and your girl speaks multiple languages, so I figured it wouldn't hurt to know what her demands are."

The rattle of his vocal cords reveals how close to the edge he is. He's on the brink, ready to explode at any moment, which both terrifies and excites me. I snuck out of his room last night because the burden of my freedom doesn't belong on his shoulders. I walked through the gates of hell hoping to be freed, so I have to deal with the blisters my walk caused alone.

Just like I'll be the one who falls on the knife when Trey realizes how I deceived him.

My fear takes on an entirely new meaning when the dark-haired man growls, "We don't negotiate with whores. We tell them what to do, and they either listen or die."

"We're not whores," I fight back in Czech. "We're mothers, sisters, and daughters. Women who deserve to be treated better than we've been." I shift my eyes from the dark-haired man to the woman he calls his *Ahren* when I recall what Trey said earlier. She may understand me. "My sister. He took my sister. I need her back. Please."

It takes me repeating myself another three times before she whispers something into the dark-haired man's ear. I can't hear anything she says through the thump of my pulse in my ears, but I'm reasonably sure she's the only woman in this compound capable of helping me. She has control of the dark-haired man's heart—just like Ana does Achim. That's why his wife sent her away. She knew it would be only a matter of time before he gave her crown to Ana. Since she didn't want that to occur, she sold his favorite whore like the commodity she is.

My grip on the glass loosens when the pretty redhead recites what I tell her to the man using his body as a barricade to keep her safe, "Her sister was here last night but vanished this morning. She wants to know where she went."

"Her sister was here last night?" the man double-checks after swallowing harshly.

"*Spala vedle mě, ale když jsem se probudil, byla pryč.*"

She struggles to understand me, but she gets the gist of what I'm saying. "She's adamant her sister was sleeping next to her last night, but when she woke this morning, she was gone."

When Trey left with my orange, I laid down next to Ana, hoping to rest through the hunger pains ripping through me. My head had barely hit the pillow when my arm was suddenly clutched, and I was dragged out of the room.

Once again, no one came to my aid.

Ana didn't even budge an inch.

I had barely escaped the man's vicious clutch when he shifted his focus to Ana. I tried to hold onto her. I gripped her to the death, shredding my nails through her arm as well as the man's grubby ones had done to mine, but my fight wasn't enough. He disappeared down the corridor with a half-asleep Ana faster than I could snap my fingers.

That's when I ran to the kitchen, unaware I was wasting precious seconds.

Tears burn my eyes when the dark-haired man shifts on his feet to face Trey. "Where's her sister?" I told you the redhead owned the key to his heart.

Trey shrugs, truly unsure. "I don't know. We've got nearly every nationality covered in this room, but none of the girls speak English."

"How many women did you bring here last night?"

"Seventeen," Trey answers him after a quick mental calculation. "Six each in the first two SUVs and four in the last."

"That's sixteen," the man roars, startling me so much I jump.

The possessiveness in Trey's tone can't be missed when he confesses, "One rode with me." The blue-eyed man appears as shocked as I felt when Trey separated me from the pack. I was scared by his attention, but if I'm honest, that wasn't the only emotion I experienced. I was also excited. Not once since the night in the butler's pantry have I been chosen first, so once again, my wailing confidence craved his attention.

Unease melds through my veins when Trey mutters, "She reminded me of India."

If I were missing any pieces of the massive puzzle in my head, I'm not anymore. India isn't a common name like Ana and Sarah, but it grew more popular when India Dvořák married aristocratic royalty, Achim Novak, in a lavish, multi-million-dollar ceremony six years ago. Citizens of Czech have a weird fascination for naming their children after important members of society—even ones that cheat, rape, and steal for everything they have.

My mind jumps from the past to the present when the dark-haired stranger shouts, "I told you not to move until I said so!"

"I did," Trey replies, nodding. "I told Rory to sit on them until you gave us word on what you want done with them."

His confession is like a whack to the stomach. I knew I had seen that man before. "That's him," I garble in Czech. "That's the man who took Ana. Rory. He has her somewhere here. Can you find her?"

A hope the dark-haired man can understand me crashes into me when he demands Trey to watch Justine before he commences searching the compound.

With everyone's focus devoted on him, I drop the shard of glass from my neck before bending in half to suck in the air my lungs failed to accept the past three minutes.

I've barely filled my lungs halfway when Trey kicks the glass I was clutching to the far corner of the room before he raises my hand to check it for damage. I thought he'd be mad about me putting his crew in danger, so you can imagine my surprise when he seems more concerned about me than anyone.

He has no reason to fret. Although the slash mark across my hand is throbbing, the scratches down my arm hurt more than my self-inflicted wound. It may be an emotional pain more than a physical one, but still, it's there, nonetheless.

"Why are you scratched?" Trey sounds angry, but it's scarcely noticeable through his frustration.

He's still on a cliff edge, but instead of coercing him away from it, I join him there instead. "Rory."

"Rory attacked you?" Justine interrogates on Trey's behalf, speaking in my native tongue. When I timidly nod, the worry on his face augments. "Why?"

"Pokusil se mě vzít místo Ana. Bojoval jsem s ním." Guilt transcends when I mutter, *"Ana nebyla dost silná na to, aby ho odradila."*

"What is she saying?" Trey's voice isn't as stern as it was earlier, but it is fortified with anger.

After taking a few moments to gauge how he'll respond, Justine tells him what I said. "She said Rory scratched her when she fought him off her." The sorrow in her eyes matches mine when she mutters, "Ana wasn't strong enough to do the same."

"He tried to take K first." Although Trey sounds like he's asking a question, he isn't. He's summarizing. The tick in his jaw announces this, much less the tight clench of his fists. "If she hadn't fought him off, he would have..." He can't work the rest of his words out of his mouth. His jaw is too firm.

From his response, anyone would think this is the first time I've been sexually assaulted. I wish it were, but that's far from the truth.

Does that mean what I think it does? Did he order for me to become a whore like Achim said? Or was that another lie on a long list of many?

I was never told the identity of the man in the butler's pantry, only that he was so angry about my deceit, I was the cause of the carnage that occurred the following morning. Our night together had tainted him so perversely, I poisoned his mind. India said that's why he turned his gun on his family and killed his father. He was so sickened about what I had done, he wanted to die.

I wasn't aware he had survived the six bullet wounds I counted on his torso when he laid across from me lifeless on the dining room floor. I was shipped away to face the consequences of my actions where I remained the past six years, and where I most likely will stay since I've once again failed.

Justine's unique colored eyes pop open as wide as mine when Trey suddenly spins on his heels and storms out of the room. He knows the direction to take in an instant. The roar sounding down the hall is like a beacon for deranged, psychotic men determined to get vengeance. "You not only disrespected me, you disrespected my *Ahren!* Disrespecting her warrants the punishment of death."

My eyes drop to the floor when my race down a lengthened corridor has me stumbling onto the dark-haired man beating the living hell out of Rory. He has him pinned to the wall with one hand while his other smashes into Rory's face on repeat.

I can't see anything but several pairs of feet, but the crack of the man's fists to Rory's cheek spells out every sickening detail on what's occurring. Even if Trey wants in on Rory's punishment, the stranger won't allow it. He'll kill Rory before he will ever permit him to leave this room breathing. I guarantee it.

My theory loses steam when the faintest voice whispers, "Enough, Nikolai." It doesn't belong to a man. It's the owner of Nikolai's heart—his *Ahren.*

After floating my eyes up from my feet, I watch Justine enter the death-scented room with only the slightest quiver to her stride. "You taught him a lesson. He won't defy you again."

Confirmation she can get through to him like no one else is proven without a doubt when Nikolai's next two hits aren't as bone-crunching as his earlier strikes. He still pounds Rory's face to within an inch of recognition, but even I can tell his focus is shifting, and we're strangers. She's calling him to her, gravitating him nearer as I instinctively navigate myself closer to Trey. Even though I'm scared as to how he'll respond when he discovers who I am, I need answers, and he's the only man who can give them to me.

Just as Justine whispers, "Nikolai, I need you," I slip my hand into the tiny slither of space between Trey and me not taken up by his balled fist.

After unclenching his hand for me, opening up to me as no one ever has, Trey peers down at me, shocked and muted. We don't talk. I can't even hear the words Nikolai and Justine exchange. I'm too stunned by the massive turn of events the past twenty-four hours to get my mouth to work. I am so confused, I'm beginning to wonder if Vladimir killed me and this is a whore's fucked-up rendition of heaven.

I lose the devotion of Trey's eyes when the thud of a lifeless man slumping to the floor booms through our ears. Nikolai has released Rory from his grasp. Shockingly, he's still alive—just. My sky-high heart rate is too loud to hear a word Nikolai and Justine share, but that won't stop me from saying it's heart-clutching. There's too much sentiment crackling between them to ignore. It's almost as intense as the zaps darting up my arm from Trey's simple hold. I doubt he's a man known for his gentleness, yet he holds my hand as if it's a delicate flower that could be crushed at any moment.

Not even thirty seconds later, Nikolai scoops Justine into his arms before he makes a beeline for the door.

Just as quickly, Trey frees my hand from his before he steps into the room.

Believing the show is over, the crowd dispels remarkably fast. Within seconds, it's just Trey, Nero, Rory, and me. A normal person would tell Rory to thank his lucky stars he's still alive. I'm nothing close to ordinary. I felt the surge in Trey's pulse before he stepped away from me, heard his mumbled comment about Rory's punishment not being sufficient.

He's not standing Rory to his feet to help his lungs fill with the air Nikolai's beating stole. He's doing it so he's forced to face the person responsible for him being sent to hell. Trey wants him to know why he's ending his life as Nikolai failed to do. He wants him aware he's being killed because he touched me.

It proves without a doubt how many lies I've been told the past six years. He didn't send me away because sleeping with me sickened him so much he wanted to die. I doubt he even knows what happened to me. He's in the dark just as much as I was only yesterday.

After wrapping the cord he removed from the curtain stretched across one wall around Rory's neck, Trey's focus shifts to me. He stares at me for mere seconds, his eyes deadly and murderous, before he drifts them to Nero. He barely lifts his chin an inch before I'm grabbed around the waist and yanked out of the room.

Although the door separating us rapidly closes, it doesn't stop me hearing the sickening crunch Rory's neck makes when Trey tugs on the thick twine curled around his throat so brutally it snaps his neck. If the initial break didn't kill him, he'll be dead within seconds. Trey's murderous smirk leaves no doubt about this.

He killed for me—twice—and I have no clue how to repay him for that.

THIRTEEN

TREY

As my thumb skims over the rope burn on my index finger, I follow Eight through the sleeping quarters at Clarks. Since Rory's death was so quick, it gave me little satisfaction. I'm still itching for a bloodbath, but since my desire to make sure K is okay outranks my urge to kill, I'm prioritizing her first.

"Did she need stitches?"

Eight strays his eyes from a body bag housing Bailey's body to me before he shakes his head. "Dok said her wound was deep, but he glued it instead of stitching it up. Some shit about it being easier to keep clean if its fully joined." He shrugs before scrubbing at the bristles on his chin. He's usually a smooth-jaw type of guy. The past thirty-plus hours must be fucking with his head too. "What's the go?" He motions his head in the direction we just left. "Is he being buried with the rest of them or..."

He leaves his question open for me to answer, which I do two seconds later. "Rapists don't deserve proper burials. Nero suggested I take him to Jim's. I'm not opposed to the idea." When we reached the door all my brothers avoid as if it'll give them the clap, I say, "Get someone to help you put Rory in my trunk. I'll be out in a few."

A *pfft* vibrates his lips. "I don't need help." He doesn't. Even though he was a pathetic pin-prick weasel, Rory was a decent build, but Eight is a real-life giant. "You traveling alone? I could come with you, if you want."

I consider his offer for all of two seconds before shaking my head. "Jim hasn't forgiven you for fucking his granddaughter." I wait for his smile to fully incline before adding, "I'm also not traveling alone. K will come with me."

"The boys won't touch her. Not after how you responded to Bailey's taunt." Everything Eight is saying is true, however, until my blood pressure returns to a safe level, I'm not letting K out of my sight. Tension is still hanging heavily in the air. It's just bristling with the unease I felt when I was blindsided by my father's unexpected arrival at Mikulov.

Knowing better than to second-guess any decision I make, Eight says, "Aight. Offer stands if you change your mind."

When I jerk up my chin in thanks, he barges me with his shoulder before stalking away. I wait until he disappears down the isolated corridor before entering the makeshift hospital room Dok commissioned within weeks of joining Nikolai's crew. Supposedly, he can't do surgical procedures in a 'standard ole room.' I don't bother knocking. The fact he's alone with K already pisses me the fuck off.

Some of the annoyance heating my veins cools when I spot K sitting on the end of a sterile-looking bed, several feet from Dok. It's one of those examination beds you find in all general practitioners' offices. It even has the stirrups I often threatened to borrow.

"You good?" Not waiting for her to answer me, I lift her chin to check the cut she made to her neck when she pierced it with the glass.

It's angry and red and has me wanting to resuscitate Rory so I can kill him all over again. If he had listened to my directive, K wouldn't have been forced to put her life on the line for her sister as I did for Cole years ago.

Cole thought taking down our father would make him the cream of the crop. Nothing would take him down. Then Achim double-crossed him as he convinced Cole to do to our family only months earlier. I should have let Achim kill him without intervening, but what can I say, I'm a stubborn prick who couldn't forget the morals our parents had instilled in us even only having half my strength.

I survived the carnage.

Cole didn't.

Nikolai helped me bury his bones in the compound his crew seized at the request of his father. It was years after Cole had died, but it was better than the corner of my cell where he was rotting and decaying like his head had never worn an invisible crown.

After taking a big breath to free my mind of memories of my past, I crank my neck to Dok, who does a mighty fine job of appearing invisible when he isn't needed. "Did you give her anything for the pain?" My jaw spasms when he shakes his head. "Why the fuck not? She'd have to be in pain."

"I agree," he replies, stepping closer. "She refused to take anything."

I return my eyes to K, smirking when I catch her gawk of my face before she can drag it away. A less cocky man would think she was staring at the droplets of Bailey's blood I can feel on my cheek. I know that isn't the case. She's not scared I have and will again kill for her. She's happy about that—quite possibly turned on.

"Is that true, K? Did you refuse to take your medicine?"

Although I'm asking a question, I don't give her the chance to respond. I plant my palms on each side of her teeny tiny thighs before leaning in really close to her face, stealing more than her words. I've got a lock on her senses as well. "Do you want me to feed them to you like you're a baby bird?"

While seeking an answer to my question in her expressive eyes, I scan every inch of her grubby face. She's so young, my cock shouldn't be twitching like it is. It wouldn't be if I truly believed she was underage. She's a couple of years younger than me, but I wouldn't put it past ten, making her legal. She just has a real youthful face the cruelest circumstances couldn't age.

After hitting her with a wink that doubles the width of her pupils, I click my fingers at Dok two times, demanding he cough up the painkillers he wants her to take. "Give me a double dose," I demand when he hands me two measly white pills.

"Trey, pain killers were one of your dependencies—"

"I wasn't asking, Dok," I interrupt, my roar loud enough to make K jump. "I'm telling you. Give me a double dose."

He isn't happy about my request, but he follows through, aware of what the repercussions would be if he didn't. Yeah, I was dependent as fuck on *any* drugs my first year here, but this isn't about me. It's all about K.

I feel the heat of Dok's heavy gaze on me when my two front teeth crunch through the first white pill. I swallow down my half without any water before holding K's half out in front of me. A smirk tugs at my mouth when she allows me to place the tablet between her lips without a single snip of hesitation crossing her features. It's the simplest gesture, however, my cock acts as if I'm notching its head into her plump and inviting mouth.

We do the same thing another three times until the four pills Dok handed me have been consumed, and K's hand shoots up to remove something from my beard. My head slants to the side when she removes a chunk of Bailey's skin matted through the wiry mess minus the grimace you'd expect.

You can't feel ill when you're nurturing someone the same way they're nurturing you. It isn't possible. That's why I killed Bailey and Rory without an ounce of remorse being felt. I knew it would do K more good than harm to know I'd do anything to protect her.

"You good?"

This time I wait for K to bob her chin before helping her down from the examination bed. After curling my hand around her uninjured one, I guide her to the door. "Have her medication in my room by the time we return."

Dok grumbles something, but I miss what he says. I can't hear anything through the pounding of the pulse in my ears.

"Jump in," I say to K after guiding her to my car Eight is in the process of dumping Rory's slumped form in. "I'll be back in a sec."

"She good?" Eight asks when I join him at the trunk.

I fold Rory's leg in half like Eight did one of Alexei's goons only days ago to ensure he fits in my trunk before jerking up my chin. "She's more than good," I reply before I can stop myself.

I said to Nikolai earlier my obsession with K is because she reminds me of India, but that isn't true. India's inclusion in my life royally fucked me over. Because of her, my father and brother are buried beneath the same six feet of dirt, and I became a monster. If anything, K's similarities to India should give me the hives. However, there's only one part of my body that swells when she's around. It can be as red and angry as welts and cause just as much discomfort, but it's usually a rash women beg for time and time again.

Feeling my unease, Eight asks, "Are you sure you don't want me to come to Jim's with you? I kinda miss the old bastard, so I don't mind dodging his bullets if he's still pissed at me. I'll even squeeze into the back seat, so you can keep your girl up front with you."

Although annoyed he's double-guessing my order, I also understand his hesitation. I haven't been this unhinged since Nikolai's crew found me on the cusp of death. "I appreciate the offer, but I'd rather you stay here. Justine will keep Nikolai subdued for a couple of hours, but we won't know how he'll react once he's out of her spell." I slam down the trunk before moving for the driver's side door. "Besides, if Jim kills you, I'll be left standing next to a pigpen longer than required. It's not often they're served two bodies in a day." Eight laughs off my worry with a playful tug of his collar. He needs to work on the panic in his eyes if he wants me to believe he isn't worried, though. "Keep an eye on P's until I return. News of Vladimir's death is only just circulating, so we can't be too cautious. If our enemies think we're busted up, they'll want to pick at the scabs."

"Aight, I'll head there now." When I crank open the driver's side door of my car, he straddles a quad just to the left of me. "Heads up." I look up in just enough time to catch the bag he tosses at my head before it smacks me in the face. "Nero said your girl didn't eat breakfast. Figured you'd have a better chance than us."

After jerking up my chin in thanks, I slide into the driver's seat. "If you get any rumblings, call Nero. I can't find my cell phone."

Eight returns my head jerk before he kicks over the quad's motor. Its healthy vibrations only just conceal his snickered, "Again." I have a habit of misplacing my electronic devices.

Although K's attention appears to be on Eight, I can feel her eyes on me. They're as heated now as they were when we dined on the delicious range of goodies Dok keeps well hidden, and it has nothing to do with the bag of fragrant-smelling food Eight just handed me. She's still liking that I stood up for her almost as much as I'm loving her lack of disgust I killed two men in front of her.

Killing is only sinful when it's done to an innocent.

I almost let Nikolai's verdict stand, but the scratches on K's arm altered my verdict. I couldn't see them when she slipped her hand into mine, but I most certainly could feel them. The droplets of blood sliding down her arm obliterated any chance of Rory walking out of his room alive. I wanted him dead no matter the consequence.

Mercifully, I don't see Nikolai disagreeing with my judgment once he emerges from his Justine high. Rory disobeyed his direct order. The verdict for that is only ever death.

I wait for Eight's quad to leave a dust trail before directing my focus to K. "Put your seat belt on, K. Don't want you getting hurt."

If I didn't already know her eyes were on me, I'm left with no doubt when they float away to locate the buckle of her belt. Her gaze was so heated, my face cooled when she moved her eyes away.

Once the familiar click of a belt latching into place sounds through my ears, I fire up my engine, shift my gearstick into first, then commence our five-mile trip.

We're a quarter of a mile away from Clarks when I dig my hand into the bag Eight tossed at me. There's an array of food inside—bacon and egg muffins that are still warm, freshly baked cookies, fruit, and enough bread to feed an army.

Although I'm dying for K's stomach to quit fucking growling, I'm not so hyped up on the adrenaline every kill awards me with to know feeding her stomach its every desire right now could end disastrously. Jim is a cool guy, but even I have issues showering at his ranch. The dude is almost blind, so he has the perfect excuse for a lack of cleanliness, however, what's his whore's excuse?

Nikolai gave him the pick of the crop when he offered up the use of his industrial fridges two years ago when we had bodies to hide and no place to hide them. He picked well when he chose Arabella, she has a nice rack and plenty of ass, but it's clear her hoover lips were the only thing Jim considered while testing out the merchandise on offer. She can't cook or clean for shit.

With that in mind, I pull a bread roll out of the bag, take a large bite out of it, then hand it to K. She waits for the dry clump of carbs to slide down my throat before accepting her share. For someone eating her first meal in almost twelve hours, she doesn't scarf down the bread roll like I'm anticipating. She nibbles at it like a mouse. Even her nose screws up during her chews.

Once she's finished her share of our bread roll, I ripped through another one with my teeth to ensure her it's safe to eat before handing it over.

When her little nibbles get the better of me, I mutter, "You better tell me your real name soon, K, or I'll start calling you Mouse since you eat like one." An unexpected smile tugs at my lips when her nose screws up even more. She's not a fan of the nickname I chose for her. "You don't want to be called Mouse?" When she peers up at me with her big eyes out in full force, the thud in my chest shifts to my ears. "I guess I wouldn't be a fan of being called a rodent either. Do you have another nickname in mind? I'll call you anything you want to be called."

I wait and wait and wait for her to answer me.

When a peep fails to leave her lips, I say, "Come on, K. I heard you talk. You can do it. You've just got to be brave enough to take the plunge."

I flick on the wiper blades when rain patters my windscreen partway down the long dirt road that leads to Jim's. This is the slowest part of the trip when it's dry, so I have to go even slower in the wet.

My tires slip and slide more than usual when K exercises her vocal cords for the second time today. "Duchess."

Even with it being dangerous for me to do, I remove one of my hands from the steering wheel so I can wiggle a finger in my ear, certain I heard her wrong. I've only ever called one woman that name. It was when I was claiming her virginity in her daddy's food pantry.

Although this is a piss-poor excuse, my head was still a little fucked-up from the drugs I consumed last night, so mixing Dok's weak-ass prescription with my already drug-laced veins could be causing a slight bout of hearing loss.

"What did you say?" When panic darts through K's expressive eyes, I'm quick to shut it down. "I'm not mad at you. I just want to make sure I heard you right. I can barely hear anything through the thump of my pulse in my ears."

I wasn't meant to say my last sentence out loud, but I'm glad I couldn't hold back when K removes my hand from my ear to place it on hers. Since her heart is beating as fiercely as mine, I can count her pulse through her ears.

Because I'm too busy staring at her, fucking lost on what the hell is happening, I fail to notice the massive pothole I narrowly missed two days ago. When I hit it front-on, it juts my car out far enough, my tires slip off the portion of road Nikolai pays to have graded every six months so his crew can travel to Jim's as often as needed without hindrance.

Since the road is in the process of being redone, the sides are high and full of loose dirt. I'm bogged in an instant and seconds from burying Rory in a shallow grave instead of feeding him to the pigs as per Nero's suggestion.

After numerous failed attempts to free my back tires from the slop, I stray my eyes to the pigsty on the horizon. It's drizzling, but Rory is as weightless as he was pathetic, so I'll have no trouble carrying him to his final resting place before asking Jim to tow me out of the slosh.

"You can wait here, K. I'll only be a few minutes..." My words trail off when she cranks open her door and slips out of the passenger seat at the same time I notch up the trunk's latch to release its lock.

Like a psychopath with a fondness for blood and gore, my cock hardens to the point its painful when the removal of Rory's naked-ass from my trunk is quickly chased by K's foot landing in his stomach.

I can't understand a word she snarls at him when she lays her boot into him for a second and third time, but I'm as confident as fuck she deserves the title of Duchess.

As Nikolai said all those years ago, not all princes wear crowns.

The same can be said for princesses.

"You good?" I ask her when the lack of nutrients in her stomach has her grappling for air four kicks later. "He's already dead, but I've got no issues with you tendering him up for the pigs. They'll chew straight through his bones either way. Kinda like someone tried to do to his cock." In my earlier rage, I failed to notice Rory's dick is all chewed up. It looks like someone tried to bite it off. Serves the fucker right. If you don't want your dick gnawed off by an angry woman, don't force it between her lips. "Pity they didn't bite straight through. Might have taught him some manners."

K's eyes flash my way. They're brimming with the strength I saw in them when our eyes locked and held. The resurrection of her will to live has me holding back on my plan to toss Rory over my shoulder. If K wants to help send the man who attempted to assault her to hell, I'm more than happy to allow her to do that.

Redemption comes in many forms.

"Just a little bit further," I assure K when her pants grow rampant. I transferred a majority of Rory's weight onto my half of our duo before commencing our sloshy trek across a muddy field, but K's help is still noticeable, especially since she has a cut-up hand. She's holding Rory's legs, which are at an odd angle since I had to bend him up to fit him in my trunk. "I can take it from here if you want to head back."

The sprinkling of rain does little to cool the heat that roars through my body when K grunts out her disapproval. She's come this far, and nothing is going to stop her from reaching her goal.

"All right. Don't get your knickers in a twist, Duchess. I was just checking." My smirk grows when her eyes shoot to mine during the middle of my reply. It isn't her nickname gaining me her attention, it's the way my voiced dipped when I said knickers. It was as British as it could be, and it doubles the tension teeming between us. I doubt any of the men who tortured her under Vladimir's watch called her panties knickers. That's the reason I used it. To remind her she's no longer under Vladimir's watch.

She is sheltered by mine.

"Ready?" I ask K after ripping Rory's body through a gate too narrow for his wide shoulders.

When K nods, we toss Rory into the pigsty like kids throw their mates into a swimming pool. Mud kicks up when he hits the sloshy ground with a thump. It dots my clothes with smelly pig shit and God knows what since Nikolai's crew has dumped multiple bodies here the past two years.

K is nowhere near as lucky. She gets it in her eyes and her face, and it has her stomach protesting to the smell with violent churns.

"Shit, come here." I drag her until she's standing under the drain spout running across the pigsty's roof, wordlessly warning her body it better not bring up a smidge of bread rolls in her stomach. I'll be pissed as fuck if Rory causes her more harm.

The flood of water teeming down her face clears away the mess in an instant. It also drenches her shirt to a point I can't ignore. She's not wearing a bra, and her rosy pink nipples are budded and staring up at me, begging to be touched.

I'm not a good man. I've told you this before, and it's proven without a doubt when I track the back of my fingers down one of K's hardened peaks without seeking permission. When her rosy bud stiffens more from my meekest touch, my cock knocks at the zipper in my jeans. We're standing next to a pigpen, the smell is fucking atrocious, yet I'm two seconds from whipping out my cock and plunging it into K's fragrant-smelling cunt no amount of manure and blood can take away from.

I wouldn't hesitate if K's head wasn't angled to the side, and her eyes were blank and unblinking. She's still here, with me, but only just.

"Look at me, K." When she fails to jump to my command, I get snappy. "Look at me, Duchess!"

I don't know whether it's my clipped tone that awards me the attention of her eyes or the grip I have on her face. Whatever it is, her stare is my undoing.

I want her now more than ever.

"I want to fuck you, Duchess. I want to fuck you so bad it hurts." I step closer to her until she can feel how thick I am beneath my jeans. Even with my cock's length being held back by an industrial-tough zipper, there's no denying my girth. "But since I won't touch you again until you say so, I'm not going to fuck you." You have no idea how hard it is to articulate my next sentence when my fucked-up head has me believing the flare darting through her eyes is disappointment. "Instead, I'm going to kiss you.

All right, Duchess? Just a kiss. I'll stop at that. I swear to you, I will."

She shouldn't believe me. Hell, I don't even believe me, but for some ludicrous reason, she does. With her eyes locked on mine and her nostrils flaring, she faintly bobs her chin, permitting me to kiss her.

"I can't be gentle, K. I don't know how to be gentle." Even though I'm trying to talk her out of it, my fingers weave through her hair that's in bad need of a brush before I steer my mouth toward hers. "But I can try and be gentle for you. I'll treat you like a real motherfucking princess if that's what you want." I brush my lips against her, uncaring if her teeth haven't been brushed for as long as her hair. That's how fucking bad I want her. "Open up for me, Duchess. Show me you want this, too."

Any worries about unhygienic conditions fly out the window when she pops open her mouth at my request. She consumed almost two bread rolls on her way here, however, nothing but minty freshness awakens my senses when I suck in her hearty exhales, hoping the coolness of her breaths will lower my unhealthy body temperature. The seductive scent of her mouth has me so eager to join our lips, I drag my tongue along the roof of her mouth long before I taste the sweetness of her lips.

"Fuck me, Duchess. From the moment I saw you, I knew you'd destroy me."

She doesn't get the chance to respond. I'm on her in an instant. With one hand in her hair, and other on her waist, I pin her to the side wall of the pigsty with my crotch before kissing the living hell out of her.

For how shy she is, I figured her lips would remain as still as her mouth when she refuses to talk. I'm pleased as fuck to announce that isn't close to the truth. Not only does she kiss me back, she leads our embrace like only one woman in my life has previously. She's bruised, cut up, and marks cover almost every inch of her, but she kisses like she can't see the chaos surrounding her. Like she's perfectly stable. Beautiful and without scars.

The knowledge of her strength has me fighting for the top spot. I bite her lip harder than necessary, needing her whimpers to cool the fire roaring in my gut. If I don't simper the temptation burning me alive, I'll fuck her where she stands, heartless to the fact she's already been used and abused multiple times in her pathetically short life. Then I'll fuck her again just to ensure she knows she'll never be touched by another man who isn't me.

After dragging my beard-covered chin across her cheek, I press my lips to her ear. "Do you know what this means, Duchess? Do you have any clue what you've just given me?" I relish the pounding of her pulse in her ears for several long seconds before growling out, "This makes you mine."

When her heart thumps faster during my confession, the darkness inside me roars. My hand is under the shirt she's wearing as a dress in an instant, her scent causing my undoing. Her cunt smells delicious, and it has me completely forgetting my earlier pledge that I won't touch her until she asks me. I need the wetness of her arousal coating my fingers more urgently than my lungs require their next breath.

An urge to piss on Vladimir's ashes overwhelms me when I notch half an index finger inside of K. Her body isn't the only thing messed up. Her insides are just as messy. Vladimir and his men fucked her over so good, no amount of tenderness will reverse their damage.

The thought of what the sick fucks put her through should have me immediately backing away. It's a pity for K I've always had a fascination for the broken ones. They're the fighters. The battlers. The women worthy of a crown. They trudged through the ashes of hell for their non-jeweled crown, so they deserve to wear it without the slightest slant.

She just needs someone stronger than them, rougher and unhinged. She needs someone tough enough to ensure her she'll never be hurt again.

And that someone is me.

"Open up for me, Duchess. Let me in, and I promise I'll make you feel good." The violence roaring through me shifts to nurturing when the tight clench of her vaginal walls around my finger loosen at my request. I don't deserve her trust, but I sure as fuck am pleased to have it.

K's head bows forward to rest on my chest when my thumb finds her clit. It's not marked like the rest of her. It's perfectly soft and responsive to touch. None of the men she was forced to endure would have touched her here as their exchanges were never about K's pleasure. It was always about them.

For how young she looks and the extent of her bruises and scars, I don't feel comfortable saying she wasn't a virgin when she became a captive. She could have very well never experienced pleasure. The thought has me paying extra attention to her clit and clenching cunt.

The weakest moan fans my chest like a feather dusting my skin when I circle the tiny nub protruding as much as the sharp cut of K's hips. It causes pre-cum to drip into the crotch of my jeans and allows me to notch the second half of my index finger inside of her.

When K clamps around my finger, uneased by the unexpected arrival of a shuddering moan vibrating through her chest, I drop my eyes to her face buried between my pecs. The rain sizzling on my red-hot skin makes my shirt appear to be painted on, leaving no place for K to hide—*thank fuck.* I need to know she's with me, not in the darkness she generally hides in during sexual escapades.

"Stay with me, Duchess," I demand, lifting her head to mine with my spare hand. Her eyes are glazed over and brimming with tears, but they're not black and lifeless. "You're not allowed to pass out until you've seen the fireworks."

Her innocence is undeniable when she raises her eyes to the cloud-filled sky, unaware my comment was figurative. They beat her, raped her, and fucked with her head, but there's one thing they never took away from her, and that was her purity. Anything you're forced to do against your will doesn't count.

I learned that three years ago.

K will learn it today.

After clearing my throat of a pride I haven't felt in years, I say, "Are you ready to be swept away, Duchess? Are you ready to be free?"

Although I'm asking her questions, I don't wait for her to answer me. I simply swipe at her clit firm enough to buckle her knees out from underneath her and for the barrier keeping her tears at bay to break.

As she silently shudders through a climax sparking her eyes with life, tears topple down her cheeks. Every salty drop that falls down her face has me wanting to go on a rampage. The only reason I don't is because they also shed away the pained expression I thought her face would never quit wearing.

She is no longer a captive.

She is now just a broken woman.

Broken can be fixed. More times than not, the jagged pieces end up even more beautiful. A kaleidoscope is a cylinder full of broken pieces, yet everyone still stares at it in awe.

Who's to say the same can't be said for women?

FOURTEEN

"Let them be," Jim chokes out in a rough, grunted tone. "They're women, so let them be women."

Even with Jim giving K permission to leave the kitchen after helping Arabella clear away the dishes of our shared meal, her eyes still stray to mine to seek consent.

As quickly as K shattered around me, the heavens opened up. We were drenched in an instant, meaning there was nothing but my wide frame to hide K's flushed face when Jim arrived out of nowhere to check on his pigs.

He's practically blind, but that didn't lessen my urge to maintain K's dignity. I don't want anyone to see her in a vulnerable state, and no, my annoyance had nothing to do with the fact my hand was still inside her panties when Jim interrupted us.

K shattered an hour ago—in more ways than one. The way she opened up to me made her even more beautiful. She's fragile but so fucking strong. Her strength ensures it isn't just her looks I'm attracted to. I also admire her grit. She has been beaten and exploited, yet her shoulders don't hold the weight of her abuse. Her heart does.

She thinks she deserved what happened to her.

I'm determined to prove otherwise.

My first thought when Jim interrupted us was to gather K in my arms and trek straight back to the safety of my car, but something altered the direction of my course. K needed a few minutes to catch her breath as much as I needed time to work out my next move. Jim's ramshackle ranch wasn't the best place for that to occur, but with my car bogged and Jim's truck slipping and sliding on the graveled portion of his road, I didn't have much choice.

The past hour has been good for K. After I sampled a small portion of the pork cutlets, mashed potatoes, gravy, and beans Arabella served her for lunch, she gobbled down her food like it wasn't the blandest meal I'd ever tasted.

Arabella's cooking skills have improved somewhat the past two years, but it still has a lot left to be desired. The potatoes were lumpy, the beans were undercooked, and the pork tasted more of the fat she cooked them in than their homegrown freshness.

K didn't seem to mind, though. She ate and ate and ate until the tiniest curve propped out of the shirt clinging to her body since I refuse for her to get changed. With how timid she's been since climaxing, I can't let her out of my sight for even a second, which is why I shake my head, refusing Arabella's request to take K to get changed.

I'm not being an asshole. I'm reading the silent pleas in K's eyes. She likes Arabella and appreciates the meal she supplied her with, but she doesn't want to be alone with her. She feels safe with me. *Regretfully*.

I can't control myself around her. My instincts go to shit the instant our eyes lock, overcome with a sudden urge to make her mine. I want to protect and shelter a woman who's already been hurt, even knowing my possessiveness could damage her even more than she already is.

You can't incinerate brokenness without first setting it ablaze. It isn't possible. But can I do that to K? Can I break her with the hope of piecing her back together? Or should I leave her alone to live in the bleakness she *thinks* is life?

My fingers tighten around the napkin in my lap when the truth smacks into me.

I don't want to break K.

I want K to break me because as my dad always said, two broken people trying to heal each other is what love is all about.

The chaos stirring in my gut doubles when Arabella spots my head shake. After splaying her hands across her meaty hips, she squawks out my name in an ear-piercing tone. "Trey—"

"No, Arabella," I cut her off, growling, pissed at both her disobedience and the inane thoughts in my head. I've barely known K for thirty hours, so why the fuck am I acting as if I can't live without her? "If you're so desperate for K to get changed, you can bring the clothes to her."

I realize Jim has Arabella on a leash far too long when she huffs out, "Fine."

She makes a beeline for a bedroom attached to the eat-in kitchen. With how messy her room is, I'm shocked by how quickly she returns. She didn't just gather up a dress either. She has an assortment of accessories, including shoes, which K appears excited about. Her expression scarcely altered, but I saw a flare of excitement dart through her eyes before she could shut it down.

It was the same gleam her eyes got before she came.

My eyes rocket to Jim when Arabella snappily requests for K to remove her damp shirt. The heat of my gaze must be hot because he pivots on his heels not even a second later.

"I'll be in the den if anyone needs me."

He's barely burst through the swinging wooden door when Arabella yanks K out of her seat with enough aggression for my jaw to tick. She may be accustomed to my brothers' rough handling her, but that doesn't give her the right to treat K like a whore. Anything she was forced to do under Vladimir's watch wasn't her choice, so I won't have her treated as if it was.

"Move." When Arabella attempts to ignore my directive for the second time, my hand instinctively rises into the air. The only reason it stays suspended mid-swing is because of the width of K's pupils. The thought of me striking Arabella for being disobedient angers her more than the idea of her being hit.

She's once again placing herself last.

That pisses me the fuck off and has my objectives changing in an instant.

After lowering my hand back to my side, I say more respectfully, "Please move."

I work my jaw side to side when Arabella's lips slant downward. She's one of the whores who likes being smacked around, so she would have happily accepted my wrath, even if it hurt K in the process.

"Do you want to wear this?" I ask K, holding up the dress Arabella fetched for her. It's skimpy, short, and I'm reasonably sure it'll have me going on a rampage when we arrive back at Clarks.

The pulse in my jaw drops several inches lower when K shakes her head. Her shirt is grubby and far too big for her tiny frame, but she knows as well as I do that it isn't the packaging that makes a person attractive. It's their uncracked insides.

With a smug grin, I toss Arabella's stripper dress onto the floor of her room. "She doesn't want your dress—" My words are cut off by K's hand darting out to touch my arm. She stares at me with wide, terrified eyes before she drifts them to the shoes Arabella is clutching. They're basic and bland with only the slightest heel, however, she stares at them as if they're Gucci. "You want her shoes?"

K's eyes fall to her bare feet as quickly as her hand returns to her side. For a second, she doesn't breathe, ashamed she showed eagerness for something she doesn't own. She wanted Arabella's mall-purchased shoes so much, she failed to consider how much they could cost her, so now she's more panicked than excited. It's clear she's never been given anything without a hefty price tag attached to it, not even something as simple as a pair of wedged sandals.

When I click my fingers two times, Arabella coughs up her shoes as if she's a genie and I rubbed her bottle the right way. "Sit." My command is for K, and the bob of her throat reveals she's aware of this.

After a second swallow, she does as requested, her eyes never lifting from the floor. I relieve my throat of its sudden dryness before kneeling in front of her to put on the first shoe. The high rise of my shirt on her slim thighs already makes her legs look like they go for miles, so you can imagine how much seduction a two-inch heel will add.

"Sit still, Duchess," I command when it dawns on me the tiny shudders trickling through her body have nothing to do with her wearing shoes for the first time in God knows how long and everything to do with my hands being on her. Is it a scared shake? I don't know. If Arabella weren't eyeballing our exchange like a freak, I'd be halfway through testing my theory by now. Alas, I have to maintain patience—again. "Arabella is a worse cleaner than she is a cook. Even if I wanted to answer your every whim here, K, I can't, so stop convincing me I can."

Arabella scoffs at my insult. K smiles. It isn't a full smile, it's barely noticeable since her chin is tucked in close to her chest, but it sets off the pulse in my ears so quickly, I'm concerned my hearing will never be what it once was.

"There you go," I mutter once I have the second latch done up. "Now how about a twirl?" K shakily accepts my hand before she gingerly pivots around. She's embarrassed by my request, but the ruddy red hue creeping across her cheeks ensures it'll occur more often from here on out.

The downpour we got caught in earlier cleared away the mess from her face and unknotted most of the bird's nest in her hair. If you can take away the paleness of her skin, her teeny emaciated frame, and the red rims around her eyes from when she cried while coming, you'd have no clue she was held captive against her wishes. That's how significant something as minor as a pair of shoes was to her mindset.

Once K is facing me front-on, I clear away a smear of gravy on her top lip before curling my hand around her. "Are you ready to get out of here?"

Her nod this time around isn't concealed like the one she did when I asked her if she wanted Arabella's shoes.

"Jim—" My words stop when he bursts into the kitchen with his coat already on and the keys for his truck in his hand.

I tell Arabella to take the next right before dropping my eyes to K. She's snuggled into my chest, sleeping like a baby. I want to say the droning lull of Jim's old motor is responsible for the peaceful expression on her face, but that would be a lie. She placed her ear over my heart the instant our attempts to un-bog my car caused its tires to sink in deeper. She's as comforted by the sound of my beating heart as I am when I hear it pulsating in my ears.

"Go a quarter a mile up, then pull over. We'll walk the rest of the way." Nikolai kept Clarks hidden for a reason. Even with hiking not being my activity of choice, I don't want to be the cause for anyone knowing where it is. "Here will do."

Ignoring Jim's grumble that Arabella is well aware of the location of Clarks, I divert my attention to K, so I can wake her up without scaring the shit out of her.

My worry is unfounded. She's awake and peering up at me.

"We need to walk from here. Do you want to test out the versatility of your shoes or jump on my back?" My last two words come out with a husky laugh when her eyes pop open at my offer. "Piggyback ride it is."

After thanking Arabella and Jim for the ride with a lift of my chin, I slide out of the cab of his old truck with K still in my lap. I could carry her through the desert-like valleys like a groom does a bride over the threshold, but I offered her a piggyback ride, and for once in my life, I'm going to do as offered.

"If your legs get sore, tap on my shoulder, and we'll stop for a few." Her legs won't get tired from our trek. It'll be from how wide they have to spread to curl around my waist. Our differences in size are starkly contradicting. She's so light, my damp jeans weigh more than her, and it's lucky if the top of her head reaches my nipple piercings.

"*Děkuju.*" I don't understand a word of Czech, but considering she said the same word every time Arabella reloaded her plate with food, I'm reasonably sure it's some sort of thanks.

By the time we reach the outskirts of Clarks, the sun is setting on the horizon. K's faint breaths hitting my neck advise the clomps of my boots didn't deter her from getting some shuteye. She slept the entire way.

When men from Nikolai's crew spot my approach, they dot my chest with the scopes of their high-powered rifles. I wait for the red dots to lift to my face before squashing my index finger to my lips. Sometimes my brothers get excited about identifying a threat's approach before the clearing, they fire shots of celebration into the air. I'm usually all for the adrenaline rush of unloading the chamber of a high-powered assault rifle, but I'd rather K stay asleep, so I downplay my eagerness.

The amused faces of Nero and Mikhail confront me when I break through the matured trees surrounding Clarks. They've seen many women cling to me the past three years, but this is the first time she's clothed, and they're not being invited to sample the merchandise. I'm all for fucking, have been since I was sixteen, but you can be as assured as fuck K will never be offered to *any* man, much less the horndogs of Nikolai's crew.

"Any word from Eight?" I ask Nero while placing K onto my bed in the middle of my room.

Nero scrubs at the stubble on his chin before shaking his head. "No birds are whistling just yet. The quiet is a little unnerving."

I jerk up my chin, agreeing with him before tugging up the bedding to cover K, wordlessly assuring her the slant of her head isn't necessary. She is still with me, she's just zoning out to protect herself, not just sexually, but emotionally as well.

The less you know in this industry, the longer you survive.

Once every inch of K's body is covered by a duvet, I shift on my feet to face Nero and Mikhail. They kept a respectable distance by staying outside my door, them too noticing the glazed-over expression K's face got when they followed our walk to my room.

"Maybe send out some feelers. We usually get rumblings long

before a storm." Men in this lifestyle love to gloat. It gets their rocks off as well as the whores they regularly sink their teeth into.

"All right." Mikhail strays his eyes to K for the quickest second before he pivots on his heels and stalks away. His glare doesn't clench my jaw as expected, probably because his stare was more filled with remorse than desire.

After stepping to the right, blocking Nero from giving K the same sympathy as Mikhail, I ask, "Where's Nikolai?"

He licks his dry lips before curving them into a smile. "Still holed up with Justine. Do you need him?"

I shake my head. "But come get me if he needs me. I'm gonna jump in the shower to wash off the pig shit from my skin. They were extra hungry today. I think we might have a new record. Consumed in under eight minutes."

Nero arches a brow at the impressive number I cited, but he'd rather focus his attention on the first half of my statement than worry about a record he'll never come close to beating. "That's pig shit I'm smelling? *Right.*"

After hitting me with a wink, announcing he knows as well as I do that the sweet smell coating my skin isn't close to the disgusting mess pigs get grubby in, he moseys down the corridor like I'm not five seconds from shoving my rifle up his ass. *Pompous prick.*

Once my door is shut and locked, I drag my eyes over K's still form. Upon discovering she's asleep, I toe off my mud-stained boots, yank my shirt over my head, then drop my hands to my belt. After flinging my jeans over the chair I slept in last night, I head for the bathroom. I won't lie. My cock is hard and throbbing with want.

I've never gotten hard over a kiss before. They don't thrill me enough to be seen as pleasurable. But our kiss—that goddamn motherfucking kiss that almost had me treating K like the monsters from her nightmares—got me so damn hard, my cock hasn't deflated an inch the past hour and a half.

I have no control over it.

None whatsoever.

It's like her kiss was Viagra, and I took the maximum dosage.

Even now, recalling her feather-like moans and the smell that vaped off her skin when she came has me wanting to return to my room. To push away the bedding and spread her legs wide. To snap off the soiled panties she's been wearing for God knows how long. To lick her, eat her, and come over every inch of her.

I want her dirty and broken.

Stripped and scared.

I want her so goddamn much, I want to be one of the monsters from her nightmares.

But if I do that, she'll only be mine once.

I want her so much more than that, so instead of focusing on what I can't have just yet, I climb into the shower, wrap my hand around my cock, and give it a long and determined stroke.

The pounding I give it for the next five minutes is brutal. I don't give the barbell piercings speared through my shaft any leeway in the tightness of my grip. I hold on tight, hurting it as it wants to hurt K.

She'll never take all of me without bleeding. She's tiny, and the scars I felt while fingering her will make her even harder to penetrate, but my God, I want her.

It'll have to be her choice. If she wants me, she'll have to prepare for the pain associated with it. She will bleed no matter what. I'll just make it pleasurable for her this time around.

If possible.

The vicious strokes on my cock weaken as I ruminate over the idea of K being capable of orgasming during sex. She shattered earlier without much initiative, but that isn't unusual. I've made many women come with only a stroke of my thumb, however, not one of them has cried during it.

Will that be normal for K? Will she always break when she gives in to the sensation overwhelming her. She'll still be beautiful once she's put back together, but I don't see it being healthy if it occurs every time.

I could show her how awesome sex is, make her an addict who depends on climaxes as much as her body requires food to live. I'll need to gain her trust, and have her looking at me differently than she does any other man. To watch me as she is now with her lips parted and her eyes wide. For her jagged breaths to match mine when she takes in my cock sliding in and out of my fisted hand.

She has watched a man jerk off before. The low tilt of her chin assures me of this, much less the dilation of her pupils, but I doubt she ever watched them as she's watching me now. The focus would generally be on her—the smooth planes of her stomach and the generous swell of her tits even with her being starved. She's battered and bruised, but more than enticing enough to double the speed of my pumps.

My hips jackknife on repeat as an overwhelming desire to come crashes into me. My body trembles as pre-cum drips from my crown. I tug on my dick so fast, even the coolness of my piercings feel roasting hot.

As I bring myself to the brink of insanity, I refuse to look at K's pebbled nipples or check her panties for wetness. Even with tingles racing from my sack to the tip of my shaft feeling good enough to come, this isn't about me. Just like the fireworks blistering in the cloudy sky above the pigsty, this is for K.

After adjusting my footing to ensure K has the best view possible, I splay my spare hand on the tiles above my head. I want to come so bad, but it's got nothing on my urge to make this the most riveting performance K has ever watched.

While increasing the pressure on my strokes, I suck in big breaths through my nose. I can smell K's heated skin from here, her cunt.

Fuck.

Its intoxicating smell is my undoing.

As cum rockets out the crown, I strangle my dick, pissed as fuck it couldn't hold back for a second longer. It shoots murky white substance up the tiled wall of the shower stall and coats my hand, jerking on repeat until it goes limp, and my lungs are breathless.

"Go to sleep now, K," I murmur through the exhaustion clutching my throat. "Go to sleep before I do something I can't take back."

I don't need to look her way to know she's sinking away from me.

The loss of her heated gaze is telling enough.

FIFTEEN

SALES DOCKET NUMBER 12574... OR IS IT KRISTINA?

Ten years earlier...

"Do you remember what Pa said, Kristina?" my mother asks as she braids the thick waves of blonde curls hanging loosely down my back. I've been growing my hair for as long as I've been living. Twelve years of growth sees it stopping just before the faintest dip in my back. "Treat people how you want to be—"

"Treated. Never less or never more. We are all equal people."

"That's right," my father chimes in, his voice full of pride. "Everyone has their place. You just need to find yours."

"I will, Pa. I'll do precisely that today." I wait for my mother to twist a ribbon through the bottom of my braid before spinning around to gain their approval on my outfit of choice. I have on my best Sunday dress, my face has been scrubbed clean, and since I'm hoping to represent an adult more than a child today, my lashes *have the faintest splattering of mascara. I don't need blush or any of those other gimmicks they sell on the boxed television in my parents' room. My cheeks are already rosy, and since I got my complexion from my mother's side of my family, I'm not as pasty as the other blonde-haired, blue-eyed children in town.*

My mom places down the horse-hair brush that's been passed down from generation to generation in our family before twisting around to face me. "You better get a wiggle on. Mrs. Novak does not appreciate tardiness."

While nodding, I run my sweaty hand down the flare of my dress before making a beeline for the door. I'm so nervous, my palms are sweaty.

"Remember to finish your schoolwork as soon as you're done," my father shouts when I break through the door of the servants' quarters.

He can't see me, but I nod my head, nonetheless. I love my parents, and we're extremely fortunate to be given a cabin on the grounds of the Novak's estate, but I don't want to be them when I grow up. I want to be a nurse, or a pilot, or perhaps a naval officer.

If you haven't worked this out yet, I haven't exactly worked out what I want to do just yet. There's only one thing I do know, I don't want to do it here. The only people I can help here are the Novaks, and they have so much money, they don't need the type of help I'm offering. I'm only applying for the position of chambermaid today so that I can put aside my wages for a degree. They're not cheap, and my parents can't afford to pay on my behalf. I'm two years younger than the starting age of most of the chambermaids, but I'm hopeful the mascara on my lashes will mature up my looks enough they'll look past the childishness of my face.

"You're Hana and Ivan's daughter, correct?"

Mrs. Novak's head pops up from my handwritten resume when I nod. "Yes, Mrs. Novak. My father is currently your chauffeur, and my mother is your head housekeeper."

"And you want to be a chambermaid? That's your career aspiration?"

I lick my lips, truly unsure how to reply. I've never been a fan of lying, so I go with straight-up honesty. "Not exactly. I'd like to be a chambermaid for now. I don't know what I want to be when I grow up."

Her expression switches from amused to miffed in less than a nanosecond. "Grow up is a fitting set of words considering your age."

"I will work hard, and I'll have no trouble keeping up with your schedule as set."

She arches a blonde brow. "Even with you being half the age and weight of your colleagues?"

I nod, preferring to lie without words. I'm strong, despite my small frame. My parents raised me right.

The knot in my stomach tightens when Mrs. Novak sighs. She only ever sighs when she's disappointed, which is often these days. "I'm sorry, Kristina. I don't see you being a suitable fit for our staff. Perhaps in a few years—"

"I won't be here in a few years. I'll be at college."

She smiles like I'm joking. It agitates me more than I'll ever express. "We'll see."

After dismissing me from the room with a wave of her hand, she shifts her focus to the next applicant on her long list of many.

"I'm sorry, Ma," I mouth to my mother during my silent trek across the ballroom-size room.

The lowering of her chin reveals she spotted my comment, but *she can't reply, or she'll risk being fired. Even suggesting for a chicken gravy to be served with turkey can get you fired by Mrs. Novak. She hates being told what to do.*

Halfway across the manicured gardens separating the servants' quarters from the main residence, I'm startled to within an inch of my life. "No luck?" Achim, Mr. and Mrs. Novak's eldest son, smiles a blistering grin when I clutch my chest to ensure my heart remains put. This is the first time I've seen him in over a year. He's attending his senior year at a boarding school far, far away from here. "It was probably the braid. It makes you look very childish."

Boarding school was supposed to teach him some manners.

It clearly didn't work.

After rolling my eyes, I continue down the path I was walking before I was rudely interrupted. My strides slacken three steps later when Achim shouts, "I can help you, you know."

Hearing his unvoiced words the loudest, I say, "With what, exactly?"

He waits for me to pivot around and face him before he answers, "You want to work for my family, don't you?" When I nod, the arrogance on his face doubles. "I can help you with that... if you're willing to do something worthwhile to be awarded my help."

I've lived a very sheltered life, but even someone as naïve as me couldn't miss the innuendo in his tone. "Thank you for the offer, but I'm willing to wait another two years."

My steps freeze for the second time when Achim mutters, "That'll be another four years stuck here, saving to go to school. Come on, Kristina. Don't act so regal. Your head will never wear the crown you're seeking. You'll always be the help, so why not accept it when it's being offered?"

I barely roll my eyes for a second, however, it's long enough for Achim to creep up on me unaware. He fists my braid so fiercely, I'm certain it'll take longer than a year to cover the bald patch of his yank. "You either accept my help willingly, Help, or I'll force you to accept it."

I'm terrified for my life, equally scared and horrified. I don't budge an inch, not even when Achim commences dragging me toward the pottery barn at the side of the garden. As vomit creeps up my throat, panic sets in. My family has served the Novaks for years, but what Achim is asking for was never part of the agreement. My parents work hard for their money, and even with their stature not being close to the Novaks', they're good, honest people who don't deserve to have their only child treated this way.

Just before Achim pulls me into the dark, scary void, a voice I'll never forget breaks through the horror setting my panic alight. It's the voice of my mother, demanding for me to come back to the main house immediately because she has some good news for me.

"If I don't go, she'll come looking for me," I speak through the lump in my throat, praying Achim is as scared by my mother as the women who work with her. "Please, Achim."

His fingers are only half weaved out of my hair when I push off my feet with a grunt, running in the direction opposite to the one I was walking. I sprint so fast, the tears streaming down my face blow off in the wind of my speed.

When I crash into the chest of my mother a few strides later, my words come out in such a flurry, I barely make any sense.

"Kristina, slow down. I can't understand you."

As my mother lifts my chin so she can peer into my eyes, I catch sight of the people surrounding us. Mrs. Novak isn't the only one eyeing me with a steely glare, so is her son. He's holding the ribbon once twisted around my braid to his nose, smiling when the scent of my shampoo streams through his flaring nostrils, not the least bit concerned I'm about to rat him out.

I discover why when my mother mouths, "Please be careful about what you say. Mrs. Novak is quite temperamental today."

She'll put measures in place to protect me when I tell her what Achim did, but I can't commence that here. She needs her job. Both my parents do. This isn't a town with money to burn. If you don't work for the Novaks, you don't work for anyone.

After licking my dry lips, I mutter, "I lost my ribbon. I'm so sorry."

"Oh, sweetheart." My mother cups my jaw in a motherly way before saying, "I'll pick you up another one. Your father and I are about to head to town for supplies."

"Can I come with you?" She shakes her head for not even a second when I switch my question to a beg. "Please."

"I'd love for you to come, sweetheart, but Mrs. Novak has agreed to put you on a trial basis commencing immediately. If you can prove yourself within a week, she'll place you on permanently." Mistaking my gulp as one of excitement, she smiles a grin so bright, the sun appears nonexistent. "You can tell me everything that happened the instant your shift is over, okay?"

Even being genuinely unsure how I can explain what happened, I nod.

"Good girl. Now go with Rosa, she'll show you the rooms you're in charge of this week."

Rosa, a lady with thick silver hair and a shadow of a mustache on her top lip, steps out from behind Mrs. Novak before gesturing for me to follow her. Since her presence guarantees I won't be left alone with Achim, I quickly follow her into the Novak estate.

"**M**a?" I question, my voice groggy since it's almost two in the morning. I fell asleep not long after finishing my first shift. Since I was so determined to show Mrs. Novak I had the *strength needed to be a chambermaid, I put in more hours than necessary.*

It also meant I was never alone.

I only left the main residence when I was forced out, and even then, it was under protest. My parents hadn't returned from town. They'd left hours earlier, and their absence is very unlike them.

A scratch impinges my throat when the face of the person entering the servants' quarters registers as familiar. It's Mr. Novak. He's nicer than both his wife and son, but he never merges this deep into the grounds of his estate. He barely leaves his room.

"Kristina, honey, I need you to come to the main residence with me. There's been an accident. The police are in attendance..."

I wake up screaming, panting, and clawing at the arms circling me as the world drains from beneath my feet for the second time in my life. "You're okay, K. You are safe."

Because the nightmares of that morning were replaced by real-life ones not long after it, I haven't dreamed about the night my parents were killed for years. They died when a truck driver lost his brakes going down a hill. He was pulling across the road to use the emergency stopping lane etched into the side of the mountain. Because he didn't see my parents, he ran straight over them, killing them both on impact.

It took the authorities so long to notify their next of kin because they were trapped under the wreckage for hours. As if that wasn't already confronting, I was given the horrifying news while standing across from Achim, who smiled like the end of my life was the beginning of his.

In a way, he was right. My life did end that morning. I wasn't raped until four years later, but that's only because Achim was so scared he'd get the help pregnant he wasn't willing to risk penetration. That's why he forced me to suck him off instead. It was his worry-free alternative.

That all changed when I gave my virginity to Trey.

Because I was no longer pure, and Achim had the solemn vow of his wife-to-be to prove it, he realized he could shunt unwanted pregnancies onto almost anyone. Who would second-guess anything he said? He's a Novak. He has the blood of royalty.

Only Trey's family blood was more regal, and look where that got him. His family legacy is dead, the whereabouts of his mother and brother are unknown. He has no one but me. A whore who wakes up in the middle of the night screaming. A woman so selfish the last thoughts she had of her parents was that she wanted to be better than them.

A woman so broken, she may never be fixed.

What was so bad about my parents' life that I desired more? They had love, light, and me—the cancerous leech who destroys everything.

If I had remembered my place, I would have never gained Achim's attention, and none of this would be happening. Trey's mind wouldn't have been poisoned, Achim wouldn't have raped me, and I wouldn't be so selfish, the desire to be cherished sees me placing my needs above anyone else's. Trey has his own demons, yet, he's here, soothing me while the nightmare of my past clings to my skin.

Achim was right. I am a whore. I sold half my soul for an orgasm, then surrendered the other half for a pair of shoes. I'm a terrible person, but that doesn't mean the hate I have for Achim is underserving.

He didn't punish me because I had sinned.

He punished me so I *would* sin.

Then he had the perfect excuse to hurt me.

I fell straight into his trap. I hate myself for it, but I hate Achim even more than that.

"*Nesnáším tě*, Achim," I garble through the bile scorching my throat. "*Nesnáším tě. Nesnáším tě. Nesnáším tě*," I repeat again and again and again until my confession of hate pushes me into a blackness so fierce, I don't think if I'll ever come out.

TREY

My eyes float up from my balled fists to the door when a knock sounds through my ears. I haven't slept since K woke up screaming. I could hardly understand a thing she said while digging her nails into my arm, fighting to get out of my hold, but one word rang louder than the rest —Achim.

That's not a common, everyday name, especially in this part of the continent. It has me wondering exactly how long K has been stateside and how she got here. This isn't an industry you choose to join. You're either purchased, stolen, or kidnapped from another organization. Could that sanction have anything to do with the name she shouted in the midst of a terrifying nightmare?

Although I'd love a few more hours to work through my confusion, the urgent expression on Nero's face doesn't give me a chance. He's a few spots down from me in Nikolai's crew, but his importance to this sanction is undeniable. He has a pretty-boy face most of the crew gives him hell for, but deadly, murderous insides.

You grow thick skin when you spend half your childhood looking like a girl instead of a boy. He's fixed the injustice now with as many tattoos and piercings as me, but no amount of body art can hide his boyishly handsome face.

"Can this wait?" I ask, still uneased by K's nightmare. She's been fragile since she orgasmed, and I have a feeling her nightmare is just the beginning of her downfall.

Nero shakes his head. "Not unless you want Nikolai's kingdom to topple before it's truly begun." My heart rate kicks up a beat when he adds, "We let feelers out as you suggested. One caught wind about a flock set to fly."

Fuck. This is what I've been worried about since Nikolai decided to storm Vladimir's off-site compound. His decision revealed he was putting Justine above his position. To his crew, it showed strength and leadership. To his enemies, it exposed he has a weakness—one they'll be more than happy to use against him. That's why I fired at India all those years ago. If I had placed her above anyone, my operation would have folded even quicker than it did from Cole's change of teams.

If I knew back then what I know now, I would have never notched back the trigger. Alas, I can't change the past, but I sure as hell can stop the same thing happening to Nikolai.

"Who?"

I could expand on my question, but Nero isn't my go-to guy for no reason. "Vasilievs. Eight spotted them armoring up. They're a mile or two out from P's."

I swear for the second time, out loud this time. "Tell the men to suit up." After dragging over my jeans, I stuff my feet inside the openings, yank them up my thighs, then hunt for a shirt. "Does Nikolai know?" Nero waits for me to pull a plain white T over my head and grab my boots from the door before he shakes his head. "Why the fuck not?"

"Mikhail—"

"I don't give a fuck what Mikhail says. You don't work for Mikhail. You work for Nikolai, so anything happening on his turf goes directly through him."

My throat works through a hard swallow when Nero says, "Mikhail didn't want you informed either." When I look two seconds from ripping Mikhail's stomach out of his body via his nostrils, Nero talks faster, "Not because he's trying to jump over your rank. Word is Alexei knows you killed Tristan. He doesn't want revenge, Trey. He has every intention of killing you."

"Then it's my right to be a part of this war, isn't it?" I don't wait for him to answer me. I once again direct him to get the men ready before moving to K's side of the bed. She appears to be sleeping. Her ruse would be more convincing if her ear wasn't squashed against the mattress, and her eyes weren't open and unblinking. I don't know if Nero's unexpected arrival to my room shunted her into the dark void or her nightmare. It could be a combination of them both.

After pulling out the blanket flattened beneath her and cocooning her within it, I push her hair away from her face. "I'll be back, all right? I know I said I wouldn't leave you, but this is really important."

I'd give anything for her to answer me. To say it's okay for me to leave. But since it is unlikely she'll ever do that, I drag my thumb over her lips that are slightly parted so she can suck in shallow breaths unnoticed before making a beeline for the door Nero's shadow disappeared from only seconds ago.

As carnage swarms around me, I take the most direct route to Nikolai's room in the compound. Even though I'm dressed, I feel naked without my gun. It's usually stuffed down the back of my jeans. Tonight, I left it sitting on my bedside table. Leaving it there was the only way I could convince myself it was okay to leave K.

She'll be safe. No one knows about Clarks' location. Nikolai kept it on the down-low for this very reason. We'll never be ambushed here. It's Nikolai's safe haven, and the only place I've ever felt sheltered.

Hopefully, it will represent the same thing for K one day as well.

A Russian curse word breaks through the door of Nikolai's room when I rack my knuckles against it. He tells me to leave with a heap of gravelly words and even more expletives.

"Can't," I reply without the slightest quiver to my voice. We've had days to prepare for this war, so now isn't the time to act panicked. "Birds have word of a takeover bid."

Another Russian curse word booms through Nikolai's door a mere second before it swings open. When I see his girl splayed on his bed, barely covered by a sheet, I drop my eyes to my boots, aware even I would kill my number two if he saw K like that. My fists twitched for a smashing when Nero peered into my room earlier, and K's body was hidden by one of my shirts.

"What is it?" Nikolai asks when he spots the annoyed expression crossing my face.

Just like my conversation with Nero, I keep things basic. "Alexei. He's heading to P's."

"The men—"

"Suiting up now. Armor was restocked when you kicked us out of Justine's apartment. We've got plenty of ammunition, but I suggest we still go in quietly. We'll need less men if he doesn't know we're coming."

Most people think there's only one route to the Popov mansion.

They're wrong.

Why go around when you can go over?

"How many?"

I shrug. "Nero didn't give me a number. Last count, the Vasilievs were sitting at around thirty or so men. Fifty when the coke is good."

That's where Alexei went wrong. He secured the loyalty of his crew with drugs instead of respect. He doesn't give a fuck about his men or the whores who service them after a hard day, and they know it.

I kind of wish Nikolai was the same when he says, "I'll lead the men in. Have the quads fueled and ready to go, then take up comms. The last thing we want is the feds interrupting a turf war."

"I'm not doing comms—" Nikolai cuts me off with a stern glare. Usually, it would have me backing down in an instant—this is his sanction, so he can do with it as he pleases—but that excuse won't fly today. "Nero said the word on the street is Alexei is doing this because he wants me. If that's true, he won't stop until he gets me."

"He won't *get* you, Trey. He'll *kill* you." He locks his eyes with mine. They're more sparked with worry than fortified with the hate they are generally fired by. "You were acting on my orders, which means retribution for Tristan's death belongs on my shoulders."

"Nik—"

"Don't make me take this decision out of your hands, Trey. You either stay here as I am requesting, or our truce will be over. Don't you know princes from different realms can't be friends?"

He doesn't mean what he's saying. He's just stressed, that's all. We're brothers. Allies. Best friends. That's why he's dealing me the hand he is. He'd rather have me as his enemy than see me buried. It's his fucked-up way of saying he cares about me.

"Get the quads fueled up but tell the men to hold until I'm ready." Stealing my chance to put forward a better argument, he shuts the door in my face.

I'm barely halfway to the weaponry room decked out with enough equipment for three wars when Nikolai and Justine nip at my heels. Nikolai's speed is so fierce, Justine has to jog to keep up with him. Her panicked expression grows when Nikolai tells her she's to stay with me, and under no circumstances is she to leave Clarks.

While my brothers strap AK-47s to their chests and don army paint like real-life motherfucking marines, I crack open a laptop and hack into the Las Vegas PD's command center. I knew jack shit about computers only a few months ago, but the head operative of the firm Nikolai hired for security showed me a few pointers. Tapping into a scanner radio takes barely ten seconds.

The bustling space descends into silence when Justine shouts, "I can't help you if I'm left in the dark! Tell me what's happening!" She has the eye of everyone in the room, but there's only one pair she's seeking. Nikolai's. "Please, Nikolai. I want to help."

"We roll out in thirty," Nikolai tells the men frozen and gawking. His wording couldn't be more perfect. Not only does it lessen the heat of their wrath on Justine, but it also gets their heads back into game mode. Alexei is a moron, but it doesn't take much more than that to fire a gun.

After inconspicuously requesting for me to join them, Nikolai strays his eyes to Justine. "*Ahren—*"

"What's going on?" she interrupts, almost sobbing.

Shock rains down on me when Nikolai picks honesty over deceit. It's a rarity for him when he's dealing with the opposite sex. "The Popov compound is moments from being stormed."

"By whom? If it's the authorities, I can help. They need a warrant and don't even get me started on the number of books I'll throw at them if they don't have one."

I smile right along with Nikolai. Justine's offer was sweet, but nothing is ever done here with a book. "We're not being raided by police, *Ahren.* It's a rival of ours, unhappy with the consequences of joining a war he didn't belong in."

Justine's lack of knowledge about this lifestyle is seen on her face when she asks, "What do you mean? What war?"

When Eight bursts into Clarks, out of breath and with an ashen face, Nikolai signals for his men to move. Eight can't get a word out since he's so out of shape, but his facial expression makes it obvious as to what he wants to say. *Hell has come knocking.*

While Eight struggles to fill his lungs with air, Nikolai continues wooing Justine with straight-up honesty. "Vladimir sought help with your kidnapping. My men couldn't get to Roman without taking down members of their crew. A man lost his son; now he is coming to get answers."

Well, mostly truthful. I still haven't given him the full recollection of events that occurred that morning between K and... K. I haven't had the time. That's why I can't let my fuck-up be placed entirely on Nikolai's shoulders. I messed up, so I should pay the price for my error.

"Let me come, Nikolai. Let me speak to Alexei. He just wants to bury his son." That was the only term he was interested in negotiating with Vladimir two years ago when his middle son's switch in enemies resulted in his death.

"No." Nikolai's denial snaps out of his mouth like the crack of a whip. After mounting the ATV he arrived at Clarks on, he strays his eyes to mine. "He will kill you, *then* he'll bury his son. You were acting on my orders, Trey, so the blame for Tristan's death is on my shoulders, not yours."

Hearing the unease in Nikolai's tone as readily as me, Justine begs, "Please don't go. *Please.*"

Forever a leader, Nikolai replies, "I have to, *Ahren.* These are *my* men. That makes them *my* responsibility."

"What about me?" Justine fights back. "I'm your responsibility too. You promised to keep me safe. You can't do that if you're dead."

When the sound of gunfire breaks through the eerie silence, Nikolai kicks over his ATV before locking his eyes with mine. "Keep her safe, Trey. That's your *only* job. Keep my *Ahren* safe."

I barely dip my chin half an inch when he yanks back on the throttle.

"Nikolai, please!" I band my arm around Justine's waist before she can take off after him on foot. "Don't leave me! I love you!" She kicks, wails, thrusts, and grunts for the next several minutes, her fight only lessening when Nikolai's ATV disappears into the darkness of the night. "Let me go." She stabs her nails into my arm like K did when she woke from a nightmare before jabbing the heels of her shoes into my shins. "Nikolai!"

Her frustrated wails are soon echoed by the women in the dormitory. They call out just as loud, and their cries are just as anguish-filled. When I nudge my head to the corridor where their room is located, Eight jerks up his chin, hearing my silent request for him to go check on them. My room is on the other side of the compound, but they're so loud, they could wake K.

With Eight's wariness as high as mine, he removes a gun from the back of his jeans when he reaches the opening. When he disappears from view, I set Justine back onto her feet. A florally scent smacks me in the face a mere second before Justine's fist does. Her gall both frustrates and excites me. Not because I'm a brain-dead idiot who enjoys being hit, it's because she socked me with the same amount of intensity K did only two days ago. Justine's hit reveals how strong K is. She may look frail and scrawny, but she's far from it. Even at her weakest, she gives it her all.

After returning my head front and center where it was before I was punched in the face, I mutter, "I deserve that... and so much more." My brothers are fighting for my honor while I hide out like a coward. A throbbing jaw isn't close to what I deserve.

I realize the universe works in mysterious ways when Eight's grunted request for help sounds through my ears. He's carrying a lifeless woman in his arms—*my lifeless woman.*

SEVENTEEN

"Come on, K."

The heat of a hand being slapped across my face rouses me from the darkness long enough for me to realize I'm in the shower. The same shirt and tiny pair of knickers I've been wearing the past twenty-four-plus hours clings to my body. I'm drenched head to toe, and the contents of my stomach are being forcefully removed by two thick fingers ramming down my throat.

"Bring them up for me, K. You're not going down like this. You are too fucking strong to let them win."

I soundlessly cry through the pain tearing up my throat when the fingers pierce through my gag reflex so forcefully, my stomach has no reason not to protest. I cough and splatter through pain medication I must have swallowed whole since they ping off the floor like they're made from the same material as the studs in Trey's cock.

"Yes, that's it. Bring them all up," says a growly British voice not as pained as it was minutes ago before he once again shoves his fingers down my throat.

This time, it is Trey's clutch around my waist that causes me to hurl. He squashes my stomach so brutally, I'll never be convinced my insides have organs.

Once my second bout of vomiting is over, Trey commands for someone to count the pills in my vomit, wanting to ensure not a single one remains in my stomach. I don't know who he's talking to. I can't see anything through the film coating my eyes. I'm not even sure we're in the shower in his bathroom. Everything is a blur.

While the black bob near the lower half of my body rummages through my stomach's contents, Trey slips his hand under my chin to raise my heavy head. "Stay awake, K. Don't you go passing out on me again. If you pass out, I will hurt you. I'll hurt you so fucking bad, you'll get back the will to live because you'll hate me so much, you'll want to kill me. You can't kill me if you're dead, K, so you need to fight to stay alive."

He pushes my hair out of my face when I slant my head back so the icy-cold water drenching my waist-length hair can remove the blobs of spew gripping my chin. "That's it, K. Come back to me. Show me how strong you are." When my head careens toward his chest, the pressurized water too strong for the emaciated muscles in my neck to handle, Trey wrenches it back. His clutch on my hair hurts, but it's nothing close to the first time Achim tried to assault me. "Don't you go falling asleep, K. Stay with me. I'll get you warm soon, I promise. I just need to make sure you've brought up all the pills first, then I'll never leave your side. You'll never be left alone again. Do you hear me? I'll always be there for you when you wake up from the dark. I won't leave your side. I should've never left you to begin with." His last sentence is barely a whisper, and it breaks my heart.

When the guilt highlighting his solemn tone becomes too much to bear, I whisper, *"Omlouvám se. Nezasloužím si tvou korunu. Nic si nezasloužím. Je mi to moc líto."*

My blurry eyes drift to the right when a soft female voice whispers, "I'm sorry. I don't deserve your crown. I don't deserve anything. I'm so sorry." Although my vision is still hazy, I know who she is. She just translated what I said word for word. Only one person has done that in this country. Justine.

"You said you'd go to war for me," she tells Trey on my behalf. "But the war had already started. It will never end."

After blinking in rapid succession, I raise my eyes to Trey's face, desperately needing to gauge his reaction when I quote, "I'll give you the crown you're craving, Duchess. It just won't be pronged with jewels."

Since he has to wait for Justine to translate what I'm saying, it takes a few seconds longer for shock to wash over his face than I am anticipating, but it arrives, nonetheless.

"You were in the pantry?"

When I nod, Justine stops interpreting his question for me, clueing on that I have no trouble understanding English.

After many seconds of painful silence, Trey asks, "Did I fire at you?" Not waiting for me to respond, he pulls back the tangled hair draped down the front of my shoulders, sucking in sharply when he spots the familiar circular singe of a bullet wound. "I hurt you."

I shake my head. "You didn't shoot me. You pushed me out of the way."

Justine is only halfway through interpreting what I said when a gruff, accented voice interrupts, "I'm only finding four pills." Although I can't one hundred percent testify it is Eight speaking, I'm reasonably sure it is. He has quite a twang to his tone considering he lives in the city. "There are only four pills. Are you sure she's overdosing on codeine?"

"I assumed that's what she took since it was what Dok prescribed. Did you find anything near her when you found her?" When Eight shakes his head, Trey lowers his eyes to mine. The panic in them has me wanting to fold in two. "What did you take, K? Was it pills? Coke? Did you shoot up?"

Even knowing there won't be any, he checks my arms for puncture wounds. It isn't that he trusts me, he just knows I wouldn't take anything that would make me more vulnerable than I already am. Drugs would do that.

When he fails to find the cause for my near-comatose state, Trey requests for Eight to reach out to Dok. "If she's OD'ing on heroine, pumping her stomach won't be enough."

While Eight rushes off to do as ordered, Trey pulls me out of one of the shower stalls across from the dorm where the other women are. When I shudder through the toxins wreaking havoc with my senses, he requests for Justine to fetch some towels from a linen closet partway down the hall. When she darts out of the bathroom, I wrack my brain as to what's happening. I'm so confused. The last thing I remember is waking up in Trey's bed screaming, but that's on the other side of the compound, so how did I get here?

As panic drudges through me, my eyes pop open. I'm not just scared about the horrifying memories slowly filtering into my woozy head. I'm petrified Trey's wet shirt is amplifying the zap of electricity surging through his body from him being tasered.

The charge of electricity buckles his knees in an instant and has him slumping to the floor as if he's dead. If that isn't already terrifying, with a mocking grin, a monster from my nightmares steps out from the shower stall next to the one Trey and I just exited.

With his head slanted to the side like a naughty dog, Achim says, "That was more fun than I thought it would be... even with his sickening display of chivalry. He has quite the fascination for you, doesn't he? *Come back to me, K. Fight for me.*" He gags like he's physically repulsed before he steps over Trey's lifeless form. "Doesn't he know he can buy you for a couple of nickels and a stick of gum?"

Determination spirals through me when he has the nerve to laugh. Those are the objects he tossed at me the first time he forced me to give him head. I took the gum willingly, needing anything to remove the putrid taste of his cum from my mouth.

When I say that to Achim, he backhands me so fiercely, the crunch of my neck isn't natural. "Don't you dare speak down to me. You're *nothing* but the help."

Something inside me snaps. I don't know if it's grit or pure hate, but whatever it is, it roars so loudly, the force of its rumble shunts Achim back almost as much as my hands.

When Achim trips over Trey's still legs, his gun skitters away from him. I'm tempted to snatch it up, but he recognizes my game plan in an instant, and just as quickly, he pulls a second pistol out of the breast pocket of his jacket.

With my heart in my throat, I sprint out of the bathroom, praying Achim will be so angry about my disobedience, he will take his frustration out on me instead of Trey.

Mercifully, my plan works. A bullet pierces the drywall next to my head a mere second before I burst into the corridor.

With Justine being hogtied by a man with icy blue eyes and black hair on my right and Eight gargling blood and clutching his stomach on my left, I head straight, praying the shard of glass Trey kicked away from me yesterday is still in the corner of the large space. It might not be as powerful as a gun, but more times than not, battles like this are mind over matter.

Since my head is still woozy, I miscalculate my landing. I skid more than necessary across the highly polished concrete floors, only stopping when my head colliding with the solid wall almost knocks me out.

While dabbing my head with my hand, praying the large bump under a mess of blonde curls doesn't burst open, I clutch the shard of glass in my hand then twist to face the door.

The jagged edge of the mirror digs into the skin Dok glued together yesterday, when my wooziness clears enough, I see the sickening image confronting me. A second man is standing next to Achim. He's holding Trey off the ground by a fierce clutch of his hair. Blood is dripping off Trey's chin. I can't see where it's coming from, but there's enough for me to be concerned my endeavor to protect him has come too late.

"No!" I shout in Czech when the man clutching Trey's hair strikes him over the head with a tire wrench, causing a large crack to both Trey's skull and my heart.

My voice is so loud, the women huddled in the corner of the room break into a painful sob. It's the same whimpered response they produced when they spotted Achim sneaking me past them so he could place me in a spot I'd be easily found.

This was a set-up. My overdose. The takeover bid that emptied Clarks within minutes. Achim's apparent annoyance about Trey's protectiveness. It was all a set-up. The only thing I can't work out is why. What benefit does Achim get from this?

My stomach rolls when the truth smacks into me.

This isn't about Ana or me.

It's about Trey.

It has *always* been about Trey.

"What did he ever do to you to deserve this?" I shout at Achim in Czech. "It was India who couldn't say no to the Corbyn men. She's the one you should be angry at!"

"What about you!" he roars back, his veins bulging. "You deceived me by giving your virginity to him..." he spits out 'him' like it arrived with a fresh batch of vomit, "... a lowlife thug who *thinks* he's better than he is." When a grin tugs on his abhorrent face, the color drains from my cheeks. "I thought a few years in a dungeon would have taught him his place." He shakes his head in a demoralizing way. "Some people never learn." His comment is for both Trey and me. He hates that he found me in Trey's bed just as much as he hates how fiercely I'm fighting for Trey. I've never shown him the grit I'm displaying now. "There's only one solution for disobedience. *Death*."

The reasoning behind him speaking his last word in English comes to light when the dark-haired man next to him raises his tire wrench for the second time.

With a roar of a woman with nothing to lose, I spring to my feet, ready and willing to send Achim to hell before he can amass another undeserving victim.

I'm halfway to the door when Achim commences closing it. Its vault-like locks clicking into place are as heartbreaking as Justine's scream when the whack of a tire wrench fracturing a skull booms through the door only a second later.

Although panicked about what I may see, I bob down to peer out the keyhole. Blood is oozing out of Trey's head, but the tiniest flutter of a pulse can be seen in its ripples. When they commence dragging him down the hall, unaware of my watch, I strain my eyes to the furthest point before seeking another way to spy on them.

The wall across from me takes up most of the view, but since it's dark, the industrial lighting wired throughout the compound bounces shadows off the stark white paint. They reveal they enter a room a few doors down from the one I'm trapped in. I can't tell exactly how many, but I am assuming five or six spots down.

When a terrifying scream rips through my ears not long later, breaking my heart further, I search the room for another exit point. My head is thumping so fiercely it feels like my brain is about to drain from my ears, and I'm unbelievably dizzy, but I can't give in like I have so many times the past six years.

It's time for me to show my strengths.

Within minutes, my only-just-gathered determination gets squashed. A large window spans one wall of the dormitory, but it's barred up and locked like a maximum-security prison, the bathrooms are across the hall, and the walls are made out of concrete, so they're too durable for me to break through.

There's only one way in and out of this room. I don't want to go near it again. The keyhole is tiny, but the noises that seeped through it during my hunt for another exit are messing with my head so much, blackness is creeping forward, begging for me to merge myself into it, to free myself from the torture I'm reasonably sure Trey is being put through.

I want to go, I want the pain to stop, but if I do that, Trey will die. That isn't a possibility. It's a fact.

"Argh!" I scream out loud, my voice brittle and scorned.

I smack myself in the head three times before spinning to face the women still huddled in the corner of the room. They stare at me like I'm crazy when in reality, they're the ones who are deranged.

They don't fight at all.

They just give in.

Like I did when my parents died.

Determined not to make the same mistake twice, I return to the door. I pry at the hinges with my fingernails and scratch at the steel material until my nails bleed, and terrifying silence fills my ears.

Silence isn't good.

Usually, it only means one thing.

Death has arrived.

"No!" I scream in Czech again while banging on the door with my fist. "No, no, no!" I shout on repeat as tears stream down my face. I'm so sick of this happening. It isn't fair. Yes, every action has a consequence, but instead of the backlash occurring to the people responsible for the injustice, it's always shunted onto the undeserving half.

Trey doesn't deserve this.

I tricked him into sleeping with me, not the other way around.

I lied.

It was me.

Everything happening is my fault.

My mini-breakdown gets a moment of reprieve when I pick up the faintest patter of a pair of boots. Anyone not trapped by their own thoughts for weeks on end wouldn't hear the faintest tap of a person sneakily approaching them. I hear every step. I'm just praying their wish to keep their approach unknown puts them on my side of the team for once.

I send thanks to my parents when I spot the shadow of a man I'd guess to be around six foot two. Achim isn't that tall. My father often said his lack of height was the reason he was always grumpy. He has short-man-stature syndrome.

A relieving sigh rattles in my chest when the body of Nikolai gobbles up the shadow I'm watching like a hawk a few seconds later. He has a gun in his hands, and a crinkle of determination is popped between his dark brows.

"There, down there," I whisper to him in Czech, praying Achim won't hear me. "They took them down there."

It dawns on me that he can't understand me when his eyes drop to the keyhole I'm glancing out of. "Where is she?" His voice is as soft as mine, his willpower just as notable.

"Tam dole. Pospěš si. Už je zranil. Trey krvácí."

I beg for him to hurry again when he tilts so close to the door, I can no longer see his face. I don't have a good sense of time since my head is still woozy from whatever murkiness is filtering through my veins, but it feels like almost an hour has passed since I last saw Trey.

If that's true, we could be too late.

Trey may already be dead.

Tears burn my eyes when Nikolai pulls down a key from the lip above the door. When he slots it into the lock I'm peering out of, I scurry back since the door swings inward. After dropping his eyes to me for the quickest second, he shifts to the women cowering away from him like he's one of the monsters in their nightmares.

He isn't. He just didn't know he wasn't until he found his *Ahren.*

After returning his eyes to mine, Nikolai whispers, "Do you know where Justine is?" He touches his chest that's splattered with blood while adding. "My *Ahren.* Do you know where they took her?" When I nod, he asks, "Can you show me?"

When I nod again, he squashes his index finger to his lips, demanding for me to be quiet. Aware sometimes silence is your only ally, I nod again before gesturing for him to follow me. My feet don't make the clomping noises his boots do when we quietly tread down the corridor. I'm not just barefoot as I have been almost every day for six years, I learned the importance of sound-less steps when Achim's room was placed onto my list of quarters to take care of after my parents' deaths. I was so quiet on my feet, I made up his room while he was still sleeping, only returning when he was having breakfast to make his bed.

After double-checking my bearings to ensure I have the right room, I point to the door across from a nick in the wall. It isn't nail marks like the walls in my old prison cell. It's too low for a fist and too high for a knee. It is more like the gun on someone's hip accidentally grazed the drywall. It's barely a scuff, but it was a great anchor point to keep me up to date on Trey's location.

My tear-filled eyes stray to Nikolai when he whispers, "Justine is in there?"

While my throat works through its dryness, I nod.

I stare at him like he's grown a second head when he mouths, "*Thank you.*" It's been a long time since I've been thanked. Not even after being assaulted against my wishes did I hear those two words.

When Nikolai points to the far back entrance of the compound Trey piggybacked me through earlier today, I follow the direction of his gaze. Considering we're in the middle of a desert, the mature trees surrounding Clarks is impressive. "They'll be safer there."

My mouth falls open when it dawns on me what he's saying. He wants me to take the captive women into the tree lines to keep them safe. His unexpected chivalry is both pleasing and shocking, however, I can't do as he's requesting. I can't take responsibility for my mistakes out there.

I also can't protect Trey.

Before I can explain that to Nikolai, a roar projects from a door two spots down from the one we're standing next to. "What do you mean! You were told to keep him there until I gave word I had finished here."

The undeniable noise of someone being backhanded overtakes the growling tone not even a second later. It's closely followed by a pained groan. Although I'd rather no one be hurt, groaning means the person being tortured is still alive. It means we may not be too late.

"Go," Nikolai demands before shoving me back toward the room that's oddly silent. It isn't a rough shove. Just one that reveals his panic. He knows as well as I do if the women commence sobbing again, Achim will be alerted about his approach, and he and his goon will kill Trey and Justine without hesitation.

With that in mind, I race back to the dorm. The reason for the rare silence comes to light when I enter the room three heart-thrashing seconds later. The captives are no longer huddled in the corner of the sterile-feeling space.

They're nowhere.

The room is completely bare.

As panic sets in, I pivot on my heels to face the room Nikolai is gingerly entering. My scream to alert him to watch his back is gobbled up by a large hand clamping over my mouth. I know who has me in an instant. His smell is nothing out of the ordinary. It's as familiar as the prick of the needle he jabs into my neck for the second time tonight.

When I fall to my knees, the toxins pumping through my veins too much to keep me upright, Achim slaps a piece of duct tape over my mouth, yanks a hessian bag over my head, zip-ties my wrists and ankles, then tosses me over his shoulder as if I am weightless.

It's lucky my stomach is empty, or the thumps of his feet as he races us across a sloshy ground would cause me to vomit. Considering my mouth is taped, that could end disastrously. My lungs are already depleted of air since I'm putting everything into screaming out for help. The walls of Nikolai's compound are built from concrete, but I'm still hopeful.

Hope encourages courageousness, and courageousness encourages miracles.

I could do with a little bit of both.

As Achim jogs us through the trees surrounding Clarks, I scream about how many injustices I've been forced to face my twenty-two years on this planet. I tell him how I hate him, and that no matter how cruel he is, I'll never submit to him. And then I scream to Trey that I'm sorry for what I did and that I hope one day he can forgive me.

If that's even possible.

Dead men can't offer forgiveness.

Thirty seconds later, I'm tossed onto a cool and hard surface. The idling of an unhealthy engine reveals I've been placed into the back of a transport van, much less the noise of its door sliding shut a few seconds later. The Novaks are well-known for choosing versatility over luxury when it comes to anything they own—captives included.

After the boom of a car door slamming shut adds to the thump of my woozy head, a man asks, "Should we wait for Alexei?"

"No," Achim replies, "I'd rather he *not* come out of this alive." I can't see anything through the bag over my head, I'm barely lucid, but I can tell Achim is smiling when he mutters, "Saves the need to find a dumping location on the way to the airport."

Their brittle laughter is the last thing I hear before I grant my head permission to slip into a shadowy void. I feel protected here. Safe. It has been my shelter for the past six years, and it will remain my shelter until I'm given a good reason to once again step out of the dark.

EIGHTEEN

Two months later…

I swish my tongue around my mouth, hopeful a bit of spit will loosen up its dryness as the conversation of two people standing next to me trickles into my ears. "How long was he awake this time?"

I could be mistaken, but I believe voice number one belongs to Nikolai. It sounds like him, just more worrying, which is surprising. Usually, nothing rattles him.

"Barely a few minutes. The doctors are lowering his sedation, but they don't believe it's the reason he's been under so long. His head was pretty fucked up, Nikolai. He may not wake up as the Trey we once knew." The only good that comes from Eight's comment is the fact my name registers as familiar. I don't know where I am, or how the hell I got here, but I know my name.

That's got to be good, right?

"Did you convince Dok to let us take him home yet?" Eight asks, his tone lowering. "Might help with his recovery. Familiarity and shit."

"We can't yet..."

The rest of Nikolai's reply trails off when darkness once again overwhelms me.

"Successful pain management for recovering addicts is just as essential as primary care. Trey is an addict, so you need to manage his pain relief with that in mind, or he'll come out of this with even more issues than some memory loss."

That's Dok. How do I know that? He'll never let me forget I was addicted to popping pain medication the months following my release from hell. He can't harp on about blow and crack, they're pretty much necessities in this industry, but he has no trouble chewing your ass out if your crutch of choice is meant to ease your pain instead of increasing it.

"Acute pain relief is treated the same way for *all* patients... addicts included," replies a voice I'm not familiar with. It's anal and retentive, a voice none of my brothers would *ever* have. "He has multiple skull fractures. He'd be in a heap of pain."

Me, in pain? *Never.* I survived hell, so whatever they're talking about would be a walk in the park. Before I can tell them that, I blank out again.

"Make sure they put on the double cheese as ordered this time. Fuckers ripped me off last week."

Laughter breaks out across the room, exposing there's more

than a handful of people surrounding me. Can't see jack-shit, though. It's all red and hazy like when you close your eyes and stare at the sun.

"You're only cranky because the nurses turned down their noses at your offer for them to suck your dick. You always get extra moody when you're without a whore for the night."

My entire face aches when my lips notch up into a smirk. Nero loves giving Eight shit about his fascination with fucking. Can't say I blame him. Eight has a face you can't help but hate. It keeps the whores on their toes even with him missing two digits.

Eight tosses me into the flames to save his own ass. "Do you think if I slip a twenty under Trey's sheets tonight, they'll make his sponge bath extra enticing?"

The laughter of over a dozen men simmers to a whisper when another voice mutters, "I bet he'd rather K do it."

K? Who the fuck is K?

"**A**re you sure this is right?" The playfulness Nero's voice had the last time I heard him has up and vanished. He sounds pissed. "Perhaps Hunter is wrong. Wouldn't be the first time he's tried to steer you in the wrong direction."

Nikolai's growl rumbles through my chest. "I went through the records myself. This is the only anomaly."

There's a short pause before Nero asks, "Did Justine decipher what it says?"

Justine? That's another name I'm not familiar with.

The ripples of a chin being lifted fans my face. It isn't as sore as it was days ago, but there's no doubt I'm busted up. I can't even lick my lips because they're too swollen for my tongue to pierce through them. "It says, *I have Ana.*"

Ana. I work the name through my head a handful of times, struggling to work out if it belongs to one of the many whores at Clarks. It sounds familiar, but that could have more to do with the fact it's an ordinary, everyday name. Everyone will eventually run into an Ana at one stage of their lives.

"Oh shit," Nero breathes out in a heavy groan. "That's what K called her sister. She barely made any sense since she was speaking a foreign language, but that word stuck out." He either scratches his chin or his head. They're both hairless, so they make the same noise when being rubbed. "Do you think K was the one who told Alexei about Clarks?"

I don't know who the fuck K is, but I hope she's picked a good hiding place. If she didn't, she'll be dead by the end of today. Second only to Vladimir, Alexei is Nikolai's number one enemy. Just him knowing the location of Clarks will throw up a ton of challenges for Nikolai.

The thought alone should give me plenty of incentive to wake up.

I just need my fucked-up head to get on board with my plans.

***

"**H**ey."

This time around, there are faces with the voices.

Many of them. It's as if my brothers brought Clarks to my hospital room. We're just missing a jacuzzi tub full of whores.

"How are you feeling?" Nero asks before he nudges his head to the door, commanding for Eight to fetch the nurse. "I wouldn't touch them. The nurses treat you like a pin cushion every time you pull them out." He places his hands over mine, stopping them from moving for the cables, wires, and IV lines poking out of several regions of my body. "If you stick around for longer than five minutes this time around, they might consider loosening the shackles."

"Good morning," says a bright, bubbly voice as she bounds into the room like she isn't a lamb being sent to slaughter. The nurse in light blue scrubs has the eyes of over a dozen murderers on her, yet, she acts like she's just walked into a gay bar. "I'm glad to finally see you're back with us."

"Finally?" I cringe at the high-squeak of my voice. Even before my balls dropped, my voice was never this high-pitched. "How long have I been out?"

My eyes almost bulge out of my head when Nero answers on the nurse's behalf, "Ten weeks."

After wordlessly checking she has everything covered, Nero frees my hand from his grip then moves to the corner of the room to make a call. I hear him tell Nikolai I'm awake before his voice is gobbled up by the nurse pushing buttons on a heap of monitors at my side. She takes my blood pressure, checks my pulse, flashes a torch in my eyes, then paces my way with a long glass thermometer in her hand.

"Bend over, Trey. It's time to take your temperature," Eight jokes from his station in the corner of the room, rousing both the men surrounding him from their half-asleep state and the nurse's cheeks.

I give him a stern glare, warning him to shut the fuck up before opening my mouth at the nurse's request. While she watches the red mercury in the thermometer rise, I scan my eyes over her name badge pinned to her enticing chest. Her name is Kendall.

"K? You're K?"

Smiling, she pulls the thermometer out of my mouth, jots down my temperature into my file, then drifts her eyes to mine. "Sorry, what did you say? I couldn't hear you through the thermometer."

"K? Are you called K?"

I rip the cords off my chest when they advise of my skyrocketing heart rate. My pulse isn't thudding in my ears, but I feel seconds from having a heart attack.

"No, I've never been called K." Kendall curls her hand around my wrist in a caring manner, halting me from removing the rest of the cords while inconspicuously checking my pulse. "But you can call me anything you'd like while taking in some big breaths for me. Your heart rate is very high."

While she wordlessly begs for me to calm down, I drift my eyes to Nero. He's no longer on a call. "Who's K?"

When Eight attempts to butt in, Nero waves his hand through the air, cutting him off. Once he's joined Kendall in standing at my bedside opposite her, he asks, "How much do you remember about the past few months?"

"Clearly, not as much as I should." I remember joining Nikolai at the club for a drink, and one of Dimitri's goons egging Nikolai for a beating, but other than that, it's pretty much blank. "Am I here because of the brawl?"

When Eight once again attempts to interrupt, Mikhail convinces him not to this time around. Unlike Nero, he uses his fists.

"What brawl?" Nero interrogates like a real-life motherfucking detective.

"The one near Cliché." I scrub a hand down my face in frustration when the name of the bar we were drinking at slips my mind. I know Cliché as well as the back of my hand. It's my regular haunt and one of the many businesses I own with Nikolai, so the watering hole next to it should be just as clear. "Umm..." My words trail off again when the scrub of my face switches to my head.

My hair is fucking gone.

I have a buzz cut.

If that isn't bad enough, there are grooves in my skull.

"Trey, please, we need you to stay in bed," Kendall begs when I flop my legs off the side of the hospital bed I'm waking up in before I rip off the remainder of the cords. Since the IV line is taped to my arm with industrial-strength medical tape, it, along with the bags of liquid dangling above my head, hobble into the bathroom with me.

I take a step back when I see the gaunt, lifeless face peering back at me in the mirror above the vanity. My beard is thicker and longer than usual, but my hair is completely gone. Although my skull is no longer stitched and stapled together, it's clear it was at one stage. It looks like a fucking patchwork quilt. My eyes are lifeless, and my muscles are barely noticeable. Even my tattoos don't look as lively as they once did.

What the fuck happened to me?

When I pivot back around to face my room, desperately needing answers, I hear Eight say, "You need to tell him who she is."

Mikhail has him pinned to the far wall of my suite. He's right up in his face, but it doesn't have me missing his reply. "That's not up to you to decide. If Nikolai wants him to know, he will tell him. Until then, keep your fucking mouth shut."

After working my jaw side to side, I slur out, "Someone better tell me what the fuck is going on!"

With the environment hostile, Kendall slips through the cracked open door, bumping into Nikolai and a redheaded woman on her way out.

NINETEEN

SALES DOCKET NUMBER 12574

"Eat!"

With his annoyance higher than my starvation, Achim yanks on the chain latched to the metal collar around my neck. His tug is rough enough to pull me off the mattress my backside has barely lifted from for the longest time—*I don't know if it's weeks or months anymore. I don't know anything* —but it doesn't arouse a response from me. Not even a squeak parts my lips.

That annoys Achim more than anything.

"Do you want me to strap you to the bed again? To have them feed you through a nasal tube?" He wrenches my head back by fisting my hair in a cruel hold. It's shinier than it has ever been, nourished by the care I was given my first few weeks back here.

Achim wants to build me up so he can break me all over again. He wants me to fight him like I did Vladimir in the videos he watched.

I refuse to give him the satisfaction.

I won't even look at him. That's how much I hate him.

He can go to hell. They all can. They can use me and abuse me. They can beat me until I am black and blue, but they'll never see the life in my eyes. I am not K to them, nor am I Kristina. I am a number on a sales docket. An asset.

And yet, I'm still too good for them.

"Answer me, goddammit!" Achim screams in my face, unaware not even the repulsion of his spit landing on my cheek will cause me to blink. I stay completely still. Motionless and mute. *Dead, yet somehow still alive.*

My lips die to crack into a smile when Achim suspends his second hit midair, but I won't allow them to twitch. That would give him too much satisfaction. This, however, doesn't. He's growing bored of the game remarkably quick. There's no joy in abusing someone who refuses to respond. His ego can't be fed from my silent cries. His dick won't harden because of my whimpers. He'll need to get his kicks elsewhere because he will *never* get them from me ever again.

I used to give in because I felt bad that my punishment would be handed to someone else, but my time in the United States taught me differently. I protected Ana. I went to hell and back for her, yet, she couldn't even share her food with me. She left me defenseless as I do her when Achim releases my hair from his grip before he stomps to Ana's side of our room.

Her whimpers almost break me.

Her cries almost fill my eyes with tears.

But I cling to the memories that I was once free. It might have only been for a couple of hours, but time doesn't matter when you're brave enough to tiptoe out of the dark.

"No can do. You heard Dok. You're on desk duty until further notice."

Grumbling that Dok can suck my dick, I make my way to the passenger side of Eight's car. I spent the majority of the summer in a hospital suite, yet Eight's pride and joy looks more haggard than me. The lower half of his schmick ride is covered with mud, and the paint on the roof looks like she's been battling the elements for longer than three months.

I think Eight is chuckling at my derogative comment but am proven wrong when he mentions my pretzel-like maneuver to get into my seat being the most action I've had in weeks. My knees are around my ears, and my crotch is an inch from my face.

"Don't fucking remind me how dire it's been. Stroking one out while wearing a heart monitor isn't an easy feat." He chuckles again when I mutter, "Still worked it, though." After pushing back my seat as far as it will go, I tug on my seat belt. "What happened to you sneaking in some whores into my room for me? I thought you were my man, Eight, but you left me hanging."

With his eyes front and center, he fires up the motor of his car. "Nikolai—"

"Doesn't understand what I'm going through. He's got Justine's pussy on speed dial." I shake my head, still shocked Nikolai is shacked up with a girl. I thought my brothers were messing with me when they filled me in on everything I had missed. Nikolai fell dick first in love. Vladimir was killed in an unexpected raid, and I spent the entire time holed up in a hospital bed because I couldn't keep my Shelby on the road after a few drinks. "Lucky we're going back to Clarks now, isn't it?"

Eight hums out an agreement, but he keeps his eyes on the road, only removing them when he pulls into the closest drive-thru at my request. The hospital food was rank, and I'm more than eager to replace it with something greasy, so Sonic is a good choice.

The quickest flicker of a pair of baby blue eyes flashes before my eyes when Eight asks, "What do you want to eat? Beef, chicken, or wings?" With my mouth refusing to cooperate, Eight socks me in the arm before ordering one of each item on the menu. "But hold on the drinks. We'll just take two bottles of water," he says down the ordering box.

After pulling up to the window, he hands the cashier a bundle of cash before accepting the two bottles of water she's holding out for him.

"You good?" he asks me, peering at me strangely.

I don't feel close to good, but I jerk up my chin, nonetheless. "Just hungry, that's all."

"Aight. It's coming. Hold your horses."

The way he watches me when he hands me bag after bag of greasy food makes my stomach churn more than the hospital's version of scrambled eggs. "If you're hoping this will get your dick sucked, you're shit out of luck, Eight. I'm all for my whore sucking your cock while I fuck her in the ass, but that's only because your cock isn't anywhere near mine. I'm not into you like that."

He laughs, but it isn't his real laugh. He seems more frustrated than amused.

With Eight's switch-up in personality freaking me the fuck out, I exit his car before him when it comes to a stop at the front of Clarks. The smell of cocaine, gun powder, and chlorine is all too familiar, but me heading for the sleeping quarters at the side of the compound isn't. My room is on the other side of Clarks, far from the dormitory-like confines we house brothers from other chapters in when they're stateside.

"You stopped for food?" Mikhail asks when I dump a handful of bags onto the coffee table between us. When I jerk up my chin, he growls out, "Looks like you got enough to feed an army. What is that? One of each item on the menu?" His eyes aren't on me. He's glaring at Eight, who's making his way into the main living area with the bags I left in his car.

"Trey was hungry," Eight defends, shrugging. "Figured everyone else would be, too."

My mouth freezes halfway to the burger I've just unwrapped when Mikhail forcefully places Eight into his seat. It wasn't a hey-let-me-help-you-with-your-load shove. It was a, you-are-pissing-me-the-fuck-off nudge.

"What's the go with you two? You've been weird since I woke."

"It's nothing," Mikhail assures me after hitting Eight with a stern finger point. "We just have opposing opinions on a matter."

"Then get *un*-opposing opinions," I mutter through a chunk of beef patty. "With Nikolai's head in a lust cloud, we need to stay focused for him. Things get complicated when women are involved." *I know that better than anyone.*

When Mikhail gives Eight a look as if to say, *I told you so,* he holds out his hands in front of himself. "Aight. I'll back the fuck up." He slouches low into his chair before lifting his eyes to Mikhail. "But when this backfires in your face, don't say I didn't tell you so."

I spend the next two hours sitting across from my brothers who stare at me like the cap I wear to hide the scars on my head is invisible. Something has changed, I just have no fucking clue what it is. The whores still prance around in their skimpy clothes waiting with desperation for me to wave them over, white lines of coke still take up a majority of the coffee table, and excluding a handful of men I'm assuming were lost during the raid, the faces peering at me are familiar. Yet, it still feels like something is missing.

It's probably my mojo. Excluding my years in hell, I could have been inducted to the Hall of Fame for fucking on many occasions. It's a part of who I am. It is what I'm about. If my cock isn't filling the cunt of a whore, it's being rammed down the throat or ass of another.

It has been in none of those places the past three months.

Confident that's what I'm missing, I scoot to the edge of my chair before *psting* at Eight to get his attention. After stabbing out his cigarette into an ashtray on the coffee table, he joins me in sitting on the edge of his chair.

"What's the blonde's name? It's slipping my mind." I nudge

my head to the jacuzzi full of women staring at me like their mouths salivate just at the idea of sucking my cock.

"Which one?" Eight asks after following the direction of my gaze. "Most of them are blonde."

"The one with the big ass and tits." I nearly say, *and big blue eyes,* but I hold back. I don't know why. "Sitting next to the African woman."

"Oh, that's Saige." His eyes snap to mine so quick, they make my head dizzy. "Why?"

Smirking a smug grin, I rub my hands together. "Because I'm going to invite her for a nightcap in my room."

"No." Eight rockets out of his chair so fast, he knocks over his drink. "That isn't a good idea. You two have history."

"History she *liked* by the hankering in her eyes."

Eight splays his hand across my chest, stopping me from scooting past him to make my way to the jacuzzi. When I arch a brow, wordlessly announcing he better have a good excuse for putting his hands on me, he blubbers out, "You don't take girls to your room."

He's right, but my head is too mixed up to admit that right now. "A change-up never hurt anyone, August. Sometimes that's what life is about. The occasional tiptoe out of the dark."

When he gets up in my business again, Mikhail tells him to stand down before I get the chance to remind him a car accident didn't lose me the use of my fists. I like Eight, but he's getting on my last nerve tonight. He's been weird since the day I woke up four weeks ago.

"Time to cut back on the drugs, E. They're fucking with your head."

I swear he grumbles, "Not as much as Mikhail is messing with yours," when I scoot past him, but I can't be sure. My heart is thumping out too much of a funky tune from me shortening

Eight's nickname to one letter for me to hear anything. I can barely hear anything over the thud of my pulse in my ears.

I wiggle my index finger in my ear to free it from my heart's echo before stopping in front of Saige. "Wanna get out of here?" Ignoring the clench of my jaw from my words coming out with a lisp, I nudge my head to the corridor my room is located down to ensure she knows what I'm referencing. I am not taking her for a steak.

My cock gives out a half-hearted twitch when she eagerly nods. She's got everything I usually go for. Curvy hips, plenty of ass and tits, and my favorable blue-eyed, blonde-hair combination, but she still seems a little assertive. Overbearing even.

"Nuh-uh," I growl out on a groan when my assistance to help her out of the jacuzzi sees her legs wrapping around my waist and her lips arrowing toward mine. "If you want to kiss, you can save them for my cock."

I push her away from me via a hand to her face before spinning on my heels and stomping toward my room, acting ignorant to the limp my car accident caused.

Saige follows like a motherfucking lap dog. Her eagerness would usually please me. Today, it's just pissing me off.

"Go wash off the jacuzzi water," I demand, nudging my head to the bathroom attached to my room. "The chlorine on your skin is burning my nose hairs."

Her nasally voice screeches my eardrums when she says, "There's no towel."

"You don't need a towel, do ya?"

I nearly roll my eyes like a punk-ass when she smiles. "I guess not. They're only needed for people wanting to dry off. I don't want to be dry. I like being wet."

When she switches on the shower faucet, my hand rockets up to cradle my skull. It's not throbbing through one of the many migraines I've faced the past four weeks, it is struggling through a flashback. I'm standing in the middle of my room, but I swear droplets of rain are gliding down my cheeks.

When you think about an unexpected downpour, it usually arrives with a calming, natural smell. That isn't the case this time around. My room reeks of pig shit... and perhaps a touch of mint.

I'm drawn from the oddity by Saige stopping to stand in front of me. She's drenching wet and butt-naked. "Are you okay? Do you want me to get Dok?" The genuine concern in her tone frustrates me more than I can explain. She doesn't know me, so she has no right to act as if she cares about me.

"I'm fine. Get on the bed."

Her pussy and ass are shoved into my peripheral vision when she climbs onto my mattress, not the least bit confronted by my snapped tone. "How do you want me? Like this..." She shakes her ass, hopeful it will see some action tonight. "... or like this." She rolls over and spreads her legs wide, fully exposing herself. Even though she's just showered, I'm confident the sheen between her pussy lips isn't water. Her cunt is salivating for me.

I can't say my cock is having the same reaction for her. He's down for the count. Passed the fuck out as I would have been if I had accepted Mikhail's many offers for a line of coke earlier tonight. Usually, I'd take up his offer in an instant. I wasn't interested tonight. Don't ask me why. I'm beginning to wonder if it was more than a couple of days of memories I lost.

After clamping Saige's knees together like the sight of her puffy cunt makes me sick, I tell her to tilt her head to the side and stay still. "I don't even want to see you breathing."

"Okay," Saige breathes out slowly before straining her eyes to peer at me standing over her, lost on where to go next.

"Don't look at me. Face your eyes to the wall."

I wait for her to do as told before dumping my cap, shirt, and jeans onto the floor. Once my boxer shorts join them, I tug at my dick, begging for it to get with the program. He's not even at half his strength, not that Saige seems to mine. She licks her lips while staring at the piercings down the shaft like they were put there for her pleasure.

"I said to look at the wall." I slap her thigh hard enough for her to yelp before crawling up her body, praying like fuck my cock will sniff out the needs of her greedy cunt and stand to attention.

When the heaviness of my dick rests on the aching bud between her legs, Saige moans, and something inside me snaps. "I said to shut the fuck up! God, what is it with you women not knowing how to keep your mouth fucking shut? It isn't hard to follow directions, is it!"

I flop onto my back before throwing an arm over my eyes. The throbbing of my brain against my temples is brutal, but it's the silence it fails to arrive with that's driving me mad.

Instead of taking the hint that I'm not interested, Saige positions herself onto her knees before she gathers up my cock in her hands. Yes, I said hands. Even in my pissy mood, I'm not ashamed to admit she'll need more than two hands to handle me.

When her lips hover an inch above the crest of my cock, I growl out a set of words I never thought I'd say, "If an inch of my cock gets in your mouth, I'll fucking kill you where you kneel."

With menace being the highest of all the emotions in my voice, Saige's backside sinks back until it's resting on the balls of her feet, and my cock slips from her grasp. "Then what do you want me to do—"

"Get out." When she remains frozen on my mattress, unblinking and mute as I wanted her to be only moments ago, I scream again, "Get out!"

After scurrying off the bed, I grab Saige's wet bikini bottoms from the floor of my bathroom, her grubby nightie from the foot of my bed, and her arm before forcefully marching her to the door. Once she and her belongings are deposited in the corridor, I slam the door shut, grip the sprouts of blond hair peeking out the top of my head, and scream like I've never screamed before.

It's a silent, gut-wrenching scream that sends my heart's racing beats to my ears as quickly as my brain thumps my temples. When it does little to ease my agitation, I shift my focus to my room. This place was once my sanctuary, the only place I ran to when I was lost.

Now it feels empty, cold, and silent.

So very fucking silent.

After upending my bed, a drawer full of clothes, smashing my television into the wall, and taking a knife to my mattress, I shift my focus to my headboard and bedside tables.

They're destroyed in a nanosecond, leaving me nothing left to ruin.

While running a hand over scars that will never be hidden, I crouch down to suck in some big breaths. I'm spiraling so hard if I don't take a moment to breathe, I'll destroy more than replaceable furniture.

I wasn't like this at the hospital. I felt cooped up and caged, but normal.

Well, as normal as a man raised in this lifestyle can be.

I don't know how long I stay crouched for. It isn't long enough to dispel the rage tearing me in two, but long enough for Eight to think it's safe to come in. He fetches up the nightgown Saige left outside my door, dumps it into the laundry basket in my bathroom, then commences straightening out my room.

Although my first thought is to help him, something navigates me to my untouched bathroom instead. I remove the stained nightie from the laundry basket, raise it to my nose, and suck in a lung-filling breath for the first time in months.

"Who is she?" I ask Eight after pulling down the grubby sleepwear from my face and storing it into the drawer he just righted. "Who is K?"

TWENTY-ONE

SALES DOCKET NUMBER 12574

I thought being beaten so horrifically, my body resembled an abstract painting of mottled purples, blacks, and blues would be the most painful thing I'd experience while being a sex slave.

It was silly of me to ever believe.

Strangulation hurts so much more.

The bulging of my eyes from his tight grip. The strain on the muscles in my neck when he wrings them to within an inch of recognition. The burn of my lungs as they scream for another breath.

They want to live.

They want to fight.

I don't want to do either of those things.

I deserve to die.

I broke like I promised I wouldn't.

I responded to his taunt.

And I'd do it all again just to see my spit slide down Achim's murderously red face.

For hours on end, he made me watch all the horrible things they did to me. The beatings. The rapes. The humiliation. He played his sick videos on repeat while holding my face an inch from the screen.

The dark comforted me, it kept me sane, then Achim switched tactics.

You can't scare a captive with scenes of captivity, but you can taunt her with how close she came to freedom. First, it was an orange and a heat lamp that resembled the warmth of a sunny Vegas day. Then, it was freshly picked wildflowers and a pork chop overcooked in too much fat.

His last tactic was the worst of them all.

It was his hand, on me, in an area he'd never touched me before.

Whether with Achim or one of the many men I've been forced to 'entertain,' our exchanges were never about me. I was *not* to be pleased. I was to give pleasure.

That's why I couldn't help but respond when Achim slid his hand into my panties. I should have taken solace in the fact he repulses me so much that if he had found my clit, my body didn't notice it. There was no buzz of excitement, no euphoria on what might occur. There was nothing but an urgent need to spit in his face, which is precisely what I did when his eyes lifted to check if I were responding to his touch.

His face went red with anger.

I'd never seen him so mad.

He was on me in an instant. He slapped me, hit me, then ripped at my hair. When that failed to startle me, he clamped his hands around my throat. With his face an inch from mine, he told me how much he hated me, how I was ungrateful and unappreciative, and that I'd never be free.

That was a little over two minutes ago.

My head is woozy now.

My mouth and eyes are dry.

I can hear the darkness calling me. It's begging for me to let go, to fall into its safety. The only reason I'm holding on is because I know this tiptoe out of the dark will be my last.

Achim Novak wants to kill me, and I'm ready to let him.

TWENTY-TWO

TREY

Have you ever felt like you're being lied to, but you have no clue why people you trust think lying is their only option? That's the feeling that hit me the instant Eight and Mikhail left my room. They helped me get my room back in order, assured me I'm not going crazy, then exited like I didn't ask them three times in a row who K really is.

They answered me, they know better than to act ignorant around me, but they lied through their teeth the entire time. I know it, Eight and Mikhail know it, and so the fuck does K.

A whore hoping to claw her nails into the back of a worthless crew leader wouldn't stir enough interest out of me to make my cock twitch. I doubt I would have given her a second sideway glance, but just the mention of the letter 'K' sets off my pulse in my ears. It's been thudding nonstop the past hour, growing in intensity the longer I stare at the drawer I shoved a grubby nightgown into.

Needing answers, I rip open the drawer with enough force to

fully remove it. Anger percolates through my veins when nothing but numerous pairs of boxer shorts reflect back at me.

Concern my almost manic breakdown has me mistaking which drawer I hid it in, I yank open the three below it. Confirmation I'm being lied to smacks into me hard and fast. None of my drawers are housing an almost see-through nightgown. There's not a single piece of female attire to be found in my room.

When my attempt to gulp down the anger festering in my gut makes me angrier, I storm out of my room and march down the hall. I'm not surprised to find Eight and Mikhail at blows in the living area. Pretty much anytime I left the bathroom attached to my hospital room, I stumbled onto them brawling each other. Usually, Mikhail has Eight pinned to the wall. This time, it's the other way around.

If any of the thoughts in my head are true, Mikhail should be grateful it's Eight clutching his neck. If it were me, he'd be dead by now.

"Give it back."

"Give what back?" Mikhail asks, aware my question was for him. "As I said to Eight, I don't know what the fuck you're talking about."

While I close the distance between us, Eight snarls, "This wasn't our agreement. We were told if he naturally progressed toward his memories, we weren't to keep them from him."

"I'm not repressing his memories, August. I'm trying to stop him from being hurt." Mikhail lowers his tone a notch, meaning I have to strain my ears to hear him when he whispers, "*You* weren't there when we found him. *You* don't know what he's been through, so *you* have no fucking right to judge *us* on how *we* handle this situation."

"But I sure as fuck can," I growl out in a gravelly tone.

With Mikhail having no plausible comeback, he keeps quiet.

"Let him go."

Eight glares at me as if I'm insane for a second before doing as instructed. Mikhail won't run. Cowards run. He isn't one of those.

He is close to his death, though. So very, *very* close.

As thunder cracks above my head, I step closer to Mikhail until I'm confident he's aware fourteen weeks in a hospital bed, three skull fractures, and a busted-up leg won't weaken the severity of his punishment if he lies to me again. "Give. It. Back."

"Trey—"

"Give it to me!" My roar silences the room. It doesn't give me the comfort it did in the hospital. It makes me unhinged.

Like Nikolai did to Rory months ago, I pin Mikhail to the wall by his throat before attempting to throw my fist into his face. I say attempt as I'm frozen mid-strike, shocked about the video playing through my head.

I killed Rory, and I did it for K.

I'm certain of it.

"The specialist said forcing memories onto you could do you more harm than good." This comment isn't from neither Mikhail nor Eight. It's from Nikolai. "Should have known better. Those fuckers might have degrees, but they don't know how our brains tick." After locking his eyes with Mikhail to reveal his absolute fury, he returns them to me. The deadliness in them reveals Mikhail will pay heftily for his bend of the rules. "Leave us." When Mikhail's lips twitch, prepared to issue a defense, Nikolai shouts, "Ignore me again, and I'll strip you of more than your ranking!" His words are nothing but menacing when he growls, "And I'll start with your snitching tongue."

With his hands held out in front of himself, and his eyes wide with fear, Mikhail tosses a dirty nightgown into Eight's chest before he makes his way to one of the quads parked around Clarks. He'll go blow off steam for a few minutes before coming back to apologize. He'd rather grovel like a punk-ass than lose his place on Nikolai's team. Most of my brothers would choose death over exclusion.

After waiting for Eight to hand over a frail material I clutch like it was my mother's, Nikolai nudges his head to one of the many couches in the living area, requesting for me to join him there.

As we pace toward the living area, low-ranked members of his crew and whores disappear in all directions. Nikolai didn't specifically ask for privacy, but his facial expression is telling enough. Once we're alone, he asks, "What do you remember?"

"Nothing about a car accident," I mutter under my breath, unable to take my eyes off the nightgown I'm wringing around my fingers like it's capable of healing the stupid-ass lisp and limp I got from my injuries.

It dawns on me just how far Mikhail's deceit went when Nikolai's brows stitch at my mumbled comment. "That's the script they're running?" When I jerk up my chin, his tightens. "We were advised to let you formulate your own response to your memory loss, not make up gimmicks." He plops into the first single sofa before lifting his eyes to mine. They're still icy and dangerous, they're just not as dark as they once were. "What do you remember about K?"

"That she smells like the rain..." An unexpected grin tugs on my lips when I mutter, "... and pig shit?"

Nikolai isn't as surprised by my comment as me. "Jim said you were under. Didn't believe him until now." After gesturing for me to sit across from him, he hands me a single print out. It's a photograph of a slender blonde with big blue eyes and ruddy lips. It's hard to tell from this image, but she looks around sixteen.

"Anything?"

I shake my head, disappointed. Other than my pulse thumping

in my ears, her face doesn't register as familiar. Don't get me wrong, her perfect nose, plump lips, and gorgeous face make my cock twitch. Its spasms are just barely felt over my skyrocketing blood pressure.

"What about him?" Nikolai places a second image onto the first one. Although he's older than I remember, I immediately know who he is.

"What does Achim Novak have to do with any of this?"

My eyes snap to Nikolai's when he says, "He's her owner."

"He owns K?" When Nikolai nods, I scoff. "That can't be right. He's married to India—"

"Who looks remarkably similar to K when she's not dirtied up by the sex-trafficking industry?" Nikolai interrupts.

The picture he hands me this time around sends blood rushing to all regions of my body. My cock, my heart, my ears, they all get slammed by an overzealous pulse, not the least bit turned off by the grubby-faced blonde with bird nest knots in her matted hair.

As my nostrils flare like I can smell K's scent off her image, I stray my eyes to the open side door of Clarks. It's dark out, however, all I'm seeing is a mess of saturated blonde hair clinging to the face of a blue-eyed woman. She's just as beautiful, if not more, than the woman in the first photograph Nikolai handed me, and she doesn't have an ounce of makeup on.

After a few minutes of silent deliberations, I blubber out, "I took her to Jim's."

Because I'm not asking a question, I don't look at Nikolai to get confirmation. I'm too busy staring at the rain, confused as to why the sight of it has me the hardest I've ever been. My cock is pressed against the zipper in my jeans, standing to attention like it refused to do only an hour ago.

It tells me everything I need to know, and exactly what I must do. "I want her back."

In the corner of my eye, I spot Nikolai shaking his head. "That isn't possible—"

"I don't care what's possible. I want her back!"

Nikolai works his jaw side to side, frustrated by my roar, but the stupid lisp my words arrive with halves his annoyance. He's looking at me more in pity than anger, and I fucking hate it. "She's the reason you were attacked, Trey. She's the reason you almost died."

Even having no real memories of K, I shake my head. I let a woman play me for a fool once, so there's no fucking chance in hell I would have allowed it to occur a second time. If I let K in, I must have trusted her. Furthermore, if Nikolai truly believes she's to blame for what happened to me, she'd be dead by now. Woman or not, he wouldn't have let anyone get away with entering his turf to fuck with his crew for no reason.

When I say that to Nikolai, silence transcends, proving I hit the nail on the head.

"Don't you want the man responsible for hogtying Justine and forcing her to watch me being tortured be brought to the courts?"

Nikolai's brows furrow as tightly as mine. "You remember what happened that night?"

As I slide my hand over the ridges in my skull, my chin dips. The memories slowly trickling in my head are hazy but filled with enough anger to know even if K is partly responsible for what happened to me, nothing will stop me seeking justice on Achim. "Alexei was doing the torturing, but he wasn't the only man in the room."

When my eyes drop to the stack of photographs, Nikolai says, "Are you sure, Trey? Justine and Eight only saw Alexei. Could your past be fucking with you?"

I immediately shake my head, doubling the throb of my brain. "We were in a shower stall in the bathroom." I lick my lips to give my brain a couple of seconds to work through the drudge coating it. "K overdosed?"

Unsure if that part of my memory is true, I peer at Nikolai for confirmation. Even though he nods, I know he's holding back. He wants me to sort through the shit like he made me do three years ago, aware when your trust is low, you don't believe anyone but yourself.

A few more minutes pass in silence before clarity breaks through the fog. "Eight only counted four pills." I feel my pupils dilate when another revelation hits me. "I was tasered..." My jaw tightens so much I'm afraid it will crack when I growl out, "... by Achim." After dragging my hand down my face, I lock my eyes with Nikolai. "How do you not know any of this? This place is wired to the hilt with surveillance."

"Our cameras were infiltrated seconds after I headed to P's." He peers at me beneath lowered lashes. "I assumed that was you. You often say only fools record themselves doing something incriminating."

Our cameras are wired to the same network as the one protecting P's, so his reply has credit. I would have cut the feed if I were given the chance. I was too busy nursing a throbbing jaw before coercing a fighter off the ledge of a skyscraper.

"Your girl smacked me in the face."

Nikolai's smirk is more smug than sorrow-filled. "She told me. You kinda deserved it." With a jerk of his chin, he demands Nero to our side of the compound. I fell so far down the rabbit hole in my head, I hadn't realized a handful of Nikolai's highly-ranked soldiers had joined us. "Show him the printout I gave you."

This isn't a paper version. Nero is all about electronics.

"What does it say?" I ask after taking in a two-worded text in a foreign language.

"I have Ana," Nikolai and Nero say at the same time.

Before I can ask who Ana is, Nero skims past a report of texts, calls, and internet usage for a date three and a half months ago—the same date of my 'supposed' accident—before he stops on an image of a woman who looks oddly similar to K. Her only downfall is her attractive face doesn't make my pulse thud in my ears.

"She's also owned by Achim," Nikolai advises, his tone somewhat annoyed. He was all about the whores before he fell dick first in love, but even then, he never forced a woman to sleep with him. Just like me, his kink isn't sex slaves. "He loaned them to Vladimir. Larks say that's why he returned to collect them when I killed Vladimir."

I jackknife back, shocked.

Nikolai killed Vladimir?

When I spot the truth in Nikolai's humored gaze, I slump low in my chair. I thought only drugs could fuck with my head this much.

Who knew a tire wrench could cause so much damage?

After working through the truckload of information I've been bombarded with, I ask, "Did Achim take any of the other women?" I'm hopeful we'll have a reason to respond. If Achim doesn't own the women under his command, he doesn't get to keep them. Point blank. That's how things in this industry work.

My hopes get crushed when Nikolai shakes his head. "But..." He leaves me hanging on a knife's edge for so long, sweat beads my temples. "He technically doesn't own K anymore. I do."

What. The. Fuck?

Hearing my silent question, Nikolai shoves a dirty piece of paper under my nose. I swear I've seen it before even with it being an industry I've never dabbled in. It's a sales receipt for a woman named Kristina Svoboda. Nikolai paid one point two million dollars for her a little under four months ago.

"When did you say you and Justine hooked up again?" Now is

not the time for jokes. I'm just hoping a little bit of playfulness will stop me from pinching my gun against Nikolai's temple. He's my brother, my best friend, but the violence roaring through me right now is so temperamental, not even he is safe if this document is legitimate.

The gun stuffed down the back of my jeans grows less heavy when Nikolai mutters, "I don't pay for whores. Never have. Never will. But..." He lifts his eyes to mine. They're the same dangerous pair I'm used to seeing. "I could pretend I have *if* required."

"You'd do that for me?" If I need any more clues on how fucked-up your brain gets when it's smashed in with a tire wrench, I don't now. Nikolai took me in when I was nothing but a home-less-looking rat with a wish to die. He's already proved how far he'll go for the men in his crew. It's why he's so well respected, and the very reason I have no intention to leave his crew any time within the next decade.

Not needing to clarify my shock, Nikolai stands to his feet. "Give me the night with my woman, then we'll head out by dawn." He shifts on his feet to face Roman. "Find out where they're holding the sale. I want to go in heavy but quiet."

Sale?

What fucking sale?

Before I can voice my concern, Nikolai returns his eyes to me. "We will get K out, but if she's responsible for hurting my *Ahren*..." His words trail off. He doesn't need to say more. His eyes are very telling. K will be dead.

I'd be worried for her if I could feel anything over the thud of my pulse in my ears.

SALES DOCKET NUMBER 12574

A chim Novak killed me. He strangled me until my lungs stopped screaming for air, and my body went limp. Then he revived me.

Now, I'm to be sold to the highest bidder.

Passed on.

Handed down.

Dismissed like a worthless, broken toy.

He's made me pretty for my new owners. He polished my exterior so well none of my cracks can be seen. My hair was washed and blow-dried out until every curl represents a golden wave of perfection. I'm wearing lipstick for the first time. I even have on a pretty dress.

If you didn't know what I've been through, you could think I was worth a few pennies.

Perhaps even a dime.

I know I'm not worth that much.

I'm broken.

Abused.

Incapable of escaping the dark.

That's why I'm clutching the tiny shard of glass from the mirror in the back of the brush Achim left in my room. It's my mother's brush, a family heirloom that has been passed down from generation to generation. Its sentimental value meant nothing to Achim when he used it to ensure I'd fetch top dollar at his auction later today. He taunted me with it. Reminded me that I'm an orphan who got everything she deserved for whoring myself out to an unknown, now-dead man.

He snickered when he said his last comment, loving the faintest flicker of despair that darted through my eyes before I could shut it down. Then he gave credit to his remark I would have never believed without proof. Twenty-one teeny tiny lines of an obituary hurt me more than anything I've experienced the past six years. It siphoned the blood from my heart as effectively as my parents' death, and saw me shattering the mirror on the back of my family heirloom against a set of drawers in my room.

It's time to end things. To take back who I once was.

I'll never be free until I free myself, and not even the dark can save me this time.

With my head tilted high, and my mind shut down, I stab the end of the glass into the vein in my neck that hasn't quit thudding out its own tune the past thirty seconds before I thrust down.

Death usually means the end of a life, but that only counts for those who have truly lived.

TWENTY-FOUR

TREY

Ten minutes earlier…

This place reeks of death and discretion, a stark contradiction to the elaborate compound scoured into the foothills of a sleepy hamlet west of Prague. Champagne is flowing, bids have been placed, and caviar is being served to pompous pricks in priceless tuxedos and over-beaded ballgowns.

None of the festivities have reached this far down, though.

The women here are glammed to the nines, but no amount of polish can clear the skank smell of desperation. If Achim's guests were to come down here, the bids of men and women seeking their own live-in sex slave would be significantly reduced.

All the money in the world would never have you forgetting the smell. I scrubbed my skin raw in a shower five times a day for months when I was released from captivity. When soap failed to free me from the putrid scent, I took to my skin with a knife. Little nicks and a handful of well-hidden cuts stopped my stomach rebelling every time the slightest breeze rustled by, but within weeks, it was no longer enough.

Confident the undeniable scent of determination would overtake the smell of desperation, I commenced working out. I lifted weights, ran for miles, and swam in a lake not too far from Clarks even in the middle of winter. My plan was working. The putrid smell I was swarmed by was slowly weakening. However, I had amassed more scars after I was freed than I had when I was imprisoned.

I hated them. They weren't just a reminder of what I had lost because I couldn't keep my dick in my pants, they showed I had failed, that I'd been played for a fool.

Nikolai didn't suggest I use tattoos to cover the marks I loathed. He merely suggested for me to join him at his favorite tattoo haunt when he was getting a mottling of scars covered by a dragon's head.

My addiction switched from drugs to tattooing shortly after. Piercings closely followed them. Although I have as many piercings as I do tattoos, my visible scars still outnumber their combined total. Some I'll never be able to conceal. They're not on my body. They are on my heart, in my head, and burned into my soul.

And my newest nick is compliments to her—K. I can't see her face as she stares at nothing, but I know who she is, I can feel it in my bones, hear it thudding in my chest. She's healthier than she was in the surveillance image Nikolai showed me. Her hair is glossy and hanging loosely down her back. A light blue floral printed dress hugs her svelte yet still enticing frame, and she's wearing a pair of shoes no amount of heel could hide the foreignness of it. Her feet are too cracked, flat, and grubby underneath to pretend she wears footwear often.

When K lifts an antique-looking brush into the air, I grab

Eight by the scruff of his shirt and pin him to the rock wall beside me. The brush has a mirror on the back of it. It's only small, but the angle of its reflection would give away our stake in an instant.

Despite the screams of the voice inside me, I can't move for K until I get word from Nikolai. He's several floors above us attending the auction as if his face is too hideous for a woman to warm his sheets without handing over a bundle of cash. He gave me the option of taking down Achim myself or freeing K.

I chose K.

I should have always chosen K.

A familiar *thud, thud, thud* booms into my ears when for the quickest second, my eyes collide with K's in the mirror. Although she appears to be staring straight at me, she doesn't blink, move, or gasp in a shocked breath. She does nothing but peer at me blankly.

I can't say I'm experiencing the same thing. The memories I lost crash back into me in an instant. K's gallop down the stairs on the heels of a woman with oddly similar features. Her inability to light a match to send Vladimir to hell. Me burning her wounds when I slid into the jacuzzi with her on my lap. They all come flooding back in, and they maim me as much as the expression on K's face a second before she lowers her mirrored brush to smash it against a set of drawers she's seated in front of.

"Oh fuck," Eight mutters at the same time I say the exact words in my head.

K is clutching a shard of glass in her hand. It's only tiny, but it isn't the size of her weapon I'm worried about. It is what she intends to do with it.

"Give me an orange." I yank down the backpack on Eight's back before digging my hand inside for an orange. I ribbed him when he packed oranges, disgusted he'd even consider eating a snack during the middle of a raid.

Now I get where he was going.

Now I understand.

"Come on, K," I quietly beg when I roll the orange across the filthy floor, praying like fuck she spots it before any of the sorrow radiating out of her cell can transpire. "Look at the orange."

I realize my error when my prayers fall on deaf ears.

K doesn't trust anyone.

Not even me.

Ignoring the tightness of my jaw, I dig a second orange out of Eight's backpack, rip out a big chunk of it with my teeth, swallow down the citrusy clump, then roll it toward K's cell again. My heart launches into my throat when she peers down at the bitten orange within a second of it tapping her shoe. She gathers it up, almost trance-like before she swivels in her seat to face the direction the orange rolled from.

Although she stares straight at me, she doesn't see me. She's completely fucking gone. Her eyes are lifeless and blank, swallowed by her miserably bleak existence.

"Go!" Eight roars when we get word from Nikolai it's time for us to move. We don't use listening devices to communicate. The healthy discharge of machine guns and the potent scent of death guides us through every raid.

"Duchess," I push out through a groan as I sprint for her cell, praying I'll reach her before she can do any of the morbid things I see in her eyes.

She wants to die, to be free.

She most likely thinks she's already dead.

I'll prove her wrong. I'll show her how your heart doesn't have to beat in your chest to prove you're alive.

Sometimes it thuds in your ears.

After taking down three men charging at me from the other

end of the dungeon, I punch in the five-digit code Hunter assured me would open the digital lock on K's cell, then throw open the heavily-weighted door keeping her hostage. Having no time to remove the glass from her hand she's intending to drag down a vein in her neck, my palm takes on the brunt of the glass's jab. She pierces it into my hand deeply before yanking it down with a groan, proving she wasn't playing.

She truly wants to die.

As the undeniable scent of blood seeps into the air, K collapses. I catch her just before she hits the grubby ground with a thud, my nostrils naturally flaring to suck in her intoxicating scent.

With K held in close to my chest with one hand, and the other gripped on my gun, I gingerly make my way out of her room. I'd rather place her down and make sure the route is safe first, but there are too many objects she could hurt herself with if she were to come around while I was gone.

I also refuse to leave her alone.

I made that mistake three and a half months ago, and look what happened. The last of the light in her eyes has been stolen. I don't know if she'll ever get it back.

Partway down the almost black corridor, Eight raises his hand in the air. He fires into the dark two times, silencing the faintest conversation of two men talking in a foreign language before he gestures for me to keep moving.

The itch for a bloodbath treks through my veins when we race across a body-studded field. Nikolai's crew went in quiet and heavy as planned. There are more bodies littering the grounds than there were when I was freed from captivity three years ago. I wouldn't hold back my desires if K wasn't my main priority. This isn't a turf war. It's an extraction.

Nikolai's crew is once again saving one of their own.

After sliding into the back seat of the SUV door Eight is

holding open for me, I instruct the driver to go. Once the tail lights are at a safe distance, Nikolai will command for his men to pull back. Then he'll meet us at the airport that has a private jet idling on the tarmac.

As the sound of a helicopter hovers over my head, I peel K off my chest to check her for injuries. Her neck is marked up and bruised, and she's far too skinny, but those are the least of her problems. Her eyes are open, but just like the pair that stared back at me only minutes ago, they're lifeless and blank.

"You'll be all right, K. I'll take care of you."

When I unscrew the cap on a bottle of water, Mikhail slides down the privacy partition separating the front half of the SUV from the back. I originally wanted Roman to fill in the spot of evacuation driver, forgetting Nikolai couldn't leave Justine without an army of her own men. Roman is the perfect leader for that group. "Don't force-feed her water. If she shuts down, the water could end up in her lungs. You'll drown her thousands of miles from the nearest ocean."

Although I'm still pissed at him, I jerk up my chin before placing the water back in its holder. I want to help K, not hurt her more.

Seemingly hearing my private thoughts, Mikhail says, "We're two miles out from the airstrip. Dok is waiting in the hangar. He'll give you more of an idea on how you can help her."

He waits for me to lift my chin for the second time before he returns the privacy partition to its original spot, freeing up some privacy. I use the time well. I drink in K's perfectly straight nose, her plump lips, and eyes as calm as an ocean.

She stares at me just as intently, however, her eyes don't blink or move. They don't even gloss over. They just stare and stare, even more so when I track my thumb over her lips to remove her ruby red lipstick.

"You don't need all those gimmicks, do you, Duchess? You're regal even with your crown missing unnecessary jewels."

I stop staring at my reflection in K's pupils when Mikhail pulls up beside one of the Popovs' many private jets. I wasn't staring at myself because I'm a pompous prick who thinks he's pretty, I was striving to work out how a man I've never met before was staring back at me in K's eyes.

I'm a monster, a cheat, a thief, and a liar. The man staring at me from K's eyes was none of those things. He was a stranger, but a man I've always hoped to become.

Dok dips his chin when I nudge my head to the stairs of the private jet. Our mode of transportation is heavily guarded to ensure nothing will come between Nikolai and his *Ahren* at the end of our raid, however, I don't want Dok examining K with a heap of witnesses.

While I place K down in the middle of the double bed at the back of the jet, Dok digs a stethoscope and a thermometer from his medical bag before pivoting around to face me. "Can you give us a minute? I don't work well under pressure."

I want to tell him to go to hell, I want to smash his teeth in, but instead of doing either of those things, I grip the lapels of his jacket and drag him to within an inch of my face. "Make it quick."

I'm not bowing under pressure, I am taking a breather before I do something I'll regret. K hasn't budged an inch in over ten minutes, hasn't murmured a peep. I can't even hear her breathe. It's as if I was too late, and the mirror ripped through the vein in her neck instead of my hand, and don't get me started on what the sick fucks did to her to have her so desperate to die.

She's been a sex slave for six years.

What could be worse than that?

———

I'm pacing the floorboards of Nikolai's private jet when he arrives off the battlefield. His grubby face reveals he got in the nitty-gritty, much less his smirk. He loves killing fuckfaces as much as me. "How is she?"

I wait for his eyes to stray from the closed bedroom door to me before shrugging. "Dok is with her. She's... ah..."

"Quiet?" Nikolai fills in when I fail to find the right word. When I jerk up my chin, he scrubs a hand across his before he plops into a cream reclining chair like his pants aren't covered with blood. "I was worried about Justine's mental stability after our raid of Vladimir's compound too." He undoes the laces on his boots before raising his eyes to mine. "Little did I know, my panic hurt her more. They're stronger than we think, Trey. They have to be if they want to be queens."

After three years of working under him, it should seem foreign that he continues talking about me as if I'm his equal, but since it's coming from Nikolai, it doesn't. He knows I don't have to work for him if I don't want to. I do it because I'd rather work beside him than across from him. That would have *never* been the case if my father's raid of Prague had been successful.

The world works in mysterious ways, and my friendship with Nikolai is proof of this.

Recalling Nikolai's earlier offer for us to return to Prague one day to restore my family's name, I ask, "Achim?"

I could say more, but I don't need to. The first syllable of Achim's name had only just left my mouth when Nikolai's jaw tightened to the point of cracking. I assume it's a bad tightening until he opens the bag Nero entered the jet with. Achim's head is inside of it. The fact his eyes are still open reveals his death was quick, but the expression on his face exposes it was also painful.

That appeases my annoyance for now.

My eyes drop to Nikolai's when he says, "His wife wasn't at the auction. That's why it took me so long to give the word to strike. I'm wary she somehow got word about our raid."

"By whom?" It's clear from the information Nikolai shared during our eighteen-hour flight to Czechia that India is well-aware of Achim's kinks. That's one of the reasons she agreed to marry him. With his family money, the Dvořáks became untouchable.

Well, so they thought. If the number of bodies I trekked past during my sprint for the evacuation vehicle are anything to go by, they just lost several key members of her crew.

I'll take care of the rest once K is stable.

It may be six weeks, it may be six years, but India Dvořák should enjoy her last breaths because they're limited.

Nikolai's chest rises and falls three times before he mutters, "I don't know, but I intend to find out. When I do—"

"That fucker is dead."

Nikolai loses the chance to reply when the creak of a door sounds through our ears. The whiteness on Dok's face is nothing out of the ordinary, he has super pasty skin, but the concerned pinch of his brows frustrates me. "How is she?"

He half-heartedly shrugs. "Physically, she's stable. She gained a little weight the past three months, and her vitamin D deficiency doesn't seem as bad."

I swish my tongue around my mouth, praying it will help with my next set of words. When I stumble them out like a teen sucking on his first tit, I realize it was a waste of time. "Was she... did they..."

I stop blubbering like an idiot when I spot Dok's headshake. "There are no bruises or tearing associated with... *that*. She has old injuries, but from what I could tell, she hasn't been penetrated the past ten to fourteen weeks."

Although appreciative she wasn't raped during my watch, something still feels off. "What aren't you telling me, Dok?"

He guides me to the back of the jet, so our conversation isn't overheard by my brothers returning from battle. "K's mental stability is very concerning. She's in what we call an acute psychosis. She has no sense of reality and is unresponsive to both touch and command." He locks his concerning blue eyes with mine. "I don't even think she knew I was examining her."

In a way, that makes me happy. The less invaded she feels, the quicker she'll come out of the dark. "How long will her psychosis last?"

Dok shrugs again. "I truly don't know. I've never seen a condition as bad as K's. Some patients go in and out of psychotic episodes within hours, some last months, even with intensive therapy." He licks his lips before breathing out slowly, "Then there are a handful who never recover." He doesn't directly say it, but I know he's placing K in that category. "I wish I had better news for you, Trey, but unfortunately, I don't. The best we can do is make her as comfortable as possible and for her to know she's safe."

I can't talk. I'm too gutted to speak. The fight in K's eyes was one of her most attractive features, and I'm devastated a prick like Achim Novak has stolen that from her. Anger surges through me as an overwhelming desire to kill echoes in my heart's beats. I want to kill a man who's already dead before resuscitating him so I can kill him all over again.

Sensing my unease, Dok whacks my shoulder in an it'll-be-all-right way before he moves for a group carrying Eight into the plane. If the way he's clutching his stomach is anything to go by, he's sporting a bullet wound. His second for me if the memories in my head are anything to go by.

When I go to help my brother in arms, Nikolai steps into my path. "Go to your queen. She needs you more than Eight."

"You heard what Dok said—"

"Yeah, I did," he interrupts, "but I also know he's full of shit." He slants his head like we don't stand at almost the same height before saying, "He said the same thing about you, and look at you now. Life is your fucking oyster, Trey, so show your queen what she's got to come back to." After another head slant, he adds, "Unless you want me to order one of my men to keep her warm?"

Nikolai snickers like a dumb fuck not in fear for his life when I pin him to the cabinets we're standing next to by his throat. I have my blade a millimeter from his jugular, and the adrenaline from a kill is already skating through my veins. He's all but dead. The only reason he's still breathing is because it was the air in his lungs that resuscitated mine long after I was freed. He also killed Achim for me without giving me the slightest bit of grief that I was choosing K over revenge because even someone as once heartless as him knows I made the right choice putting K first.

She will always be first.

The fury bubbling in my veins reduces to a simmer when Nikolai says, "That's what I thought. You want your queen, and you'll take down any fucker stupid enough to say otherwise, so why are you still standing here? Why aren't you bringing her back from the madness like only you can. If you want to save her from the blackness, Trey, show her how hell is darker than death, and it's one hell of a playground if you play your cards right."

After pushing me away from him without making a move for his beloved knife he's never without, he returns to the middle section of the jet. "Let's get this wrapped up. My *Ahren* is waiting for me."

He tells the two emergency whores the men always pack for long trips to piss off to the front of the jet before he lays on a three-seater couch as if it's a bed. After tossing an arm over his eyes, he instructs for Mikhail to wake him once we land. His admission that he's planning to sleep the entire trip lowers the bottom lips of the whores hoping to entertain him, unaware the opportunity ended the instant his eyes locked with Justine's.

It was the same for K and me—and it will be again.

I'll make sure of it.

TWENTY-FIVE

TREY

"Can I borrow that?" I ask Dok, freezing him partway out the door.

He just finalized his third check-up on K the past eight hours. I stayed for the last two, too worked up by Nikolai's comment to let anyone alone with K.

Dok is one of the good ones, but I don't care if he's a saint. No one will *ever* touch K without my permission, and even then, it'll be a rarity and never in the manner she's been touched previously.

Dok spins around to face me with his brows pinched. He thinks I want to borrow his thermometer or blood pressure machine. It couldn't be further from the truth.

"Your iPod. Can I borrow it?" Dok would be lucky to be thirty, but he's as old-school as they come. He still has his iPod from his college days, and his medical bag looks like it belongs on a British sitcom. "You have weather noises on there, right?"

His lips curl before he lifts his chin, shocked I've watched him close enough to know one of his quirks. He shouldn't be surprised. It's the quiet ones you need to watch the closest.

"They help me sleep."

After placing down his bag at the end of the bed K and I are resting on, he pulls out a set of wired pods from his pocket, rolls them around his ancient iPod, then passes them my way.

Just as I'm about to snatch them up, he yanks them back. "Can I take a look at your hand first?"

"Dok..."I growl out, pissed he's attempting to negotiate with me. I told him hours ago my hand is fine, and I'd appreciate it if he'd fucking listen to me.

"The wound looks deep. If we don't flush it out with some saline and clean it, it could become infected." When I fail to budge on my glare, he huffs. "Fine. Lose your entire fucking hand instead of a finger like Eight." His facial expression turns mocking when he spots the shock on mine. "Let me guess, you all think Eight lost two fingers in turf wars?" He doesn't wait for me to answer him with a hell-to-the-fucking-yes grunt. He just pushes out, "He would have been called nine if he had listened to me."

Taking my silence as approval to be an A-grade moron, Dok fishes a stainless steel kidney dish from a cabinet in the bathroom before he pulls some medical equipment from his bag.

Once he has my wound clean, he searches the open cut for tiny shards of glass. I'm surprised when he finds three micro pieces in the lower half of the slash mark. "Your palm is designed the way it is for a reason."

After dumping the glass into the kidney dish and giving my wound another thorough washing with saline, he peers at me through the ridiculous pair of glasses balancing on the end of his nose. They have lights on each side of the lenses. "Stitches or glue?"

"I—"

"Stitches or glue?" he repeats, knowing I was about to say it's fine how it is.

The tightness of my jaw is heard in my reply, "What will get you out of here faster?"

"Glue—"

"Then glue it is."

Halfway through the gluing of my hand, I'm tempted to cement Dok's lips together. It isn't because his question annoys me, I just have no clue how to answer it without sounding like a soft cock.

He asked why I want his iPod.

I wait until he has my palm glued up and he's reaching for a bandage before I say, "Rain reminds me of K. I'm wondering if it could be the same for her."

"Did something significant happen to her in the rain?" When I lift my chin, he asks, "A good thing?"

For the first time in my life, I'm unwilling to share my sexcapades with one of my brothers, so I once again nod my head. Usually, I'm all about sharing details of my hookups. There's no eagerness this time around. That afternoon in the rain changed things for K and me. I'm just praying it was noteworthy enough to help her find her way out of the dark.

"Do you think triggering her memory is worth a shot?"

Dok finishes bandaging my hand before locking his eyes with mine. "It won't hurt her. Just keep your expectations low." He drifts his caring eyes to K lying still as a plank as she has the past fifteen hours before returning them to me. "She isn't the only one who needs to tread cautiously right now."

"I'm not a headcase, Dok."

"I never said you were." He stands from his seat, tucks it back under the vanity mirror at the side of the room before shifting on his feet to face me. "You just need to ensure you're helping her because it's what *she* wants, and not what you *think* she wants."

"How can I know what she wants? She can't communicate with me even when she's alert."

"Are you sure about that?" Dok asks, smirking. "Because from what I'm seeing, she's stronger than I realized."

I glare at him like he's certifiably insane, my eyes only leaving his when I follow the direction of their gaze. To someone who hasn't been watching over her for the past fifteen hours straight, they'd believe K is still unresponsive and shutdown.

I know that isn't the case.

She moved her head. Not enough to have me believing she's close to leaving the dark, but there's no doubt she angled her head so she could see me in the reflection of the full-length mirror in the bathroom. I've been lying beside her for the majority of our trip, but my change in position to the end of the bed so Dok could patch up my hand put me out of her line of sight.

Acting ignorant to the panic beaming out of me, Dok shoves his iPod into my hand. "Be gentle with her, Trey."

"I don't know how," I reply before I can stop myself.

He acts as if I never spoke. "Track 37 is my favorite summer afternoon rain track. It only goes for around four minutes, but you can play it on repeat."

Not speaking another word, he leaves me alone with K. I'm not going to lie. I'm shitting my pants. Gentle isn't in my vocabulary, but I sure as fuck want to be gentle for K.

Can I do that, though? Can a man who's raised his hand to women shelter one who has been beaten beyond recognition?

If you had asked me that very question only three months ago, I would have said hell no. Now? Now I'm willing to give it a shot. The most euphoric thing in the world is watching the light switch on in someone's eyes long after they've been trapped by the dark.

I swear Nikolai's ego still feeds off his feat now.

After unwinding the cords around Dok's iPod, I push back the curls fanning K's face before popping a pod into her exposed ear. The other half goes into mine. Once I've pressed play on the track Dok suggested, I lay on my side so I can watch K's face for any indication she can hear the patters of rain on a tin roof.

Dok picked good. This track sounds exactly like a sprinkling of rain hitting a pigpen. All I need is the smell of pig shit, and the scene would be set.

My eyes pop out of my head when a lightbulb inside switches on.

"I'll be back in a sec, K. I know I said I wouldn't leave you, but this is really important."

Ignoring the similarities between this comment and the one that had K taken away from me for three and a half months, I remove the pod from my ear then hightail it out of the room. Nikolai is awake, alone, and eating toast like he wasn't responsible for the death of over thirty men last night.

"Who hid in the stables before the raid?"

He stops munching on his toast to arch a brow. Although curiosity is his highest expression, he hates being interrogated more. "Nero and Shaun..." I race down the hall before all of Nero's name leaves his mouth. "Why?"

"I need shit. Lots and lots of shit."

Nero greets me with a grin like he isn't in the process of getting his dick sucked by a whore. "How's K?"

"Good, but I need your boots." I drop my eyes to his muddy boots parted by the naked backside of a brunette slurping away on his cock as if it's a lollipop. "Did they have pigs in the stalls you hid in?"

Nero fists the brunette's ponytail to hold her down on his cock until she gags before shrugging. "I can't recall. I don't know the difference between a moo and an oink." He jerks up his hips two times, producing a prolonged moan from the whore before a smug grin curls his lips. "But I sure recognize the moans of a horny woman."

With his shirt showing signs of an oozing wound, he's being extra pigheaded today. He's probably also drugged up on pain medication. If you've got a good doctor on call, that shit can be better than the best blow.

"Give me your boots, Nero." I commence untying the laces on his left boot, ensuring he's aware I'm not taking no as an answer. "If your dick gets anywhere near my face, I swear, I'll bite it off."

"What the fuck, T-man?" He thrusts his hips up in a way that makes my stomach roll. "You're the one cutting the queue 'cause you want my nasty-smelling shoes."

The men surrounding us laugh, but I barely hear their chuckles over my second light-bulb moment for the day. Although shocked revelations like this usually have me wanting to drop one campaign to take up another, this time around, I don't need to. They're both about the same person—K.

With Nero's boots thrust under my arm, I make my way back to the room at the other end of the jet, stopping by Nikolai's little alcove on my way. He almost chokes on his last slice of toast when I say, "K tried to bite off Rory's cock." While he coughs up the breadcrumbs lodged in his lungs, I explain. "When I took Rory to Jim's, K laid the boot into him... *after* seeing teeth imprints in his cock. You saw how drugged up he got Ana. She wouldn't have been able to chew through his skanky cum much less his dick." Nikolai sits up straighter, understanding where I'm going. "If Vladimir was letting members of your crew hook-up with his prized girls, what were they giving him in return?"

I hear his back molars grind together before he spits out, "Do you think it was just Rory?"

I want to say yes, but my suspicions are too high to allow that. "I don't know, but I suggest you don't quit looking until you find out." When he lifts his chin, agreeing with me, I add, "I also suggest you look deeper into your purchase of K..." Before he can remind me he doesn't pay for whores, I push out, "Not because you pay for whores, but because her sale wasn't placed in your name for no reason. Dok said K was looked after the past three months. None of the women housed with her were. I don't even know if the blonde in her cell was breathing when I raced out of there."

I should feel guilty about the number of women we left behind, but I don't. We would have never extracted K safely since the number of rescuers was less than the number of captives.

Nikolai lifts his chin for the second time before locking his eyes with Nero's boots. "What's with the boots?"

After hitting him with a cocky wink, I say, "Not even the darkest night can hide the brightest star."

Leaving Nikolai to unravel my riddle alone, I enter the only door next to the couch he's spent the past fifteen plus hours on.

K is still as stiff as a board, but her eyes appear more sheened than they were when I left.

The gloss of her tears has me switching tactics for the third time this evening.

While struggling not to hurl, I tap out the dirt from the bottom of Nero's shoes into the washroom sink before scooping it up in my hands and depositing it into the soap holder in the shower. Once I have the water switched on and at a similar temperature to a Vegas summer shower, I snag a t-shirt out of the bag Nero dumped on the floor hours ago before moving to K's bedside.

My hands jitter like a virgin undoing his first bra when I peel back K's hair enough to locate the zipper of her dress. As it slides down to the two dimples in her lower back, my jaw works through a bad bout of stiffness. Her whip marks have healed, but they've left a nasty set of scars on her back.

Endeavoring to keep my head out of the darkness of my past, I shimmy K's dress down her slender frame before rolling her over so I can see her face. Her wide and un-terrorized eyes are the only things capable of keeping me out of the dark. They can even surpass my wish to kill.

I'm a cruel, faceless monster... until I'm standing across from K.

Then I'm anyone she needs me to be.

Once I've slipped my shirt over K's head and pulled her hair out of the collar, I tug off my jeans, yank off my shirt, remove Dok's iPod pod from K's ear, then gather her in my arms. I don't carry her like a groom does a bride over the threshold. I plaster her body to the front of me, gluing her to me as I plan to be glued to her until she fully emerges from the dark.

With the bathroom steamy, the muddy slop I dug out of Nero's boots is highly noticeable when we step into the compact space. It doubles the faintness of the pulse in K's neck in an instant, and has me hopeful she might leave the dark sooner than I'm hoping.

"Come on, Duchess," I mutter as I step us into the shower stall. "You're stronger than this. You fought Satan and won, so don't let this beat you." My arms tighten around K's torso so fiercely I'm afraid I may have broken one of her ribs when her eyelids dip for the quickest second. It wasn't a full blink, but it was noticeable. "Didn't you want a war, Duchess? I brought you the war. We played the fucker at his own game and won, so you can come out of the dark now."

Another blink.

It's even longer than the first one.

"We could dye your dress in his blood. Parade his beheaded carcass through the streets of Prague." I step her back until the lukewarm water pumping out of the showerhead flattens her curls. "We started a war without firing a single bullet, and we ended it the same way. His life wasn't worth the price of a bullet, so we beheaded him instead. He's dead now, Duchess. He'll never hurt you again. I promise you that."

This time I get two blinks and a single tear. It hasn't fallen from her eye just yet. It's clinging to mascara-coated lashes on the lower lid of her right eye.

She's too brave to cry, too fucking strong. She is the most courageous woman I've ever met.

When I tell K that, her tear plops onto her cheek. I wipe it away in an instant, its worth inconsequential. She isn't broken, she's fighting to come back, to claw her way out of the darkness.

"Look up, K. It's time to see the fireworks." My heart thuds in my ears when I place the hand not holding her body hostage to mine under her chin so I can carefully crank her neck back. "I want to kiss you, K. I want to kiss you so fucking bad it hurts. But I won't touch you without permission. No one will *ever* take away your rights again. I'll kill any man stupid enough to try. I don't care who he is." After working my jaw side to side to weaken the fury of my tone, I say, "But that means I need your permission, K. I need you to come out of the dark and tell me this is what you want. I need to know you want this as much as me."

When I stare into her eyes, waiting for the light of life to return, they do a lengthened blink. "It's not enough, K. I need more. I'm far from a fucking saint, but I can be your light. I can protect you better than the dark." After tugging her in so close, the material of her saturated shirt and my drenched boxer shorts become one, I say, "The dark won't last forever. Even on the blackest nights, stars still shine through. Let me be that star for you, Duchess. Let me guide you out of the dark. Then I can kiss you as often as *you* want." I bring my lips an inch from hers before murmuring, "I know it's safe in the dark, but that isn't living. You can't exist if you're locked up in your past. Let it go, K. Show them how strong you are. Fight for you and *only* you..."

My words fade out when K proves she's always been more brave than afraid. Her lips are on mine—*only just*—but it feels like the most intimate thing I've ever done.

A better man would stop at a peck kiss. I've told you before I'm not one of them.

She's only just tiptoed out of the dark.

I want her fully emerged from it.

But if I do that, I could lose her forever.

Since that's the last thing I want, I don't act like the man I was raised to be, nor the one I've faked since I was freed from hell. I commence being the man I saw in K's eyes when she peered up at me lifeless and lost.

I will be the man she *needs* me to be.

The thump of my heart in my ears doubles when I slowly notch my head back so I can peer into K's eyes. She's back, but her grip on reality is loose, proving I made the right choice.

After clearing away the hairs fallen in front of her eyes, I issue a promise I plan to keep even if it kills me. "While Achim played for the castle, we took down his whole fucking kingdom. I promise you, Duchess, your crown is next. It just won't be pronged with jewels."

TWENTY-SIX

TREY

Nine long months later…

Killing doesn't faze me. I experienced all types of murders long before Nikolai found me shackled to a wall, naked and on the verge of death. I could end a life without the slightest increase in my heart rate and eat an almost rare steak only minutes later. My stomach didn't twist, and my brow didn't mist with sweat. I was the monster I was raised to be.

K changed me.

Don't get me wrong. The man hanging from the second-story balcony of his home, bleeding and whimpering for his life won't get any leniency from me. But women, in particular, beaten, sold, and raped women, they're not on my list anymore. I'll kill the men responsible for what happened to them. I'll slit their throats *after* cutting off their cocks and feeding it to them, and I'll torture the ones stupid enough to *think* they can come between us.

That's what's happening here tonight. An errant, low-bottom-gangster wannabee *thinks* he can play Nikolai and me as fools. My sidekick and I are determined to prove him wrong.

K isn't responsible for a single nick on his body. From her vantage point in the foyer, she doesn't even know his cock is hanging out of his trousers, ready to be removed. Her presence merely ensures the thudding of my pulse in my ears keeps my head in game mode and not on my past when torture and deprivation of liberty were above me.

Lester would have been dead an hour ago if it weren't for K. This way, I'll get the information I'm seeking *and* the adrenaline high K loves feeding off after every raid.

Eager to get that side of the festivities started, I say, "Let me make sure I have my facts straight, Lester. You've never heard of Zoran Davis, and you don't know where he is. Is that correct?"

He can't answer me since he's gagged, but he has no problems nodding even with a rope burning his jugular. He's tiptoeing on a chair like Justine did mere seconds before Vladimir kicked it out from beneath her a year ago.

I've always had a fascination with adding a personal touch to the shakedowns Nikolai passes down to me. Sometimes you have to put the sick fucks through the pain they've made others experience for them to grasp how fucked-up they are.

It's a theory I've been running since Nikolai discovered the real reason K was 'supposedly' purchased by him. Achim didn't gift K to Vladimir because he wanted Ana back. He did it to get to me. He had no clue there were two separate entities being run under the Popov name during the planning stage of his ruse—Nikolai's and Vladimir's.

Finding Vladimir was easy, but Nikolai and his crew's location was a lot harder. Nikolai kept Clarks' location wrapped up tight, knowing a hidden bunker was one of his strongest assets, second only to the love of a good woman.

With Ana's inclusion in Vladimir's arsenal of sex slaves going unnoticed by Nikolai's second-in-charge who Achim was convinced had a fascination for blonde-haired, blue-eyed women, K was microchipped without her knowledge, then gifted to Vladimir with the hope the *real* woman from my dreams would bring me out of hiding.

In a way, Achim's planned worked. It just took weeks longer than he would have liked.

K was his favorite whore, and for every day he was without her, his quest for vengeance grew more rampant. That's why he organized K's mocked sale. If Nikolai hadn't fallen dick first in love for his defense attorney, he may very well have collected the woman he'd unknowingly handed over one point two million dollars for—or better yet, he'd send his second-in-charge.

K confessed to messaging Achim on my phone as drummed into her during their many chats about how she'd be released from his 'service' the instant she handed over Ana, but flight plans prove Achim was already on his way to the US long before K had sent her text. The instant the chips in K and Ana's shoulders were picked up at a second location, Achim's plan was activated.

I'll give it to Achim, he was smarter than he looked. He didn't want to instigate a war with a man he knew he'd never win against, so instead of hitting Nikolai's compound alone, he sided with one of his enemies. His plan was almost foolproof. No one in Alexei's crew knew about their once-off merger, and Achim left no evidence he was ever at Clarks.

He just forgot one vital part in his equation.

The significance of a woman who can make your heart thud in your ears.

I had my skull cracked open with a tire wrench. I died twice on the way to the hospital, and three times on the operating table, yet, the faintest scent of rain on the horizon had me remembering eyes the color of an ocean and a grubby, underfed face.

K brought me out of the darkness, taught me how to be gentle, and how I can forgive even if I never forget.

She also showed me only the most damaged cocoons produce the most stunning butterflies.

She's stronger than she has ever been—both mentally and physically. She can put Eight on his ass when they go a handful of rounds in the ring, eat like a trucker, and can climax without crying.

The latter part of my confession was her biggest challenge, but I'm pleased to say she overcame it. I'm sure there are days she's tempted to tiptoe back into the dark, but for the most part, she's here, with me, always at my side.

I've been trying to loosen the invisible lead I curled around her ankle nine months ago, but it's a slow process. Eight has taken her for the occasional drive when he's collecting supplies, and the once-whores-now-cooks steal her away from me as often as possible, but anywhere I go, she comes with me.

Even now, she sits on the entryway table, swinging her legs like the effortless movements won't irritate the tattoo Jarmon finished for her earlier this week. Her tattoo is beautiful. It's a phoenix that goes from the exit wound of the bullet that ripped through her shoulder blade seven years ago to the tiny grazes on the lower half of her stomach from when Vladimir dragged her down a glass-littered hall by her hair.

K's favorite flowers are mottled throughout the bird's long tail feathers that hug her enticing, yet still tiny curves. They add a touch of color to a symbol known for rebirth, life, growth, and longevity.

The tattoo was K's idea. Everything she's done the past nine months has been her choice. The size of her tattoo, its placement, and its design were purely her decision. As was the tiny diamond stud hidden by the tender folds of her pussy.

Jarmon wasn't given the pleasure of piercing K. She wanted me to do that. In all honesty, I was opposed to the idea at first. I didn't want to hurt her any more than she'd already been hurt. It was only while recalling the reason for my many tattoos and piercings did I change my mind.

K doesn't look at herself and see beauty. She sees scars and irreversible damage.

Her piercing didn't make her feel more beautiful, but it brought her out of her shell and broke away the ugliness she thought she was shrouded in so she could commence her metamorphosis.

I doubt she'll ever peer at her reflection and understand how truly beautiful she is, but I'm hopeful one day she will believe she's worthy.

Annoyed an insolent man is keeping me from stepping K closer to that day, I pierce the tip of my blade into the shriveled skin around Lester's cock. He's uncircumcised, or should I say *was* uncircumcised. He's not anymore.

"This is your last chance, Lester. My woman is waiting for me. Her time is precious, so I suggest you stop acting as if it isn't. Where. Is. Zoran?" I space out my last three words to ensure he knows his balls are next on my hit list.

"P-P-Puerto Rico," he stutters out, his words pushed through a howl from my blade jabbing his walnut-size nut.

"What was that? I couldn't hear you."

"P-Puerto Rico," he repeats, louder this time. "He's at a vacation home in the name of his old mistress. I can get you the details. I have them stored in my phone."

When I click my fingers two times, Eight magically appears out of nowhere. He's good like that. He is always at my side watching my back as I do K's. Excluding Nikolai, he's the only man I trust with her, and even then, he is wary about what he does and says around her.

"Where, exactly?" I ask after scanning Lester's blood-stained face with the facial recognition software on his phone.

When I enter the contact app, I automatically scroll to the very bottom, seeking the Zs. My thumb stops mid-scroll when Lester answers my question. "It's under the 1s." His panicked eyes dart between mine when he confesses. "I store my clients' details in my phone under the docket numbers of their purchases. Janice's was 12573. I remember hers as it was only one digit different from my favorite mistress' number."

I'm not the only one who balks at his blubbered comment.

I felt K's ripples from here.

Her sales docket number was one number away from Janice's as well. It was the number I used to free her from captivity, and the date cited on her mother's headstone. India was such a sick bitch, she suggested for Achim to use K's mother's date of birth as her sale document number. She hated how her family's wealth and stature couldn't weaken Achim's obsession with K, so she made K's life as miserable as possible.

Even with K being the help, Achim wanted her on sight and was willing to do anything to have her. He didn't count on a Corbyn man stealing his ultimate prize. I was supposed to bed his wife-to-be, not the jewel of his eye.

Knowing K gave her virginity to me willingly gutted Achim more than India nursing my brother back to health so they could plot their own takeover bid on the Novaks. That's what got Cole killed. Achim had spies in many places. India's chambermaids were only one of them.

Although no bones have been found, rumors are India was killed by Achim not long after she suggested he gift K to Vladimir. She may have been a more royal version of K, but no amount of glitz can replicate the fight in K's eyes. When Achim finally learned that, he supposedly strangled India like he did K nine months ago.

He just failed to resuscitate her.

I've never been a man to believe rumors. I've seen firsthand how the dead resurrect when least expected, so although my hunt for India has ceased, my watch will never end. If she resurfaces, I'll take her down just as quickly as I have every other person who has caused K harm. It'll make me a monster, but since it will also ensure I keep my promise to K while coercing her out of the dark, I'm willing to step into the nightmares of my past for her one more time.

As I am now.

Lester sighs when I tuck his penis away, stupidly believing he's safe from dismemberment. He is dead fucking wrong. If any of the inane thoughts in my head are true, the loss of his penis will be the least of his worries.

"K, can you come here for a sec?"

My pulse quickens when she enters the elaborate galley of a mansion thirty miles from Vegas. Her hair is wet and clinging to her face compliments to the sprinkling of rain we dashed through while sneaking into Lester's home unaware, and her white dress is grubby and almost see-through.

I see so much of the girl who galloped down the stairs of Vladimir's compound twelve months ago tonight. She's just stronger now. More determined. *Fucking perfect.*

After telling my cock to calm the fuck down, aware I could never remove a man's appendage while mine is pressed against the zipper in my trousers, I ask K, "Do you recognize him?"

She joins Eight and me near a balustrade that curves up and around four floors of opulence so she can take in Lester's features with due diligence. My cock hardens even more when the scent of her rain-soaked hair streams into my nose. She has a seductive scent not even the hardest conditions can detract from. It's a scent that reminds me of bad decisions with deadly consequences but with a touch of purity I've never experienced.

My addiction to her scent helped her heal faster than expected as does my dedication to ensure her pleasure forever comes before mine. She never kneels to suck my cock until the apex of her thighs is drenched by multiple orgasms. Just like we've never fucked without her eyes locked on mine.

Even before she learned a word of English, I could read her thoughts in her eyes. They guided me through the many exchanges we've had the past nine months.

As they do today.

Ignoring Lester's wordless pleas for her to say no, K shifts on her feet to face me. I'm pleased to say even with her heels bringing her tiny five-foot-two height closer to my six-foot-three stature, there isn't the slightest wobble to her stride.

Shoes were the first thing I spoiled her with.

Orgasms were a close second.

"Yes."

"Yes, you recognize him?" I double-check. Nikolai said I could leave Lester breathing if he gave us what I wanted. He was a mere accountant working for the wrong man.

Now, I'm not so sure.

"Yes, I recognize him." K's English is still developing, and her voice is heavy with an accent I fucking love, but even if she couldn't speak a word of English, she'd have no trouble communicating with me. I can see the truth in her narrowed eyes, feel her anger slicking her skin with sweat.

This fucker isn't just an accountant.

He touched my girl.

And now he'll die for it.

"Wait in the car with Eight for me, Duchess. I won't be a minute." The restraint I'm struggling to hold back is heard in my voice. I want to hurt, I want to maim, but more than either of those things, I want to continue being the man K has encouraged me to become the past nine months.

Most men can't be both a monster and a saint. That isn't the case for me.

A good man doesn't cause his woman additional problems.

A bad man makes them all disappear.

Most women either accept one or the other.

A duchess deserves both, and I'm going to make sure she gets exactly that.

KRISTINA

Nine months ago, Achim Novak killed me. He siphoned my will to live with nothing but cruel, vindictive words full of hate and maliciousness.

Only hours later, Trey Corbyn revived me in the same manner. He breathed life back into my veins by draining the black, hate-filled blood the darkness filled my heart with.

I thought the dark was my safety net, that it would keep me safe during my bleakest days. Over the past nine months, I slowly learned that isn't the case. It sheltered me from the horrid things happening to me against my wishes, but it stopped me from using the fighting strength Trey swears he's seen in me since day one.

He sees something in me no one else ever has. He thinks I'm special, where, in reality, I was once just a young girl from Czechia who dared to dream for a better life. There have been a handful of times Trey's attention has made me want to tiptoe back into the dark. It wasn't anything he said or did. When he isn't fulfilling his role in Nikolai's crew, he's charming in his own barbaric way. It's believing I don't deserve his attention that's my biggest struggle.

My family was treated as lesser-valued members of society for longer than I've been born. We were devalued because our blood was neither royal nor tainted with evil.

Now I feel as if it has a touch of both. Trey's blood is royal in a way where he doesn't need to balance a jeweled crown on his head to hold his chin high. His family's legacy, although not as well-known as it once was, is still respected across the globe, and the reverence it demands ensures I'll forever be safe.

Even now, while sitting in the passenger seat of Trey's car as it's being loaded with a body, I feel safe and protected. Lester hurt me. Not as bad as Vladimir, Achim, or Rory, but he still died because of it. As did Achim.

Achim's head was returned to the United States minus his body so he'd be denied a proper burial. Most of the Czech Republic's population are atheists, therefore funerals are more based on a person's accomplishments than their religious beliefs, but the Novak's had their own strong spiritual beliefs. To them, all the horrible things Achim did in his life would be excused during proceedings. They'd confess his sins on his behalf, which would give him a free pass to heaven.

Neither Trey nor Nikolai were ever going to allow that to happen. They wanted him to rot in hell along with Vladimir. Although his head is stored in below-freezing temperatures, I'm confident his soul is experiencing a starkly different set of circumstances.

I stop smirking like a vindictive witch when the crank of a door breaks through the silence that forever shrouds me, or should I say, used to shroud me. Although my English is still developing, I'm not close to being mute.

Trey jerks his chin up about something Eight says before he slides behind the steering wheel of his Shelby. Fond memories flash before my eyes when he says, "I need to make a quick stop at

Jim's before heading to the restaurant Nikolai's party is being held at. Since you're ready to go, you can travel with Eight if you want?" His smile when I grunt sends blood rushing through all extremities of my body. "All right, don't get your knickers in a twist, Duchess. I was just asking."

After signaling for Eight to go, Trey kicks over the engine of his beloved car. Although I've been sitting in his passenger seat for the past forty minutes, I wait for him to request for me to put my seat belt on before I do. I love that even though I'm no longer battered, bruised, and on the verge of death by starvation, he still doesn't want to see me get hurt. It's one of the things I love about him.

Yes, you heard me right. I love Trey Corbyn. I may have commenced falling for him before I knew his true identity, but unearthing who he really is hasn't weakened the intensity in the slightest.

There's nothing more beautiful in the world than a broken man doing everything in his power to fix a broken woman. He could have ended up more scarred than he is, but alas, a shattered heart will forever beat louder than an untouched one.

"K..." Trey pushes out in a gravelly tone when I unclick my seat belt a few miles out of Vegas. "We're already running late without adding in a detour to Jim's. I won't have time to make sure your thighs are drenched before filling you with my seed, so don't fucking tempt me."

Ignoring the way his tone both worries and excites me, I continue with my mission. The scent of rain-soaked ground is lingering in my nostrils, my dress is still damp to touch, and the blood of a man who hurt me dots the sleeves of Trey's shirt. This is inevitable.

Only months ago, the catastrophic range of emotions pumping into me would have caused me to shut down. I would have blanked out long before I took the time to work out why they arrived out of nowhere. Now I hold on for the ride, knowing that every exchange we participate in adds fusions to the cracks nowhere near as unsightly as they once were.

Like a cat wanting attention from its owner, I rub my cheek along Trey's beard, breathing heavier when the thud of his pulse in his ears reaches mine.

I couldn't feel love before him.

I couldn't feel freedom.

I also couldn't hear my heart thump in any place, much less my ears.

Now I hear its beats as loudly as I do Trey's.

I should hate how unstable he makes me, how dependent, however, each beautiful pump of his heart triples mine. It beeps in my chest, my ears, and in a region of my body I swore would never be fixed.

Within weeks, the horror I felt when touched was replaced with fascination. I was mesmerized that a big brooding man who towers over me even when sitting could be so gentle. He took his time with me, showing me that even events I once hated could be enjoyable if the right person was doing it.

I won't lie. There were days I cried when the guilt of enjoying what he was doing to me became too much to bear. There were times I thought I got everything I deserved because only someone wickedly immoral could experience pleasure after being so brutally hurt. Then, there are days like today, where my hunger is so rampant, even if the nightmares of my past want to surface, they wouldn't be strong enough to stop me from taking what I want.

Trey says I'm a fighter. What he doesn't realize is my biggest battle is fighting my addiction to him. I feel alive when I'm beneath him—cherished and unbroken. It's a strange but highly welcomed feeling I crave as much as my stomach once begged for food.

"Please," I whisper in Trey's ear in Czech, knowing out of all the words in the world, he'll understand that one the most. I've used it on him many times when he refused to touch me until I begged him to.

With his hand gripping my nape to hold my mouth hostage to his, Trey pulls his car down a deserted side street. His hold thrills me more than it scares me. He's not holding me roughly because he wants to hurt me but because he can't kiss me like I've never been kissed if he wasn't being him while doing it.

That's how he broke through my defenses so quickly. Trey says he can't be gentle, but he holds me in his arms for hours when the horrors of my past rear their ugly head. He brushed my hair to ensure the bristles of the brush didn't irritate my tattoo its first few days, and even now, months after our first shared meal, he still tests my food to ensure it's safe before allowing me to eat it.

He's gentle when I need him to be and rough when his once jittery and scared woman tiptoes out of the dark so far, the light almost blinds us both.

"Ah, fuck, Duchess. You're destroying me. Utterly and fuckin' wholly," Trey says after inching back his kiss-swollen lips. His beard is thicker now than it was last year, but not even its inches of wiriness can take away from how plump his lips look. He looks thoroughly kissed, which makes me want to kiss him more.

Feeling daring, I lock our lips again.

This kiss is almost violent.

It goes above and beyond any of our previous ones.

It's the most real we've had.

"Jesus, K. Fuck." I love it when he calls me K. Duchess will always hold a special place in my heart, but he called me that when he didn't know who I was. K ensures me he's with me, in the present, not in a dingy butler's pantry in a country far from here with a woman undeserving of him. "I have to have you now. I can't wait." Eager to move along with his plans, my hands shoot down to his belt buckle. "Nuh-uh," he growls under his breath, stopping the slither of my hands. "Duchesses don't get fucked in the driver's seat of a Shelby." His smile when I pout doubles the throb between my thighs. "But on the hood of a Shelby on a cloud-filled, rain-scented night sounds about right."

Not waiting to see the flare of excitement darting through my eyes, Trey cranks open his door, then slides us out of his car. Considering his leg was broken in three places during Alexei's assault, it shouldn't be an easy task. He makes it look easy, though.

The droplets of rain on the hood of Trey's car sizzle when he splays me across the gleaming material. It's summer, so the temperature can't be blamed for the shiver that darts through my body when Trey steps back. It's the admiring glint in his eyes when he drags them up my body causing my shuddering response. He stares at me like I'm not broken, was never used and abused, and like all my dreams came true.

In a way, they did. I just took the long track instead of the short, uncomplicated one.

"Tell me, K. Tell me right fucking now before I do something I can't take back." Trey's voice is rough and crammed with need. It has my thighs squeezing together as well as the tugs he does to his cock through his jeans. He's most likely begging for it to calm down. He has done that a minimum of once a week for the past nine months.

He locks his eyes with mine when I breathe out, "Touch me."

They're dark, dangerous, and the very reason the light inside of me shines brighter than the darkness. "Where? Spell it out. Tell me exactly what you want me to do and exactly for how fucking long, Duchess." His eyes drop to the gap between my thighs when

I spread my legs wider. It's rare for me to answer him with words. Mercifully, he has no trouble reading my every desire without a word being shared. "Good pick."

After hitting me with a wink that pushes me within an inch of the finish line, he tugs my backside forward until it sits in front of the air vents on his hood before he slips his index finger into the waistband of my panties. As his finger traces the seam, he runs the barbell piercing in the middle of his tongue across his teeth. Even with his head inches from my pussy, I can feel the zap that roars through my body when our piercings collide. You'd swear they were wired with electricity for how potent their zaps are.

I immediately shake my head when Trey asks, "Is your tattoo still sore?" Jarmon finished the last of the phoenix's tail feathers earlier this week. The buzz of his gun usually frustrates my sensitive skin for a week or two at most, but it wasn't as long this time around since Trey was extra attentive with my tattoo wound care.

He had a good reason for his chivalry. The longer I'm out with an injury, the longer he goes without touching me. For some reason, not having his hands on me is the equivalent of Trey being tortured. For someone who never thought they'd feel desire again, much less be desired, his frustration tears at my heartstrings even more than him forever gaining my permission before touching me.

"Tell me again, Duchess. Show me how much you want this."

"*Prosím,*" I repeat without pause for thought. "I need you."

TREY

I check K's eyes for any signs of distress before pulling her panties to the side to marvel at the feast I'm about to consume. With tonight being Nikolai's thirtieth birthday, she's been polished and gleamed as if she never endured the revolting world of the sex-trafficking industry.

Her dress is designer, her heels cost more than what her parents made in a month, and her panties have me reasonably sure I'll kill someone before the end of the night, however, there are parts of her that'll never shine as brightly as they should.

She's scarred, far too skinny, yet still so fucking perfect. She's messily beautiful. A duchess worthy of the priciest crown, and the only thing better than that is the fact she's mine.

Seven years ago, she *gave* her virginity to me. She wasn't forced, coerced, or placing anyone's needs before her own. She gifted it to me of her own accord, preferring an unexplained immediate connection with a stranger than having it cruelly stripped from her as Achim and Vladimir tried to do to her self-worth.

This will make me sound cocky, but I don't give a fuck. This is straight-up honest, so do with it what you may. Our fuck in the butler's pantry of the Dvořáks' estate is what kept K's spine as hard as a rod during six years of torment.

For her entire life, she was told what to do, how to do it, and for precisely how fucking long she was expected to do it... until that night in the pantry.

She pulled my cock out of my trousers.

She lined it up with her fragrant-smelling pussy, just like *she* drove our exchange home by impaling herself on my cock with one quick plunge.

Everything was taken away from her *except* that. She didn't know who was kissing her, she couldn't see in the dark any better than me, but *she* decided her fate that night.

As she will from here on out.

"Scoot up onto your elbows, Duchess. Let me see those eyes."

I slant my head to hide my smile at her eagerness when she jumps to my command. I'm a cruel fuck who usually wouldn't give a shit about the needs of the women I was getting myself off on. That shit doesn't fly with K. Her needs will forever come before mine.

"This is gonna be quick. We have a party to attend, but I'll make it up to you tonight, all right? I promise."

Just like my pledge I'll never come before her—she can accept this guarantee just as readily. I've never made her a promise I can't keep. Take the tilt of her chin, for example. Even though she's peering down at me, waiting for me to devour her, there's no shadow on her neck. Her chin is held high in the air to ensure her invisible crown has no chance of falling.

"Are you ready for me, Duchess?" I swish my tongue around my mouth while silently warning my cock to calm down. The scent of her cunt alone has pre-cum seeping into my pants, and I'm not going to mention the catastrophe it causes from being mingled with the fresh smell of rain.

The soft cotton of K's panties is no match for my hand when she bobs her chin for the quickest second, choosing light over dark, happiness over dread, herself above anyone.

After dropping onto my knees, I peel open the slit in her dress, push it up her milky white thighs, then band it around her waist.

"Christ..." I have no other words to explain what I'm seeing. Her pussy lips are glistening in the moonlight. They're even brighter than the diamond stud hidden by delicate folds of flesh. "I want you so fucking bad, K. My tongue is dying to shred through you. To eat you. To fuck you. To claim every inch of you." For each word I speak, K's backside lifts off the hood of my Shelby more and more.

Once she's an inch or two from my face, I run the back of my knuckles down her clenching slit. "Always hungry." I lock my eyes with hers over her thrusting chest that's extra plump due to the three meals a day I ensure she eats without fail. Cockiness fills me when our eyes collide. She's still here, with me, not the least bit tempted by the frantic calls of the dark. "I'll happily accept your cunt's insatiable demands over your hungry stomach any day."

I wait for the fire in her eyes to shift to yearning before spearing my tongue through the folds of her glistening cunt. The beat of my pulse in my ears doubles when she clamps her thighs around my head, overwhelmed by the buzz of our piercings connecting. I stole a bit of ice out of Eight's drink before sliding in the driver's seat of my car, aware Lester's death would most likely lead us down this path. K gets off on me protecting her as much as her rain-soaked hair makes me the hardest I've ever been.

After giving her clit the attention it deserves, I blow a cold breath across her swollen and wet pussy, ensuring her piercing gets a tinge of the iciness from mine. She shudders in an instant. Her shakes have nothing to do with the coolness of my breath. My woman is coming undone, both mentally and physically.

"That's it, K, give me more of that sweetness to devour," I mutter through a groan before returning my mouth to her shuddering cunt. I eat her like I'm starved. Like her pussy wasn't on my mouth only hours ago. I can smell her arousal in my beard, taste it on my lips, however, it still isn't enough. If I had it my way, I'd only let her cunt leave my mouth to suffocate my cock.

When K's hands move for my hair, I poke my tongue inside of her, acting as if it's my cock. She has a tight, little cunt that's super responsive to touch. Just my beard scratching at the scarred skin between her drenched slit and her ass stretches her orgasm from one to two. She's soaked front to back and riding my face as if she's yet to come.

For years, she placed herself last. She still does it now without even realizing it, but when my head or cock is between her legs, no one is placed before her. Not even me.

I fucking love that about her.

Yeah, you heard me right. I love K, and I'm not ashamed to admit it. I've fucked many women in my almost twenty-nine years, but not one of those exchanges came close to what I experience when K is shuddering beneath me. There was no love attached to those interactions, no feelings. I was there to get off. Plain and simple.

Now, I'd rather go to bed with a sack full of sperm than have a meaningless romp with the whores who keep my brothers entertained after a long day. My cock doesn't even twitch at the thought of a drug-fueled gangbang I'd forget within an hour of it occurring.

The only thing that twitches when the guys give me shit about being a one-woman man is the itch to kill. For the most part, they're stirring me, but I've seen the way some of the men eye K when they think I'm not looking. They want a taste of the magic, convinced I'll eventually give them a slice of my pie.

There's no fucking chance of that ever happening, and I have no troubles expressing that with my fists when word of their hope reaches my ears.

Just them thinking they can get a taste of what's mine has me eating K faster and hungrier. I grip her hips to stop their sways before dragging my tongue up her slit to circulate it around her clit. As my beard soaks up the remnants of her two climaxes, I coerce a third one out of her. I rub at her clit faster with my tongue before notching a finger inside of her. She's still as tight as fuck, and her insides are all types of messy, but my fucking god, the greedy sucks of her cunt have me wanting to fill her to the hilt for every second of every day.

"I want to fuck you, Duchess. I want to fuck you so bad it hurts, but I need you to come again first. I need your thighs drenched and for my name to tear from your mouth." The pumps of my finger are brutal, but they, along with the growly delivery of my words, send her freefalling for the third time. She rips at my hair as my name shreds from her throat in a mangled groan. "Yes, Duchess. Give it to me."

She's barely shuddered through the brutality of her third climax when she slips off the hood of my car, falls to her knees in front of me like the gravel isn't cutting up her delicate skin, then yanks at my belt. "Please," she begs like she can't wait to taste my cum for a second longer.

I wait for her to free my cock from its tight confines before scooping her up off the ground and replanting her naked backside onto the hood of my Shelby. I'm a cruel, heartless fuck who loves her desperateness to suck me off so much, I can hold back my desires for hours just to force her lips to remain on me longer than necessary.

Just like her kisses cause the shards inside of me to shine brightly like a kaleidoscope, her blowjobs make me feel invincible. Like I can have both her and my kingdom.

I can, but regretfully, I don't have hours to spare to show you that right now. I told Justine we'd arrive at the restaurant hosting Nikolai's surprise party before Nikolai. I'm forty minutes out from breaking that promise. If my pledge were attached to any other man, I wouldn't give a shit how late we are, but since this is for Nikolai, I'll do my best to keep it.

"There's no time for cock sampling today." K almost whines, but the bracing of my cock's head at the entrance of her seeping pussy holds it back. She doesn't breathe while I coat myself in her juices. She doesn't move. She just stares straight at me, ensuring she's with me, at my side, and not tiptoeing toward the dark.

"Are you ready to see the fireworks, Duchess?"

When her chin tilts, I could blow my load right now. That's how fucking turned on I get by her strength. She's so fucking strong. So perfect. *So mine.*

My last two words release the beast from inside me. With my hand gripped on K's nape and our eyes locked, I thrust my hips forward, impaling her with one ardent pump. She's drenched front to back, but the clench of her jaw is undeniable. She's hurting. She just now knows the difference between a good hurt and a bad one.

"Stay with me, K." I lower my hand to her clit to stimulate it before slowly dragging my cock back out. "I can protect you better than the dark. You'll always be safe with me. You've just got to be brave enough to believe that."

Like a real-life monarch, the fire in her eyes roars to life. She adjusts the spread of her hips, widening herself for me, before digging the heels of her shoes into my ass, demanding for me to move with a regalness I'm going to ensure she has for real by the end of this year.

Nikolai is right. K is my queen, and together, we will build an empire.

TWENTY-NINE

KRISTINA

I giggle like a child playing a schoolyard game when Trey throws me over his shoulder before he continues our sprint for the restaurant where Nikolai's surprise party is being held. I've gained some much-needed pounds the past year, so my legs should be more than capable of pumping out the steps needed to beat Justine and Nikolai's race for the same entrance. They're just exhausted from the number of times Trey made me come.

Who knew something I once thought was hideous could fill me with so much euphoria, the weakness it arrives with seems inconsequential? Usually, I hate anything that makes me seem scrawny and pathetic. My small stature already has me putting in double the workload of those around me.

I don't face the same issues when it comes to sex.

When you think about it, orgasming is as intimate as kissing. They're full of passion, love, and devotion, and more times than not, I feel drunk after every one of them.

Perhaps that's why my legs don't work? I can barely stay

upright after a glass of wine, so imagine the controversy four back-to-back climaxes cause.

Once we break through the entry door of a pricy restaurant, a mere ten seconds after Nikolai and Justine, Trey sets me back onto my feet. Nine months ago, I would have anticipated being punished for making him late. Now, I'm smiling as largely as him. He's not happy we're late. He loves my smile as much as me. There have been plenty of times for me to smile the past nine months, but it's taken almost this long for my fucked-up head to realize it's okay to show happiness. Trey won't hurt me because I'm happy. If anything, he'll probably spoil me more.

"Come on." He curls his tattooed hand over mine before guiding me through the restaurant brimming with men and women of all ages. "The quicker we get this done and dusted, the faster my head will be back between your legs."

See? Crude, yet undeniably cultured.

The sweet smell of heat-slicked skin streams into my nose when Trey stops us just in front of Nikolai and Justine. "Hey, sorry I'm late. I was a little tied up."

As heat creeps across my cheeks, Justine leans in to pop a kiss on my flaming skin. The brightness illuminating my cheeks pales when it dawns on me why the scent of sweat-slicked skin doubled when she leaned forward. It appears as if Trey and I weren't the only ones seeking solace in modes of transportation tonight.

After inching back, Justine says, "Kristina, hi. How are things? I hope Trey is treating you well?"

"About as well as Nikolai is you," I reply in Czech, my tone cheeky and somewhat apprehensive.

I don't really know Justine. She doesn't come to Clarks often. I don't know if that's her choice or Nikolai's, but whatever the reason, we've only seen each other in passing the past few months.

She's busy keeping Nikolai's men out of jail, and my spare

time not gobbled up by Trey is used for studying. I don't know what degree I want to do yet, but I'm leaning toward nursing. Dok has his hands full, so I'm sure he'd welcome an additional team member. This way, I'll remain glued to Trey as long as my heart desires. We can even do that at Clarks if he wants.

Once I learned that the women who prance around Clarks half-naked despite the weather are there of their own accord, I grew to like the idea of Clarks. The women are free to come and go as they please, so I have no issues with how they choose to live their lives.

Like all groups of women, some are polite and friendly. Others are rude and bitchy. Then there are a handful like Ana. It won't matter how much I stick my neck out for them, they'll forever place themselves first.

Unfortunately, selfishness is ingrained in some people. Even being a sex slave didn't have Ana believing she was my equal. She forever placed herself above me.

I don't know what happened to Ana, and in all honesty, I don't care. Trey tells me he'll find out for me when the time is right, but for now, he wants the focus to stay on me. It's comments like that that had me almost tiptoeing back toward the dark. The guilt is horrible, but haven't I been punished enough to let the focus be on me for a change? Nine months ago, I would have *never* agreed with that judgment. Now, I'm a little more open to the idea.

Justine's smile reveals I'm on the money about her pre-party entertainment with Nikolai, much less the faintest pink hue coloring of her neck. "Good," she mutters, only the slightest bit embarrassed. "I told you he was a keeper."

Happy to shift the focus off her, she greets Trey in a similar fashion she did me. My stomach gurgles when she scrubs away a blob of red from Trey's cheek, believing it's lipstick. I'm not hungry. My stomach is upset I've become so focused on myself lately, I didn't notice Lester's blood was on Trey's face until now.

It dawns on me I must have missed something between Trey and Nikolai when Trey mumbles under his breath, "What? I didn't have time to shower."

The smugness in Trey's eyes grows when Nikolai's roll skyward. After giving Trey an inconspicuous nudge with his shoulder, Nikolai guides Justine to the other side of the room. I recognize the dark-haired man he's approaching. He was one of the men who freed the women from captivity, however, his wife seems new to this lifestyle. Her knees knock as obviously as mine when a middle-aged waiter suddenly stops in front of me with a platter full of funky-looking bite-size snacks.

"What is it, K?" Trey asks, his voice almost a roar. "Do you recognize him?"

The waiter looks on the verge of pooping his pants when he spots Trey's murderous glare. I had wondered if Trey's quest to rid the world of the men who hurt me was circulating beyond his crew. The waiter's response reveals it is.

The waiter sucks in his first breath in almost thirty seconds when I shake my head. "I've never seen him before. It's just the food he's holding." I throw a hand up to clamp my mouth when my reply comes out with a gag. I don't know what that black beady stuff is on crusty clumps of bread, but it makes my stomach heave.

When he reads the rest of my reply in my eyes, Trey pushes the waiter away from us via a hand to his face before he guides me in the direction opposite the way Nikolai and Justine went. My stomach stops flipping shortly after the fishy-smelling dish is removed from under my nose, but the pounding of my pulse remains, even more so when Trey asks, "When was the last time you bled?"

I peer up at him in both shock and fear. He'd never physically hurt me, but his response when I answer his question could shunt my mental stability back by months. I can't recall the last time I had my period. Due to inadequate nutrition and a body forced to age backward, it was absent for months after I was freed from captivity, and it only returned once around four or five months ago, much to Trey's disgrace. He hated when I got my period even more than when I chose a tattoo that would cover my entire back and half my stomach. He loved the design I had chosen and its location, he just hated that it took me days to heal between each tattoo session.

"You two good?" Eight asks when Trey races us toward the exit we only just bolted through.

Eight's brows stitch when Trey doesn't answer him, and my stomach violently flips. Silence isn't Trey's strong point. He was silenced for years, so he doesn't seek it often. He's generally only quiet when he's upset.

Now I wish more than ever that I could speak English better. I want to tell him he has nothing to worry about. Even if my period is late, that doesn't mean I'm pregnant.

Achim and Vladimir didn't just mess up my outsides, they fucked with my insides as well. I can't fix the damage they did with pretty tattoos and piercings.

My damaged insides are unfixable.

My heart breaks for Trey when he walks us to an all-night drug store two blocks up from the restaurant. He shakes like we're in the middle of winter as he scans the shelving for a test to confirm if his worst nightmare is coming true.

"I'm not pregnant," I say in Czech. He can't understand me, but I've got to try something. Every second his focus is on anything but me refractures cracks he's worked hard to fix.

I hate that he won't look at me. One of the things I cherish about him the most is that he doesn't look at me like everyone does.

He's never seen me as a sex slave, a sales docket number, or even Kristina. He sees me as K. *His K.* And now stupid, out-of-whack hormones have gone and ruined that.

"Can we use your bathroom?" Trey asks the cashier as he throws a bundle of cash his way. He's paying way more than the tests are worth because no matter how hard he tries, he can't hand the pregnancy tests to the cashier. Shame could be behind his motive, but I'm genuinely unsure. I'm having a hard time reading him right now. He gets jittery when he's both angry and scared, so perhaps tonight he's being hit with a combination of them.

My heart launches into my throat when the cashier says in broken English, "No bathroom." I'm not gasping about his lie. I'm stunned at Trey removing his gun from the back of his trousers to aim it at a wrinkle in the cashier's head.

"Trey..." Although I don't think he'll kill the cashier for denying his request, I have to do something. The middle-aged Indian man doesn't deserve Trey's wrath because Trey is unhinged about something he has nothing to do with. "Please."

When Trey's eyes drop to mine, the world shifts beneath my feet. Something has changed in them. They're as icy and cold as they are after he's killed, but they don't belong to the man who unclicks the safety on his gun and curls his finger around the trigger when it's pointed at an innocent person. "Five... four... th—"

The cashier tosses a plank of wood across the counter. It has a single key attached to it. "Fourth door on the right out back," he garbles through the panic clutching his throat.

After staring at me for what feels like two lifetimes, Trey lowers his gun, stuffs it back into his jeans, then uses the same hand to drag me out of the pharmacy. I really shouldn't say drag considering how I've been treated in the past, but there's definitely aggression in his guidance.

I don't know why Trey bothered gathering the key when he kicks out the lock on the bathroom before he gestures with his head for me to enter the dingy room before him. I gag again when I spot the stall he wants me to pee in. It's almost as bad as the bathroom in my room at Vladimir's compound.

"No." Even if Trey can't understand a word I speak, he'll have no trouble seeing my denial. I'm shaking my head so fiercely, I'm hit with a severe bout of dizziness.

"K..." He drags a hand over his hair that's almost back to its normal length when his one letter comes out super husky. Once he's confident he has a better hold of things, he tries again. "I need you to do this for me. I need to know." He strays his eyes to the filthy bathroom stall. "I'll hold you above the toilet. You won't get near the fucking lid, I swear."

His promise shocks me. He doesn't usually hand them out unless he intends to commit to them. It reveals how important this is to him, how he won't look at me again with the eyes I'm used to until I do this for him.

With my teeth gritted, I snatch up one of the tests out of his hands and enter the first stall. Trey stops shadowing my walk when I close the stall door behind me and fix the latch into place. I've been humiliated in more ways than you can imagine, but I've never used the washroom with a witness before. I don't want tonight to change that.

Trey's forehead rests on the door a mere second before his tattooed hand clutches the top of it. "You need to take the test out of the packet. There's a cap on the end of the stick. Remove that, then when you're peeing, dip that part into the stream of your pee."

I don't know what upsets me more, his knowledge on how pregnancy tests work or the fact he knows I'm so naïve I have no clue what I'm doing.

Men like Achim and Vladimir didn't worry about tests. They just kicked you hard enough you bled even when you weren't due for your period, and don't get me started on the women whose babies held on with everything they had. I can hear their screams now. They're as heartbreaking as Trey's breaths rattling the door separating us.

Doing my best not to get my backside anywhere near the grubby toilet seat, I pee on the stick as per Trey's instruction, recap it, wipe, then flush. The instant the water whizzes around the bowl, Trey knocks on the stall, demanding for me to open the door. I don't understand his eagerness. Even someone with a life as deprived as mine knows these things aren't instant. They usually take a few minutes to show a response.

Well, so I thought. This one pops up two lines almost immediately.

Jesus Christ. I'm pregnant.

"K..." Trey pushes out in panic when he hears my sharp gasp. "Let me in." His third word scarcely leaves his mouth when he commences kicking down the door. His size is no match for the flimsy material, much less his strength. He has it hanging on its hinges in seconds, and even quicker than that, his eyes snap down to the positive test I dropped to the floor like it's capable of undoing all the good things we've achieved the past nine months.

"Holy shit," Trey mumbles under his breath after taking in the result. "Holy fucking shit!" he utters again, louder this time. "Now you've got to say yes, K. If you don't say yes, you'll fucking gut me. You'll kill me more than any bullet that's ripped through my body. Don't break my heart, Duchess. I like hearing it thud in my ears. It's only ever done that with you. I don't want to hear it from anyone else."

I'm lost to where he's going with this—even more so when he falls to his knees like he did earlier tonight. Although disgusted about the gunk he's kneeling on, I'd be lying if I said my heart wasn't pounding in three distinct places. A violent and dirty world brought us together. No amount of sheen will ever have me forgetting that.

"Say yes, K. Please say yes," Trey begs as he digs his hand into his pocket to remove a pronged ring that's missing a diamond. "You can put any gem you want in there, Duchess. A ruby, a diamond, Achim's nuts." He smirks during his last comment. "I didn't want to assume what gem you wanted any more than I didn't want to assume you'd say yes." He lifts and locks his eyes with mine. They're back to the same icy blue pair I've adored the past nine months. "You can say no if you want. The choice is yours. I'll never do anything against your wishes. I just really fucking hope you don't say no, especially since my kid is in your gut."

Hearing nothing but unbridled hope in his voice, I dip my chin. Although it weakens the worry in Trey's eyes by a smidge, he's not willing to let me off that easy. "It's not enough, Duchess. I need more. You're stronger than that. You're going to give honor to the Corbyn name. Your veins are carrying my DNA. A dip of your chin isn't enough."

Smiling like a woman stupid enough to believe in fairy tales, I join Trey in kneeling on the floor, cup his chin, then whisper a word I've said more often than 'no' the past nine months, "Yes."

THIRTY

TREY

My brothers rally around K and me when Eight screeches out, "Listen up, motherfuckers. The T-man got married!" He's as high as a fucking kite, doped up both on the good shit the Popovs have distributed by the truckloads the past year and the testosterone pumping out of me when I made K my wife at the Chapels of Flowers thirty minutes ago.

She may have said yes only hours earlier, but I wasn't taking any chances. I wanted her to be my wife more than my cock is dying for a hug of congratulations from her tight, wet cunt.

Nikolai was right. Those pompous pricks in white coats don't know how we operate. They said the odds of K getting pregnant were virtually nonexistent. The sick fucks who brutalized her didn't stop at her head. They royally fucked her over. Yet, here she is, once again proving she's stronger than anyone thought possible.

Anyone but me.

I've seen it in her from day one. I just needed the head on my shoulders to overrule the tattooed one between my legs. Thank fuck not even a tire wrench to the skull stopped that from happening. Otherwise, if Achim had it his way, K would have his ring on her finger and his spawn in her gut.

The thought alone has me planning a trip to Jim's so I can piss on Achim's face. It'll be my third trip this month alone. What can I say? I'm an unforgiving prick who can't be as compassionate as K. You could fuck her over backward, and she'd still find a way to forgive you if you said you were sorry.

You won't get the same response from me.

I'll watch you snivel like a bitch to my woman until she finds it in her heart to forgive you, then I'll knife you the instant she's out of earshot.

You don't fuck with my girl and live. Lester found that out the hard way. He's still in my trunk, dickless and nicked up. I'll take him out to Jim's in a few. Celebrating our nuptials with K is more important than worrying about the pigs being fed a rotting corpse. They'll take Lester anyway they can get him—kind of like me with K. Grubby, polished, or deliriously happy like she is now, I'll take her any way I can get her.

After waiting for my brothers to stop humping my leg like a bunch of dogs on heat, Eight says, "Let's say a few words while we have a round of drinks to celebrate."

"Do you mean a toast, fuckface?" Mikhail ribs Eight, laughing. Their relationship is better now than it was nine months ago. They still get into the occasional fisticuffs, but for the most part, they tolerate each other.

The platinum black metal circling the ring finger on my left hand clinks against a glass of god knows what Eight hands me. He's a shit mixer, but since I'm not planning to hang around long to celebrate, I'll stomach the injustice.

Before passing K a can of Sprite, Eight takes a swig out of it to ensure it's safe for her to drink. If it were anyone but him taking up the role I was born to play, I would have smashed his teeth in by now. Alas, even someone as possessive as me knows there will eventually come a time I can't be at K's side twenty-four-seven. I'm just really fucking hoping it isn't any time soon.

I raise my glass of frothy pink shit into the air along with thirty or so of my brothers when Eight says, "To Trey and K. May they fuck like champion thoroughbreds, breed like rabbits, and get a less soundproof door so my brothers and I aren't squashed against each other every night while stroking one out."

He sprints to the other side of the living quarters during the last half of his sentence. It's for the best. If he were still standing across from me, he'd be dead by now. It took months for K to learn it's okay to moan when she comes. If Eight's rile causes her to backstep on that even a smidge, I'll fucking gut him where he stands.

"I'm joking, man. I swear on my ma's grave." He crosses his heart like a punk-ass moron before locking his eyes with K's wide pair. "You know I'd never let anyone hear you, K. You're like a sister to me. They'd be dead before they made it halfway down the corridor." The truth in his comment lowers my annoyance. Eight does treat K like his sister. It's why he's the only man I trust with her.

Noticing the loosening of my jaw, Nero says, "To Trey and K," before he clinks his glass against mine and throws down his drink. After swallowing Eight's idea of a cocktail, he screws up his face before pivoting toward the bar. "Anyone need a chaser after that rat shit drink?"

I swear nearly everyone surrounding me puts up their hand. Only K remains quiet, happily sipping on her can of Sprite as if it's a bottle of Dom Perignon. Real duchesses know crowns aren't just worn on your head, they're also embedded in your soul.

"What's the matter?" I lean in closer to K to press my lips to her ear, ensuring my words are only for her. "Is your stomach playing up again?"

K stops pushing her food around her plate to lock her eyes with mine. Although she doesn't say anything, I can see her answer in her expressive gaze. Her food is fine. She's just lost her appetite, which is very unlike her. Once I've proved her food is safe, she usually polishes off her plate before anyone else. She isn't upset I rushed her down the aisle within minutes of her saying yes, she's smiled at her ring too many times for that to be considered. It could be the whores. They're prancing around fully naked tonight with the hope they'll nab their own husband-to-be from Nikolai's crew. However, K is used to their antics. If they stay away from me, she barely gives them a once-over.

That can only mean one thing. One of the many men enjoying the feast the once-whores now-cooks made to celebrate our nuptials is pushing her buttons. Eight is seated on the opposite side of her, so I know it isn't him. It must be coming from someone across from her.

When my eyes stray to the three men directly across from K, Eight, and me, my jaw gains a tick. One of the men I've known as long as Nikolai. He'd never say a bad word about neither K nor me, but the other two are from Vladimir's debunked crew. They're older than my brothers and badly trained. Vladimir let them get away with far too much for way too long. Nikolai is in the process of shortening their leads, but I'm open to the idea of giving him a hand.

"Which one, K?" I only speak three words, but the violence roaring through me is heard in my voice. I'm about to maim for my girl, I'm about to kill, and I'm not the least bit deterred it's occurring on my wedding night. I told K I'd eradicate the world of the scum who hurt her, so events worth celebrating won't factor into it. "Which one hurt you?"

The obvious sticks out like a sore thumb when the man directly across from K mutters, "*Držte ústa zavřená.*" His narrowed eyes aren't on me. They're on K. That infuriates me more than anything he could possibly say. "*Nebo odstraním váš potěr pomocí ramínka.*"

When a chair scraping across polished floorboards sounds through my ears, I assume Eight is responding to the menacing gleam in West's eyes. He's forever on point when it comes to protecting K, so you can imagine my surprise when K makes it halfway across the table before my brain registers the fact she's moving.

West howls like a motherfucking baby when K stabs her fork into his hand resting on the table. Before his free hand can do any of the murderous thoughts in his eyes, Nero pinches his temple with the barrel of his gun while Mikhail squashes his knife against his jugular.

Their quick thinking ensures West's hand gets nowhere near K's face.

She's untouchable.

The same can't be said for West.

He's a dead man no matter what.

I've just got to decide if I should punish him or let my brothers take care of business on my behalf. If K weren't screaming in West's face, calling him a pig and the many other derogative words she's taught me in Czech the past nine months, I'd blow his brains out where he stands.

Regretfully, I have issues killing when my cock is knocking at the zipper of my jeans, begging to be released. K is upset, but the light inside of her is roaring brightly.

The Duchess is at her coronation service, ready for proceedings to begin.

Since I'm right there with her, I band my arm around K's waist, yank her away from West, then commence walking her down the corridor to my room.

K fights me all the way. She digs her nails into my arm, kicks out her legs, and tells me to let her go in more ways than one. Her fight loses some steam when the undeniable noise of a bullet cracking through a skull barrels down the corridor. Nero prefers quick, clean kills over gruesome ones. Eight and I give him hell about it all the time.

With K still struggling against me, I head for the bathroom instead of the bed I planned to subdue her on. The water that pumps out of the showerhead when I switch on the faucet is fucking freezing, however, it does little to weaken the hardness of my cock. I've never seen something so erotic in my life. K is half the size of West and a shit-ton shorter, yet she was up in his face, ruling her monarchy like a real-life motherfucking princess.

"You showed him, didn't you, K? You proved only real duchesses rule their kingdoms with dignified strength." I step deeper into the shower until the water flattening her golden locks removes the gunk on her face she only wears on special occasions. "Nuh-uh," I say on a growl when her hands shoot up to remove the smears of black mascara rolling down her cheeks. "I like you grubby. Messy. Real." I bite on her lips for each of my words, loving how the roughness of my nips switches the gleam in her eyes from murderous to needy in less than a nanosecond. "My duchess doesn't need gimmicks to be regal. She just needs to be strong." The fire in her eyes I've admired since day one shines brightly during the last half of my comment. Desire has surpassed her wish to kill. Just like me, there's only one addiction she's yet to overcome. Me.

It's proven without a doubt when her hands drop to the belt in my trousers. I'm not wearing jeans like the night I stole her virginity. With Nikolai willing to put on a monkey suit for Justine, I backed up his campaign with a pair of slacks and a button-up shirt. He can keep the vest and tie, though. Not even the marriage celebrant telling me it's tradition to get married while wearing a bowtie got me over the line. K likes my crudeness, so who am I to take it away from her?

"Slow down, Duchess. You're with kid." My fucking god, you have no idea how good that felt to say. I wasn't shitting my pants when I bought one of each pregnancy test at the drug store. I was doing everything in my power not to fall to my knees and pray like a soft cock.

Dok is a rare good one in this industry. He took care of K the best he could, but when certain issues extended outside his perimeter of knowledge, he hooked us up with another doctor—a female one. Although she was sympathetic for what K had been through, not all her news was good. I could fix K's self-worth and mental stability, but I couldn't do sweet fuck all for her insides. Dr. Laura was so convinced K would never get pregnant, she didn't rib us like Dok when K's contraceptive pill went untouched for months on end.

My focus returns to the present when the heat of K's cunt wraps around my cock's head. She's so impatient, she didn't bother removing her panties. She just pulled them to the side like a hungry little nymph.

"Nuh-uh," I say again when K wiggles in my arms, wordlessly requesting for me to loosen my grip so she can impale herself on my cock. "Tell me you want my cock first and for how fucking long you want it 'cause your every wish is my command, Duchess."

"*Prosím,*" she replies in her sexy little accent as her eyes rise to mine, forever aware my dick will never be inside of her unless she proves she's not close to tiptoeing toward the dark. "Two."

"Two what, K? Two minutes, two hours, two orgasms..." My words trail off when a flare darts through her eyes during my last two words. "Two orgasms it is." After securing a better grip on her soggy dress with one hand, the other weaves through her long locks. I then swivel my hips to get her tight, little cunt to open further for me. "Are you ready to see the fireworks, Duchess?"

Her chin barely lowers an inch when I thrust my hips upward. Her moan is felt all the way to my balls. That's how hearty it was, and I've barely given her the first four inches of my cock.

With Eight's rile playing on my mind, I seal my mouth over K's before pushing in another two inches. I can't understand a word she speaks around the exploration on my tongue, but I'm reasonably sure it's a Czech version of "Oh my god. More. Please. More."

"You're so fucking tight, Duchess. I can barely fit in," I say on a moan as I stuff in another three inches. "This is why your thighs are supposed to be drenched before I fuck you. My cock wants to hurt you."

"No," she begs when I twist to face the shower stall exit.

"We're not going anywhere. I just need you in a better position so you can take all of me." I carefully push back on her shoulders until the weight of the top half of her body is taken up by the tiled wall my cum squirted up almost a year ago today, and the lower half of her body is distributed on my cock.

"Ohh..." K moans as she begins to shudder.

"Yeah, that's what I thought. A much better angle for you to take all of me." I notch in the last bit of my cock before adding a roll to my hips. It doubles K's moans in an instant and has my chest swelling like the steamy air my lungs are sucking in is made from helium.

People say possessiveness kills relationships.

I say they're full of fucking shit.

Possessiveness shows love. If you don't feel threatened another man is going to swoop in and steal your woman, you don't love her. Point blank. I'd rather be a neurotic, possessive, jealous motherfucker than have K ever believe I don't care about her.

When I defend her, she sees how much I love her.

When I kill a man because he hurt her, it assures her she'll never be hurt again.

Just like when I promised her crown would be the first thing on my agenda once she was fully healed, I meant it.

She has my ring on her finger, my heart in her chest, and my kid in her gut. Next, she will have her throne.

I just need to work two orgasms out of her first.

THIRTY-ONE

TREY

"Doesn't count if I weren't invited," Nikolai grumbles under his breath when he takes in the black metal band wrapped around my wedding finger.

He's acting pissed K and I got married with only Eight as our witness, but I know that isn't the cause for the crinkle between his brows. He's as uneased about the news Justine was given last night as I am. The Popovs haven't handled a takeover bid since Alexei and Achim joined forces to pulverize my brain with a tire wrench, however, that doesn't mean we're sitting pretty. Even Rico agrees with me about this.

Although Nikolai's reputation is fierce, it has no authority on the other side of the country. The Gottles have had a stronghold on the East Coast for decades, not to mention the fact the town Nikolai is planning to take Justine is swarming with members of the Italian cartel. Even if he's simply visiting that side of the country, his stopover won't go unnoticed. It's as risky as fuck, and one of the reasons I'm here, hoping to talk him out of it.

After returning Nikolai's shoulder barge, I mutter, "Certainly feels fucking real." I scrub at my chin, exhausted. With West's interference still high in her thoughts, I had to work extra hard to keep my pledge to K last night. She climaxed twice as requested, but it took me fucking her to the point of exhaustion before she succumbed to the sensation she strived to ignore her first couple of weeks out of captivity. "We'll do it again when all the shit dies down." I stray my eyes to the flight plan Nikolai was in the process of approving before I interrupted him to ensure he's aware of what I'm referencing. "This is risky, Nikolai. I don't like it."

"I'm going in heavier than we did at Prague. Only a fool would consider acting now."

Although I agree with him, my gut still has a niggle I can't ignore. "The men in this industry aren't known for their smarts. We've fed off their ignorance the past four years."

"And we will continue to feed off their ignorance now. You're not the only man capable of cutting out the tongues of insolent men, Trey. I've had my fair share the past twelve months." He smirks like he's aware I removed West's tongue before feeding him to the pigs at Jim's this morning. He probably does know. There isn't much that gets past him.

With that in mind, I take a moment to conjure up another way to get through to him. If I were honest, I'd admit this isn't solely about Nikolai. We've traveled the globe the past six months ridding the world of the men stupid enough to bid on Justine. We had a common interest. Most of the men who bid on Justine placed down deposits on a pretty blonde sex slave who didn't speak a word of English. However, K traveled with us then. She was at my side as she has been the past nine months.

She can't do that this time around. Rumors are just that, rumors, but if any of the ones about the Vasilievs moving to the

East Coast after their failed bid are true, I can't risk taking K there. Achim is dead, the drenching I gave his head with my piss this morning assures me of this, but he wasn't my only enemy. The Dvořáks were high on my list as well. If they're aware of Achim's one-off siding with Alexei, K's safety could be in jeopardy.

I swore I'd protect K. I can't do that by dangling her in the face of danger.

Seemingly aware of my inner workings, Nikolai says, "I sent a crew to Hopeton last night. Their mission is to solely sniff out any rumblings of a takeover bid. Rico's contacts have been updated about our visit, and we've made it clear my visit has nothing to do with business." After moving to the other side of his office, he takes a seat in his big leather chair. "I'm not stepping into this lightly, Trey. I've put measures in place to ensure my queen..." he stops before correcting himself, "... *our* queens are safe. I'll slit the throats of a thousand men before I'd let anything happen to Justine. You have my word I'll do the same for K."

As air whizzes out of my nose, I slump into the chair across from him. I want to believe everything he's saying, and in all honesty, I do, but the niggle in my gut won't fucking quit. Something feels off.

Nikolai does his best to eradicate my worry. "I told Justine she'd have the world when she claimed her throne. I'm a man who keeps his word." When my brow pops up, he adds, "*Now* I keep my word. Things change." He returns my jeering smirk before he mumbles, "You know that better than anyone. We don't marry whores, Trey. We fuck them, spill our seed inside them, then go home... *alone.*"

"*Fucked* whores. We don't fuck them anymore." After working my jaw side to side to weaken its grip, I say, "Besides, K wasn't a whore." Usually, Nikolai's riles roll straight off my back. I must be feeling a bit temperamental today. "Don't fucking start, Nikolai. I'm taking enough shit from the guys. I'm not up for more crap."

My grumbled comment wipes the smirk right off his face. "What shit?"

I want to tell him my brothers are as wary of his plans as me, but since that'll most likely cause him more issues, I direct our conversation in another direction. Nikolai worked hard to gain the honor of his crew, I don't want him thinking he's lost it just when he needs it the most.

"Just the same shit we've been hearing the past twelve months. The whores are whispering in the men's ears, worried your relationship with Justine hasn't just seen their nail marks removed from your back."

He clues on to my remark rather quickly. "They are worried they're being replaced?" When I jerk up my chin, he growls out, "They're not going anywhere. Whores are a part of our industry. Justine understands this."

A chuckle rumbles in my chest. Justine may understand whores are a part of our lifestyle, but she is far from okay with it. There's only one time she's come to Clarks the past nine months. It was when we arrived back with K. If we didn't need someone to speak on K's behalf, I doubt she would have stepped foot in the place the past nine months.

"What?" Nikolai sneers, annoyed when he reads the truth from my eyes. "The main compound is off-limits because it's our home. I want Justine to feel comfortable here. But there are no limits at Clarks. If they want to fuck a whore an hour, so be it." After pushing away a sheet of paper with more aggression than needed, Nikolai lives up to his namesake. "If any of my men have an issue with my rules, they can bring it directly to me. But be warned, they won't be breathing by the time I'm done with them. Everything they have, *whores included*, is because of me. I also don't take kindly to assumptions that I'm being led by my cock."

I'm an ass for smiling, but I can't fucking help it. If anyone had any doubt Nikolai wasn't born for this lifestyle, they won't now. Hell is empty again because the devil is once again walking amongst the living.

Upon spotting my grin, Nikolai warns, "You won't be smiling when I slit your throat for goading me."

With a laugh, I hold my hands out in front of myself. "I wasn't goading, just testing a theory. Your reply pocketed me two freshly printed Benjamin Franklins."

"Testing a theory? Whose theory?"

"Rico. He's so convinced you're under the thumb, he bet two hundred dollars that you'd have the whores extradited to Russia before sundown." I wish I were lying, but I'm not. I bumped into Rico on my way to Nikolai's office. He was peering around the parlor, lost as fuck on where all the whores had gone. Vladimir was a pompous prick who preferred to display women as trophies instead of actual accomplishments. "He seems to have forgotten he's the only one bedding a kitten too timid for our way of life."

My comment brings Nikolai's attitude down a notch. *Just.* "Speaking of playthings, where's Rico? I thought he and Blaire were traveling back to Ravenshoe this morning."

"They are." Rico said that exact thing to me only minutes ago. "He just had some old memories he wanted to recreate before his flight." I hit him with a frisky wink to ensure he gets the gist of what I'm saying. Rico wasn't on the hunt for a whore when I bumped into him. He needed a strip of condoms. Something about party balloon tricks? Fucked if I know. He didn't stick around for an interrogation when I handed him a three-strip of rubbers from my wallet.

After shaking his head to rid it of the horrid image I forced in there, Nikolai gets back to business. "Have the men traveling with Justine and me ready to move by this evening. I want to touch down in Hopeton before sun-up because every man knows a devil has never seen the sun rise."

Although wary he's still moving forward with his plans, his comment reveals he isn't taking this lightheartedly. My first thought, when told of his plans, was for him to move in the darkness of the night. Even a soft cock like Achim knew about the benefits of a 3:00 a.m. raid.

"Who do you want at the helm while we're gone? Zyron has shown great improvement since Andros gifted him to us. He still has a long way to go, but it might smarten him up a little." Zoran is the nephew of Andros Smirnov, the richest man in Russia. He's rich because he has sanctions like the Popovs and the Yurys protecting his assets. If he had entrusted anyone else, he would have been broke by now.

Nikolai shakes his head. "Zyron is a good kid, but he doesn't have the balls needed for our line of work."

I twist my lips, wordlessly agreeing with him. Zyron can kill, but only if he has no other option. Nikolai's crew works on a kill-now-ask-questions-later motto.

I arch a brow, telling Nikolai to get the fuck out of my head when he says, "I need a man who will kill without thought. One who'll never second-guess any decisions I make. I need a man as ruthless and as brutal as me, while also understanding my greatest asset has blood running through her veins, not white powder, lead, or liquid gold." He locks his eyes with mine. They're all sentimental and shit. "I need you to cover me while I'm gone, Trey, to keep our ship on course."

Although pleased as fuck he still considers me his equal, notoriety doesn't count in this industry. My family's legacy became as worthless as a piece of paper when Cole killed our father. He broke the rules we lived by and dishonored a sanction once worth millions of dollars. Could I have turned it around when Nikolai found me? Possibly. But at the time, I didn't have the strength to do that. When you break the rules in this industry, you pay the highest price. Cole's was his life. Mine was knowing I'll forever be number two.

"I can't. That's not allowed." I cock my head and arch a brow. "I'm British, not Russian."

Nikolai laughs as if he's not precariously placing a lifetime of injustices on the line for me. "I'm well aware of your heritage. It's one of the reasons I made you my number two guy."

I straighten my shirt, all pompous-like. "And here I was thinking it was because of my roguishly handsome face."

It isn't the time for jokes, however, I'm lost for a better reply. If shit hits the fan as I'm anticipating, this won't just place Nikolai's life on the line. It'll put his legacy in my hands. I did a shit job with my family name, so I have no fucking clue why Nikolai is being so trusting.

I get an inkling of an idea when Nikolai says matter-of-factly, "I need someone I can trust. We're still on unsolid ground since Alexei's death. If we're blindsided by a second takeover bid, I need someone at the helm who'll maintain control. I trust that man is you, Trey."

His words floor me. Jaw unhinged, air-free lungs, floored. He's my brother, my best friend, but still, this is a fucking shock. Just like K, Nikolai doesn't trust anyone, so this isn't only unexpected, it's making me feel all teary-eyed and shit. Even my pulse is thudding in my ears. It's nothing like the thump it hears when K is around but enough to have me convinced we have some sort of bromance forming.

After rehinging my jaw, I ask, "Are you sure this is what you want, Nikolai?"

He makes light of the shock in my tone. "It's only for a few days. I'm certain even a *vyperdusch* like you won't fuck things up that quickly."

"Ah, you make my heart tingle with your sweet words." My mouth inches into a smile when he flings his letter opener to my side of his office. The fucker is blunt, yet it still manages to nick me.

Smirking about his ominous jab, he stands to his feet. "Offer for Rico to travel with Justine and me but warn him I'm traveling heavy." His smirk shifts to a genuine smile when he growls out, "His little kitty might faint when she sees how things truly operate in our industry." When I give him a look as if to say *and Justine won't?* he adds, "My *ahren* was born to lead. She doesn't kneel for anyone."

With his mind elsewhere, he leaves me to finalize his plans. After gesturing for K to join me and instructing Eight to get the men ready, that's precisely what I do for the next three hours. I organize for a dozen men to go over Justine's childhood home with a fine-toothed comb, organize a heavy presence at the private airstrips Nikolai's jet will land and depart from, then forward my schedules to Roman. He'll give them a once-over to ensure I haven't missed anything while I take K to her first appointment with Dr. Laura. Because we still want to keep Clarks' location on the down-low, we'll go to her office in town instead of her coming to us like she did at Dok's request months ago.

"Jesus Christ," I mumble under my breath when I crank open the passenger side door of my car for K. I dumped Lester and West at Jim's this morning, but my car still reeks of death and desecration.

After slipping in behind the steering wheel, I roll down the window, then fire up the engine. K's eyes shoot to mine when I say, "West must have shit himself when you pierced your fork through his hand. Serves the fucker right. If he didn't want to die, he shouldn't have threatened a momma bear with her cub." I smirk at K's shocked expression. It lowers my anger by a smidge. "That's what he did, wasn't it? He threatened our baby?"

When K dips her chin, I keep my cool—barely. I wring the steering wheel with my hands instead of pounding it with my fists like I really want to.

"How?" K could say more, but she doesn't need to. Her eyes speak the words she's yet to learn.

I hit the steering wheel with a handful of firm squeezes before sharing a story I've never told before. "Your eyes had the same fighting gleam my mom's had when they dragged Cole away from her. She didn't want my father to pick her. She wanted him to save Cole." I lick my dry lips before continuing, "His decision drove her mad. She killed herself five months later. Our sister perished right along with her."

When shock crosses K's features, I explain myself better. "She didn't kill her daughter. She was pregnant when they tried to take her. It's why my father wouldn't let her go. He thought Cole would fare better than them." My sigh exposes how that turned out. Just like K, our baby is the only direct descendant to my blood line. It doesn't mean I ever want to be in the position my father was placed in, though. "Don't ever make me pick, Duchess. I never want to be in that situation. If you put me through that, I'll have to hurt you. I promise I wouldn't do that, so don't force me to break my promise."

Fear is usually the first thing K expresses when threatened with pain. Today is pride. She knows I won't physically harm her.

I'm referencing the hurt I'll put her through when I pick her over our baby.

For six years, her feelings always came last. That shit won't fly with me. Her needs come before anyone's, including those who share my blood.

K stops fiddling with the flimsy paper gown she's wearing when I flatten my palms on each side of her teeny tiny thighs. "You good?" It takes me placing my hand under her chin for her eyes to lock with mine. "You've got nothing to worry about. I won't let anyone hurt you. You know that, right?" My heart thumps in my ears when she nods without the slightest pause for consideration. "Then what's got you so worked up? You weren't this jittery last night when you married a madman."

With her lips itching into a smile, her eyes stray to our right. When I follow the direction of her gaze, my heart beats out a funky tune. There's a heap of medical equipment you'd expect at any gynecologist's office, but a box of condoms is unexpected—especially since it's sitting behind a dildo-looking instrument.

"What the fuck is that?"

Dr. Laura's eyes pop up from the report she's compiling on K. When she notices the direction of my gawk, her throat works hard to swallow. "That's an internal ultrasound wand."

"*Internal?* As in, it goes inside of her." I very ungentlemanly-like gesture what I mean with my hands. It whitens K's gills even more.

When Dr. Laura nods, I shake my head. "Nope. Nuh-uh. Not happening." I nudge my head to the coat rack holding K's clothing. "Get dressed, K. We're heading out."

Dr. Laura jumps up from her desk as quickly as K leaps off the fancy bed with stirrups tucked under the sides. "If my dates are correct, we won't need the internal wand." Both K and I freeze like statues when she garbles out, "From what I felt during my examination of your stomach, I'm guessing you're around four or five months along."

"Months?" I double-check, certain I heard her wrong. My pulse is thudding in my ears, so poor hearing can be excused, and I'm not going to mention the fact K's stomach is as flat as a tack. There's no way she's hiding any kid in there, much less one that'll grow to my size.

Dr. Laura nods again. "Months." She shifts on her feet to face K. "Do you remember the scan we did to check your ovaries and uterus?" She waits for K to nod before adding, "That's all we need to do. If you're as far along as I'm thinking, the internal wand won't be needed."

When K's eyes lift to mine, I shrug. "It's up to you, Duchess. It's your body."

After a few seconds of deliberation, she returns to the bed and lays down as per Dr. Laura's instructions. Once she has a tube of warm lubricant in her hand, Dr. Laura opens the front of K's hospital gown so she can squirt the liquid onto her stomach. Her aim is a little lower this time around than the examination she did months ago.

"If we can see the baby's gender, do you want to know what it is?" Dr. Laura asks as her eyes bounce between K and me. She smiles when we nod at the same time.

It's fucked I even need to say this, but I'm kind of hoping it's a girl. If she's small and petite like her mother, she'll be less likely to damage K's insides more than they already are. She's been hurt enough. I don't want her hurt more.

After clicking on the machine next to the bed for a good three or so minutes, Dr. Laura shifts her eyes to mine. They appear wiser than her thirty-five years. "I was right. She's just shy of five months."

"She? We're having a girl?"

I both crap my pants and mentally give myself a pat on the back when Dr. Laura's chin careens toward her chest. "Due on the last day of November." Three black and white printouts shoot out of the machine K and I were staring at only minutes ago before she hands them to K. "We will need to organize a more in-depth ultrasound in the coming weeks, but I'm happy with how she's progressing. Her length is above average, and she weighs approximately half a pound." After standing to her feet, she wipes the gunk off K's stomach. "Do you have any questions?"

With K too in awe of the printout she's holding, Dr. Laura drifts her eyes to me. Tiny creases wrinkle around her eyes when I wordlessly request for her to give us a minute. She's not squinting, she's smiling about me putting K's well-being first. K is still here, in the light, but she's a little unbalanced.

"I'll meet you in the reception area once you're ready." Dr. Laura squeezes K's hand in support before she exits her office.

I wait for her door to click shut before joining K near the monitor still displaying the outline of our daughter's face. "You good?" It takes her longer to nod this time around than it did earlier. "She won't be hurt, K. Not only will I protect her, so will you." When the light in her eyes dims a little from my comment, I add, "And she'll have Nikolai, Eight, and Nero. Fuck, she'll probably even have Mikhail wrapped around her little finger." I push back hair that smells like rain even in the middle of a drought before returning the tilt her chin should never be without. "She'll never be alone. I promise you that."

Most people believe K's life was screwed over after our fuck in the pantry. In reality, it was years before that. Achim may not have raped her until after she gave her virginity to me, but his mind-fucks started long before that. He knew she had no one to turn to, and he milked it for all it was worth.

Just the thought of what he put her through has me replotting ideas I've been working on the past few months. They'll end with more than the streets of Mikulov being littered with the bodies of the Dvořáks' men.

A new monarch will be crowned.

THIRTY-TWO

TREY

Six days later...

"Anything yet?"

When Eight shakes his head, I tug off my jacket and place it over K's slumbering form. She's resting on the sofa in Nikolai's office. Our early rising is noticeable on her face, but I'm wary that isn't the sole reason for her frozen state. She's tiptoeing toward the dark, as haunted by her past as I am when news broke that Nikolai and Justine are missing.

If I were to believe any of the reports circulating throughout morning news broadcasts today, Nikolai and several members of his crew were caught unaware by a Petretti raid last night. Dimitri Petretti, now leader of the recently reformed Italian cartel, was found amongst the carnage. He was surrounded by numerous deceased members of the Popov crew and sporting a set of nasty bullet wounds.

Although the rivalry between the Popovs and Petrettis is well-known, I'm still struggling to comprehend what the fuck happened. Dimitri helped Nikolai last year. If it weren't for him, Nikolai would have never located the warehouse Vladimir took Justine to in time. Dimitri's assistance netted him a pardon from Nikolai. That's practically a golden ticket in this industry, so why would Dimitri go against Nikolai now? It doesn't make any sense.

"Move." Once Eight shifts out of Nikolai's seat, I seize control of a computer that could take down half the world's mafia entities with one strike if it were placed into the wrong hands. While I seek missing pieces of the puzzle, I nudge my head to the foyer of the P's. "Get word to the Yurys about a possible takeover bid. Go light with details but advise assistance may be required." The Yurys are a Russian-based entity the Popovs were founded from when Anatoly Popov moved stateside many moons ago.

"If they want more details?" Eight asks, uneased I'm calling in backup only hours after Nikolai failed to check in. I'm not jumping the gun. I'm being prepared. Even with Nikolai's first five days on the East Coast occurring without incident, my gut hasn't quit niggling. It's only done that twice before—when my father arrived at Mikulov earlier than anticipated and when I held my gun at K's stomach and fired—the same stomach now holding our daughter. My past could be fucking with my head, but I'd rather be cautious than be seen as a fool.

I lift and lock my eyes with Eight's. "Tell them they'll have to come through me."

I wait for him to jerk up his chin before rummaging through the information he unearthed between advising me at two this morning about Nikolai failing to check in after having dinner with Rico and now, which is almost twenty-three hours later. The evidence is shit at best. It has murky FBI prints all over it, and there may even be a handful of CIA smudges. I don't care how much shit this gets me in, those rumors about the CIA colluding with members of the cartel are true. They don't care who they have to work with to get their man. Dimitri's sister, Ophelia, learned that the hard way two years ago.

Two hours into sorting through the steaming pile of shit the Bureau logged into their mainframe earlier today, K suddenly jack-knifes into a half-seated position. Although Dr. Laura proved without a doubt she's five months along, you wouldn't know it from the flatness of her stomach. My shirt she's wearing as a dress falls straight to her thighs when she stands to her feet.

After snatching up a printout off Nikolai's desk, she makes a beeline for the door. "Let her go," I say to Nero when he blocks her exit with his big, brooding frame. He thinks she's stuck in the throes of horrifying blackness. I know that isn't close to the truth. She's too strong for that. Too fucking brave. She hasn't been quiet all day because she's tempted by the dark. She's seeking answers in the only way she knows. With silence.

After logging out of Nikolai's computer to ensure his secrets remain that—secret—I follow K's trek through the Popov mansion. To anyone unable to see the fire of life in her eyes, they'd think she's snooping. Once again, I know that isn't true. She's hunting. For what? I have no fucking clue, but I trust her enough to know she wouldn't waste my time unless she thought it was important.

"You don't want to go in that room, K," I warn her when her hand circles the doorknob of Vladimir's private abode a few minutes later.

Nikolai all but banished Vladimir's name from the Popov compound after his death, but his room remains untouched. I don't know why. It could be a reminder of how far Nikolai has come or the fact even with Vladimir having many whores, this room also belonged to Nikolai's mother. Her perfume bottle still sits on the top of a stack of drawers K stops in front of a few seconds later.

"That's Nikolai's mother, Oskana," I tell K when she lifts a photo off the bedside table. I don't need to tell her the identity of the man photographed with Oskana. She knows all too well who that piece of shit is.

My brows stitch when K runs her thumb over Vladimir's face. It isn't a nurturing gesture, she's more clearing away the dust coating the glass than anything, but the expression on her face is concerning.

"What is it, K?"

Frustration slicks her skin with sweat when she struggles to find the correct wording to explain what angle she's working. She has no reason to fret. Even with a massive language barrier parting us, she forever finds a way to communicate with me.

After tracing her finger across Vladimir's eyes, she does the same thing to Oskana and then to Dimitri's driver's license printout. My brows draw close together when she does the same movements again, except this time, she does my eyes, her eyes, then runs her finger over her nonexistent baby bump.

I'm still fucking lost to where she's trying to take me, but I give it a shot to understand what she's saying. "Eyes? Is this about their eyes?"

K's face lights up like a motherfucking Christmas tree before she nods. After tapping the photo frame she's holding two times to return my attention back to Vladimir—*I lose focus anytime her face lights up*—she highlights Vladimir and Oskana's eyes again before saying in a thick accent, "No devil." After a quick swallow, she drops her eyes to Dimitri's license printout. "Nikolai."

"That's not Nikolai. That's Dimitri. They look similar, but

they're not close to being related..." My words trail off when the truth smacks into me. Well, I assume it's the truth. It is farfetched, but if K's hunch is correct, and Nikolai and Dimitri are somehow related, this could be more than a turf war. It could be a takeover bid.

"You're so fucking smart, K," I mutter over her lips before kissing her hard on the mouth. Eight, Nero, and I spent hours looking at this with the wrong set of eyes. Now I have a new direction to focus my attention on.

"Get out," I demand when I re-enter Nikolai's office with K on my heel. When the group of six men ignore my direct order, I growl out, "If I'm forced to repeat myself, you'll be buried alongside the brothers we lost last night." My brow cocks when a bottom-dweller wannabe grips K's elbow to remove her from the room along with him and five of his brothers. "You better get your hands off her before I remove them with my knife."

The acne-faced punk has bigger balls than I realized. "If this is a business matter, she has no right to be here. Women have no place in this industry, *especially* one like her."

As my hand slips behind my back, I lock my eyes with K's. "K..." One letter and she slants her chin enough her crown isn't close to toppling, but her face won't be hit with any of the blood of fuckface's brain when I lodge a bullet between his eyes.

As Eight drags the unnamed foot soldier out of Nikolai's office by the scruff of his blood-soaked collar, grumbling about how he's lucky his death was quick, I demand K's eyes to mine.

It takes them longer to float up from the floor than I'm happy about, but I'd rather a delay than no response at all. "I didn't have a choice. War or not, I couldn't allow him to speak to you like that. You are worth more than any apology he could have *ever* given you. Do you understand? I'd take a thousand bullets before I'd ever let anyone speak to you like that." Nothing I can say will erase the guilt I feel knowing I fired at her all those years ago. Just like nothing I can say will undo the damage Achim and Vladimir did to her, but that doesn't mean I can't try to show her she's worthy.

I gave up seven years ago. I let Cole and Achim get the better of me. I'm not doing that this time around. This isn't my kingdom, but K is my woman, and she's more valuable than any castle.

"Come here." The funky beat of my heart rises to my ears when K immediately jumps to my command. I'm not a chauvinist pig who wants his wife to be a submissive doormat, I'm relishing the way her scent can settle the storm brewing in my gut in an instant. We're in the middle of a fucking war, yet one sniff of her hair keeps my head in the present instead of my fucked-up past.

After propping K's backside onto Nikolai's desk next to his computer and removing a handful of blood droplets from her cheeks her hair missed, I ask, "You good?"

Only once the fire in her eyes matches the bob of her head do I commence working out if her theory has any credit. For Nikolai's sake, I'm hoping his blue eyes are a recessive gene, but I'd be lying if I said part of me isn't hoping K's theory also holds merit. Women in this industry are seen as Sir Now-Brainless said—they have no authority or respect whatsoever.

However, if K is right, her assistance today gives credit to my belief that this industry needs to change. Not just for the sake of our daughter, but for the kid in Justine's gut as well. Nikolai commenced making adjustments the instant Justine surprised him with news of their pregnancy on the way to Hopeton, and I've backed him all the way, except now, I'm drafting a new set of rules.

Nikolai won't be required to follow them, but the insolent men who believe my family's legacy ended when Cole killed our father won't have a choice. If they want to play on my field, they must abide by my rules.

I don't see that being an easy feat. They thought my father's rulings were harsh. They'll learn otherwise when the new ruler of their kingdom is crowned. He has years of injustices to correct. That'll take more than a bloodbath.

Luckily, I know more than a few men willing to get bloody with me.

THIRTY-THREE

I block out the groans of a man being tortured pumping out of the computer monitor's speakers with my hand before saying, "Again. Ram it down his throat like it's your cock, Eight, 'cause I swear to god, if he doesn't do what I'm asking this time around, I'm gonna order you to blow a load of lead down his fucking throat."

As Eight follows my instruction to a T, I stray my eyes to K. She's resting on Nikolai's couch—again. Her third night in a row. She's not eating enough, sleeping enough, and the past three nights have been the longest I've gone without her quivering beneath me for months. I'm fucking pissed, but more than anything, I'm over disrespectful fuckfaces who think it's a free-for-all since neither Nikolai, Rico, nor Justine have been sighted the past three days. Not even Dimitri knows where they are, and he was there when Nikolai's crew was blindsided by an unknown crew.

In case you're wondering, K's theory stacked up. Vladimir had a ton of kids, but not one of them was born with icy blue eyes.

Nikolai's eyes are icy blue. They're identical to Dimitri's in every way. Even their hair coloring is a match. As is their DNA.

My eyes snap back to the monitor when a muffled, "Seven," sounds through the speakers.

Aware the Popovs' family lawyer won't be able to speak with a gun stuffed down his throat, Eight inches it back out.

"Seven…" I hit the old geezer with a threatening look, warning him what will happen if he denies my request again. He'll be a dead man, and Eight will take his time driving him to hell. He's a sadistic little fuck who likes messing with his victim's psyche as much as he loves fucking eight whores at once.

Mr. Schluter succumbs to peer pressure rather quickly this time around. He wouldn't do that unless he believed Nikolai is dead. No one double-crosses a Popov and survives. Not even me. "Seven, three, two, nine, A for apple, C for Charlie, a comma followed by an exclamation point, then the letter J."

If I needed any more proof Nikolai has Petretti blood running through his veins, I don't once I place in the final letter Mr. Schluter deciphered to me. The once-locked file on Nikolai's computer doesn't just contain the results of a paternity test Nikolai ordered over a decade ago, it has a court transcript from when Nikolai went against Vladimir and lost. Nikolai was only sixteen at the time. The shit he accused Vladimir of doing to him isn't just sick, it slots in the final piece of the puzzle. I'm shocked Nikolai held out as long as he did. I get this industry has rules we must abide by, but fuck, it would have taken him a ton of willpower not to slit Vladimir's throat when he caught him unaware not long after his sixteenth birthday. I don't know if I would have had the same gall, and my father wasn't a monster like Vladimir.

After swishing my tongue around my mouth to loosen up its dryness, I search the file for the document responsible for me breaking Nikolai's trust. I find it a few minutes later at the very bottom of the screen—Nikolai's will.

I won't ever consider the prospect that Nikolai is dead, and I'll never stop searching for him, but I need to know who his assets will be distributed to if the coroner believes the pool of blood found in Rico's apartment is enough to rule Nikolai's disappearance as a homicide.

In this fucked-up world, even with K having my ring on her finger, my kid in her gut, and my last name, she is still owned by Nikolai.

I refuse to accept that. I'd rather kill K with my own hands than ever see her back in the industry that stole the light from her eyes. Then I'd turn my gun on myself. That's how far I'll go to protect her, so hacking into Nikolai's private file should barely create a rippling of guilt, right?

Fucking wrong.

My guilt is horrendous, even more so when I notice Nikolai awarded me an equal share of his assets along with Rico in the event Justine is incapable of accepting the terms of his will.

Although I could own fifty percent of K, it isn't enough.

She's mine wholeheartedly.

I'm not willing to risk that for anything.

"I need you to execute a sale transfer receipt..." When the pin-dick weasel on the monitor in front of me immediately commences shaking his head, I talk faster. "I wasn't asking. I'm telling you what you're doing. You will execute a sale of an asset like you did many times for Vladimir before his long-winded demise."

While Eight works Mr. Schluter's face over with the butt of his gun, I log out of the file and into my personal banking app. Eight's beatdown splits open the old geezer's right brow, but not enough he can't see what he's doing.

Once I've transferred the $1.2 million-dollar payment men in my industry believe Nikolai paid for K from my account into Nikolai's personal account, I pull up the asset transfer software the Popovs use for all sales. My already woozy head gets thrust into a black void of my past when the transfer receipt number is eerily similar to the number Achim used when he gifted K to Vladimir. If you switched out the last two digits, it would be the same number I punched into the lock of K's cell.

With my head teetering between the past and present, I fill in the document as if it was done by Nikolai last month before forwarding it to Mr. Schluter's law firm's email address. "Execute it." When he shakes his head, I grip the screen of Nikolai's computer like it's Mr. Schluter's scrawny neck and scream, "Execute it... or I'll execute you! Five... Four... Three... Two..."

I suck in my first breath in what feels like days when the whoosh of an email landing into my inbox sounds through my ears. It's the executed sales document that proves without a doubt that I purchased K from Nikolai weeks before he disappeared.

After slouching low in my chair, I lock my eyes with Eight's through the monitor. "Let him go."

"You sure?" He drags his teeth over the piercing in the corner of his lower lip to hide his smile. "This fucker made you count. I know that's not your strong point."

I'm about to hit Eight with a stern finger point, but before I can, Nero darts into Nikolai's office, out of breath and red-faced. "They found them... her... on the freeway. In Vegas."

While he takes a moment to catch his breath, I drop my eyes to Eight. "Get back here now." My last word has barely left my mouth when he strikes Mr. Schluter across the temple, knocking him out before our connection is lost.

After joining Nero in the doorway, I ask, "Who was found?"

"Justine. Courier spotted her coming back from a run. She's pretty nicked up—"

"But alive." *Thank fuck.*

Nero bounces on my shoulder like he did when Eight announced K and I had married. "Yep! Now we just need her to lead us to Nikolai."

"How far out is she?"

Nero checks his wrist like he's a soft cock who wears a watch. "Guess would be ten, fifteen minutes. She was a fair way out. Nothing much out there but sticks and canyons."

After calculating how long it will take Eight to get from the Schluter & Fletcher Law Firm to here, I tell Nero to wake Justine's brother before sending word to the men at Clarks to suit up. If Justine is alone, we'll need to go in heavy, as there's no way Nikolai would have let Justine leave his side unless it was vital. He's as protective of her as I am K.

I grab Nero's elbow before he hightails it out of Nikolai's office. "Keep things simple with Maddox. Until we know whose team he's on, treat him as you would Dimitri. He didn't have a Petretti visiting him every month in prison for no reason."

Nero jerks up his chin before he races for the stairwell that leads to the sleeping quarters. I wait for him to disappear down the landing before shifting on my feet to face K. She's awake and peering at me through scrunched brows. She knows what I'm going to say before my head even formulates how to say it.

"I need you to go with Eight for a couple of days." She immediately commences shaking her head. "I wasn't asking, Duchess. It's not safe for you here right now. I shouldn't have kept you here as long as I have."

Guilt for snooping into Nikolai's private life is partly responsible for my decision, but I also know this is the right thing to do. Whether this is a turf war or a takeover bid, blood is about to be shed. Justine was found near Vegas. That means the carnage will occur here. That makes it unsafe for both K and our baby.

Just as I reach the sofa K is sitting on, still shaking her head, a pair of headlights beam into Nikolai's office from outside. Since most classic cars have the old retro curved design instead of the modern square shape of Nikolai's armored fleet, I scoop K into my arms. Although it would be safer for my nuts to carry her like a groom does a bride, I'd rather my family jewels be damaged with a knee than steal K's chance to stand up for herself. She's only just learned how to do that, so I'll avoid having it lost for anything.

As I walk K through P's, she kicks and thrashes against me like she did last week when I dragged her away from West, but this fight comes with a handful of tears and heavily-accented begs. "No. Trey. Please. I stay. We stay."

When Eight spots K's tear-stained face a second after we burst through the back entrance of P's, he curses into the humid night air before he races around to the passenger side of his car to open the door for me. "Where do you want me to take her?"

"The last place Nikolai's enemies would think to look," I grunt through the brutal whacks of K's fists.

Her nails drag down my back when I peel her off me to place her into Eight's car. "No, Trey, *prosmi*."

It fucking guts me when her tears dampen my beard when I lean across her body to latch her seat belt into place. The only reason I continue with my mission is because I'd rather my beard absorb the saltiness of her tears than be tinged with her blood.

After yanking on the seat belt hard enough to convince it it's been through an accident, I press my mouth to K's. For the first time in almost nine months, her lips fail to part at the request of my lashing tongue. She's angry. Rightfully so. I told her she'd never have to leave my side if she didn't want to.

I'm not upholding my promise.

But what she doesn't realize is that I have to break one promise to keep another, and it comes before any promises I've made—to keep her safe no matter what.

I suck in a hearty whiff of her hair before pressing my lips to the shell of her ear. "Go into the dark, Duchess. I'll bring you back out when it's safe."

In an instant, she stiffens like a plank. She's not tiptoeing into the blackness she once thought was her safety net, she's being unwillingly swamped by it. I tugged on her seat belt too forcefully for it to loosen its grip when she attempts to follow my departure from Eight's car, then I leave her utterly defenseless to the nightmares of her past when I slam Eight's car door shut a mere second after he slides in behind the steering wheel.

She's still with me when Eight commences driving away, but I lose her to the dark long before her eyes are ripped from my visual. She's gone, wholly and without constraint, once again lost to a miserably bleak existence, and I'm one teeny tiny step behind her.

I stole my duchess's crown to hand it to another woman. If that doesn't expose how badly I'm being snowballed by my past, nothing will.

THIRTY-FOUR

KRISTINA

Nine months ago, Trey pulled me out of the blackness. He made me feel safe and protected, cared for and cherished.

Now, I'm not feeling any of those things.

I feel alone, hollow, and empty.

So very, very empty.

It's an emptiness that grows to a point it may never be filled when Eight pulls his car down a long and windy road. The nightmares of my life began long before I arrived here, but this place made them ten times worse. I was beaten here. Starved and left for dead. I had my back whipped, my dignity stolen, and my self-worth squashed to within an inch of recognition.

This compound doesn't feature in my nightmares. It *is* my nightmare and the last place I'd ever feel safe.

As Eight's car comes to a stop at the front of a set of stairs I raced up in fear for my life twelve months ago, his dilated-with-worry eyes stray to mine. "No one will think to look for you here, K. You'll be safe here."

Safe from who? I want to ask him.

My nightmares?

The demons of my past?

Me.

I'm not safe here.

Not mentally anyway.

This place makes me so sad, I forget what happiness feels like. That's more damaging than any amount of torture could be, and it has me emerging into the dark as Trey suggested mere minutes ago.

The light makes things look easy.

The dark proves you have to work for everything you want.

I think they're both as evil as the other.

THIRTY-FIVE

I stop seeking Eight's taillights in the dark when Nero calls my name. When he's awarded the attention of my hooded gaze, he nudges his head in the direction of the sleeping quarters. "She's here." While striving to ignore the burn of K's nails down my back, I follow his climb up the stairwell. "The courier said she's pretty incoherent. I was going to call in a physician but wanted to get your thoughts first. Usually, Dok handled this type of stuff." His comment gives credit to my decision to send K away. Dok was the first causality positively identified by the FBI. He died on the operating table after enduring three bullet wounds to the chest.

When we reach the landing, I stray my eyes to a door two spots down while digging my wallet out of my pocket. "Request for Dr. Laura to do a house call. Tell her it's for me."

"All right." Nero jerks up his chin before he finds a quiet spot to take his call. With most of P's quarters occupied by Vladimir's old crew, things got rowdy days ago. Anyone would swear they were celebrating instead of commiserating. If I find out that is the case, Nikolai's crew will face a second slaughtering within hours of him being found.

After shaking off the funk coating my skin with sweat, I tap on the door of Nikolai's childhood room before pushing down on the handle. I'm not surprised to find Maddox standing to the left of the couch Justine is resting on. His presence has been noticeable the past three days even with him barely speaking a peep. His silence might have more to do with the fact he's failed to tell me why he's searching for his sister on this side of the country instead of the side she went missing from than an uncomfortableness for this life-style. He only got out of lockup a week ago, yet he's already knee-deep in shit. Not even a low-ranked bottom-feeder wannabee gets himself in that much trouble in a week.

"Has she said anything?"

After taking in Justine's sun-hardened skin and blood-tinged hair, Maddox shakes his head.

"Where's the blood coming from?"

Not speaking a word, Maddox pulls back a chunk of Justine's hair to reveal a large bump in the back of her head. Breathing out of my nose with the hope it will keep my head in the present, I crouch down in front of Justine to check her pulse. Her skin is as hot as fuck to touch, but her pulse is robust.

When Maddox snags a water bottle off the table next to him, Mikhail's advice from nine months ago smacks back into me. "Don't give her any water. You could fuck her over more. Nero is organizing a doctor to come check on her. She'll be here in a few..." My words trail off when Justine groans. When it's closely followed by a giggle, I crank my neck to Maddox. "Does she generally laugh in her sleep?"

"I wish." He gives his jaw a good workover before adding, "I haven't heard her giggle like that since she got them." During the 'them' part of his comment, he nudges his head to the scars Nikolai's slowly convincing Justine to be proud of. They're bite marks from when she was mauled by a dog on the Petretti compound.

When Justine rolls over with a groan, I scoot closer to her. "Justine..." Her brows furrow as she stuffs a pillow between her legs. K has done something similar the past three days, but I think it has more to do with Nikolai's hard couch than our daughter's demand for space. "Justine, can you open your eyes for me?" I get another groan, but her eyes remain shut. "Justine..." My lips tug into a smirk when her eyes slowly flutter open this time around. "Hey."

I give her a couple of seconds to scan my face. When recognition flares through her eyes, I help her to sit up. "W-w-what happened?" Anyone would think she'd drunk a gallon of whiskey for how slurred her words are.

Concern for his sister is seen all over Maddox's face when he jumps into our conversation. "You don't remember?" His worry lowers my suspicions by a smidge. Not a lot, but enough to realize he isn't Justine's enemy. Nikolai, on the other hand, I'll save my verdict for a more appropriate time.

When Justine shakes her head, her eyes bulge out of her head as her throat works through a hard swallow. I'm about to catch her vomit in my hands, but Maddox saves the day by shoving a bucket between us.

While Justine brings up some funky-smelling puke, Maddox asks me, "Where was she found again?"

I nudge my head to the left like the freeway can be seen from here. "By Interstate 95. One of our couriers thought he was seeing things."

After scrubbing the back of her hand over her vomit-smeared lips, Justine garbles out, "Hold on. I was found along a highway?"

I nod. "You were a few miles from the private airstrip you used last week. We figured that was the location Nikolai told you to use in case of an emergency."

My reply seems to confuse her more. "Why was I on Interstate 95? Blaire and Rico's apartment is miles from there."

Shock is heard in my tone when I ask, "Blaire and Rico? What do they have to do with anything?"

Justine peers at me as if I'm slow. "We had dinner with them last night. You know this because Nikolai called you on our way."

Before a single word can leave my lips, Maddox slots his ass into the spot next to Justine, then gathers her hands in his. "You had dinner with Rico and Blaire three nights ago. You've been missing ever since." He waits for her to absorb that truth before hitting her with another. "You're also in Vegas. Trey meant Interstate 95 on the California border, not the one in Florida."

"That can't be true." Her wide and terrified eyes bounce between ours. "You don't just lose three days of your life." While straying her eyes over the room, she asks, "Where's Nikolai? He'll prove we were with Rico and Blaire last night." When her hunt fails to find the man we've been searching for the past three days, she drops her eyes to the bucket of vomit. "That's the rosemary chicken Blaire prepared for us. She used herbs that would help my queasy stomach..." Her words are stolen by the worry clutching her throat. With her breaths labored, she raises the hem of her shirt to peer down at her stomach. Although she's not as far along as K, her stomach is more curved. Usually, most people would see that as a good thing. I don't. Her stomach is covered with a massive bruise. It's as mottled and damaged as K's skin was when she was freed from hell twelve months ago.

When Justine jumps to her feet and races into the bathroom, I follow her retreat. She's so confused by the disheveled redhead peering back at her in the mirror, she doesn't notice I'm standing behind her until I say, "You truly don't remember, do you?"

Tears well in her eyes when she shakes her head. "All I remember is having dinner. The rest is blank."

When Maddox joins us in the bathroom, he has the audacity to wordlessly request for me to leave. I don't know who he thinks is running the show around here, but it sure as fuck isn't him. When I fold my arms in front of my chest and shake my head, air whizzes out of his nostrils.

After hitting me with a glare that's too weak to respond to, he moves to the shower. He switches the faucet on full pelt before shifting on his feet to face Justine. "Why don't you shower while I get you something to eat? Once you've filled your belly and taken a nap, your confusion may lift." When Justine nods, Maddox runs his hand down her arm. "We'll be just outside."

He waits for Justine to nod again before he moves back into the main section of Nikolai's room, closing the bathroom door on his way. "What the fuck do you think you're playing at? She doesn't have time to have a nap. If she's concussed, the worst fucking thing she could do right now is sleep. Furthermore, she may be the only person who can tell us where Nikolai is."

"That's my sister in there. Her well-being comes before anything and anyone."

The fact he's playing the sibling card already gets my guard up, much less his lack of worry for Nikolai. "If you truly give a fuck about your 'sister'..." I air quote my last word like a soft cock, "... you'd know that the *only* person she needs right now is Nikolai." My reply is the equivalent of jabbing a knife into my chest. I had no choice. I had to send K away, but it doesn't make it any easier to swallow, though. "Are you here for Justine, Maddox, or to claw your way into a sanction you have no right to be a part of?" When he scoffs like I'm being ridiculous, I hit him with enough facts to knock him on his ass. "Did you and Dimitri have conjugal visits during your four-year stint at Wallens Ridge State Prison? Or did he have you suck his cock in front of everyone so they knew whose bitch you were?"

I laugh in his face when he fists my shirt to bring me to within an inch of his face. "Shut your mouth before I shut it for you."

"I'd like to see you try, twatface."

After pushing him off me via a hand to his face, I straighten my shirt just as Justine enters the room in nothing but a towel. "We were attacked, bombarded without warning. Men came from all angles. They were wearing balaclavas and knew things about Nikolai not many know."

"What type of stuff?" Maddox asks at the same time I encourage her to continue unlocking her memories. "Then what?"

Justine proves my earlier comment to Maddox was true. Her focus is dedicated to finding Nikolai. "A battle ensued. Nikolai and Rico were outnumbered, but they held their ground until..." I hiss along with her when her hand caresses the nasty bump in her head. "A man grabbed me. He was so large he didn't need to extend his arm to hoist me from the ground."

"That's good, Justine. Keep going," I encourage after recalling my own tiptoe out of a foggy mist ten months ago.

"Nikolai threatened him, told him he'd kill his family if he didn't let me go." I nod, fully aware that is something Nikolai would say. "That's when another man entered the equation." Her eyes flicker as her memories slowly trickle back in. "Maxsim. Nikolai called him Maxsim."

I jack-knife back, shocked. "Maxsim?" I double-check. "Are you sure?"

Justine nods. "If he's Alexei's son, then yes, I'm sure. They argued about Nikolai killing Alexei and how Maxsim would use Eli to take Nikolai's place."

"How did Nikolai respond?" I'm assuming violent if his blood pressure was anywhere close to the level mine is now.

"Umm... he said he had changed the rules, that Anatoly's rulings were no longer relevant." Wetness almost slides down her cheeks when she mutters, "His reply angered Maxsim so much, he signaled for his goon to hit me."

Anger steamrolls into me hard and fast. Although it is Nikolai's queen standing in front of me, my fucked-up head is absorbing everything Justine is saying as if she is K. I know Eight will do everything in his power to protect K and that he'd die before he'd ever let her be taken from me as she was nine months ago, but I'm so fucking angry I had to hand her protection to another man.

It isn't Eight's job to keep my wife safe.

It's mine.

The fury making my blood hot chops up my words when I ask, "Do you know what happened to the men Nikolai and you traveled with? Roman? Rico?" Justine stops shaking her head when Maddox adds, "Dimitri?"

"Dimitri was shot."

Wanting to test a theory, I give credit to Justine's comment, "Dimitri is under watch at an undisclosed location. He was found by the Feds surrounded by numerous deceased members of a Russian association. They're seeking the death penalty."

Just as suspected, Maddox's pupils dilate to the size of saucers.

This fucker isn't here for Nikolai.

He's here for Dimitri.

Lucky for him, his sister keeps my head screwed on straight. "What aren't you telling me, Trey?" She's rising to the podium as K did only last week, except she doesn't want K's crown. She wants the man who vowed to keep both our queens safe.

Mistaking my time of reflection as malice, Justine snickers out, "Don't lie to me, Trey. You know the consequences if you do."

Although amused by her gall, I do my best to double the flame flickering in her eyes. "Nikolai's DNA was found on the scene. A pool of his blood was located next to a man only known as a myth *Ubiytsa*."

"Killer?"

When I nod, the color drains from Justine's cheeks. "Rumors are his father was a Ukrainian weightlifter and his mother an operative at the Russian soviet. With his childhood devoted to beating his mother's lineage into him, his seven-foot-eight height never matched the maturity of his brain. His mental capacity only reached that of a young teen." He was as brainfucked as I would have been if Nikolai didn't find me.

My focus shifts back to the present when Justine asks, "Was he the man who held me hostage?"

I lift my chin. "We believe so."

Although I'd prefer he didn't, Maddox rejoins our conversation. "What are you saying? Nikolai killed a man, and in retaliation, he was killed?"

I hit him with a pompous glare instead of my fists like I really want to. "We don't know. Dimitri was the only man found alive."

Not hearing the snark in my tone, Justine asks, "Because he was too injured to flee?"

Tsking, I shake my head. "He was left as a warning. If this was a takeover bid, Maxsim needs the word spread that he toppled the king. Dimitri is his equivalent of a town crier."

"But Maxsim didn't topple the king. Nikolai isn't dead."

Uneased by the authority in Justine's tone, Maddox tries to coerce her off the ledge. "J—"

"No!" she fires back, her eyes fully lit. "Nikolai isn't dead! I'd know if he were dead. I would fucking know it." As a queen rises to command her monarchy, her pauper of a brother falls into line.

"I somehow got from Florida to Vegas with my life intact. That wouldn't have occurred without Nikolai's help."

With another theory at the ready to be confirmed, I say, "The Vasilievs used a subsidiary entity to bid on you last year. You're only alive because they see you as an asset."

Maddox doesn't blink, move, or breathe. He does nothing. He either has no clue who I'm talking about or he's a skilled actor.

I give it another attempt to poke the bear. "I'll call a physician to check you over. He's very discreet. I assure you, nothing you tell him will *ever* leave this room."

This time Maddox's facial expression alters from peeved to concerned. However, his response has nothing on Justine's. "I don't need a doctor. I wasn't raped. Nikolai would never let that happen. He'd kill any man stupid enough to get within an inch of me."

"He couldn't protect you from the grave, J."

I want to ram Maddox's words back into his throat with my fists, but before I can, Justine takes him down in a way only a sibling can—with a disappointing stare. "Then I'm lucky he isn't dead, aren't I?"

As she races to a set of drawers in the corner of the room, her towel slips off her body. I instantly drop my eyes to my feet, not just out of respect for Nikolai but for K as well. She trusts me because I've never given her any reason not to. Well, until tonight when I forced her into Eight's car.

After yanking on a pair of sweatpants and one of Nikolai's shirts, Justine pivots to face me. "Where are the men?" A mask I've never seen her wear slips over her face when Maddox steps toward her with his hands held out like she is a child. "Where are my men!"

Happy to remind Maddox about who runs the show here, I say, "They're in the den."

Justine is out the door before half of my reply leaves my mouth. After flashing Maddox a shit-eating grin, I chase his sister down. "What are you planning?"

The fogginess in my head lifts a little when Justine replies, "I'm going to fulfill the role I was born to live. I'm going to be Nikolai's queen."

Then perhaps you can help me make K mine?

KRISTINA

I blink through the grogginess coating my eyes when a familiar face pops into my peripheral vision. Although it isn't the bearded face I was hoping for, it's still comforting. "Hey there, baby sis. Welcome back," Eight says with a smile before scooting back. "You hungry?"

Even though I shake my head, he digs through a backpack sitting on the corner of the blanket I'm waking up on. Although appreciative I didn't blackout forever, I would have preferred waking up anywhere but here. We're on the lower level of the compound where Vladimir imprisoned his captives. The concrete pillars holding up the second story protect us from the harsh Las Vegas weather, and the blanket saves my skin from being covered with the soot no amount of rainfall will clear.

Tears prick my eyes when Eight commences peeling an orange. I'm not tearing up because the citrus from the peel squirted my eyes but from what he says while peeling it. "Trey said if you won't eat for you, do it for bub. If she's anything like her daddy, she'll be hankering for a feed twenty-four-seven."

After splitting the peeled orange in half, he hands the bigger portion to me. "No," he replies with a shake of his head when he reads the silent questions beaming from my eyes as I accept my share of our breakfast. "They're close, though. They found Rico, Blaire, and Eli. Nikolai should be next." When my eyes dilate more, he adds, "They're a bit shaken up but alive." He runs the back of his index finger down my screwed-up nose like my dad used to before saying, "Kinda like you, eh? You scared me, sis. You were out a while."

When I lean to the side so I can peer up at the gaping hole that was once enclosed by a wooden roof, my jaw drops. The sun is barely hanging in the sky. It's well into the afternoon.

Spotting my shocked expression, Eight moves a chunk of orange to the side of his mouth so he can laugh. "I said you were out for a while." He licks juice off his lips before asking, "What brought you back? I tried all Trey's suggestions. Nothing worked."

Shrugging, I pop a wedge of orange into my mouth.

"Oh well, at least you're back now." He stands to his feet to dust soot off his backside. "I better give Trey an update. He lost his shit when I told him our location. If he knows you're back, I might not have to change my name to Seven."

I am a terrible person for smiling, but I can't help it. I'm not just grinning about Eight's lack of care for his safety, I am smiling about discovering the reason for my return from the dark. It wasn't the rain track on Dok's iPod he gifted me months ago, nor the scent of Trey's shirt Eight tucked under my head as a pillow. It was the teeny tiny flutters in my stomach.

Although my anxiety is still high, I'm confident the trembles in the lower half of my body have nothing to do with nerves or hesitation.

They're excitement over dread.

Light instead of dark.

Life not death.

It's our baby. I'm certain of it.

When the faint flutters hit my stomach for the second time, I leap to my feet, shocked as hell something so weak could cause such a massive impact to my heart. Our baby would only be the size of the orange Eight and I just shared, but her feeble movements make it seem as if I can move mountains. It doubles my determination in an instant and has me convinced I have what it takes to survive the ruthlessness of this lifestyle without any additional scars.

Mistaking the expression on my face as eagerness to steal his phone, Eight chuckles out, "Give me a sec to have my name scraped off his hit list, then I'll hand over my phone. It'll do Trey some good to hear your voice." When my expression switches from determined to worried, he adds, "He's all right. He's just struggling with guilt. He thinks he can't rule Nikolai's kingdom with honor without borrowing the crown he wants to put on your head." When shock blazes through me, confused as to what he means, Eight's smile picks up. "He wasn't joking when he said you'll have your crown, Duchess. He wants to give you the world."

"I have the world." My English is terrible, but Eight looks at me as if I spoke it like a true queen. I blame the heavy undertone of sentiment in my voice for that. My life isn't close to ideal, but compared to what it was, I almost feel regal.

"Think of it this way," Eight says, stepping closer. "His entire life is wrapped up in you and his kid, so the knowledge he nearly took that away would be a hard pill to swallow. There are days I can't tell the difference between a bull and a cow, but even someone as stupid as me has no issues understanding how guilty he'd feel knowing he fired at his now-wife and soon-to-be mother of his children. It makes his protectiveness of you somewhat manic." Remorse fills his eyes when he murmurs, "Then he's got all that other shit to wade through." He doesn't directly say it, but I know he's referencing the abuse I endured under Achim and Vladimir's watch.

I wish Trey wouldn't feel guilty about that. He may have kissed me all those years ago in the pantry, but I instigated everything that occurred after that. *I* undid his belt. *I* lined up his cock. *I* chose to give my virginity to a stranger just like *I* paid for the consequences of my actions. Nothing that happened after our kiss was Trey's fault. If anything, his family's downfall should be on my shoulders. If I hadn't done any of those things mentioned above, perhaps his father and brother would still be alive, and he wouldn't feel the need to choose between Nikolai's monarchy and his debunked one. He'd be the governor of his own realm and free from his nightmares.

I smile like I can't feel the darkness calling me when Eight mutters, "It's probably best we keep our little chat between us, though. I didn't tell you this because I want you to feel bad. I just want you to know why he sent you away. He didn't do it to hurt you, sis. He's just trying to keep you safe. Aight?" When I dip my chin without pause for thought, he smiles. "Good girl. Now finish your orange so I can tell him you ate."

I'm not hungry, but I swallow down the remainder of the citrusy clump coating my hands with sticky residue without chewing. Trey and I worked too hard on my recovery the past nine months to let *anything* undo our efforts. Although I would have preferred to stay by his side, Eight's comments have flattened my annoyance to barely a blip.

Nikolai freed Trey from hell, gave him shelter when he saw something in him no one else could, and reminded him that the sun still rises after the darkest nights. He was Trey's beacon all those years ago as Trey has been mine the past twelve months. Those facts alone should assure Trey he doesn't need to pick between Nikolai and me. I'll happily hand him my crown if it assists him in honoring a man who respects him just as vehemently. I will never judge him on his decisions today. If anything, they will have me respecting him more. He fired at me years ago because he was raised believing blood came before anything. Today, along with many other times the past twelve months, proves he doesn't believe that anymore.

Blood makes you related, but loyalty makes you family. That's why Eight calls me his sister. We're family even with us being born in different countries. Justine said *once you're bratva, you're bratva for life.* She was right.

My focus shifts back to Eight when he holds his cell phone into the air, seeking a signal. "I swear the service is worse now than it was this morning."

While following his slow track through the lower half of the compound, I rub my juice-stained hands down Trey's shirt I'm wearing as a dress. A real duchess would use a washroom. It's lucky for me, Trey likes me grubby.

When Eight takes a right at the stairwell, I peer up at the grandeur I failed to notice twelve months ago. I was so eager to get out of this compound, I practically dragged Ana down the stairwell that's wide enough to fit an army tanker. The wooden balustrade was demolished by the inferno Trey and I lit, but the steps I galloped down remain since they're made out of concrete. Most of this warehouse-type building is built from the same durable material.

I slant my head when I notice a set of footprints in the ash coating the stairwell. They're not faded as you'd suspect. They almost look recent.

Curious, I cautiously climb the stairwell. Since I'm barefoot, Eight fails to notice I'm moving in the opposite direction to him until I reach the soot-covered landing. "Be careful up there, K.

Some of the roof's beams held during the blaze, but they're not stable."

His acknowledgment that he's been through this part of the compound weakens the nervous knock of my knees. I explore more out of morbid curiosity than fear. I don't want to say I've overcome the damage this place slapped my mental stability with, but I'm most certainly on my way to reaching closure on that part of my life.

After taking in the room I was given my first night here, then the one I was freed from almost twelve months ago, I move to the room Vladimir entered and never exited. Although the walls and floors are badly smoke damaged, most of the roof remains intact. The soot and fire-licked walls add to the eeriness of a room that claimed more than the lives of innocent women. It also sent Satan back to hell.

Soot kicks up around me when I bend down to clear away the ash beneath the pully I was chained to when whipped. A handful of the blood droplets hidden under the mess belong to me, but I don't believe it's responsible for the copper smell in the air. A larger pile of ash sits to the right of where I'm kneeling. Its long and slender stack almost conceals the smallest slither of a red thread stuck between warped floorboards.

As my heart thuds in my ears, I pull at the thread, prying it free from the blackness as I was freed. Horrid memories fill my head when I remove enough of the ash covering the ribbon to spot its bright red and white dot coloring. It's been an incredibly long time since I saw it, but I swear this piece of ribbon is a similar length, pattern, and width to the ribbon my mother placed in my hair before my interview with Mrs. Novak.

Achim wore it like a bracelet for years, forever taunting me with it when I outwitted his chase by keeping someone with me at all times the first two years after my parents' death. It grazed my cheek the first time he forced his dick between my lips, and it was there when he slapped me after India told him what I had done with Trey in the butler's pantry.

With my mind trapped between the past and the present, it takes me a little longer to notice the faintest shimmer of a light peeking through the crack I dug the ribbon from. It's coming through the floorboards. It's too bright to be a candle and too dim to be the rapidly setting sun.

Motivated by vile curiosity, I dig the steel end of a shackle into the gap in the warped wood before leaning on it with all my might. My breathing grows shallow when a section of the floorboard pops up a few seconds later. Although the wall behind it is burned away, the stairwell beneath the floor is in one piece. That isn't surprising, considering it's made from concrete.

When a flicker of light breaks through the blackness at the end of the hidden stairwell, I almost call for Eight. The only reason I don't is because I refuse to add another victim to the long tally I've amassed the past seven years.

Furthermore, Nikolai is missing, and I've found a hidden bunker. Perhaps this time around, my placement in Trey's life will do him more good than harm.

After weaponing-up with the shard of metal I opened the trapdoor with, I gingerly make my way down the stairwell. A stable woman would call out—I'm nothing close to stable. In this life, sometimes silence is your only defense.

My heart batters my ribcage when I soundlessly slip off the last step of a long, spiraling staircase. Although the accent of the voice at the end of the corridor usually instigates horrid nightmares, they're not as bad as they once were since I've been surrounded by the same accent every day for the past nine months. I'll never find a Russian accent as comforting as Trey's British twang, but I won't fear it again any time soon, either.

I'm stronger than I was twelve months ago, I remind myself when I almost chicken out partway through my mission. *I am braver. I'm a duchess ready to rule her monarchy.*

I'm also a fool who walks straight into the blackness without remembering to blink.

"Hello, little girl," greets a thick Russian accent when I enter an opulent bedroom hidden in a bunker under Vladimir's compound. "Do you still taste my cum when eating peanut butter and jelly sandwiches?"

TREY

"Come on, Eight, answer your fucking phone." It's late, the sun commenced setting hours ago, and I haven't had an update from Eight since this morning. The last time I heard from him, K was as lifeless as a plank of wood, unblinking and unspeaking. She'd been that way since Eight carried her into the compound where she was raped, beaten, and sodomized.

I get why he chose that location, and I understand it's the one spot Nikolai's enemies would never consider looking if Nikolai's disappearance was about more than a turf war, but my fucking god, am I fretting our actions today will set K's recovery back by months?

You can't teach someone to swim by throwing them into a pool and hoping they'll stay afloat. The same can be said for the nightmares of your past. More times than not, forcing someone to relive the experience fucks them up even more. I'm living proof of this.

Nikolai's disappearance was because a man wanted a

monarchy that wasn't his. He took the rules we lived by, bent them to suit himself, then stormed in with the aggression Cole used when he thought he was wronged by our father.

It got men killed, women and a kid victimized, and has put my head into such a dark and temperamental place, I'm worried not even K will be able to yank me off the ledge.

I was born for this life. I was raised by a killer to be a killer. I can end a life without the slightest flip to my stomach and sit down for a meal only seconds later, but I wasn't taught how to handle any of the things I've been bombarded with today.

Love fucks everything up. It screws you over like you spent a thousand dollars on a whore only to discover she has a dick between her legs and will have you wondering why you ever signed up for this shit in the first place. But, even in the darkest of moments, it will also convince you that you can't live without it. It'll have you craving it like it's a drug and have you begging for another hit before you've even snorted the first line.

It'll even convince you that no matter how loud the dark calls for you, you don't have to walk into it. My past fucked with my head today. It screwed me over and had me convinced I'm not cut out for this life, but instead of letting it get the better of me, I fed off it. I dared it to push me harder and try and break me.

All it did was make me stronger.

What I said all those months ago was true. I didn't want to break K, I wanted K to break me.

Today broke me, yet here I am, still breathing and alive. That wouldn't have been the case if I hadn't seen the slightest flicker of life in the eyes of a grubby, malnourished sex slave. K was forced to walk through the gates of hell unaccompanied, but instead of letting it consume her, she whizzed through the place like she owned it. That's why her crown will never slant even in the windiest conditions. She's a true duchess who knows even a pawn can become a queen if you play the game right.

After pulling my Shelby behind Eight's car, I throw open my driver's side door and hotfoot it up the stairs K raced up when I separated her from the pack.

My brutal speed slows when I spot Eight's phone sitting at the foot of the internal stairwell. I know it's his phone. His screen is proof of his namesake. You can't see his eight fingers since they're occupying two of the eight whores surrounding him, but they're not the only part of his body my brothers referenced when considering his nickname.

When I bob down to gather up Eight's phone, the faint murmur of a set of voices hits my ears. I think one of them belongs to Eight, but I can't be sure. Although they sound like they're coming from below me, something steers me toward the stairwell. It could be intuition or the fact my pulse thuds in my ears the more I approach the stairwell.

After removing my gun from the back of my jeans, I climb the soot-covered stairs two steps at a time. Unlike today's mission to find Nikolai, I go into this operation with complete silence. K taught me that silence can be your greatest strength when you live in a world with people who refuse to hear your words even when you speak the same language as them.

My gun enters the room Vladimir was killed in before me. Although the accented voices trickling into my ears still sound like they're coming from beneath me, this is the only room reflecting any light.

"What the fuck?" I murmur to myself when I discover the light is beaming out of a trapdoor in the corner of the room.

Most of the theories I ran with today were based on Vladimir escaping the inferno K and I lit twenty minutes after Nikolai took him down with a knife to his chest. Justine's representation of the noise Vladimir made when she removed Nikolai's knife wasn't close to the gargle that left Kliment's mouth when he stupidly touched Justine without permission earlier. Add that to the fact the information Maxsim had on Nikolai was only known by a handful of people, and I was convinced we were dealing with a ghost.

It wouldn't be the first time a ghost has resurrected from hell. Now, this adds credibility to my theory. The trapdoor is mere feet from the spot Vladimir laid dead when Nero threw gasoline over the walls. He could have rolled to safety. He could still be alive.

I gallop down the stairwell at the speed of lightning. My heart is pounding in my ears, but for the first time in years, I'm not seeing it as a good thump. Vladimir kept K in the room across from his. He only ever did that with his favorite whores. If he's alive, and K is missing, that can only mean one thing...

No! I refuse to say it.

She's free from that life. I promised no one would ever touch her without her permission. I'm going to keep my fucking promise.

With my blood pressure sky high and my finger curled around the trigger of my gun, I enter a bunker-type room at the end of a pitch-black corridor. My stomach heaves in disgust about the skank smell streaming into my nose, but my wish to find K keeps my head screwed on straight.

The smell of a rotting corpse is not my brother.

He's buried thousands of miles away from here.

He can't come back from death for the second time.

I jack-knife to the right when a thick Russian accent says, "Don't be shy, little one. I'm not going to hurt you... yet. If you behave, I can play nice too."

My chest rises and falls in rapid succession when I take in the wrinkled face of Vladimir Popov. It's grainier than I remembered, duller. That probably has more to do with the fact I'm peering at him through a bank of security monitors than seeing him in the flesh.

When he shifts to the right, my blood turns black. K is cowering in the corner of Vladimir's private suite. Her cheek is red like it was recently slapped, and her eyes are brimming with wetness, although not a single drop flows down her cheeks.

I almost pivot on my heels to sprint back up the stairs. The only reason I don't is because I cleared Vladimir's room only minutes ago. It was as black and lifeless as my heart now feels—as dark as death.

With a roar of a deranged man, I fire at the surveillance monitors like I wish I could have done to Achim and Vladimir. I gun them down before I discover the ending of Vladimir's stalk to K's side of the room. He has a gleam in his eyes I'm all too familiar with. The same savage glint that brightens my eyes anytime I look at K. The wolf is hunting his prey. He's going to hurt my duchess.

I continue firing at the now-mangled security system until the faintest snivel steals the devotion of my gun. I aim it in the direction the cry came from before stepping deeper into the dark. "You didn't listen. No matter what I said, no matter what I did, you never heard a word I spoke. You wanted the castle, I gave you the entire fucking kingdom, but it still wasn't enough for you, was it?" As I inch back the trigger, I hear someone call my name. Well, I assume they're saying my name. I can't hear anything through the pounding of my pulse in my ears. "Is this where you hid when he brutalized her? Did you sit back and watch the videos of the sick fucks raping her over and over again?" As the evil inside of me roars to life, I scream, "Did you ever feel one fucking day of guilt! She could have given you the world, but you were too fucking stupid to see it. Too fucking blind. Her head would have *never* worn your crown because it was too tainted for her level of royalness."

"And here I was thinking the Corbyn men cared about no one but themselves," says an unfamiliar but heavily accented female voice.

My eyes blink in rapid succession when a light is suddenly switched on. I blink and blink and blink, but nothing takes away the image of my nightmare sitting directly in front of me. K is tied to a wooden chair, a hessian bag is pulled over her head, and my gun is pointed at her stomach. Eight is on her right. Although he doesn't have his head covered, he is gagged.

They shouldn't have bothered impacting his speech. His eyes tell me what he wants me to do. No matter what, he wants me to pick K.

Although I appreciate his loyalty, I'd rather gun down the bitch responsible for K's slumped form than play a second game of roulette.

India smiles with smugness when I direct the barrel of my gun at the crinkle between her brows. "What the fuck is your issue?" I'd take her down without any questions if I hadn't seen the pistol she has butted up against K's ribs. She could survive a bullet wound to the stomach, but our daughter most certainly wouldn't. "Did daddy spoil his little princess too much she'd rather run his legacy into the ground than see it thrive?"

I realize I hit the motherlode when India's eye twitches out. "Quite the opposite, actually. He'd rather betroth his only daughter to a monster than make her feel one of a kind."

If anything she's saying is true, why is she taking her anger out on K? She's been Achim's victim for far longer than India. Hasn't she suffered enough?

When I say that to India, she replies, "Because she took what wasn't hers! First you, then Cole." When I balk in shock, India smiles like a vindictive cow. "Oh, you didn't know? You're not the only Corbyn man with a fascination for the help. *I* nursed him back to health. *I* showed him how he could re-seize his throne, then he tossed me aside the instant *she* was placed on his radar." K's whimper is silent when India pushes the muzzle of her gun deep into her stomach, but I feel every painful scream bubbling in her chest. "We were supposed to destroy our fathers as they had us before ruling together, but he was too obsessed with her." Her eyes come up to mine. "Why do you think Achim killed him? It wasn't for me. He couldn't care less that I was sleeping with Cole. But he was never going to let another Corbyn man touch her."

Hate makes my blood run hot when her dig of K's ribs this time around sends a pained sob rippling through my ears. India tilted her gun to ensure K's stomach won't be the only thing pierced by her bullet. So will her heart.

If I fire at her, she'll kill my wife and daughter with one bullet.

"What do you want?" The fact I'm negotiating reveals how lost I am. As Nikolai said months ago, we don't negotiate with whores. We tell them what to do, and they do it or die, but this is different. My entire world is strapped to that chair—I won't risk them for anything.

My brows stitch when India replies, "I don't want anything." I realize just how vindictive she is when she adds, "From you. You've done enough, now you can leave the rest up to us." With a smile as hideously ugly as her insides, she nudges her head to the right.

"You fucking piece of shit," I growl out in a roar when Maddox steps out of a darkened nook in the corner of the almost pitch-black room. He's holding an automatic weapon in his hands and has the sneer of a murderer stretches across his face. "Not even your sister will save you from this. Do you hear me? You're a dead man walking."

"Blood isn't always thicker than water, Trey. Thought you'd know that better than anyone." After dotting my chest with the scope of his rifle, he adds, "I heard lots of stories during my time in lockup. Failed takeover bids. Men being brought back from the brink of death. Duchesses so desperate for a crown, they fucked with the wrong family over and over again."

My brows draw together when he shifts the red dot on my chest to India's. I'm not the only one shocked. India is just as taken aback. "Wraith..."

Wraith? Who the fuck is Wraith?

"I don't know what shocks me more, the fact you think I didn't scan the face of *every* person surrounding the cage my sister was mauled in, or that I didn't hear your disappointed sigh when Col agreed with my barter of my life for Justine's." Maddox adjusts the perimeter of his scope from India's thrusting chest to her head before he says, "You were so fucking desperate to be top dog, you didn't consider who you were taking down in the process." When he breathes out, "Dimitri says hello," I growl K's name in a mangled groan.

K's chin has only just balanced on her chest when a bullet from Maddox's assault rifle pierces through India's skull. The impact is so direct, only the wall behind India's head gets splattered with her brain matter.

When she slumps to the floor with a thump, in sync, Maddox and I take aim at each other. He may have just killed one of my enemies, but he did it while speaking the name of another. That puts him on the opposing side of my team.

Although Maddox's rifle is aimed at my chest, he tries to weasel his way out of our confrontation. "I couldn't lure India out of hiding without offering up an incentive."

"Admitting you brutalized my woman won't do you any favors."

"What would you rather, Trey? Your girl tied up and safe or lying lifeless in a ditch with her stomach barren of your child?"

When white-hot anger flares through my eyes, he spits out, "Yeah, that's what I thought." He works his jaw over three times before he lowers his gun. "If it weren't for Dimitri and me, she'd be dead in four months." He nudges his head at K during the 'she'd' part of his reply. "Why do you think India wanted her brought in alive?"

My finger curls around the trigger of my gun when he digs his hand into the pocket of his jeans. Like an idiot not in fear for his life, he smiles. It would have been his last if the sale docket he tosses onto the table K and Eight are seated behind had any association with K.

"Who's Audrey?" I ask after taking in the name of the woman sold in a similar fashion to K. Her sale receipt is slightly different than K's, though. It mentions she's eight months pregnant.

My eyes snap back to Maddox when he replies, "Dimitri's wife. Well, she *was* his wife before that piece of shit tested your theory that blood isn't thicker than water." After glaring at India lying in a pool of her blood, he returns his eyes to mine. "Up until twenty minutes ago, Dimitri wasn't your enemy. I guess only time will tell where we go from here. Things get hostile when a mutual nemesis is eradicated."

After smirking like a smile will stop me from shooting him in the back, he pivots on his heels and stalks toward the alcove he was hiding out in. I should gun him down like he did India, then feed him to the pigs. I should remind him that he's on Popov turf and that nothing happens here without Nikolai's permission, but instead of doing either of those things, I suck in the scent of rain-soaked hair and dirt on sweat-slicked skin, aware Nikolai would most likely issue Maddox a pardon since he killed for Justine.

Within seconds, K's scent brings me out of the darkness. She reminds me that there's more to living than hate. This lifestyle is a part of who I am, but it isn't *all* I am.

I am a husband and a father-to-be.

A brother and a son.

I'm also a survivor who isn't ashamed to admit his past fucked with his head, but he's strong enough not to let it steer his future.

A king isn't born.

He's made.

And it's time for this king to return to his realm.

EPILOGUE

TREY

Five years later...

Standing toward the back of the hall, I follow K as she weaves through the dozens of people separating us. Even with our son stretching her stomach beyond possibility, her steps are feeble and faint. She draws the eye of so many people, her endeavor to get where she's going is slowed by those so desperate to admire her, they approach her without permission.

If they weren't my brothers, I'd gut them where they stand. Alas, the grandeur I'm standing in wouldn't be here if it weren't for them. The battle was hard, but like all things in life, the reward far exceeded our efforts. The Corbyn name has been restored across Europe. Instead of it being slotted across from the Popovs as I was worried, it stands beside them as a joint unit.

My victory can be accredited to Nikolai's crew as much as it can be mine. We fought side by side as we have the past nine years, and as we will continue doing until our children take over the reins. If Elisa has it her way, it'll be a partnership by law instead of mutual respect. She has quite the fascination with Nikolai's son, Toby. Even with him currently residing in a country thousands of miles away, she talks to him every day. Their kinship is understandable. Even with K being due with Elisa a month before Justine, since Justine was carrying twins, K only delivered Elisa days before Justine in my room at Clarks.

I should have known K was so strong, she wouldn't tell me she was in pain until it was hours too late. Elisa's head was already out before I got Dr. Laura on speakerphone. She talked me through the rest of the delivery. I'm a heartless, cruel man who can still kill without a smidge of remorse but delivering our daughter rates highly on my list of accomplishments. It is only just below a rain-sodden ground and grubby face.

My room in Clarks was my sanctuary. It was the only place I ran to when I was feeling lost, so it's fitting our daughter was born there. Within minutes of her birth, she was surrounded by murderous Russians who would die to keep her safe. She's been bounced on the knees of whores, burped by men who believe women are valueless, and promised herself to a mafia prince from another realm, yet she's not even five years old.

I'd be worried if K wasn't her mother.

She'll keep her head as well screwed on as she has mine the past six years.

Just as K breaks through the people surrounding us at our compound in Prague, I sink back behind a concrete pillar to conceal myself. With a drug shipment going wayward in the United Kingdom, I had to make an unexpected visit to my old stomping ground. K wanted to come with me, but with Elisa having a dance recital tomorrow afternoon, she had no choice but to stay put. I was supposed to be gone for three days. My addiction couldn't hold out that long. I left at four this morning, and it's now a little after ten at night.

Eight howls like a dog when I sock him in the stomach before I pull him into the darkness of my hidey-hole. I'm glad he's following K's every move as instructed by me this morning, but he can fuck off now.

My duchess only needs one protector when her king is home.

"Aww, look at you home early. I won't have to find new stroking material tonight." I punch him for the second time, harder this time around. It doesn't stop his stirring, though. "I was joking. In all honesty, just thinking about you two getting it on makes me all types of queasy." He could have saved his life if he'd learn to keep his mouth shut. "You're too damn noisy. I can barely hear K's moans with all your grunting and shit."

Somehow, the little fucker gets out of my hold before I can strangle him.

While stepping backward, he smiles a blistering grin. "Go spoil your girl. Elisa has been out for hours, and the men are so doped on the departing gifts Nikolai sent, they're not going to move from their spot for hours." When my jaw ticks, he adds, "They'll be good to go by Friday. Everyone is eager to leave this icebox for a couple of weeks."

With Nikolai's second son due in days, my men and I are returning to Vegas. We will hold down the fort for a couple of weeks while Nikolai plays house. Our arrival will ensure Nikolai's enemies know that even when his guard is down, he's not to be messed with.

Nikolai will return the favor when my son arrives in three months.

I wait until Eight disappears into the mass of men enjoying Nikolai's generosity before continuing my stalk of K. I'm not surprised to find her in the pantry at the back of the industrial-size kitchen. She went hungry for weeks on end, so even when our children are in her belly, she ensures they don't face the same injustice.

After taking a moment to relish the sound of my pulse in my ears, I gather an orange off the counter at my side, rip a large chunk out of it with my teeth, swallow down the citrusy clump, then roll the uneaten portion toward K.

I can tell the exact moment she spots it. Not only does she gasp in a sharp breath, but the sound of rain hitting a tin roof also jingles into my ears.

While removing a wireless ear pod from her left ear, K spins around to face me. Considering this part of Prague hasn't felt the heat of the sun in weeks, the scent of a summer storm in a desert shouldn't be lingering in my nose. It is, though. Very much so. And it's accompanied by the faintest smell of pig shit. Don't misconstrue. My wife has the most delectable scent I've ever sampled. I just can't help but recall fond memories of my past whenever she's close to me.

"Hello, Duchess," I greet her with a growl when her provocative smell doubles at the sight of me. "Did you come down here for a snack? Or to take down an entire fucking kingdom without firing a single bullet?"

When her smile matches mine, I read the answer from her eyes.

She came for both, and that's precisely what I'll give her —again.

The End!
The next story is Dimitri. You can find it here:
Dimitri

Be sure to stay in touch!

Facebook: facebook.com/authorshandi

Instagram: instagram.com/authorshandi

Email: authorshandi@gmail.com

Reader's Group: bit.ly/ShandiBookBabes

Website: authorshandi.com

Newsletter: https://www.subscribepage.com/AuthorShandi

Nikolai's, Asher's, Rico's, Maddox's, Dimitri's, stories have already been told. All the other great characters of Ravenshoe, Vegas, and Hopeton will be getting their own stories at some point during 2022/23.

Join my newsletter to remain informed:
https://www.subscribepage.com/AuthorShandi
If you enjoyed this book, please leave a review.

ACKNOWLEDGMENTS

I swear to God, this is the worst part about any book. You'd have to be over reading these as much as I am writing them, right? It's the same old shit every single time. *To my readers, my husband, and to myself for not strangling the kids while writing this book, yada, yada, yada.* You get it. I love you guys, but my fucking God, do I hate writing the acknowledgement page. I'd pick to write blurbs for twenty-four hours straight over this shit. I'd even wipe my ass with a cactus. Yet, here we are, all over again.

To my beloved readers...

Please fill in the rest on my behalf. While you do that, I'll get started on another book.

Love you forever,
Shandi xx

PS: I love you, my husband, my kids, my mom, my editor, my betas, and every damn person who read this and laughed!

ALSO BY SHANDI BOYES

Denotes Standalone Books

Perception Series

Saving Noah *

Fighting Jacob *

Taming Nick *

Redeeming Slater *

Saving Emily

Wrapped Up with Rise Up

Protecting Nicole *

Enigma

Enigma

Unraveling an Enigma

Enigma The Mystery Unmasked

Enigma: The Final Chapter

Beneath The Secrets

Beneath The Sheets

Spy Thy Neighbor *

The Opposite Effect *

I Married a Mob Boss *

Second Shot *

The Way We Are

The Way We Were

Sugar and Spice *

Lady In Waiting

Man in Queue

Couple on Hold

Enigma: The Wedding

Silent Vigilante

Hushed Guardian

Quiet Protector

Enigma: An Isaac Retelling

Enigma Bonus Scenes (Two free chapters)

Twisted Lies *

Bound Series

Chains

Links

Bound

Restrain

The Misfits *

Nanny Dispute *

Russian Mob Chronicles

Nikolai: Representing the Bratva

<u>Nikolai: Resurrecting the Bratva</u>

Nikolai: Ruling the Bratva

Asher: My Russian Revenge *

Trey *

Nikolai: Bonus Scenes (10+ chapters from alternative POVs).

The Italian Cartel

Dimitri

Roxanne

Reign

Mafia Ties (Novella)

Maddox

Demi

Ox

Rocco *

Clover *

Smith *

RomCom Standalones

Just Playin' *

<u>Ain't Happenin'</u> *

The Drop Zone *

Very Unlikely *

False Start *

Short Stories - Newsletter Downloads

Christmas Trio *

Falling For A Stranger *

Enigma Bonus Scenes (Two free chapters)

Nikolai: Bonus Scenes (10+ chapters from alternative POVs).

One Night Only Series

Hotshot Boss *

Hotshot Neighbor *

The Bobrov Bratva Series

Wicked Intentions *

Sinful Intentions *

Devious Intentions *

Deadly Intentions *

Martial Privilege Series

Doctored Vows *

Deceitful Vows *

Book Three

Omnibus Books (Collections)

Enigma: The Complete Collection (Isaac & Isabelle)

The Beneath Duet (Hugo & Ava)

The Bad Boy Trilogy (Hunter, Rico, and Brax)

Pinkie Promise (Ryan & Savannah)

The Infinite Time Trilogy (Regan & Alex)

Silent Guardian (Brandon & Melody)

Nikolai: The Complete Collection (Nikolai & Justine)

Mafioso (Dimitri & Roxanne)

Bound: The Complete Collection (Cleo & Marcus)